# WEREWOLF, TEXAS

## D.J. Palladino

Genius
Book Publishing

Milwaukee, Wisconsin USA

Published by:
Genius Book Publishing
PO Box 250380
Milwaukee, Wisconsin 53225 USA
GeniusBookPublishing.com

ISBN: 978-1-947521-83-4

220417 Trade

The world never ends! It will go on forever. Life on Earth died off a number of times. We come back. We are related to two percent of the fossils in the Burgess Shale that made it through to now. We were shrews under the feet of dinosaurs when the asteroid hit 66 million years ago. It never ends. Life always comes back.
　　—John Graham


Homo homini lupus
　　—Plautus

*For Diane and Zac*

*And in memory of*
*Steve Carlson*

# 0.

Once upon a time I was married to a ghost. We took the vows in throes of passion knowing full well the asymmetries involved. After all, I was fervent earth and up for anything while she was molecular air, antimatter maybe, structured around sorrowful memories. I was a poor ragged man and she came from the invulnerabilising power of money, and loads of it.

But we were lost to love. The hasty wedding happened in a magic moment but you had to wonder what future we were heading for. My daddy's mud barn or her father's mansion? Cohabitation presented problems with one foot on the ground and the other in aether's swirly realm. She thought: Love will triumph over sense and sensibilities like it always does. I thought: It's all wait and see. Let our kids sort things out. Though what such creatures might look like was wildest conjecture.

Coarse, but touched by unexpected grace, for a while I was actually changed. Not by an angel, mind you, but by breathless revenant love.

But one day, the haunting turned into a haunt. Tell you what: She's just spoiled, and that's all there is to it. Father distant as the moon above, mother stewed on the stuff the whole time she was growing up. In the beginning she was fun, though, God. You could tell she was wanting it despite all the internal damages. Thought the best thing would be some kind of take her and then take her hard and that was right on. She opened like a tangerine, booyah, first shed the covers then all fall into moist sections. Sad but that didn't last any longer'n it takes an Austin singer-songwriter like me to mention his truck. Spirit and flesh was how our marriage went awry, I guess. Particularly those last few months, what with her gliding through the house no louder than a soft moan, eyes wistful, remembering, recriminating, no appetite, and so vague you could almost see through her. See through everything she does. Used to come right up behind and ask what I was doing. Made me jump and then get madder, all the time madder at her, the ghostly wife.

And on another day, my little ghost just disappeared for a few days, like spooky girls do. I took her on a bit when she came back, I feel bad 'bout that.

But she changed, not me. My lovely little phantom said, "I can't do this anymore."

I said, "Please come back to the sugar shack." And she said no.

Then she said, "What about this? I'll pay rent, but I want my stuff to stay at our old place and me with it in the bedrooms upstairs, you in the kitchen and dining room below till you find something better."

Matter of time, I thought, before this moody soul wants to reintegrate.

Then I overheard her on the telephone, speaking to some other someone, a presence unknown. She said: "Meet me in the park, like back in the day."

And now here I am in said park mad looking for my little lost ghost. Mad to sad, turning into one of my own done him wrong songs, slinking down past the jammed-in tendrils trimmed to the edge of this dying place: poisonous oleander or tender evergreen shoots. They grow so lethal and sweet over there. Here we have edibles everywhere: cleaver, hackberry, neglecta, pawpaw, and spatterdock. Lady's Thumb. Also reckon yucca, otherwise known as Spanish Dagger plant, a succulent, sensibly adapted to desert, though bizarre to behold.

Creeping up this row of hedges planted by settlers who fled. Maybe I should flee too, you know? I mean to say: if *my* ghost is out here, are others? And carnivores abounding in this here frontier between settlements. The salmon evening turned Zane Grey. Maybe bears. Beware. Meanwhile, write a song about it; watch the full moon rim's silver hues about to rise above the desert's dim blues. A bad song.


But a big sound. Dark despite the artificial light. She's somewhere near. With her boyfriend maybe whilst her husband, me, is starting to bitch, belch, and complain. His feet hurt in his pinchy boots, his *pinche* boots. I hear crunching on the pathway.

Then: "Baby?" Her ghost voice rises.

Not summoning me, it turns out, calling him. It. Patient, attentive, it's skulking the low country too; learning to herd me. Guarding and guiding from the lighter places on the evening trail into blue shadows, to end it in darkness.

"Baby? I answer. Didn't recognize my own shaky voice.

Ran into strangers who were not amused. Gunshot you missed me. I slow down looking, but I was looking for my baby, I said. I broke out into the Moon Tower clearing and heard soft padding come from behind. In the dark below the fake moon.

"Show yourself!" I said, the once tough guy sweating in the shadow of the tower.

Then the thing glides out into the clearing too. Exhale through its black nose. Its face ringed with fur and walking like a lowdown thing, growling and sniffing the warm summer air beneath the tower with its own moon above it. I mean I heard what the government said, a plague of these things. But I didn't believe it. They was just trying to curtail my lifestyle.

"What the fuck," says me the blue-jean bro in his off-white wifebeater in the warm evening.

"What the fuck is that," and, like I was in some archaic *danse*, I bow and square off with the shadow in the changing shadows. On jelly legs, the pit of my stomach roils. I'm burning beer and whiskey now, the smell of the booze ascends over desert perfumes, flowers of abandonment, in the brush beyond the dinosaurs. Nice boy, nice doggie. Circle and dip. Allemande left. Charge and cut off. Growling low now.

"There's nowhere to run," says me out loud looking frantic around and suddenly I throw up.

"Nowhere to hide," I think she answers from somewhere ghostly near. "There there."

The moon in all its phases, she told me, strictly cyclical yet it always felt like a chance encounter. Regularly wax and wane over the tilted planet, as we go crazy about our business. Never knowing when; come out your evening class or your Sixth Street tavern and there it was in a different part of the sky, in a phase you never expected. Yellow like old teeth or flashlight white, auraed in the sky with haze. Stillborn. Complete beauty, though note terror of solitude and a life haunted by terrible dreams.

Alone, brush tangling in my boots, I fall and jump up, pure willpower, but overwhelmed at once and advantageous it passes. And nicks me. Rushes my blood.

Time to gasp then it passes to slice me again, deeper. Almost surgical. The sharp push, pull, and cut scared to shit when it hit. Sobbing for air as I stand up and realize my Achilles tendon is cut. Stumble down and there is blood. The next hit drove up the old adrenaline to superhuman. I leap up and even with my right foot flapping manage to run and run hard, blood run down everywhere.

Heard someone screaming and realized it was myself. How many am I? In a lit grove is she nearby watching? Is God watching? How many of His Persons are?

And then silence. The moon shone down, no clouds anymore. A rush forward toward where the tower towered. Artificial moon. I hit it hard as the creature hit a chain link fence. Pulled myself up steel rungs. Wolf can't climb, I thought. Something howled, long and expectant.

One day there will be a ballad about the beast below, I thought. Chester Burnett. Dogs begin to bark, hounds begin to howl. I saw the distant remnant lights of Austin. Wait a second: There aren't any wolves out here: Even I knew that. Bears, mountain lions, maybe.

I rip off my t-shirt to make a tourniquet and at about the same time the terrible pain arrives. My blood all over the girders. Reeking of Beam and beer back, I pull myself up farther into the naked iron branches of the tower, and the moon sails far from the clouds once lined with silver, the world and the blood below actually pools. Another howl and I shiver in the warm evening air.

I'll huff and I'll puff and I'll.

Below a soft crunch.

"Baby?" I say, surprised at my own quavering pitch.

I look down and can see nothing but a wind maybe moving the sage around disturbing the air with incense known to cowboys and rattlesnakes. "Baby," I whisper.

Then the thing is on my arms, teeth sunk in so deep and the flesh torn along sliding lines, blood sluicing into the mouth that brought itself back up. Release and reattach, then it tore. As I look down in eyebulging shock my arms mangled to the bone, shreds of tissue hung from coatwire. The visible man. How the human anatomy appears cut in layers to one of my deeper selves. The thing was crawling up the wall, a lover passing over his beloved's body at the neck and tearing me down on the ground tear away my face why my face and eyes without a face and went from fear into a pained paralysis and then the spasm of my body's last drives for survival trying some mad jerk away that only made matters worse and the fear turned into the horror and that turned into the darkness of weak belief and then just black.

Was the last thought I ever had as a man. For an absurd moment beneath the pain looking up at the moon I wondered if eternity would be always colored by this last despair, sagged-out dreams throwing me into an endless room reserved for those deathborn to regret. But more likely, it was just nothing and it would be nothing, the kind we can't even consider, more unfathomable than God's inactivity, an everyday nothing that nullified the entire universe and all of time and us. And all of us. Nothing, not even a ghost left behind. Tell you what, though, we will always think there's more to the goddamned story. Has to be.

# 1.

Young John Shaney scored big in the Lone Star State, though a more vivid evaluation from a more specific mind might argue that falling for Lila May Wulfhardt brought him to his unexpected joy. Indirectly, that is, in the way of the world, but not without dragging him first through a dense moraine of other people's troubles. By joy I mean fruitful endings, and by troubles I mean the law, slaughters, maimings, plagues, and that general climate trauma everyone shared; the one we dithered about, forgot, feared, and then got.

Lila meanwhile never seemed to fear anything. And if you know her, and who didn't in those days, this maybe won't surprise you. One cool customer she was, though also hot like an Austin Friday night behind the club stoned in front of the food truck. And therein lies the rub and the reason Shaney stayed in Texas too long and then just long enough to get saved.

He came to UT Austin (hook em horns) on a chemistry fellowship. You know, as in, better living through… But the proudest achievement of his science life came earlier during his undergrad career in Santa Barbara, California on the day he learned how to synthesize a stronger version of psilocybin to give it wings of pictorial flight. It was to regular mushrooms what 3D IMAX was to watching movies on your telephone. John Shaney's roommates thanked him, blessed him for his scientific tremendousness. "Awesome" was the word most heard around those sparkling Friday night soirees. Awesomer, awesomest.

He matriculated Texas, Austin because the school thought he had potential in the biochemical arena, helping the body itself manufacture changes. Things like tumors transmogrified into pussycat boils, which could be removed by first year veterinarians if necessary. He enjoyed playing with reversible transformations, too, erasing cellular constructs— he would have morphed shit back to food if he could; just for the fun of it, you see, if it was possible, just to watch it happen. But the real reason he came was that he was lost, needed time to develop his own chemical makeup. Where better than school in a hipster town known for vivid youth culture? And they'll pay me for it, he thought, learning of grad school's myriad stipends, fee waivers, and fellowships. Aimless research might come later, he figured after hard work and hard partying. O Brethren and Cistern, Amen, I say unto you. Praise the lord and pass the tuition.

Enter Louis Lamel into the tale, later Shaney's frenemy. Lamel was then between adjunct jobs after grad school accepted his dissertation on Ovid and the Transgender, the topic made him hot but his unwillingness to leave the vicinity and his bad teacher evaluations made him hard to employ. Besides he was cursed.

Lamel sought a room to let from some grad students near Sixth Street downtown, the white hot heart of the city, arriving for a roommate interview the same time Shaney did. Lamel was well-heeled that year, having wrestled the parents' bequeathal into an early settlement of massive funds. But Shaney was a grad student like the rest of them. At first, they couldn't choose between them, made them wait. They would think about it, get back to you both they said.

Meanwhile, the full moon.

It was the night before Shaney and Lamel were due to hear from the residents who called themselves the Trinitarians, after the streetname and meant to ironically underscore that they did not believe in any Three-Personed God. That night Louisa Priddy, the prettiest roommate, was heard screaming outside the door at 3 a.m. Everybody in the house woke. When they got down there in a big cowardly group, there was nothing. Oh, what's this? A little sprinkling of blood on the Welcome Pardner doormat. They called the cops, who were more bemused than sleuth, but managed to establish nonetheless the blood likely belonged to her. Her presence absence question is still on the books.

Turned out Louis got first pick for the vacant room, by Parliamentary vote. A few days later they hesitantly brought in Mr. John Shaney, who somehow wangled temporary college housing, to see how he felt about moving into Louisa's room. He was weirded out, of course, but was living alone in an abandoned dorm named Santa Ana with skittering night sounds surrounding. What if the dead woman came back? He wondered aloud. They understood his hesitancy. First of the month, on the new moon, he changed his mind and came. Thus Shaney and Lamel found a new home in that big craftsman on Trinity Street, and three persons in one place became five.

While Louis was gone a lot, Shaney was always home. Too studious and confused by the sudden reorientation to go out at night, he told himself he was testing his new time zone and feeling out the new city gradually, acclimatizing his soul to the subtle forces of the notorious town. Tasting the terroir. Too bad, he missed a lot of fun. Austin is supposed to be an alternative space in the straightbacked American south, but it's actually a much more pure form of Texas, which is a well-tended and rigorously defended culture made up of equal parts fierce pride of place while insisting on outsider status. Austin looks equally towards the cosmic and simple pleasures simultaneously, a lone star says it all. The silence of the dry or grassy plains, great clanking music, laconic expostulation, whisky, beer, and easy access to dope. Yet Shaney remained cocooned as his roommates partied on all the above substances and arrived home late speaking loud and incoherent. Even after classes, they tumbled through the door arguing, excited, flush with ideas; the most trifling occasion, like grocery store odysseys, induced high spirits come home giggling all the way to bed into hopscotch rooms. Commodification and transgression were buzzwords back then. And those kids did both. He, monastic, didn't fit in at all with all the buying and yelling, the loose reducing and gross enlarging.

The others were just about to regret his inclusion when one night the whiff of BBQ drew Shaney away from home, three weeks to the day of his first settling. Maybe it was unfair to smirk about his homebody ways, since he did go to campus nearly every day and was fully engaged there. Though fresh-minted as a grad student, he was expected to teach undergrads, a responsibility presented in the offhand way academia has of granting expertise automatically with diplomas. He never got any training and really he was a coupla years and three weeks older than the kids he was guiding. Yet he was surprisingly apt and committed to the job. First years would approach him with doleful eyes and piteous tales expecting him to agree that the professor was insane to heap them with all this. Who could remember elements with names like Ununnillium or Bismuth? He, always fascinated by the table, its compounds and catalysts, felt and showed little sympathy. He helped nonetheless.

Especially her. She was suddenly in his hands, delivered by a blustery day when he was just about to abandon his shared office for the trip home alone. She walked in, a mess. Her hair tangled by whipping winds and dirty from studied neglect. It was that era when really pretty girls dressed themselves dorky on purpose: fat barrettes pinning back greasy hair and bra and slip straps displayed as if they accidentally crept out over the shoulder gap in thrift store blousenecks. On her it looked good, though. Lila.

At first, Shaney thought she was awkward and maybe even grade grubbing. She needed clarification about some obvious chemical reaction.

Seriously? he thought. This chick either craves attention or is stupid. Also, her breath was sour milk like a child's.

As the class cycle progressed, the contacts between him and the varyingly-talented undergrads grew into unexpected bonds. Some he came to enjoy, others he almost dreaded for their stuck record, none-so-blind-as-he-or-she-who-will-not-see minds. He came to respect Lila, though, and once when he told a joke, a bad pun about a micellar membrane as the place where he would stand if a tornado came, she winked at him and that act seemed both anachronistic and racy. Not giddy, merely winked. She was capable of fun. After a while, he got to like her breath and the smell of her tied-back greasy hair. It was her he liked. He thought, uh-oh.

And then, speaking of aromatics, came the BBQ smell day wafting in one Friday night as he stood dumb contemplating yet another bowl of pale ramen illuminated with pork and shrimp bits. He was indoors and he caught the odor near a window, like some animal smelling parts per million, he wondered at the actual chemical content of the breeze: char, vinegar sauce, and flesh. Shaney followed his nose to Sixth Street past the disconsolate old hippies smoking in front of blues clubs, past the Ripley's Believe It or Not emporium, and past the bars that seemed designed to recede into vanishing points, the void beyond dead drunk, past all life in lively motion to the end of all the nightclubs where the homeless congregated in hungry packs. He passed unnoticed amongst them, perhaps they sensed his famished tongue, his breathing out off a deprived stomach longing for salty flesh. Up a few blocks and he found it at Stubbs.

Inside the long dark room, the dank room, sooted over and glued down with grease, smoke, and sweat, he ordered the brisket sandwich from the man behind the bar even though he preferred the sound of the pulled pork. When in Rome, he reasoned. Brisket was what Texas preferred, this land of giant cattle ranches, so brisket it would be. First he ordered a sandwich and to chase it a blond beer. The meat had a satisfying bark of crunchy blackened fat, flesh, salt, and herbs surrounding a tender, thick core of the beefiest beef. He was soon back ordering more of the same, wiping his fingers at the high dark wooden bar where the slightly imperious waiter stood jotting down, taking money, and issuing numbers to be displayed at the table for the waitress's benefit. It tasted like heaven opened up to in his poor calorie-, flesh-, and fat-deprived grad student body. Everything tingled and the beer spread like a warm tide through his human tributaries.

Wavering with pleasure, he stood billowing though nowhere near drunk and so he left through the front door onto the semi-desolate street wishing only that propriety had not forbade him ordering yet again. He hungered and he thirsted, still.

"Pulled pork?" he said holding up his finger to an imaginary waiter in the air outside, which was surprisingly chill-tipped. "Fuck you. Texas? Your awesome brisket wins."

He walked across the street to a dim liquor store and bought a half pint of something in the whiskey family rather too expensive for this neighborhood. He smoothed it into his student corduroys and walked diagonally over to the club called Memmo, which the kids called Meme-y. (Who knew why.) He joined a small unexpected queue inside, showed ID, got patted down and yet got away with the booze smuggle, paid a small cover, tripped awkward on brick flooring inside and stumbled clumsy right into gorgeous her.

# 2.

"Well, well, if it isn't the prof making his play," said Lila May ravishing in a white Mexican blouse discreetly embroidered loose over her unnerving curves and then, lower, hanging loose over a tightly pasted-on pair of real denim jeans, un-designered. She handed him back to himself. "And you smell like pulled pork."

"Not actually a prof," he said sheepishly grinning and trying to suavely regain somewhat his fallen dignifity. "And it was the brisket I had. I thought that was what Texas is all about."

"Oh," she said. "Another one of those come here to discover what Texas is all about. Bluebells, longhorns, and Lone Star beer. There you have it," she said and pretended to turn around. "Y'all. My daddy made his money in aw-all."

"Wait, please," he said. "I'm just a teacher's assistant."

"Yes?" she inquired mock-impatiently.

"Well, since I'm not your professor, actually, then maybe it's okay if you chill with me? I mean we can be friendly, since I'm not your professor."

"Okay with whom?" she said taking a large glug of a wheat beer.

"Okay with the bartender," he said as he held up two fingers to the bedheaded lunk who had been staring at Lila May but now wanted discourse of Rieslings, bocks, and single malts—not that this crowd was into much more than Pabst Blue Ribbon, a bunch of cheap sheep. (Stink pink for frugal ewe.) He scurried to pop a deuce of longnecks.

"Do you presume to beer me, sir?" she said holding her arms back and thrusting out with her ample chest.

He did likewise. "Aye?" he said, not conversant in spontaneity's ways. "And thou?"

She laughed. "I'll stay for one quick one. But 'Aye'?"

"Don't be cruel. I may be a science dweeb but I've been dragged through the nerdosphere in my Santa Barbara days, from cosplay to Klingon. Had a girlfriend once who knew the Pini's collected *Elfquest* and shit."

"Oh God," she said. "Ren Fair damsel denizen?"

"Worse," he said.

"Jesus, you poor lamb. RPG. Did you ever have sex not in costume?"

"A painful personal question, but no. And, um, what is sex again? Dost thou mean the beast with two backs?"

"Aw, Christ. Too much information." Her blue eyes actually glowed at this point.

"I agree. This is moving pretty much way too fast. Wanna go watch the band?"

She grabbed his arm, which gave him a jolt, though he played along fake calm. They wandered outside where a small stagefull of t-shirted musicians were tuning up and one of them said one-two-three, the drums crashed and another made the universal a-whoo-ing howl as Lila May walked by.

"Hey hey Lila May," said the drummer, a roll of greased offal and fat wrapped in skin. "If I said you had a beautiful body, would you hold it against me?"

Shaney stopped and said, hey. And the drummer said may I help you? The other guys in the band swarmed around him like an amoeba-borne intervention, antibodies on a germ. They asked the drummer to fuckin' apologize in any moment he might find convenient. Like now.

The percussionist pig glared at Shaney and Lila May and grunted, turned, and hopped off the stage, walked right by roomie Louis Lamel who was inconspicuously there too.

The drummer said sorry like a fifth grade moron, turned on a dime, and hopped back on the stage, a considerable feat considering his girth. Shaney was too caught in the hot aftermath of the macho exchange, chest puffed.

Louis lurked just outside of Lila's sight.

And then the band played on. One-two-three and the guitarist struck a screaming note and distorted it into a musical howl that made Lila May laugh.

Meanwhile, the sky's silver orb emerged from a cloud as if in response to the plaintive tone. The long low savage note penetrated minds and bodies, but particularly John's roommate. People said whoa as the feedback grew and arced into a roar and then resolved into a rapid tuneful strum. Louis had to leave.

Shaney was electrified a different way and grabbed Lila's hand. Dancing. She pulled back and looked at him but Shaney was abandoned to the entirety of an electronic song's allure, his eyes bouncing orbs and a smile, almost all bared teeth, pasted his face. He gentled up with a shrug and she had to admit to herself that something right there and then turned over in *her*, a new *leif*. She squeezed his hand. It wasn't all cheap moves.

They played sweet then the band stopped a shuffle mid groove and began discordant shrieky interludes ending in a melodramatic but pleasurable resolution. John was down with this band, despite the drummer's loutishness. Tune up and amplifier adjustments ensued and John said he liked.

"They're called Oil Can What," she said. He laughed.

She said she didn't understand the joke, assumed it was random? But Shaney got it right away. It's an insider *Wizard of Oz* reference, he said. I'm pretty sure. Shy suddenly. The Tin Man, well, if I have to explain it, it's lame. No, go ahead she said with widened eyes. Shaney somehow managed a non-mansplainy voice. Remember they find The Tin Man rusted shut and he calls out "Oilcan?" with a rusty jaw? Muted? Dorothy understands and heads for the lubricant. But the Scarecrow wonders aloud, well, the band name. Oil Can What?

You get it?

Oh I never did, it's very funny. Though she wasn't laughing, more admiring. And the last shred of her resistance to infatuation disappeared.

Besides, they danced and it worked. He had his shoulders up that white boy way and was on and off the beat like someone struggling with a second language. But when he shyly smiled at some flub and recovery she smiled too and his shoulders soon dropped. He shook. With the luck of those doomed to fall in love, the music suddenly shifted into tribal drums and screaming anthem melodies of transcendence. The stupid drummer glared at him. Smiling, Shaney moved closer for the kill. She had sexy moves when he did. Now there was no thinking involved. The rest of the set was good for her. Even when she smelled his percolating sweat through musty clothes, she liked it: It was *her* heart and she was giving it away in pieces tonight, all night, she decided.

He sensed he was doing well, and at the break bought more beers but remembered him of the half pint in his pocket. He guided her over to a secluded corner where they couldn't see the band, but also couldn't be seen by oblivious bouncers, and produced the Scotch. She gladly accepted the first swig. It burned, she sighed as relief and release translated to her veins.

"Like them?" she asked, meaning the band.

"I'm getting over the first douchey impression. They've got a good sound. I like the name."

"I like it now too. It was his idea, believe it or not. I never thought he was clever."

"Whose idea?"

"The drummer. They used to be Saliva Sativa, which wasn't too bad, probably more the way they sound."

He thought about band names, meaningless and meaningful, everybody knew when it was right. Then it dawned. "Wait a minute, how came *you* to be master of intimate Oil Can What trivia?"

"Oh. I thought you knew I know them. I thought you knew that was why I was here. And besides it's Mistress of Trivia, I think?" she said, pert.

"So. Not here to meet me?" he said. "Wait another minute, you *know* the jerk drummer," he said shouting over the rising psychedelic din, his throat hoarsening.

She looked him straight on, not quite defiantly. "In the Biblical sense," she said, just as the crescendo ended and her shout rang out over silence.

"That would be a good name for a band, too," he said after a few openmouthed seconds passed between them. She said, "In the Biblical Sense, a long while ago."

She squeezed his hand and knit her brow. "I gotta inspect the plumbing here," she said, winked, and headed for the loos. He agreed to wait, bobbing his forehead. The drummer came forward on stage and looked at him. Made an obscene gesture that implied oral sex with a woman and laughed. When Lila returned, looking a bit flush, the band was swarming back from the short huddle break. They then played a somnolent set as Lila May smiled and the moon showed its face above them. Not many short tunes later, the band stopped and the singer said thanks Austin we're Oil Can What. Thunderous applause intruded and then died. John pulled out the whiskey and they drank deep and he wondered how he could spirit her away from here. He heard some screams not far away.

The shithead drummer came back on stage and introduced a guy named Thorhammer, who stood in for him on a jammy solo but it was clearly a fake-out preface to a grand finale, oldest trick in the books, they had taken a bow but now they started playing their local hit just as Lila returned. "Nothing Doesn't Change," with its deft theft from Dino's moon in your eyes like a big pizza pie that nobody got anyways. But everybody danced in pleasure until it was over.

By then Shaney had to pee like a racehorse, excused himself heading for the bathrooms, which were down a long hall behind the stage and to the right. Shaney saw the stupid drummer enter the same facility where he was heading: Drummer Pigdog, her old lover. He had been ready to deck the guy in his fantasy life, but now that he was heading into the smelly intimacy of the men's room Shaney didn't feel so cocky, so to speak.

It was a huge bathroom and when he walked in, he saw the drummer in front of a row of faucets lock-eyed with himself in the mural-sized mirror. He didn't say anything as the drummer acknowledged him over his own shoulder through the glass brightly. Shaney didn't return any dude or bro greetings figuring that'd fix him.

"Wait, man, I know you," said the musician. Shaney stopped and before he could reply negatively, the drummer said. "Watch out for her, man. Lila May, goddammit."

Shaney was deeply, poisonously, embarrassed. He had no idea what to do, or say, turned out, he's not a fighter so he turned his head and the rest of him mumbling some vague threat that made the drummer chuckle. Shaney retreated past the row of ivory-colored urinals and feeling unmanned ducked into a stall and unzipped to be alone with his shame. He just met the woman and here he was betraying her honor with silence.

He wanted to lay into the fucking drummer. Take him out. But. He drooped his head and fell into a surprising long deep funk, a spell. He heard voices growling and he found himself standing, drawing out a long veil of toilet paper. The drummer said something like fuck you asshole and then it changed into sort of a woman's voice. Was he fucking some groupie in a stall? A short shriek rose from and fell to the silence of the tiled floor. After a second, Shaney flushed but sat down. Blood rolled under the door and he stood up as did the hair on the back of his head.

He would be a man not a mouse. There was a rivulet that widened and ran from the first stall where sat the drummer staring blankly back at him with a look of certain horror. He was seeing It, thought Shaney. It had frozen him forever, that which he saw. Dreamland abandoned forever and ever, the idea of the nothing, that idea hostile to what our senses teach us, was what he was heeding now. There was blood all over his plaid from his neck torn open. His neck was open. Shaney was breathing deeply. The dead drummer, name of Wally Shug wasn't breathing at all. Shaney holding onto the aluminum wall of the stall looking at the bloody man worrying about germs swarming off the wall, worried whether his fingerprints were printing on it in exchange. Should he wipe it down, he thought, thinking like a television criminal. How many millions of people came here and left prints? Was there a camera? Actually, if there was he would be exonerated, right? He decided to back out and tell someone if he could find someone who wouldn't panic. He had intended to beat the guy up. Somebody else did far worse. Shaney thought he heard a rough snuffling from somewhere behind him. He walked out and nobody, not one person saw him because they were all looking at the arrant proud rock stars goofing off and riffing. John found a beefy guy. Asked if he was security. "There's a dead man in a toilet stall." The guy looked at him and trundled off.

John remembered Lila May. He turned and, stomach clenched, went to seek her in the moonlit courtyard where they first met. She was standing in exactly the same spot where he left her, posed exactly as he last saw her in his beating mind's eye. She put her hand up and jerked her head gently up. Yo. He nodded and swallowed the image of the man dead on the toilet, her onetime lover. Someone shrieked.

"Someone attacked the drummer," he said. "I think he's dead."

And she said, "Okay. Let's go."

He looked for a second at the stage and the hubbub, it took time to get through the crowd and by that time an ambulance was splashing harsh light outside the door. The door where he tripped entering. That was fast.

"Okay," he said. "Where to?"

She looked stern. "For a walk," she said. "Under the moon, full and bright," she said. "It's full and I want to feel out in it." She sounded rebellious. That was cute.

Some screaming. Shaney thought about the Beatles, his mother told him girls in movie theaters screamed when *Hard Day's Night* was playing. Lila extended her hand. It was moist and cool, and John tried to tug her forward. She didn't move along willingly.

"He's dead," she said.

A longhaired dude with his eyes round and glazed walked by. Lila May just stared, but then the dude said, "I think the drummer is dead.

Probably O.D.ed. Horse?" said the longhair looking at Shaney. "What big eyes you have."

The hippie walked away.

"Walt? The drummer?" She let go Shaney's arm and then a host of security guards swarmed out from the club looking for someone. Shaney thought they were looking for him but they ran past. Lila ran back to the bathroom. Shaney followed but Lila was nimbler and got there just as a bouncer formed a pick outside the archway. He wanted her to stop but she said something in his cauliflower ear and he smiled and let her go by. Shaney could not imagine what secret word or pointed quip could possibly melt a burly guard into such willing relent.

She came back silent. When he asked her what, she held up a hand. They left mum; left the club and walked the slight downhill slope to Sixth Street, which was beginning to coalesce. The street's buzzing carnality included straight hookers and trannie hookers circling out from shadows to make contact in storefront light. Nobody had to sell hard—all the rides were smooth and the fares reasonable. Of course, more blasé hustle offers went down, too—boys on girls and boys on boys and girls girls girls as a couple of signs said. Drug deals and cons, winks and even fights. Music floated from every quarter accompanied sharp by the clank of beer bottles. They walked by the museum of oddities, a poor cousin of Madame Tussauds'. This swiveled their heads momentarily to take in the promise of a dogfaced boy named Jojo, prompting them separately to consider the valuation of life from a freak's point of view. Specifically, does life's brevity seem a blessing to those deformed and held to ridicule? Neither shared their identical reflections. Down by Congress Street she took his hand. He thrilled.

She stopped and asked if it was okay they went inside this little coffee house, this one? He said, sure, of course. She smiled wanly. "It was the drummer, Walt," she said.

He nodded. She doubled up and ungracefully puked.

Somebody walking by said, "Aw fuckin' drunk," and John let off holding her tender to walk over to the loudmouth, "What did you fuckin' say?"

The guy sized up his scrawny opponent but he also took in John's burning eyes. He mumbled something vaguely like an apology and walked away backwards. Almost out of hearing, the somebody said, "An asshole and a drunk. That just about sums up the Sixth Street shuffle after 10 p.m."

Shaney started down the street but she grabbed his shirt. "That's okay," she said, weakly. "My hero."

They went inside the coffee shop, which turned out to be a Lesbian of the Wiccan Persuasion hangout. Shaney picked up a plastic menu and even though the outside bore no signage, the top of the document read: Tea Is for Texas. Shaney snorted but Lila May remained quiet within. One look at Lila brought two swart waitresses over immediately offering balms and succors ranging from a glass of ice water to an herbal tea from the shady side of the Andes, which, being barely legal, was offered in breathy urgings. John was intrigued and held up two fingers and said please. His humility duly noted brought forth a bustle of crisper activity. Water and then the blend, which one sipped from a leather cup through stainless steel straws soon loosened their bodies toward each other. He asked her if she was alright now.

"Sure. I'm sorry. He was gross but always sweet to me."

I asked how she got past the guard. Told him who I am, she said.

"Every woman in that room wanted that drummer, at some point." She asserted the fact plainly. "And now he's cold forever?"

"The drummer," Shaney said. "Your friend?"

"You found him. Makes you a suspect." She smiled and then the waitress asked her if she needed more hot water. Shaney stared at her.

Meanwhile Lila was off on another topic, chirping about the Sixth Street scene, she had apparently overcome sadness for her ex lover. Nonetheless, she still looked a little green again. "I saw blood," she said, "a lot of blood." He took her hand and comforted, there there.

"You *are* a sweet nerd scientist," she looked up and smiled through her pretty eyes goggling with tears.

"Aw, now you're making fun of me. I always wonder where people get the gall to call themselves stuff like scientist, or athlete or artist." He skipped over the real issue.

"Maybe money makes the difference. You're an artist when it sells. I'm a poet, for instance."

He gulped. "I don't make much money."

"O, don't worry, I do. I just published a poem in the newspaper. Want to hear it? They paid me $22.50. The topic was the moonlight on the desert."

"Please," he said.

The sky above, the dust below,
Shenanigans my horse
Beneath the mantle of the moon
Trots on a half mile course

We flew together sky above
We left the dust below
Shenanigans the silver moon
Is full tonight you know

He lifted his weird tea cup to her and clinked. He didn't understand contemporary poetry, though it all sounded nice to him. This also seemed a little old fashioned too at the same time, rhyming and stuff. "Word nerd," he said. "That was beautiful."

"I didn't really publish that. I just made it up. I did publish an essay in the Austin paper about my horse, Shenanigans. Got paid a hundred bucks for it. Someday I'll tell you my whole sad story." She swallowed tea, tears, and snot and laughed.

Shaney was suddenly lost. It seemed too hard to proceed along these lines. Too hard.

"How about this Austin weather," he asked. "And what should I know about moonlight in the desert?"

"Unbearable after spring, but we make do," she said. She deeply appreciated that he held his end of the small talk like he held her when she was throwing up. Tender. That's what matters. Softness. People wandered in. Maybe some were from the show. Nobody seemed freaked out. If the word was loud on the streets, it had not infiltrated this far down Sixth Street into this female warrior enclave. The banality of evil is a phrase she remembered to remember.

Both felt a sudden overwhelming urge to pee, then decided the weird simultaneity must be connected to the mystery tea. Whatta ya gonna do? Anyway, they got up same time and announced excuses with the same exact words and laughed with the same tones. He said, after you! like a cartoon chipmunk and she, knowing the reference from ancient television said no, no, no, I insist! So they left together, heading to a dark hall off the main room leading toward commodes.

When they got there, they spied with their four eyes a five-pointed star illuminated by candles and tiny twinkling white lights. Cleverly canted, it was the iconic Texas flag but rotated to one side, to more closely resemble a pentagram, a pentangle, or whatever mystic shit you want to call it.

"I can't go back there," she said.

"Why on earth not?" he asked.

"I can't," she said with a solemn finality. "I'll go next door to the bar bathroom, take care of my bidness, and meet you there at our favorite table. You go ahead hence." She pointed toward the terminus alit. Omen moment.

"Well, okay then," he said as she went straight for the front door, blew right, and evaporated. He walked down past the mystic sign, whizzed in a flash, washed hands, returned to the table, paid the bill, and left a large tip fearing the robust women running the establishment. Outside he caught neither hide nor hair of her.

Walking to the door on the right with its steamy windows, he met a burly bouncer who was a cross between the dish soap genie and a professional wrestler.

"Gonna bet you're the prof," said the deep-voiced, gentle giant.

"I'm not really a professor," he answered.

"And that's the secret password," he smiled a gap-toothed smile and hooked his thumb over his broad shoulder indicating. Herself was perched inside and it turns out their favorite table *was* a nice one.

On the crisp linen already was a neat scotch for him which turned out to be a stunning single malt, the likes of which he had never sipped.

There was licorice and petroleum, flowery sprays, and iron walls in it. She had champagne, bubbles winking on the brim kinda thing. He was confused by her abrupt departure, the change of venue for their *tete a tete* and, as much as anything, the swift appearance of nice booze. He picked up his glass and clinked against hers. She wasn't exactly avoiding his eyes, though, downcast smiling and shy smiles returned to him.

"Cheers," he said. "What gives?"

"Can't a girl buy a boy a drink? Does that seem predatory? I'm hoping you're not hung up on macho machismo."

"No," he said. "Prefer my sex roles scrambled, thank you. Remember, I'm a science nerd? I haven't got much besides my brain. But really, what was up back there with the pentagram avoidance? Are we born again?"

"Are we born a first time? I mean, how do we really know?"

"Okay, if you don't want to talk about it. Who am *I* to ask?"

"Depends. Do you have a girlfriend? You mentioned a girlfriend."

"No. That was long ago in a land far away."

"Then you must be my boyfriend." She smiled, didn't wink.

He smiled back not really knowing what to answer. "O-kay, then," he said slowly.

He looked at her and found every bit of her darling. Her nose, lips, and ears. He thought that exact word, "darling," though the delicacy of her looks was clearly underscored by something deep and wild tumbling from her throat and caught up in her spooky laughter.

"Whatever," he added, willing to employ the generational mantra.

This room, this swank bar was buzzing unlike the insulated calm of the lesbian café. People were leaning together; at the very next linen-covered table somebody was mumbling. "His neck was covered with blood and his shirt was red and he was dead, translated into the aether. Who knew? So much blood," said the close-cropped wigging pretty boy at that table. John could have sworn a group of people were pointing at him and Lila May.

"Are you okay?" he asked her softly.

"Enough about me," she said. "What do *you* think about me?" She looked up from her booze enhanced spell.

"I think your boyfriend and girlfriend idea is good, on balance," he said.

"Well of course it is," she said looking at the door with unease and then smiling at him.

Given the strangeness of the circumstances, talk came easier now. They even got to know each other like a movie; met cute. She wanted to be a research director and her father was happy about it. He does that too, she said. He told her about his research including the sexy drugs, which he often played down. She wasn't big on drugs but she liked science fiction movies. "I go to Vulcan Video and look for hours. Junky good stuff like *Them* and *Day of the Triffids*. Horror and science fiction are real good drugs."

"Austin still has video stores? I loved them," said Shaney sincere. "You could meet girls and talk 'em into watching scary movies at your place and then, bajing." He was a little embarrassed then. "Not that I ever did it, but the possibility was there."

"You mean kadoosh, don't you?" He was cute when red embarrassed. She said there there. Then music—they both loved Deerhoof, Animal Collective, and Grizzly Bear. Gossip flourished too. She knew all the college gossip, which, of course, fascinated him, the new kid. He learned more buying her two Brave Bulls after the bubbly than he had from roommate talk all quarter long. Turns out, the entire faculty was dusting itself off from a decade of effulgent bisexual dalliances. But now sex was out.

"Why?" he asked.

"I think it's a seasonal thing, like animals have whatyoucall estrus."

He laughed, though who knows? Western Civilization certainly seemed to swing between waspishness and ribaldry. In and out of rut? Meanwhile, Shaney couldn't help notice how attentive the staff was to them and, though never really paranoid, he felt people staring at them, like they were celebrities. When he looked up, the eyes averted just like that. It was both uncomfortable and exhilarating.

Then there were lights, police lights, outside roaring down Sixth Street one way, screeching to a halt, yanking their wheels around and returning, sirens in the Doppler-shifting outside world that seemed more beautiful now after the tequila on top of the scotch and the tea. The lights and sirens stopped outside. Wouldn't it be funny if they were coming for us, he thought. Then there were three uniforms inside the door and everybody turned to observe cops as phenomena. One of the hosts turned towards them and mouthed, "I'm sorry," while pointing them in the right direction to make the funny wish he had come true. As the blue parade headed towards their table, Lila May said, "Shit, I was afraid of this."

# 3.

"Okay, Lila, as you might have surmised, we gotta go," said the tallest cop who bared his head and doffed his cap towards Shaney's date. Polite. But his voice allowed no scintilla of accommodation.

"Now, see here," Shaney said, hearing the hollow, stilted bravado of his own voice. "You can't just march up to a table and arrest somebody like that. Even in Texas."

This remark drew surprised looks from the lawbringing trio.

"What are you saying about my state?" asked the roundest one, more puzzled than offended. "Was that some kind of disparagement, slur, impugnage, whatever?"

Surprisingly, Lila joined the balding cop. "Yeah, John. What does that even mean?"

"I simply meant that you can't just barge in and order us around. It's not the old west. Mr. Dillon, Mr. Dillon," he said, flapping his arms around doing a decent Chester imitation. Shaney might have been a little buttered at this point.

"Who mentioned arrest?" asked the first constable. "And was that a *Gunsmoke* reference? I watched that show once. The whole set—Dodge City, right?—feels like a retirement home hallucination."

"And yet it was the longest running television program in history, until *The Simpsons*," said the youngest lawman. "Which must mean something."

"I'm still not sure what *he's* implying," said the tall gun. "Can I see your I.D., sir?"

Just as Shaney reached for his license, remembering there were 28 hits of his homemade hallucinogens zippered in the wallet, the officer's radio blew its nose. The cop held his hand out to abey John's proffered wallet, and, relieved, John abeyed.

A kazoo voice uttered phrases from the microphone receiver.

"Okay, okay, ten-four, and then we snore. She's coming in," the cop said, annoyed.

"And then we roar," corrected the round cop. "Lila, *sil vous plait?*"

Shaney's "girlfriend" rose looking nonetheless like it was a lark.

"What about me?" Shaney said, happy to put away the drugs. His date was now officially in *interruptus*. "I mean, what are the charges against this woman?"

They laughed at him again. Lila gave a little helpless wave as she swept out and off with the officers. "See you soon, boyfriend," she said.

"Bummer," said the busboy at his shoulder. All the help seemed suddenly cooler to the touch after Lila May exited pursued by cops. It wasn't anything actually tangible, but the mood of the room transmogrified. Shaney picked up the check and left a tiny tip for the waitress named Minnie Jo who signed with hearts dotting her I's.

Outside, the full moon was lost behind cloud cover sailing; Shaney thought he saw Louis Lamel stumble by. "Hey roomie," he said. Walleyed, his roommate rolled past.

Shaney stared.

"Whoa," said a busboy outside smoking through his break. "You see a ghost or something?"

Shaney explained nothing in discombobulated fashion. He mentioned the drummer's death and the cops taking his date though. Somewhere a cat hissed.

"The wolf is back," said the young man moving out of shadows.

"What're you talking about?" Shaney said.

"It's the full moon and we haven't had one of these unexplained murders since, well, last full moon. You ask any Austinian."

"I will, indeed," Shaney said, thought about Lila and watched the clouds. Down the street he could see Louis rooted to a corner. The sky was moon-brightening, peekaboo.

"There's this legend," the busboy said, "about the Wuff-man livin' in Austin. Awoowuff. Every time somebody gets killed so the police are baffled, it's blamed on the wuffperson.

"They even blamed it on a thing happened at my house," Shaney said, happy for a concrete distraction.

"What thing?" asked the busboy grinding out his cigarette in a fountain of sparks.

"Our roommate Laurel disappeared. By a lycanthrope was her demise." Said Shaney trying to sound like Yoda.

"Dude, werewolf in your crib? No wonder they took Lila away from you," said the busboy pulling out another smoke.

"What do you know?" asked Shaney, then straightened out. "Hey, I've got to go get my girl, um, my friend, man. Gotta save Lila May."

"Don't worry, man. Lila May is always safe, 'specially with the cops," said the bouncer. The sky's light was broadening. The busboy shrugged and went back in the bar. Shaney asked Mr. Clean where the police station was and got a little growl for an answer.

Meanwhile, not too far away, Lila May was entertaining a cadre of cops sitting not four blocks from the place from whence Shaney embarked as hero.

"You hear about the guy with five penises?" Lila May said at the cop shop, staring directly into the eye of the sole policewoman in the group. She sat on a desktop shapely leg crossed over shapely leg.

"Do tell," said icy-voiced Lieutenant Mary Peapes.

"This guy with five penises goes into a doctor and the doctor says, 'My God you have five penises. That's amazing, I've never seen anything like it,' says the doctor. 'How do your pants fit?' says the doctor. 'Like a glove, says the guy.'"

"He had five penises," said the woman slowly drawling. "That's why a glove."

Meanwhile, outside, John Shaney is stopping people on the street to find out where the precinct station just might be.

He was lost even though the neighborhood was a grid. Panic, slow growing, had changed his physiological functions—raised them to the animal level; sounds, flashing lights, and scents were concatenating as he strode through the mix of urban businesses and old houses. Once in a while a yard would explode into dog howls and inhaled snarls and it pushed his body, his already beating heart and heaving lungs, into overdrive. His search was not systematic and his thoughts kept exploding into pissy rhetorical protests. How could the police do this? Wasn't this America?

Meanwhile.

"Okay one more," Lila said. The police gal moaned. "This woman takes her dog to a vet for a checkup and after a clean bill of health asks the vet what was up with the dog's hairy ears. If you don't like it, says the vet, I recommend a depilatory. What's that? You can get it over the counter in any drugstore, says the clerk. Just ask. So she goes to the pharmacy asks for it. A hair remover, the druggist says. You want Nair. He gives her a bottle and tells her some of the precautions. If you use it on your legs, don't sunbathe for a couple of days. On your underarms, don't use strong soap. But I need it for my Schnauzer, the woman says. Then don't ride your bike for about a week."

The policewoman covers her eyes and pretends to cry. Everybody else is wolf howling with laughter. Schnauzer the policeman screams. One of the detectives arrived to drive Lila home, a courtesy.

Shaney found the building seconds after they left. It had no obvious markings, the better to harbor the fascists, Shaney said out loud. *Achtung.* Entering, he found an empty lobby with an old telephone on an end table between two shabby couches of an early 1970s vintage—plastic passing itself off as Corinthian. Radar red.

He picked up the phone. "Night dispatch," said the voice on the line.

"Hi," he said.

"Can I help you please," said voice without body, obviously practicing patience.

"I'm looking for a woman, um, name of Lila May, who was brought in tonight."

"Yes?" said the woman flattened into a blue uniform.

"Um, falsely, I believe," he said.

"Listen, I don't care much about your beliefs, please. Was this Miss Lila May arrested? I have no record of any Miss May, arrested or brought in here."

"Shit, I'm sorry. Her last name was Wulfhardt."

"Oh," said the woman. "Why didn't you say so?"

The door buzzed and it took him a second to realize it had been unlocked for him. He caught it just in time. The hall loomed long. The hall loomed empty.

A door opened and a blue-capped head poked out. "Down here," it said noncommittally. "You all just step right in, please."

The policeman looked puzzled when Shaney came through the door into the unhealthy light, bulbs that seemed to buzz with cancer-causing carcinogens. "Where's your friend?" said the cop.

"Excuse me?"

"The guy that was with you in the hall."

"Nobody else. Just me myself and nobody else," Shaney said.

"Nonsense," he said. Then the brittle-chinned cop poked his head out the door. "I could've sworn…"

"Please," said perplexed and vexed John Shaney. "I need to see Lila May."

"Are you her cousin, uncle, brother?"

"No, not… I was with her when she was arrested and I'm here to straighten things out. You see I was with her all evening and she was never in any, she didn't do anything. That is, she was arrested for nothing, which I can testify."

"Arrested," said the officer returning to a crowded desk. "Why was Lila May arrested?" He picked up a phone and barked questions. He grunted an agreement and groaned as one would at a bad joke.

"Just like I thought," he said coming back into the room. "Now you're sure nobody was with you? Anyway, she's not arrested. We just made sure she went back to Wulfhardt. Her ride came."

"She's not here."

"She went home."

"You didn't arrest her."

"Now why on God's Green Earth would we arrest Lila May?"

"You keep asking that like you know her."

"Who doesn't?" asked the officer, now patently annoyed.

"Can you tell me where she lives?"

"Okay, now I'm pissed. Look we have a possible murder at a nightclub. We have the usual Saturday night in downtown Austin. And now I have a guy trying to bilk the police for a rich girl's home address. I fuckin' let you in, but now I wish I had not."

"She's my girlfriend," Shaney said, though his heart was not behind the phrase. Shaney was confused. Why did he say they took her back to Wulfhardt? Wasn't that her last name? "I better go look for her," he said mostly to himself.

"Don't leave mad, buddy," said the other cop.

"Yeah, calm down and go," added a voice from behind a computer, been there the whole time, a voice he hadn't noticed till this second.

He wandered the streets in a kind of sawtooth diagonal, unthinkingly heading for home. The buildings in this neighborhood seemed to alternate between houses of faith and places of low intoxication and assignation. Pick up redemption parlors. To be fair, he too was on a pick up date, and wondering about his cosmic destiny at the same time, well, most of the time.

John Shaney decided then and there his date wouldn't be over till he knew his "girlfriend" was safe. Arriving ahead of himself—he almost didn't notice he was in front of his own home till he saw his car in the street—he entered with the heavy Schlage key hoping someone would be up chatting in the dining room. Someone to set him straight about Lila May, who he had concluded, was known to everyone. Nobody home, darkness and dark ghosts swirling, so upstairs he fired up the old laptop.

Of course, he found her right away on Facebook, but of course, the information was superficially offered, like a gnomic poem without scholarly notes decoding. Friending her now would be a little awkward. Besides, her boyfriending him had superseded it. He would be her rescuer, not her buddy. Fuck it, he *would* rescue. That was not a decision so much as a wave of whatness. Contact he wanted. Her page said she liked Boethius and Harry Potter. In the bar, she admitted to liking Ovid and Kafka, both Metamorphosi. She was currently obsessed with Kinks songs, in particular the one about people swarming like flies around Waterloo Underground.

He shook his head and Googled "Wulfhardt."

Aha.

A town *and* a family. Which was named for which? That remained mysterious. What was clear, though: Lila May was the daughter of a very rich Texas oil, cattle, and drug manufacturing lord of the land, respected and feared by plain folk living in the namesake town (well, that much might be conjecture). In fact, she was, they were Wulfhardts from Wulfhardt, a town less than an hour's drive from Austin up into the hilly lands. He went back to her page. Her face, younger yet beckoning him into the future. He decided to find Lila, then and there, Amen. There was even a street address for her papa's home in, of all places, an online phonebook. They had a landline. He packed up the laptop and thought he could be there before midnight, or well before. He would sing outside her window, baying at the moon.

The old green Hybrid ran great, but had suffered from the specific brand of neglect that student economies engender. Everything was nearby, so he rarely drove. Thus, with no gas, oil low, windows dirty, and tires, well… more on that later. But he turned it over and she started right up. Shaney had glanced at a Google map then printed step-by-step directions to take him from his rickety front porch to the porticoed, antebellum columns of Wulfhardt manse in the city of Wulfhardt. He whispered goodbye to absent roomies, didn't leave a note. Last second, he chose a shortcut route through mountains knowing it might end up a winding one lane road. Getting stuck behind some rube in a rusty tractor at this hour seemed unlikely. It was not quite ten as he threw the car from P to D and headed toward the onramp moving all wayward hearts west with headlights lit gold and silver. But something came tumbling after.

In the evening's course of concert and bar Shaney had five drinks but felt no ill effects, he told himself. As precaution, though, he stopped for coffee with refuel at a poison-yellow-lighted highway minimart, and choked down the bitter brew with only Cremora and sugar to dull its grating edge. Tank full and hopped up on the road, Eric Burdon and the Animals singing "Gotta get outta this place" on the radio, he laughed and then tuned out as the radio signal began drifting like a ghost around an FM universe. It sent him eerie half-messages about home security and credit card catastrophes. Gradually caffeine entered his sluice veins and took over.

Shaney saw himself in the dark car window and wondered what the hell he was doing. He was a man of science. Ruled by natural law tamed by logic—the scientific method: you know, theory and proof. His heart was pounding now because he was on a hunt not tempered by reason, but by a supposition too vague to name. The proof was this act, a pudding he could not resist. The vision in the windows was of a mysteriously self-assured night stalker moving with dark grace towards a destiny too murky for even him to understand.

But this reflection on self-reflection lasted less time than station identification on the drifting radio signal, now playing "The Lion Sleeps Tonight," as Shaney, inside his hurtling car twenty-five minutes later headed into scrub-forested hills above Austin city. He saw deer eyes in the bushes; rabbits dared the road ahead of him. He would have no mercy; he was driving hard and being driven to remit his girlfriend's captivity.

The map called it a highway, but it looked like a pitiful stretch of crumbling asphalt with the Harry Potter-ish name Fangtooth Lane posted above bullet-riddled highway signs. Ha, he thought, good thing I don't believe in omens.

He did wish, however, that the night wasn't such a heavy black blank. The road wound up into dark, and the moon was back in clouds.

Sometimes glints and reflections below suggested broad rivers or maybe wide lakes lit by streetlamps. It probably was scenic, by daylight. His radio meanwhile had gone crazy. He listened in on a conversation hailing from Nebraska all about the proper use of sheep dip and the horrors of hoof and mouth.

And then like it was right in front of him, Shaney saw the drummer Shug horribly askance with blood flowing from his neck. He shook it off, Pee-tee-ess-in-deed. Then the moon came out, the road reappeared, and Shaney muttered a dark curse. Try not to think of a dead man on a toilet seat.

And by now the asphalt part of the road was losing badly to the dust and rocks beneath it and beneath that sand and sandcrabs stretching to Pacific seas. Probably. Signs were farther and farther apart. The night was buckshot with stars but they seemed distant in this high country by moonlight.

Coming around a long sweeping-to-the-right bend, he suddenly had to curse and stamp on screaming brakes. There ahead of him in the road stood a zombie. Hair long and furiously unkempt, its face glowed white with an expression of frozen thought: as if its affect had been shut off forever. The manthing began walking towards Shaney in the halting spasmodic way of cinematic terrors evolving from Val Lewton to George Romero. How this horror had stepped out of a movie and into this roadway was the mystery. One answer might be: hallucination.

Waving his hands over his head, "Hey, man," the zombie drawled, "thanks for stopping, dude."

John got out. His car had died in the sudden screeching halt, and he heard a terrible hiss emanating from the front end. What it might mean chilled him far deeper than this apparition with stoner voice.

"Bummer," said the zombie, looking down in the vicinity of tires. "Don't guess you have two spares, man."

He looked at the supposed monster and saw now a shabby man, out late, possibly a stroke victim, in an earlier age, another era, a polio catastrophe.

"Are they both flat? Shit," said Shaney, surprisingly calm.

"Well one is de-eh-finitely fuh-lat," said the lone walker. "Both are as bald as my dead Papa," he laughed. "T'other might leak slow enough for us to limp it over to Uncle John."

Shaney looked at the formerly undead man, uncomprehending, now lost in self-pity and seeing his romantic quest disappear at the sudden onset of bad circumstances.

"What is that, Uncle John?" said Shaney. "A garage? Won't be open this late," he said, despairing sigh in his voice harmonizing with two tires hissing air into the air.

"What. Your… no… your Uncle John's is a kinda cuh-rash pad and puh-arty house right nearby. Somebody there drinkin' nice keg beer and somebody there can fix tires."

"You think," said Shaney, dubious.

"O I know, bra," he said. "Let's hop uh-in and ho-hope fer the best."

They did after changing the left tire quick, motivated by said hope. The drive *wasn't* far. The zombie gave assurances and the wheels held over the rugged terrain. Shaney had doubts about this guy, especially after smelling him: a gaggy combination of campfire, BO, and sickly sweet alcohol breath. But also something fundamental—so to speak—in his scent. It wasn't death. It was likely unchanged underwear.

"You were scared a me for a second," said lurky man, who gave his name as Junior Lee, like the funk icon robber.

"Seen too many horror films," Shaney said. "Your appearance in the headlights…"

"Thought I was the fuckin' walking deceased," he chuckled low. "Well, you're not too far off. Turn right here," he said pointing to an unlikely opening in the low brush. It was unmarked if it was a road.

He negotiated the turn but everything felt mushy and the car dipped and scraped bumper in a dry culvert across the dirt road. Where are you taking me? John Shaney wondered.

"It's not far, ruh-eally," said the strange fellow now seriously stinking up the coupe. "You know what lupus is?"

Shaney muttered something vague, "A wasting disease." He looked over.

"Yeah. I think I have it. Buh-hummer, huh? You know the name means red wolf? Huh? You know it's not contagious? You know, it's not curable and you know people can't explain why lupus sufferers have it one day and not the next. It comes and goes. What a we know? Most doctors agree that it's a good idea to avoid sunlight if you have it. Hence the zombie lifestyle. You know what exacerbate means?"

"Yeah," he answered. "Sunlight makes it worse. But what difference does it make, if you don't know for sure if you have it?" It's an age of hypochondria, Shaney thought. We live with too much information, and nary enough wisdom.

"What does it all fuckin' mean? Oh, fu-huck, almost missed it, turn here. Avoid the sunlight. It means I'm turning into a monster, fuckin' Duh-racula."

"More like a werewolf, I'd say," muttered Shaney too busy avoiding a boulder to be tactful or sympathetic. His wise-ass American boy self took over.

"That supposed to be fuh-huckin' funny?" asked Lee.

"No man. I'm sorry."

"You are? Pu-ull in here."

Easy for you to say, he thought.

"Wipe that grin off your fuh-face," said Gangster Lee, AKA Junior.

"What the fuck are you talking about? What fuckin' road?"

"Don't mind the stuttering. It's the lupus talking, and don't worry, you're on the road."

"I don't know a lot about the disease, but I don't think it affects language patterns. It's not, um…" Shaney said, trying to think of the name of the disease that made people curse and such. A syndrome. His mind threw up a block. Meanwhile he was stopping in a spot designated by Lee's shaky finger. As he got out of the car, a small gaggle of shadows swarmed out from a dark, bushy area, the shadows exclaimed salutations and introductions entailed as spooks became bodily. Many motley mountaineers here had animal surnames; Rooster, Weasel, and even a Duck.

"Anyway you're wrong," said Lee into his face as they crossed the darkling plain towards a bonfire.

"Actually, I really *don't* think lupus effects speech, though your walking, well…"

"What's wrong with the way I walk?"

"Don't be so sure, man," said one earnest thronger leaning forward while handing beers and joints, a loaves and fishes thing, as they neared a roaring fire by a dark home. "Diseases have a life of their own, doctors don't know a lot. In the 1950s and 1960s they had theyself a lot of ulcers, blamed it on the rat race. Come to find out it was a virus and not a national malaise, y'all. Stress ain't disappeared but hardly nobody gets ulcers nowadays. Then they was this Yuppie disease where everybody was enervated and tired like all the time. Again, they blamed it on the culture. Just went away like ulcers. About five years ago all my friends started having panic attacks. Didn't even know what the word was but they's so dizzy they'd haveta pull off the freeway. Makes you wonder huh? Everybody's depressed right now. Some day they gonna find out it was a virus, you betcha. I betcha WWI and WWII were virus attacks. People go crazy kill each other. You ever hear tell of the sad virus, my good old friend?"

"Can't say's I have," said Shaney now drawn into the bosom of some boozy fellowship.

"And he's a scientist," said Lee, though Shaney couldn't remember telling him anything such like.

"Okay, Doctor Science, listen to this. About a year ago, I got a flu going around. It was a weird one, I admit. Didn't have those classic syndromes or symptoms, and the fever came on so slowly, I didn't even know I was hot till some girl told me."

"You give me fee-vah," said one of the clan between slurps from a jar, going all Peggy Lee on it.

"Anyways, I succumb to this malady and my friends took care of me. But once in a while I found myself alone in their house. And when I was I would think about things and sometimes stumble across some bad memory or dismal meditation, you know."

"Like you do," said someone.

"As you must," said someone else.

"And then I just started bawling. I mean crying my eyes out, great blubbering, nose-draining lamentations."

"Lachrymosity," said a gaunt man leaning against the house Shaney saw in the black surroundings, in the dark surrounding the heat blaze.

"So anyways, I get better, back on my feet and I get back in the race only to run into some goodtime buddy in a crosstown bar and he says, where y'all been. I told him I was sick, some weird flu. And he says me too. He was a little drunk you could tell. And he sidles up to me and says, 'The damndest thing. Every time my old lady left the house I started cryin' like a baby.' Three days later, five friends told me the same thing."

"You talk to a doctor?" Shaney asked. Everybody laughed.

"Must be a college boy. One what has that, whatayoucall in-surance stuff we read about up here," he drawled accent on the "in."

"Think about it, though. My emotional life controlled by a microscopic parasite. I was transformed from the he-man you see before you into a baby girl bitch wailing for her mommy. The implications are staggering."

"Vis-à-vis identity and fuh-ate alone," said Gangster Lee.

"Vis-à-vis," said the man on the house, echolalic, "fate."

"Hey," said one of the good old boys, who were mostly in their early thirties, "speaking of priests."

"Here we go," said another.

"How do you get a nun pregnant?"

This caused considerable head scratching and finally Lee said, "I give up, Dogboy."

"You fuck her," he said, accent on the verb.

Howls of laughter and knees slapped, but in the midst of it, Shaney heard a low, long lamentation. Someone is always crying, he thought.

Then the longest and scariest wolf keen he ever heard outside a horror movie rolled across the horizon and rang in valleys filled with dark night, causing a deep silence among the roisterers.

"She's out there tonight," said someone.

She? Thought Shaney.

"So what is it you want here, partner?" said the lanky man by the house directly talking to John, who was still wondering who "she" was.

Then he realized he was being addressed. "Oh, me," he said.

"Oh my," someone else said.

"I got a flat back on the road and ran into Mr. Lee here," said Shaney as a chorus of Mr. Lee, Mr. Lee, Ooh Mr. Lee broke out behind him.

"You cannot fix a flat?" asked the gaunt man with an unmistakable tone of disapproval, contempt actually.

"Two flats," said Lee, chiming in. "One spare. By the way, Uncle John, this man is a professor from the University, a man of science."

"Why did you not say so in the first place?" said Uncle John moving with catlike grace down from the porch and face to face with Shaney. "An intellectual. An academia nut" The man had a long face ending in a pointed beard, not quite Mephistophelian but more sinister than a Carradine brother. His face caught shadows and gave off deep secret vice and easily offendable honor.

"I'm just a grad student," said Shaney. "A research fellowship that hasn't actually begun. Next quarter next," he stammered. He was frankly unnerved by Uncle John's animal magnet field.

"Where you headed tonight, doc?" asked the bass voice host.

"I'm uh-off to Wuh-wulfhart."

"He talks like you, Gangster," he said. "Hope it isn't catching. What's goin' on in Wulfhardt, uh duh-hoctor?"

Shaney looked up, recovering. "If you can't fix the tire, I understand. I was just doing what our mutual friend here suggested. I'm sorry for intruding."

Uncle John considered the man in the firelight, the light that danced on the windows of the house and on the wire-rimmed spectacles of the onlookers and dully in the glass of the beer bottles in every hand. "Don't be like that," he said. "We're glad to help you, partner. I just forget myself bein' up here amongst the jackalopes and ky-oats."

"Now you're makin' fun of us, boss," said Gangster Lee.

Uncle John snorted. "Here friend, have a beer and maybe a toke of this good hill country dope while I look at the damages."

Shaney tried to ward off the proffered joint, but people weren't hearing it. The stuff tasted kind of funny and as he headed towards the car with

Uncle John, he felt an enormous load leave his spirit. Here at last, he thought, all prayers to the mute and deaf heaven will actually be answered before articulation. John turned to him and said, "I'll take a look, don't bother yourself none. Head over to the fire and get acquainted. But I might need the key."

Reluctantly, Shaney dug out the chain on which his whole life hung. New home, the lab he had barely been allowed to touch at school, his storage bin back home, containing all the ingredients for the psychedelic party fuel, of which fruit, he suddenly remembered he was holding. Uncle John bopped off with a young woman in tow, he hadn't seen her previously, the rest of the crowd being decidedly male. Uncle John said, "No worries," over his shoulder.

At first, the conversation around the fire was promising. People began telling stories about their own long trudges through academia, with an overwhelming tone of wistfulness. "What are you all doing now?" asked Shaney, genuinely interested.

After an awkward silence, one of the more thoughtful-looking amongst the throng said, "Well, my friend, you know, I was an economics and communications double major and after a brief but exciting internship at the state capitol in beautiful Austin, I'm expecting to be a made barista at the Brown Water Fusion Emporium just down from the shadow of the legislative house. Sometimes I see my old boss. Motherfucker."

"Enough about us, perfessor. We never did hear what yer business in Wulfhardt might be so urgent on a Saturday night or is it Sunday morning?" drawled one particularly red-eyed firemate.

"I'm looking for a woman," he said. "The police dragged her off and I'm trying to figure out what happened," he answered, though surrounded by good old boys grilling him, he knew it sounded hollow.

"I had a woman once," said someone across the flames after reflection time passed.

"What's her name and occupation, doc? Maybe we know her."

"Lila May," Shaney said.

That sent ripples of laughter and nudges through the group. "Next thing you'll tell us, it's Lila May Wulfhardt, since you's gointa Wulfhardt and all," said another amidst renewed peals of laughter.

He looked at the group and said nothing.

"Oh, shit," said one of them. "It is her, iddunit?"

"Oh fuck," said another. "Why diddun you say so right away?" He went off calling Uncle John. As he left the fire another long howl rolled across the hills and vales. The group suddenly seemed sober.

"You know her a long time?" asked one of them silently.

"Just met her. Actually she's in my section. I'm her TA."

They looked at him as if he spoke a foreign language.

Uncle John returned. The woman with him looked concerned. "Why didn't you tell me?" he asked.

"How would I know, whatever," Shaney said.

"Come with me," he said and led Shaney into the brightly lit house. "Hungry? Help yourself," he said. There were slabs of beef brisket and mountains of ribs heaped on a table pooled with meat juice, blood. Beans bubbled nearby. Uncle John pulled out another joint (drugs not meat) and made a big deal out of lighting it as if the wind was beating against him. He handed it to Shaney. "Why didn't you tell me?"

"I'm not fucking sure what it is I didn't tell you now."

"Lila May was arrested?"

"Oh, yeah."

"You saw them read her her rights?"

"Well, not exactly."

"What did the pigs say?"

"Some bullshit about making sure she went home."

"Good, that's good. Tell me now, don't make me guess. Was she at the concert where that guy died, the drummer?"

"*Soleil cou coupe*," said the woman, reading from a book in the living room.

"Wow word travels fast. Yes, she was. With me. I'm John," he said thrusting out his hand to the woman. She grasped it weakly and then turned it over to observe his palm.

"*Non*," she said. She looked at John.

"Well that's a relief. You protecting her and all. I'm gonna go out on a limb and say she knew the drummer."

"I guess yes. How did you know?"

"I'm gonna fix your car and I'm gonna suggest you go home. I mean home to where your parents live. Somewhere safe. Meanwhile take a toke of this. And a beer. By the way, usually people bring something when they come to a party."

"I wasn't prepared. Didn't know I was coming."

He looked unconvinced. "Think. I bet you have something to share, maybe wisdom."

"Wait a second, there is something." He realized he could kill many birds with one stone and took the psychedelics out of his wallet. "There's about 30 hits there," he said.

"Fuckin' A," said Uncle John. "You did bring something. See?"

Pretty soon the crowd was crowding around feasting on the little blotter hits, some took two or three. Shaney didn't care much. For one, he was beginning to feel the effects of whatever it was that was in Uncle John's joint. (He doubted it was pot.) Besides, there were sheets of the stuff back in his room and binders full of it in his storage space back home. He had made the batch of molecular-altered hallucinogen a year ago with his student loan money. It cost him in the low five figures. He had profited like a pig from that batch and now was quite happy to give back to the community that had made him fat.

The drug was fast-acting. Unlike regular stuff that took half an hour of insinuating change, his formula, nicknamed Waterbear, came on like a rocket with spectacular special effects but less of the mystical. You got high without considering the omphalos of the universe in everything, and usually got happy too. Some people creeped; not often.

Soon the place was roiling in pleasure's grip. Uncle John, who had delayed his gratification, smiled ear to ear over the salubrious mood that had overtaken his midnight barbecue. He had come in after 15 minutes working on the tire and washed his hands, free of grease but not of his many sins. He liked the idea of transcendental fun: from wake and bake to nodding out. He took Shaney by the arm.

"Now they will be ready for anything, including the end," he said.

Shaney, a little fuzzy about the implication, or maybe whether or not it was a quotation, a book or a movie, pointed at an iron bent into the shape of Texas hanging by the door, maybe it was a triangle to call the diners forth and hence.

"What is it with you guys down here," he said hiccupping. (No dope ever had made him hiccup before.)

"What what?" said the bearded host Shaney, idly spitting toward the fire. "What guys down where?"

"Texans. The state you live in is some sort of talisman to you. You know, or maybe you don't, most people in America save their patriotic fervors for their hometown if anything. Yay, Brooklyn, Frisco, whatever. Californians, who have every right to consider their state as a kind of paradise show no similar—hic—obsessive possession by location, bilocations—hic—the boundaries, the morphology of some artificial delineation brought about by rivers and political motivation mostly. To make an arbitrary shape into an icon you'd hang on your garage door. It's as if it were a crucifix posted to let others know why you are the way you are. I'm a Texan, it says, and it doesn't matter if you're a hipster—hic, hic—from Austin or a hick, a hick from the mud country up near Louisiana, you are the Texan—the proudest child of the second biggest state."

"Are you through?" asked Uncle John. He made a sign with hands flat, one roofing over the other at right angles.

"Time—hic—out?" said Shaney.

"T is for motherfuckin' Texas," said the host. They crossed the small pasture land and neared Shaney's car. "Aww, goddamn," said the deep-voiced Texan. "My girl said it would be done but where the hell is she?"

"Looks done," said John feeling ready to launch.

Just then some clouds cleared above a long line of trees and the full moon shone down on the land. Shaney thought it was a Universal Pictures kind of moon and remembered the long, low howl of that which his newfound friends referred to as a "she." On cue, the thing rolled out its most baleful wail yet, sounding much, much closer now.

"A coyote, right?" said Shaney noticing that Uncle John's steps had become a little stumbly, if that's the word he wanted.

"Motherfuckin' wolf," he said. "Where's the girl?" he asked, though the question sounded almost rhetorical. "Let's head back. We must've missed her going up the other way." He took a long look at the car and reversed his steps.

Shaney looked around and, even though it was dark then, bright now with a moon that cast shadows, it seemed pretty clear there was no other way that they would have failed to see the young woman charged with changing his tires. "Hey, man," he said. "Looks like she's almost done. I'll just take it from here. I got to get on the road."

"What's your hurry?" said Uncle John. "You got it bad for her?"

For a split second, Shaney thought he meant the wolf. "Lila," he said, realizing. "She's my girlfriend," he added, chuckling.

"Really?" said John. "Really. How nice for you."

They had reached the fire where, by now, the whole pack was engaged staring into the flame in throes of ganglionic ecstasy.

"Heard the wolf, anyone?" said John sarcastically. "Seen the girl?"

"*Chupacabra*," said one of the more diligently transfixed coterie.

"O, don't get started on that, again," said somebody.

"No shit," said John. "It's just some misplaced angst about illegal aliens."

"*Chupacabra* was here first. The wolf came from up north."

"What is it?" asked Shaney.

"Mexican werewolf."

"Except there's no *were* there," said the cohort's owl-eyed grad student barista dreamily. "The *chupacabra* was never human. Besides it eats only goats."

"Then Unkie John is fucked. The goatman saith hey, where is the fucking girl?"

"Okay, all of you. You know where I stand on this issue. Draw pentagrams, drink a beer, or go away, fuck you, I stopped caring. As for you," he said to Shaney, "come over here." He motioned impatiently toward the house. "I can't blame you for getting everybody so high. It was my idea. Downright generous of you," he said, though his tone seemed to deny his gratitude. He rummaged through an end-table drawer and suddenly grunted. "Here," he said holding out yet another tiny pin joint wrapped in yellow paper. "Have a hit of this before you go, it'll protect you on the road."

"What is it, wolfbane? I think I've had enough drugs and medieval lore for one night."

"You fuckin' kiddin' me?" said Uncle John, who seemed to get larger and gruffer as he spoke. "The wolfman isn't from the Middle Ages. No. The wolfman was invented in Hollywood. Sure there was lycanthropy since Freud and before I guess, but all of the stupid warning signs and vulnerabilities—silver bullets and shit—were invented by a coupla screenwriters."

"All the more reason to…" The howl came again.

"Yeah. All the more reason to fear the thing in and of itself. It's cinema, and that means bigger than life. Only God is bigger than life, amigo. And he most decidedly does not exist. Smoke it and I'll honk your horn in five minutes or so. Oh, and give these dogs here some idea when they're coming down and what vitamins to take afterwards. I might need 'em after all."

He trudged off to the house and pulled out a rifle, the moon well past the rags of cloud coursing high. There was a box of kitchen matches. John Shaney decided to light it, take one hit and throw the rest in the fire. Turned out one was more than enough.

"I think it was the wrong joint," was what he was trying to say from the back door to the happiest campers by the firepit. How it came out was, "I'm mink in the Hmong void."

This amused the crowd, though nobody noticed Shaney had had trouble opening a screen door, so he ripped through its scrim and stumbled across the short clearing between the stoop and the bonfire as if the walked-upon earth had suddenly become a tipping ship. When they did stop laughing at his unintentionally absurd declaration, they still found themselves amused by his attempted careen to the car, which ended far short in soft bushes.

Shaney lay down now over compressed baby tumbleweeds. (Excellent eating, by the way.) He had some desperate thought about how his trip down to Wulfhardt had not gone exactly as it was half-assed planned. He concluded the conscious moments of the waking hours constituting his "day" with a fascinated survey of some dirt inhabited by night-walking ants. He thought they probably did not sting. He thought about hope and hopelessness; will and surrender, He signed off with that thought merrily ringing in his ears, they don't bite. Then a distinct usurpation of the local laughter by horrible shrieks he sort of heard coming from the fireside.

# 4.

Who knows to tell you all this mooncrossed saga of Shaney en route to Lila, *his* Lila at this point. At this juncture. In his mind. Whose eyes saw it all? Whose nose sniffed and what big ears? And who did go drive with Shaney then followed him home and then out along the sidewalks rich with fragrant debris stuffed down in hedges and behind old scraggly trees, skidding comically at stop signs and red lights and then out onto the open road together? Followed him, the art of racing. The freeway frontages and escarpments, the pavement still warm from sunlight, past culverts with little trickling gutter streams, then galloped as the country opened up as the highway closed down to two lanes of dogwoods and cottonwoods and deadwoods, sage and the dust blossoming cactus flowers. Who ran in the wind, what sidereal life, whose moon-tormented face?

Past Fergus, Kyle, Texas. Winds split and blow the hair with air from bellowing lungs, blowing through the changes? Run. Never tire.

Texas, is the answer, me. Though, funny you all never ask such stuff about the movies. Irised eyes, the long shot from outside the spaceship. Who is shooting it? Space Ghost? God is a space ghost. The better to narrator you with.

Didn't actually do it all, running alongside. Reports were made. Though some of these conversations speculative, some words approximations backed up by theoretical intimations or inter-interpretations involving imagination's participation. The poet Yeats once said concerning phases of the moon: "Separation from innocence is misdirected to limitation, modified by spiritual arrogance bringing limitation modified by emotional intellect separated from natural law." Nobody saw it all.

Which leads us out of the forest and into the fire. The sweating men around the pit, the man and the woman by the car, all plump with long, graceful fingers. Acadians nestled in pine boughs to hide. The howl again, the warning and the exclamation point, Shaney stumbles into this cohort uneasy in the dark though the gathered enjoy exalted fellowship.

Did he hear screams? Was his dream *his* dream? Or merely his mind grappling with external stimuli? In a world where everything conscious dies and happiness and sorrow distribute from a random hand, why do we lean so heavily on explanation? Another howl and it all comes true. The moon is a white breast. Shaney, pushed down into bushes by a hand of chance sees the dim sea in his sleep. Sleeps in the woven shade. Trust me on this. What choice do either of us have?


He woke with his face lying half in the sun feeling burned on the one side like that guy in *Close Encounters*, a Richard Dreyfus affair. How did the night pass? He thought perhaps he woke up once or twice though he went down hard. And the dreams: those dreams were the two worst kinds, the worst genres of dreams, he thought, all fancy like a college boy ought to think, in French: genres. Nightmares, filled with horrifying presences: offstage ghosts with giant voices. Blood-curdling screams. Then the *very* worst, one of those perseverating loops where nonsense things turn and turn over nonsense details: the importance of the Gabor sisters, and which one was which from Eva trumping Zsa Zsa. He shook his head. It hurt and his mouth was dry. But he wasn't hungover, was he? Isn't fuzzy.

Standing up, he saw little around him to help jog his memory of the night before. There weren't even beer crimes around the firepit now gone past dead into the stinking embers. He thought maybe he saw a bone among those sooty coals but turned his head away. He headed for the house, awkward-self-conscious but so bladder-swollen that niceties seemed hardly relevant. "Yoo-hoo," he croaked from the door but sounded to his own ears oddly like a parody of the howl he now remembered haunting his niggling and fearful dreamscapes.

There was an open bottle of nice champagne there in the kitchen, cold as he felt it and so he drank it off. That would help his big head. He walked in and saw nobody. "Hello," he cried in the whispery self-conscious voice of the recently awoke. He laughed and then got real: "OOO-ooo-oo!"

He went boldly into the bathroom passing a most extraordinary sight he vowed to re-visit after need was satisfied. Long release of pressure and toxins down the bowl, ahh, zip up, and return to respectability. When he went to wash his hands, however, he noticed black stuff caked underneath his fingernails. It ran crimson under water and soap. Maybe it was the barbecue Uncle John urged him to try congealed. But he had not sampled. Weird. He tried to not think about it.

Leaving the bathroom, Shaney expected to encounter damaged merrymakers but then remembered what he wanted to see again. There in a big rumpus room between the kitchen with its honey light poured down and the dark hall he saw what he guessed was an abstract painting on the wall that looked like a giant smear of red red gore. Maybe it was supposed to be funny art wink wink. He didn't understand modern art, contemporary art. Whatever. Art as prank.

God knows these hippie cowboys had developed odd strains of risibility. But it didn't seem to be art the closer he got. Maybe that was the point.

"Chupacabra" he said out loud to the room. He remembered the word and felt it might lend the wall's perhaps fake incarnadining some meaning. The "painting" disturbed him even when he talked to himself about it. It was oddly familiar as if copied from some movie or art piece he saw back in his boho days back when. He would have to look it up.

Then he remembered his car.

Then he remembered his, whatyoucall, mission. Lila May Wulfhardt, though, by now, his noble act of romantic heroism was nullified, driving west to save her probably seems mundane by light of day. Her tardy knight errant.

Maybe not, though: It did occur to him that showing up at her folks' house after dark might have been a bit more than foolhardy, likely rude to a rich person, scary weird. By the light of day, with maybe some roses in hand, it might seem less crazy, even gallant though maybe he was rationalizing from defeat. Rushing out to the kitchen, he saw that it was only eight a.m. and 75 degrees by the time and temperature clock near the sunlit window. But was his sweet ride still hobbled? Maybe that's where the gang was. Over the rise, after the dead coals and there (down there!) his car sparkled in the middle of a pasture. Its bald tire replaced with a hairy one.

As he moved closer, he saw the keys laid gently on the hood. It was time to go. He did wish for a shower but hated to impose on the lovely people who lived here. As he turned around he noticed a scarf hanging from a tree. The French girl's; he knew it. He walked towards the woods. There was an intense buzzing sound like a honeybee hive. There inside a clump of trees he saw a heap presided over by flies, criminal partners of the conqueror worm. It was, no doubt, a dearly departed deer. He felt nothing.

"Chupacabra," he said out loud.

He looked up on the ridge toward the house and thought he saw someone, but the shape disappeared. He thought maybe he had seen some clothes near the heap that the flies were busily fizzing through. He thought maybe he saw some clothes. It was time to go, he was late. Maybe he needed to go back up to the house and see if someone was there to thank. He got in his car. It started right away and the radio came on loud giving him the only real start of the morning. He backed up and swung around heading for the road leaving a fantail, a cock's plumage of dry dust behind.

The ride was smooth. On the road again. He remembered he hadn't paid for anything. Maybe with drugs, maybe on the way back, check in?

The road wound upwards but crested soon thereafter and headed down, down, down. After about ten minutes of negotiating hard-packed dirt, the highway, a street actually, which had changed names to Wulfhardt Avenue (encouragingly) changed surfaces to macadam. A sign indicated his proximity to his girlfriend's namesake place, and his clock said it was only seven in the morning. The kitchen clock was wrong, he guessed. But how did his face get so sunburned so early after sunrise? Around a bend he found a café advertising home cooked food. He was surprisingly full, or, at least, unhungry. Coffee, though, and ice water might perk his dusty mood. There was time to kill now, not much farther to go. To kill.

He pulled in at an angle. The rust-orange roof sat low over the white stucco cinderblock digs. A dog, sitting on the porch, growled low in his throat and slunk away into the shade around the corner.

Shaney opened the door with its humorous "Hippies Enter in the Rear" sign and plunked himself down at a table that seemed ridiculously well set for a diner in the middle of hot nothing. The waitress, more buxom than Pachamama, shuffled up to him and said without commas, "Hi dearie coffee?"

He smiled. She batted her made-up eyes and asked him where he was bound so early in the sun's journey over the Lone Star State. She actually said, "bound."

"I tell you what," he said and then he told her wherefrom and asked her in which way hither to he might find the home of his lady love, last name Wulfhardt? And she giggled, popped the gum, and said, stay on this road, sugar. "You'd have to be mighty distracted to miss the object of your quest."

He asked her what was good on the menu and she made the old joke; Nothing, I cleaned them this morning. He gawked, she said maybe the chile guisada and eggs would bring warmth and nourishment in that order.

"Chupacabra?" he asked, murmuring.

"No, sugar," she said. "Guisada. Where'd you hear a thing like that? Good thing the goat farmers roun' here wudden around to hear you."

Shaney said he wasn't hungry but would love to have some toast and black coffee. She said, sure shug. She brought a strange plain doughnut with the coffee, said in lieu of toast no charge. He loved it.

The Austin morning newspaper had the rock concert debacle, but suggested an overdose death of the drummer on its first page below the fold. It didn't seem like any big deal. But the reporter half-truthed the terrible event into melodrama somehow. Fans, wrote Monty Salvador, were stunned to learn that Oil Can What drummer suspicious circumstances backstage at Memmo club eyewitnesses police cordons pathologist declared drummer massive amounts of self-administered drugs.

"Terrible thing, huh?" said the waitress nudging awful close to Shaney as she poured his morning brew, black lapping white porcelain in brimming tiny tidal waves. Looking outside at heatwaves she said "*Soleil cou coupe, n'est ce pas?*"

He looked up from the paper. Déjà vu? "*Pardonne moi.*"

"French lit major, University of Texas," she said in a completely different voice. "Not a lot of call for Apollinaire most mornings. Looked like you might understand."

"Bio major, though I once took a class in children's lit and mythology."

"Cute girl?"

"Ravishing professor. There were a lot of maidens and monsters in it and mazes and shit."

"*Chupacabra?*" she asked.

"No I just heard that word up in the place where I crashed last night. A party. Bonfire," he said, wondering why he was confessing to her: probably those eyes, so blue-ringed with indigo and dotted large black in the center.

"Uncle John's place, though it looks like you crashed in a ragweed bush."

He was beginning to wonder how she read him so easily when his own eyes failed to take in her almost unfathomable beauty at first, she seemed to have metamorphosed in front of him from dowdy waitress to exotic, singular apparition.

"Going to see my girlfriend," he croaked softly. "Got a flat on the dirt road."

She wheeled around witchfaced, the spell broken.

"I was there at the show, I saw it," he said, pointing to the headlines, not knowing why he needed to impress this girl. He was in love already. "Found him first."

"Besides that, how was the concert, Mrs. Lincoln?"

He looked at her as she leaned over the table exposing the tops of her fleshly, rounded breasts which seemed to exhale scent, a co-mixture of bitter perspiration and incense and citrus-flavored eau de toilette. He was dizzy due to inner-released chemicals stimulated by hers in his bloodstream traveling through dendrites and neurons and attached or displaced stuff that tumbled into his heart.

"You motor of emotion," said the jukebox, an old-fashioned Wurlitzer beautiful with bubbles coursing through tubes of mollifying waters of strange tints.

"It was weird," he said. "I know that sounds callous or whatever but the whole thing seems unreal to me."

"Does reading the newspaper make it any realer?" she asked.

"I should go," he said.

"You're going to see your girlfriend," she said, gazing into his soul, creating a tingle. "Though it's pretty early on a Sunday morning for most fabulously rich girls name of Lila May." She leaned closer. A wavering arc of invisible light swept the field of nothing between them. How did she?

Just then, as fate, angelic arrangement, or random chance would have it, a troupe of arguing middle-class choir kids burst into the door dissolving the second spell that had begun to be woven by these two. She shoved a bill onto his Formica tabletop. He plunked down money with an awesome tip included just in case he ever again this way without interruptions came. He reluctantly left, but only then as he opened his door realized he didn't know her name, while she knew even where he slept last night and who he was seeking. Excellent witness, she would make, had there been a crime.

Then he was off down the road, not rested but at least caffeinated, blood-sugared sufficiently to stand up to social niceties and, who knew, even weather an awkward moment or two. The road led down into a valley of green swathes and dry dirt of a tan blond nature. He wished he was a geologist when he roadtripped, a marine biologist when he rowed and, of course, an astronomer as he ran beneath the starry welkin.

Wulfhardt's first outposts proved to be liquor stores closed early Sunday morning, then churches, barely creaking open themselves. It wasn't nine yet, which, he knew was too early for unexpected visits, yet his body brimmed with anticipation outweighing any reluctance based on those goddamed social niceties. At a park with scrawny trees, he yawned and pulled over, fell promptly asleep at the wheel and awoke also promptly at 9:30 a.m. It would be warm, though breezes began to mitigate the early heat. He saw her house, as the waitress promised him, there, ahead surrounded by gate walls, wires and within a garden of tropical trees. The address was right too. This guard house for Paradise's entry was not protected by a sword-bearing angel. For that they had an intercom.

Shaney rolled the car smooth up the little driveway leading to the gate. He pushed a button. Nothing happened. This was unexpected: Should he risk rudeness by pushing again or slink back home a failure after so many odd adventures? Hell, he pushed the buzzer again wondering what kind of sound it made, gong, klaxon horn, or gentle toll at the other end. He tried not to push impatiently. Again silence. He waited for what seemed an era. Sweat began on the back of his neck and the base of his spine. Been through so much, he thought, to get here. The questioner inside his own mind mocked: You fell asleep at a fire after toking up a weird joint. It might have been worse had you shown up late last night.

He rolled down the window again leaking air-conditioned air out and was about to reach for the buzzer a third time when a voice, crackling and sage, said too loud, "May I help you please?"

It made him jump.

"Here to see Lila May Wulfhardt," he answered in unconfident voice.

"And you are?"

"It's kind of a surprise."

"Thank you for coming, sir, but I'm afraid Miss Wulfhardt is off at school. Again, thank you and goodbye." The thing went dead. He felt ridiculous and exposed like those dreams of sudden public nudity we all have. But safe inside his car—and not naked—he had a bold idea.

The plummy voice returned after two assertive button jabs.

"Please tell Miss Wulfhardt her bio professor is here. I've brought the taxonomical charts. That is, if she wants to pass the class."

There was silence.

"That is if she's there."

"Her professor," said the voice emanating from a metal box between the breezy road silence and the implicit bliss inside stucco gates.

"Quite," said Shaney, a tad jesty now.

After a short silence the gates began to swing inward. He put the car in gear and started up a long straight drive that ended in an island of gigantic cacti and flower-topped trees that seemed like the maneating plant from Roger Corman's *Little Shop of Horrors*. "Feed me," said Shaney, negotiating the circular ride around the island, pulling his dull coach up beside an honest-to-God Jaguar XKE from the same era as the just-mentioned horror film. "Nice," he said. The massive oak doors swung open from the massive portico just as his size eight dusty desert boots hit the tiled drive.

"Seriously?" he asked. The portly butler gave a slight incline of his whole frame meant to imply a bow. He said, "Walk this way, like that Thin Man movie imitated in *Young Frankenstein,*" the butler said. Shaney was struck self-conscious, out of his league with the help? Whatever frothy mix of hormonal and pituitary juices brought him here seemed shaky now. John felt dulled by the power and glory implied by these wealthy surroundings. Humbled by the banister; laid low by tasteful gilt.

The butler introduced Shaney to a stiff antique couch.

"I will summon Miss Lila. Please ask for Talbot if you require more assistance," he said. Shaney wondered to whom he might address such requests. Was the butler making fun of him? Yet Shaney also felt the hushed manor seemed almost comical surrounded by the high plains of central Texas.

He began to wade deep in doubt when he heard her voice chime down the room's melodramatic staircase. "If it isn't the professor, my boyfriend. What in the name of Buddha possessed you to wash up on my lonely shore?" she said, appearing, a ravishing sight for sore eyes even in her casual dishevelment: hair tangled and pouffed out, jammies wrinkled with a Belle and Sebastian "Tigermilk" tee shirt half tucked in and also out; pink slippers with googly eyes and fur ears.

"I came to rescue you," he croaked.

"Of course you did," she said. "From what?"

"The cops last night, all that fuss about taking you away and not letting me know what was going on. They were so secretive."

"*They* were rescuing me, love," she said wearily. "Always the boys in blue come sweeping through my life. Save me! O save me," she said in a decent imitation of the *Perils of Pauline*. Then her eyes fixed on the present. "When did you talk to the cops?"

He told her then about his evening after her departure. Her eyes grew wider at every plot point of his narrative, which, by now, he had reviewed and shaped into an amusing tale—though he glossed the hours between flat tire and butler. "You spent the night on the ground alone, to check up on me," she said.

"Of course," he replied, and meant it.

She grew ever more amazed listening and came down the stairs step by step with each travaille, to stand even with him, then held his hands. He liked the contact and drew her close, she almost fell on him but he caught her. Hand flat on her torso without meaning a cheap move. She remembered the dance and suddenly everything else. She hugged him and he didn't move backwards, she felt melty then grabbed and pushed him up the stairs which split at the top heading to separate wings, hers to the left, and (he learned later) her parents' to the right.

He guessed, he hoped, they were heading to her bedroom now.

"You're quite the detective yourself, darling," she said, impressed, outside her door. He loved this kind of moment, the equipoise before. She pushed him in, closed the door and before he could think wrapped herself around him in their first, second, and third real kisses, each one expanding to twice the duration of the one before it. They were standing in a kind of den, but he could see a large disheveled bed through an open door. Each kiss came accompanied by flourishes from fingers, palms, and the tightening of space between. Always approaching unity of purpose. O, they were inching to her bed, he grew quite excited.

But, first, she said, stopping: "Darling?" with wrinkled nose.

And he said, "I smell not so great?"

"Smoke and sweat. Would you like to take a shower first?"

O, he liked the sound of that *first*. "Maybe it's pointless, I'll just be getting back into these same old dirty duds," he said.

"Uh-uh," she spoke resolute. "You won't. I'll go down to my father's rec room and steal you some loose stuff, though he's a tad more muscled than my sweet professor boyfriend is."

"Sorry," he said. "That's all of me. And not a professor. Yet."

She reached down between them. "Seems like there's more of you all the time."

She walked him backwards to a sunny, tiled bathroom, across from her bed bigger than the whole space he rented in downtown Austin. "Start the water, jump right in and I'll be bawk," she said all Arnold Schwarzenegger *Terminator*.

He was momentarily dazed standing but soon got naked in her girlie bathroom. She was moving fast, and he was getting farther than even his fantasies had allowed him. He got into the steaming tile and glass stall and felt the water burn away his exhaustion and nervousness. As he raised his hands to sweep wet hair from eyes, though, he saw rehydrated red stuff (dried blood?) running from the cakes under his fingernails, crimson rivulets. There then gone. Evidence gone, he thought. Then wondered what he meant. He began to sing some bass notes like a hook, then broke into a croaking falsetto. I've got sunshine. He felt the rejuvenation and reached for the Ivory soap with its promise of purity. On cue she pushed the bathroom door open swirling the steam and said, "You're howling, my dearest. Don't give the help too much to talk about, please." She peered in. But her expected pleasure turned to mild horror. "Oh, my! Why are you dripping blood!" she said staring.

His heart lurched. Looking down, he saw red again on the shower floor, but more than he expected. "What the hell."

"No see-ums," she said. "Look, on your otherwise sexy legs. Don't they itch like that hell you mentioned?" To Shaney's surprise, his legs were dotted with hivelike protuberances, small volcanoes. He never even guessed they were there. His ears filled with water and he couldn't hear for a moment. She was outside the steamed-up shower and her image fell on the glass, a ghost moving its lips. There was no blood on her glass lips. But then she was flesh again framed in the open shower door.

"What?" he asked.

"Itch? Jesus, John. That many bites would've driven me immediately mad." She pulled the spaghetti-strapped t-shirt she wore over her head revealing a light red bra.

This would be the appropriate place to register his emotion: a cartoon wolf eyes bulging, mouth turns to horn, "Awooga" followed by a howl, all this remained repressed as he stood ogling her.

"Wow," slipped out though as he looked leaning back against the smooth wall. "You take my breath away."

"How sweet," she said, demure.

"Mmm," she said moving in for the nuzzle while reaching around him to secure some arcane brand of peppermint shampoo. She made him bend down to her shape and nuzzle her neck with hypnotic willpower while she lathered up a patch of electric foam and began bestowing it on him: hair, shoulders, and below. He reached gracefully under her arms and lifted her whole body to bring her lips up to be kissed. It wasn't Astaire and Rogers, but it was slick. It did the trick.

They washed each other and he brought maybe a little too much concentration to bear on her curled-hair crotch. She shrieked softly and said, "Now, now," though she clearly meant hold on for later. Looking up into his eyes with the gaze of an inebriate of pleasure she firmly stopped the spigot and said, "Shall we?"

He needed no more encouragement, in fact, a little break in the mounting wave of caresses probably did them both some good. The towels were magnificently thick and soft and he gallantly assisted her. She even found them terry robes to drape them warmly to her turned-down bed in the waxing morning light, a place that was simply too much for his saturated senses to appreciate. He closed his eyes and rolled in with her between soft cotton sheets.

Animal lust carried him past any awkwardness. Thank God we can depend on that. She was a little overwhelmed; frightened almost, at times by the steep grade of his need and the fierce way he took the hill. Both of them worried for at least a moment that he wouldn't last and they suddenly stopped. Protection was briefly discussed in windy words; assurance given. Then a second wave, slower. Then a tidal wave that carried his mouth down between her legs and a stifled scream, unbridled yet covered with an arm to prevent the maids and kitchen staff from either laughter or alarm. He was inside. He came too.

She huffed happily, touching him with something like awe. He was almost as surprised as she was; felt that some force bigger than himself had opened and flowed through him. The wanky grad student was a man today, at least for now. He swallowed gulps of air and tried to think of something witty and endearing, but, lucky for him, had nothing. He kissed her tenderly. She melted.

It was to be a short nap afterwards. They spooned and he drifted on settled nerves after sleep deprivation and a short fierce countdown to ecstasy. Next thing he knew, coming up from the underground of dreams, she was telling him they had to dress before her parents returned from church.

"They go to church?"

"Worse than that, they come home afterwards."

"Don't meet many churchgoin' folks whay-ah ah come from," he said. She ignored the regional slight. "This is different. They built the church," she said, though she meant her grandfather, a German emigrant who brought his High Lutheran society together under a magnificent edifice built on the oil money he gained by an almost accidental claim. But her own father had made many improvements and a German-born populace meanwhile moved into the building and its dusty surrounding demesnes becoming the backbone of the little town that bore her grandfather's name. Meanwhile Shaney was washing, combing, and then dressing in the roomy athletic clothes borrowed from said father. He felt weird in daddy's clothes considering. But ready for anything, he thought.

She disappeared briefly and he did the new lover reconnaissance. The books in her bookshelf (Austen? Twain?), the few CDs (Boston?) and even vinyl (Shania Twain?!) lodged near her expensive stereo system; he was just about to pick up her iPhone and snoop out its musical rotation when he heard the door open behind him. Turning around slowly so's not to look guilty he was shocked to see *not* his lady love Lila but a Mexican servant who looked like the Greek actress Irene Papas in her prime. First off, he thought, bet the old man is on top of this one. Then he thought, why did I think that?

"It's not what you think," said the maid as if privy to his vulgar private thoughts.

"Pardon me," he said, now embarrassed, though unclear why.

"Let me see your hand," she said, advancing forward with an elegant, well-oiled gait.

She took his hand firmly but gently and lifted it palm up for inspection.

"I'm sorry," he said, thick. "Who are you?'

"Ssshh," she said, the sibilant Sybil. "I need to see to concentrate. There is something incessant and red running over the stiff course of your sad life. I'm suddenly afraid," she said gripping his hand now with a tight hold he could never break by force of will.

"You have gone through a something. And I'm seeing something else beneath the crimson veil. Oh my God!" she exclaimed and looked him in the eyes, blinking crazily. "The Rubicon is crossed, yes. And something wicked this way comes."

"What is it?"

"Blood. Sausages. And sauerbraten for dinner. Or maybe Mexican food. Where's Lila May? You have her here?" She peered. "Did you perform well?"

"I'm not sure what you mean," he said, offended.

"Shut up," she said. "I know who you are. On your hand, the mark. It's too late for everyone. Please," she said.

"What?" Shaney asked cold now in the bright room.

"Please leave before it gets dark, before moonrise." She straightened. "Is there anything else you need?"

"Else?"

"Maria Ignacio," said Lila May from behind Shaney, a bad ventriloquist's voice, or a haunt's.

"Si, *m'hija?*" said Maria as obsequious now as she was Cassandric seconds ago.

"This is Mr. Shaney, he's the T.A. of my evolutionary biology class."

"You helping Lilita. I always see her studying?" Suddenly pidgin, Spanglishy this lamb-cloaked she-wolf.

"I'm sure she can…"

"Evolutionary," she said. "Oh yes," said Maria Ignacio, as if consulting a computer file now opening like a rose beneath her brow. "Of the knowledge pertaining to our ancient ancestry with the animal kingdom, you weel find her surprisingly well-versed."

"Shut my mouth," Shaney said.

Maria Ignacio giggled and Lila May just looked perturbed. "We'll go back to our studying now."

"Perhaps I can bring coffee and some *pan dulce*. Your parents want you to eat an early dinner before they close up shop tonight. Shall I set a place for your handsome T.A. at the table?"

"Oh, I couldn't," he began to say.

"Please," said Lila May, suddenly tense. "Please, for my sake, join my family for Sunday dinner. We love to have guests and cook is amazing." She left him dangling in the air with this sudden shift to neediness. "Amazing."

"I blush to hear it," said Maria.

"You're the cook?" he asked, confused.

"Oh, my no."

"Her daughter who grew up in this house same as me, came back from college and begged Daddie to let her stay. Cook for us. For him."

"It is her passion," said the proud mother, eyes full with some private squall. "Please see for yourself. I'll clear it with your mother and father and tell you if it is inconvenient."

"It won't be," said Lila May with ice assurance.

"Then I accept," he said.

Lila May turned around, half-circled Maria, and opened the door. The maid, or whatever, held and then turned. "A full moon tonight."

"Goodbye, Maria, *pan dulce* would be awesome," said Lila May inexplicably exasperated. "Let's get back to the books," she added.

But soon as the door shut she was back in his arms. "I can smell me on your face still," she whispered. He could too. It was a lovely thing, like an undertone of seriously expensive perfume. It was heat and need and already a part of his memory banks, burnt in and ancient. He wondered if Maria Ignacio could smell it too.

"She protects me," said Lila May. Seems like everyone here heard his inner monologues. "And she's a little coocoo. So what *do* you say to actual studying? I mean, books."

"So old school," he said. "Bet you have a superbad laptop."

"Daddy buys me the best," she said, suddenly Southern.

She pulled him over to a low table like they have in grammar schools with modernist wood and chromium chairs. She popped open the computer and said, "Show me some tricks."

"Okay little missie. Here's a little somethin' I like to call Monster Taxonomy."

She sat back in awe as the computer booted and with clicks and finger-mousing opened a schematic vista of Life on Earth. Called the Taxonomical Project, it offered a massive tree so large that only its splash exposure page offered whole structures of life. He began touring zoological truth for her. (Somewhere in there, sweet pastries and strong coffee with cinnamon and clove whispering up arrived.) Beginning with amoebae and ending, not as one might suppose, with humans, dolphins, and the lion, King of the Beasts, but in three branches: Bacteria; Archanea, and Eucaryota, of which one branch is simply named Animals. The beauty of this website was that one could click down through the categories to find ever-more-involved webs that, since this was a tree, culminated in something, always, the last a leaf. It had pretty pictures too.

"You can't do that with a slide rule," he drawled.

"But where are the monsters you promised?" she asked demure but anticipatory.

He began showing her the insectivores with their alien appendages and eye clusters; the denizens of the ultra-deep with illuminating panels and scissoring bright fangs and teeth. Then, last, but most prevalent on this planet we constantly picture in sunsets over alpine meads, the vast variety of micro-organisms that rolled, segmented, and flagellated themselves through all media of flesh, fowl, and plant matter, the better to attach, destroy and, sometimes, often enough, aid their hosts, the more gargantuan members of the branching reaches of vivacity.

Her knee was bobbing and she clutched him sometimes, giggled and frequently groaned, but after a bit said it again. "No. Where are the real monsters?"

A deep male voice suddenly sounded over a recessed wall intercom making Shaney jolt. "Darling dearest," it intoned.

"Daddy?" She answered in a voice Shaney wondered at, a new version of Lila.

"Is it true you have company up there?"

"Yes, Daddy. He's a professor, a real egghead, who, get this, has some interest in the field of biochemistry."

"Another one of your drug dealer beaux, my sweet?"

"O! You are hilarious! He's the TA in my bio class," she said winking at me. "Say hi, honey," she whispered.

"Hello, sir," said Shaney, polite, having been raised in an abusive home.

"And a good morning to you, friend," he said. "He sounds nice. Dinner will be in precisely one hour. Have a cocktail before?"

"Bloody Mary Day!" she said, jubilant. "I almost forgot. Be down in half."

"I await you both with pepper on the rim."

She said, turning off the device, "Enough books. We have just enough time to see if that last time was just a fluke." She scampered over to the door and locked it firm. She pulled her t-shirt up and shook her hair down.

"Proof," he said. They giggled and had a lovely long fuck as the sun in waves of particles fell on the house. "I think we might have something here," he said, a full 23 minutes later.

She blinked slow and shook her head as if to clear some perceptual passageway. "I think so too. Eureka," she added in a soft voice. They forgot to make jokes while they slowly washed and dressed. The words they used were awed and quiet.

She pulled him down the stairs dangerously, yanking away at any stagefright timidity. He tried to remember if he had *ever* met the parents of his last two girlfriends, much less in the minutes after intimately exploring and invading same underneath parental noses. Well, technically, somewhere over their heads, as the kitchen, bar, and dining room turned out to be on a lower of split levels connected by long tubelike halls. From the outside, the home looked colonial, but behind the street façade, the ultramodern interiors were graphite- and polymer-lined warrens dug into the earth protecting its inhabitants from the baking heat and freezing winter of the high desert. On the walls were contemporary artists of significant fame that even a chemistry bio grad student had heard of. A soup can (Warhol, natch) gave the dining room an instant elegance and panache. If it was only a print, who cared, it was a picture speaking volumes about the hosts who might just as well have featured the works of Nieman or, more likely, Waterhouse, in the typical fashion of high country billionaires.

When Shaney met the mother he knew instantly where Lila's cool textures came from. Lila May introduced them quickly and yanked again at her new beau eager to let Daddy meet the conquering hero of her heart. It was Father whom she worshipped, though Shaney was still getting over the sight of La Belle Dame Wulfhardt, lush, small, and delicately dressed in a Japanese silk blouse with embossed animals of prey pouncing across the wide wooden buttons. It was clear that not far underneath was a body of surprisingly lush proportions and, from the visible skin, contained under its own brand of slightly sun-kissed silk. He wanted to stare but did not, once smitten, twice shy.

Shaney stood across the bar from the formidable pa of the clan.

"Drink?"

"Frequently, sir," said Shaney, perhaps emboldened by his duo of morning delights.

"Traditionally we serve Bloody Mary before Sunday brunch, though the bar is well-stocked with well-aged Scotches. Afraid we're low on water right now," he said.

"Call me a traditionalist, sir," said Shaney.

"Bloody Mary it is and please," said the mixing patriarch, "my name is Lionel, though I'm told that behind my back quite a few of my daughter's friends like to call me Wulfie. Or Big Bad Wulf, which is likely it. Call me sir again…"

"Lionel Wulfhardt," said Lila May back in the room, "May I present John Shaney, Esquire? John is the TA of my biochemistry class, Daddy. He's attending your alma mater on a fellowship. Studying the effects of certain alkaloids on psychological states. Right so far?" She asked John pointedly.

"Affirmative, partly, in fact," he said bending over to taste the proffered cocktail with pepper and lime meeting his taste buds borne on the air, "Though I don't remember us discussing much of what you just recited."

"Internet I bet," said Lionel "Wulfie" Wulfhardt.

"Quick look Facebook," said Lila May.

"No secrets anymore," said Mrs. Wulfhardt, nee Gwendolyn Conliffe wistful but also hip to the jive. "That's what the web is for."

"Did Lila May tell you what my company does?" piped up Lionel, faux innocent.

"Actually, no, but there was considerable talk about you at an impromptu barbecue I attended last night."

"Without me," said Lila May, whirling around and waggling her forefinger, warning as much as reproving.

"The place I told you about," said Shaney. "Where they fixed my tire. Anyway, good old boys told me you were interested in petroleum and had lately diversified your interests into medical, um, stuff."

"Eloquent old boys," said Mrs. W. who now seemed more fatally alluring as she stretched luxuriously then raised her arms over her head yawning like a disinterested lioness. She fell upon the bowl of marcona almonds with alacrity.

"Medicine, I suppose. Pharmaceuticals, for sure," said the father. "Lunch bell," he said, responding to a tone perhaps pitched above most human perception. "Bring your drinks. Though there will be wine today."

"What's the occasion, Daddy?" asked Lila, who seemed to be asking playfully like it was another Wulfie injoke setup. But Papa only smiled. Lila took Shaney's arm, but, then, again, so did Gwendolyn.

"We have company. Maybe I want to bring him into the family business, maybe but first I want to loosen him up."

Shaney was reeling. At the table a cork popped behind him, and someone slipped behind him filling a conical glass with fuzzing stuff that proved invigorating after just one sip. So he gulped another. His head was so loaded it nearly exploded. That was how the Strawberry Curls Girl song went. Maybe Gwendolyn had strawberry curls down below. There were strawberries on the table too.

"Daddy, I believe you made him blush."

"Nonsense, anyone who pioneered the altering of psychotropic molecules as fearlessly as this man, and allegedly tested them on himself and his friends regularly would not be even slightly abashed by a windbag like me."

"Pardon me, sir," said Shaney amazed and finding himself suddenly in a surreal canyon. "How do you know this, um?" He was about to say "shit about me."

Lionel laughed. "Who the hell do you think granted and funded your fellowship, Mr. Shaney?"

"Lobos Petrochemicals," he said. "Oh, Lobos, wolf. Wolfie. Wolf as in Wulfhardt. Don't be embarrassed. It's our charitable wing. I didn't figure out who you were right away either. The old memory bank has been overdrawn these last few years."

"At a loss from the sauce," said fair Gwendolyn.

"The wrath of grapes," said Lila May joining in the family fun. "But mostly it's me that wears him down."

"I'm very grateful for the opportunity…" began Shaney. "That is, the fellowship."

"Nonsense, son, you earned it. Only thing that irritates me is that you're being made to TA. Why hasn't the fellowship money kicked in? Why aren't you in the lab right now?"

"That was *my* choice, sir, I mean, Lionel. I got here a semester early to study with Dr. Ocdivarius, then they offered me the paying gig. Figured it would help me orient myself vis a vis the Austin college populace."

"And right away you met our daughter," said the mother, icy now. "That's fast orienting, pardner."

"Oh Mama, I picked *him* up. You know me."

By this time food arrived, an unbelievably complex version of the lowly enchilada, blazing with cumin and backed up on electric guitar with fiery chiles that burned all around the tongue like a stinging ballet, a symphony. He gasped at how good, and, surprisingly, how well it went with the sparkling white wine that kept filling up like magic at his table. The mélange of tortilla, cheese, and onion in red sauce was followed by a crisp salad of romaine leaves coated in an unguent film of lemon, olive oil, anchovies, and garlic. Then came brisket and beans. Voracious eaters, male and female, gnashed and sighed. Yet, the talk was lively and lasted a sparkling hour in gentle jokes and miniature truths. Conversation soon turned to Shaney's work.

Papa Wulfhardt asked if the young scientist saw a future in alkaloids and fungus. Shaney said his days of self-experimentation had been wildly exaggerated, but such as they were, had been replaced by animal trials some time ago. Lionel said he knew. Ready to defend such experimenting, Shaney was surprised how quickly the topic pivoted to research he had begun at UCSB and hoped to continue here. And how interested they truly seemed. Shaney wondered at the smallness of the world where he found such connection after leaving his room for barbecue. Other intimacies (like great sex before fine food) propped up his sense of some tiny private order manifesting into some further un-guessed destiny. Communally they inhaled air sweetened by musky table flowers; let out garlic and yeast. Meanwhile, Gwen kept giving him approving eyeballs. Gulp, he thought, she is so hot for me.

Then dessert came. Shaney and his new lover passed on the profiteroles, but ate the fruit and cheese as Lionel droned on and on about his own company achievements.

"You know sir," said Shaney. Lionel waved aside the honorific like a pest insect. "You know I would hope—that is I would be proud to intern there when my fellowship ends. Just saying," he added to be comic.

"What the fuck?" said Lionel, bringing Shaney upright. "Am I not speaking clear here?

"Can't you relate mate?" said Lila.

"There is a job waiting for you at Lobos P. whenever you are ready," said Lionel. "The sooner the better. *Now*, say?"

Shaney was tingling, dumbfounded. "I'm, uh, I'm speechless," he said.

"You sound like Bert Lahr," said Gwen.

"Work for you, like part time?" mumbled John.

"I can get you yanked from the TA business and put you in a lab next week if you would like," Lionel roared. "Think I will."

"And I would accept with gratitude." Shaney thought he was joking, kinda.

"Good, I need someone on the werewolf problem. That's my priority."

Gwen started coughing. Lila handed her a glass of water.

"The what, sir?"

"Come on, John. We've got more studying to do," said Lila May, leaping up from the table like a capering lamb.

"Hit the books, snooks," said Lionel and Gwen in comic unison. Gwen rasping.

"Don't forget our problem," said Lionel. "I'll call the college, get you straight, hell, set them straight," he said, muttering with his head turned looking out the window where a red-crested bird, a cardinal, sat on a ragged branch of alderwood no longer blooming.

Meanwhile, Lila May was dragging Shaney by the hand towards and up the stairs, while he spoke thanks over his shoulder. Infatuated as he was, Shaney wasn't sure he had another boff left in him. He wasn't at all sure what was next for him in a life grown suddenly wealthy with surprise.

"That was weird," he said.

"Why?" she asked.

"They were so nice. It was so easy."

"Dawg, they loved you. Especially my mother," she said, ice tones creeping forward.

"Not your dad?"

"He offered you a job, bitch."

"I know, right? I feel like my entire future got decided between last night and now."

"So, where *did* you camp last night?" she said, turning on a television set that was set into her pastel walls. She turned it off then too. The sun outside looked lethal with heat.

"Some guy named Uncle Tom, or…"

"Uncle John," she said.

"That's it."

"Funny. I was there too," she said.

"That's not possible. It was after the police took you away."

"Uncle John's soirees tend to take place from morning to following morning, O, dontcha know. They were unkegging some beer at 10 a.m. to celebrate putting the rubbed brisket into the smoker. I think they had another keg 24 hours earlier when they rubbed it."

"Were you there for both?" he asked genuinely wondering. Giant Texas seemed small.

"No, silly," she said running her fingertips down his arms. "I was in section with you in the morning, and, if memory serves, was getting hustled by you about the time dinner was served."

"Oh I hustled *you*."

"Didn't I say rustled?" she said leaning into him with all her petite might, which was considerable. She pulled the curtains back. "It's fall, you know, and they turned back the clocks, or they will. Look how low the sun is on the foothills already. I always thought the whole landscape here looked rusty and worn out by the sun. But it looks mighty perfect under the moon. Moonstone. Speaking of which, you better get gone soon."

"My," he said. "Don't act so sentimental. We just met."

"Seriously, folks," she said. "I got to get some real studying done and I think Papa would be much ungrumpier if you left at a respectable time."

"Yeah, well," suddenly he was mopey and horny too.

"Oh don't be like that. It was the perfect day, maybe the best I ever had. You're kind of a wild animal," she giggled inclining her head to the unmade bed. "Let me wash up and tidy and then I'll walk you to your car. Watch T.V. in the meantime."

She hit the remote again and the giant screen sizzled on to local news. There were some national stories about the faltering economy, a Fortune's Wheel gone mad back in those days. Newscasters loved success and failure stories—bear and bull baiting—and this one traced the rise and fall of a hot sauce store called Ay Chihuahua. But that story ended when a "this-just-in" began.

Police are investigating the site of a gruesome slaughter outside Austin in the foothills on the ramshackle habitat of one John Della Croce known to the neighborhood as Uncle John, after a keg delivery service found blood on the wall of the primary residence. A weekend barbecue and camp-over was visited by a monstrous series of violent acts, details of which have been trickling into the station from sources near the investigation, though police had nothing specific yet to report, confirm, or deny. A camera crew sat outside the compound, which reporters kept referring to as the murder site, on that street, what was it called, O there was the sign, just off Fangtooth Lane, which sounded less now like a Harry Potter place.

Not that Shaney was pop culture observant. In fact, he was crazy nervous now, his stomach clenched and his heartbeat went hard hollow-thudding and dismal—in the back of his mind something seemed to be saying see I told you so. He thought he had seen too much of death. He thought that phase of his life was over.

Then he saw the camera alight on some police puzzling over something on the ground, pointing. One of the officers came down the hill and whispered to a man who straightened and the reporter reported that they had found tire tracks that did not belong to anybody there. They were calling in a crew to take impressions. It was surprising how much one could learn, the policeman said, from patterns in the shifting dust.

Bullshit thought Shaney—they're bluffing now. He could tell. But just then another camera lit upon a haggard figure limping like a zombie across the gravel road.

This was real trouble.

Shaney heard the loud sound of a truck shifting down on the highway far far away, a lonesome highway, he thought he wanted to traverse. A hand rested on his arm and he jumped.

"Jesus," he said.

"Is that where I think it is?" Lila asked

"I'm pretty sure, yeah." He knew. "Apparently John or John's crew was murdered. Maybe after I left?"

"What do the cops know?

"Nothing at this point but they can track the killer down literally like an animal. Only with his tireprints, whatyoucall."

"Oh, bullshit," she said. "What about this guy?"

"I don't know his name but he was there last night." Shaney didn't mention that he let the zombie in his car then drove him to the murder site, at first because he thought the stranger was a real zombie, then because he was embarrassed he wasn't; picked him up in his car, drove him to the killing grounds, told the gaunt stranger his name, wondered now that he would be fingered by a stumbling midnight stalker. He would know me, he thought. Gangster Lee.

"Doesn't he have lupus or something?" she asked her mouth hanging open curiously as she stared numbly at the molecule-agitated screen.

"Yeah."

"You never know when that stuff will come on, like migraines, it's a real curse. Better for two years and then you turn. Monstrous."

"Like migraines," he offered. He wondered at her lack of concern. It could have been you, she might have said.

"I'm glad it wasn't you," she said in a numbed voice. He supposed she meant murdered. Did she think about the drummer too?

They watched for minutes and the newscasters moved on to sports. "Like I said, you better go, honey. Daddy will be getting restless."

He stood up and for a second the world whirled around him. He almost fell over from a blood pressure shift but she didn't notice, preoccupied with a commercial for a weight reduction plan that turned obese slovenly men and women into neatly-attired sex objects. She thought deeply about how a body changes, not just the years but even from one end of a spa to the other. Factory lines. She was changing. Uncle John changed. But who changed him? She had a strong idea.

And then the voice. "Are you seeing this news, Lila, darling?" the intercom boomed.

"Yes, Daddy," she said. "Uncle John."

"What can your John tell us?"

Before he could answer, Lila asked, "Was Mama safe last night?"

"Of course, dear, but please don't talk about such things. John? What happened?"

"I fell asleep by the fire, when I woke up everybody was gone. I called out and then I left. I didn't see anything."

"Do you need to see my lawyer?"

"Do I, sir?"

"If the police ask? Nevermind, if you need, I'll give you my legal representation. Their phone."

"Daddy, I believe him."

"Of course, so do I. Meet me at the door. When you leave."

"You woke up and they were gone. You're certain," she said. Now a worry on her face.

Shaney nodded, satisfied. "Gotta go. Better go. Your father."

"Daddy," she said. "You and Daddy. Write down your address before you go. My mother always sends a thank you note to luncheon guests."

"Your mother," he said. But he was thinking, shouldn't I thank her? In person?

Wordless they glided down the stairs and across the dangerously waxed tile floors past portrait rooms of ancestors and a fake parlor filled with a grand piano no one used. He thought of Disneyland's haunted mansion and wondered which spook would be riding home with him. In the old glass mirror he saw his own reflection aura-ed out, a soul outgrowing its body. His was roiling, thinking about last night. And whatever happened. It was stuck inside him somewhere. She, on the other hand, seemed to have moved on with her own thoughts. She held his hand dry. No fear. Like the popular clothing line.

Papa Wulf handed him a card. Get out of jail free. "You don't need to face cops alone."

"Think I should turn myself in? I mean as some sort of witness?"

"Hell no," said Wulfie. "Drive safely home."

Outside, the air was stiff with heat as early evening came down out of hills that curved around them like a scythe. He would be heading away from that sunset into stratums of darkening already blue.

"Can I call you?" he said. "Will I see you?"

She looked at him and cocked her head like a cute labrador considering an insect. "Of course, honey. I'll see you Tuesday in section. And, oh yeah, for the rest of your life. Did you forget you're my boyfriend?"

He laughed and said, "Forgive me my insecurities. I have been wounded in love," he said joking, melodramatic, though regretting the L-word.

She leaped into his arms and twined around him with her legs. "From now on, I am your wound," she whispered.

He laughed nervously and kissed her wondering if the help or the parents were taking in this carnal display from windows above. Fuck it, he thought.

After necking shamelessly a bit, she broke the spell. "Do I have to move to another section? Ethics of conflicts of interest or, or, whatever?"

Oh, that. It *had* vaguely concerned him, the intermingling of TA with student—he did lead her across the fields and groves of Academia into dark lands.

"I guess. I didn't think about it. I do have to recommend your grade. Aw, shit," he said. It crossed his mind that she had no qualms about his connection to Uncle John's atrocities, but this worried her. He thought about the flies buzzing in the little stand of woods and the painting like a smear of gallons of blood. He thought about the drummer dripping blood. "Every silver lining has a cloud," he said, mumbling on the edge of his own distraction.

"Ain't that the truth. Listen, when you drive, don't go by, well, you know." She meant Uncle John's with cops. At least now he knew she was cognizant of the crime. "There's another way to get to the highway faster and even more desolate. My dad had it built and maintained so he could get out there quickly."

She gave him written down easy directions but warned him not to lose faith if the stretch of road seemed treacherous or scary. He laughed.

She said don't laugh and spun around leaving him next to his dusty car with the new tire. Shit, he thought. A new tire: if they were reading that as a print, it could go either way, since I didn't come in with it. Just the same, my old tire is up there at the crime scene, I guess. Up there by itself, but where? For a few seconds he made a fantasy raid on the police-taped area seeking out his incriminating evidence. He wore a black watchcap and those black jeans and t-shirts he liked. Did he have his favorite cardigan? All his sneakers were dirty white, though. Damn. Then he thought: What exactly is keeping me from just going in and telling the police what happened? Then he remembered the blood underneath his nails flowing down the drain and got into his car and fired up the engine and pulled onto the highway, free.

# 5.

The shortcut involved a nerve-wracking search for a pumpkinhead rock. Per Lila's note. A number of false rocks appeared: basketball, Oprah Winfrey head, carousel, he was ready to give up and go the regular highway, even risk the police gathering at Uncle John's slaughter when, undeniably, Jack-O-Lantern appeared.

Turn right and go a few miles uphill to La Llorona Boulevard, it said. Hispanic and French. He was having home thoughts, drowsed by anticipation. Remember, John Shaney just went out for a bite Saturday night, and hasn't seen his lovely bed (free from dust, twigs, and no-see-ums) in a long day that felt like two, in which love and work worlds were upended. Cars kept passing him.

Traveling tired along the top of a ridge he began to notice twinkling lights of the earthly firmament, a city in the distance. He didn't know if it was Austin, but what else could it be? He made a wish on one of the city lights, then supposed he was putting faith in the glow from atop a hamburger stand. It would all end in tragedy: Burger King Lear.

Then it happened the first time.

The car simply died. The steering wheel was no good; it needed power to operate. The brakes didn't work; they felt mushy and congested. But it didn't matter because the car, radio, and lights just gave out on a stretch of road planted in hawthorn and oak. A canopy of darkness overcame him. A sudden whoosh across the darkness. His heart might have stopped, too, and he wondered what that would actually feel like on that one day when it inevitably did.

Then, just as suddenly, the car jolted back to life and he became irritatingly razzed-up. Relief mixed with shock as the engine, lights, and radio resumed functioning—the radio was playing "Get a Job" loud, fucking up his head with the odd coincidence. "I just got one," he said to the radio, pissed.

The night was pale with moonlight hidden behind long torn rags of cloud. Each silver lined. His mind considered the incongruous pines here at the summit. The events of the day kept playing. Her smell was heavy on his face and hands and, no doubt, in nether regions too. A gloat spread inside of him with night and his stabbing car beams lit random details, bush, wall, and sign. Around the curve he traveled too fast at the posted speed where the road went straight and into trees, he jerked alert. La Llorona Wilderness, said another sign. Then a little dip in the road, poorly paved over a culvert and the wheels lost contact with earth and he got a jolt. So he tried to martial his sleepy brain with thoughts, logic, and science stuff.

He tried to address some of the chemical and molecular issues raised by his last round of experimenting on the alkaloids. How 4 PO DMT can be amalgamated into the synthetic construction 4 ACO DMT; with the operative variants being nebular clouds around the tryptamine. The variant he handed out to the fireside boys was something closer to LSD, though. He chuckled at invisible puns. Then felt sad. Run out of thoughts.

Immediately, the car died again.

This time he didn't even try to reignite it. He sat back in the darkness under the darker trees. The sky was full of clouds but the moon was out. Somewhere he heard a whistling, keening, maybe. What was it? A dread began to gather inside him, deep where the bones produce marrow: He was cold and he instinctively reached across to the backseat where he usually threw a hoodie or a thrift store cardigan. Neither there; he was really cold. Wait. He had a cardi when he left. Right?

The keening grew louder and a dreamlike quality filled the air as odd ideas crossed his train of thought in irregular shapes and with divergent paths of implication, a game of Chutes and Ladders. The keening seemed to be punctuated with sobs.

Somebody is crying, he thought, somebody is always crying. Voices converge in the darkness of the living room after death. He found his mother there and had to call the police and his father wasn't in the room. There there. She was kind of crying. The crying he heard now seemed to be surrounded with blue, a fog of whispering atmosphere.

The first rag of her cloth whipped out from the gap between the oleander and the pine, borne on winds that did not exist. He was seeing into the heart of the tearful voice, the sound became flesh, not words. She was translated from emotions, objectified, a nebula of blue clouds.

The woman walked out onto the road swinging her arms in a parody of carelessness. There was visible static electricity surrounding her and she looked both ways before crossing the street, the empty mountain road. He was beyond cold now, beyond disbelief, shaking. The head turned around and looked at him, her face without features. The crying sound rose and turned then to shrieking pain.

She looked him in the eyes. Shit. The phantasm recoiled from Shaney as if *he* was the terror. He cried out involuntarily. She froze an awful moment, leaned forward towards him again, then straightened, put her eyeless gaze back on her old course and renewed her puppet march, sweeping emotions from the road. Swept up into her robes went envy and revenge. She passed into the bushes with dismay and sorrow. The shrubbery did not part for her and Shaney thought he heard the inchoate cries turn into a voice. A low growl. It said something he half-remembered but left the air suddenly still.

He sat there teeth chattering. Dark. What next? Oh, indeed, what? And then the engine screamed to life and the radio was loudly playing "Tracks of My Tears" with its ooh-baby-baby. He nearly shit. He heard a long howl in the distance.

He put the car in gear and shot off down the road.

This was not normal: this was not normal. Yet on some basic mental computational level, he accepted it. After all, it occurred before his open eyes. He knew what sleep and dreams felt like, and he was sure he hadn't drifted, though his mind was meandering there for a few seconds. No.

The car hit the crest of the rode and leaped a little bit and swayed. The trees had been left behind. Down the spine of the mountain stretched the road. And far below was Austin, sparkling in the more sedate city-lights dance of a Sunday night. She had been right; this was a significant shortcut. Except for one thing, right? Have to stop for ghosts.

Now he started with the explanations, rationalizations. Rejecting dream and hallucination, we are left with spirit, ghost. Shit he felt cold again. On the positive side, this more or less proved that the soul exists after rot consumes flesh. Sub-query: this presumes the being was a ghost, in other words, had formerly possessed body leading to the counter-presumption that an afterlife, kind of reassuring, check, might also hold legions of demon creatures, a minus, transporting themselves here from realms invisible to this mundane sphere. Angels too he guessed. Still remotely possible: hallucination, given his proclivity for psychedelic experimentations. Though this did not "look" like your basic trip vision which tends to be more like flapping edges and abstract patterns. He could also be fucking crazy. Now, that's for sure.

The moon slid out from the long-wisped clouds, full, serene, and, yet, now imbued with sparking powers, he felt. He rode down the hill past gas stations with mini-marts, the sphere mundane. But if the cosmos had cracked to let out a sprite, couldn't it have the common courtesy to suck back some of *our* monstrous creations? Corndog and blueberry Slurpee: Go back to Hell. Which world did he live in? Surprisingly meditative for a murder suspect that definitely just saw a ghost. What did she say?

The car skittered on the freeway. His driving was good but the car might have "issues," as the kids today say. He found an exit that led to a long road through the suburbs into town, a long straight and narrow road that no doubt once was a farm-servicing lane. The tract was called Maleva Estates built by a famous Russian actress who taught Lee Strasbourg everything he knew. Weird Austin was close to Hollywood in its incarnation as Holly-weird: indie film festivals, Robert Rodriguez, and the boojie Alamo Drafthouse.

Wait, now he remembered. The ghost said, "free me." The ghost said, "from the changes."

It was about three miles from home when he first thought he saw it running alongside his car, a long, loping shadow like a sleek dog only heavier. Shaney was getting tired now, also tired of his own mind's courtship with terrors. The moon was large in the sky and bright even when tangled in suburban trees.

When he stopped for a stop sign under the fruit-empty trees, the shadow stopped as well, blending into the subworld of all plant shadows.

He pulled out. It pulled out with him. What the fuck is next, he wondered. He turned on his high beams hoping for more peripheral sight. It only made the shapeless thing more durably dark. By now, all of this seemed an abomination to the streets of suburbia, his high beams; so much light piercing windows interrupting snug weekender's dream worlds. Or maybe it was just him. Shaney's mind itself was the base intrusion into this middle class life. Nope. There it was: the shadow loping like a greyhound, that's what it was, like the figure emblazoned on those big interstate buses. Nope, this was much more muscled and its hind legs were obscenely long. Shaney thought he saw incisors glinting in the shadow's mouth, but, of course, that was ridiculous. Again, he had to stop and once more the beast of shades went into the ambient dark now raked and mown by the long thin fingers of the full moon sweeping from up above like a beacon to warn lost souls.

He rolled out again and, without doubt, it came too; pulling itself like sticky gum from the dark underneath of evergreen and oleander hedge. Unglued and in pursuit it glided, nosing down the dark streets. He gunned the car and drove like a bat out of hell. It was then that he saw real bats swarm over the moon, a very common occurrence in Austin, but now it felt obviously cartoon omen-ish and disturbingly clichéd like horror story chic. He chuckled angrily wondering if the bats above and the hound below might be supernatural enemies, like caribou and wolf. Nope. He was the caribou. He punched it harder, going about 100 miles per hour through streets where daylight parents rolled soft perambulators. By God, he had lost the shadow, but he was still about one half mile from home. He slowed fearing policeman now more than any hound of hell. He came to a stop sign that he meant to run. The car died for a third time. Always in threes, pissant symbolist stuff.

"Fuck shit," was what he said out loud. He rolled to the curb down a tiny hill. The ignition turned, produced no sound beyond an ominous click and the lights were fading, so he thought he might want to scoot, hoof it, but he was scared to go outside. He pulled out his cell phone—he rarely used it—and its batteries were still dead. He grabbed again for the sweater that still was not there. Fuck shit, what if he *had* left it at Uncle John's? By now his body had forgotten completely its earlier post-sex ease. Now he was worried and could not recall the sweater's last contact with his skin. His heart made more sludging big beats, he was sickened afraid. As he sat in the dark, breathing through his mouth and gulping air, he jerked into action as if on strings. How do heart attacks feel?

The Whatever Shadow was nowhere in sight and outside the car's cocoon Shaney convinced himself it was left behind, far behind, if it ever existed outside his own mind. Probably got tired of the chase, the lure of home and doggy bowl overruled whatever sport this shadow named Shadow enjoyed while chasing me, Shaney thought. Bats flew over the wide moon again. He got out. He looked again warily and locked the car door. He began walking towards home beneath that wide moon.

It was so quiet he could hear music piping from downtown. That seemed ridiculous until he realized he wasn't far from the scenesters and their lurkspots, particularly the rogue west end of the nightclub world. Austin was a funny place, suburb, city, and wild spaces intertwined without transition, little frontiers of brush between open land and civilized earth.

He walked by a dry creek and thought of the coyotes that, he read, traveled it like a highway, huddling beneath shrubbery when daylight surprised them. He saw a yellowy streetlamp with particles dancing in the light, moths, perhaps, or fledgling bats, making the light almost liquid with a diseased hue.

He heard it but wouldn't admit the truth at first. It wasn't slinking with a creeping hunter's gait, it was plodding, prancing, pre-victorious. He could read its movements as if through some previously unknown medium; a fog of electrons colliding against a sense, an organ of perception, never used before. If he turned around, the dog or whatever would be visible. So he didn't turn, he played ostrich in the open air. Shaney crossed the street and into a tree-hooded stretch. No sound followed, perhaps the beastie walked on soft pads.

Then he heard the rasp of bellows breathing. He stepped up the curb and went into the moon-blocking trees for about 100 yards and then he heard a loud gun-report twig crack, a cliché but more undeniable than death's inevitable fact.

Nothing left to do, he turned around. Nothing. The street was empty and Shaney felt foolish and relieved. Likely his nerves were stressed after the crying figure, or whatever, perhaps that too was a figment of his stressed nerves. Then he thought about the cardigan and wondered again where he might have left it.

In his mind's eye, he saw it lying by the firepit: a very intelligent-looking policeman, picking it up, perhaps with a pencil, and examining the smoke-smelling sweater as one would peer down the nose at an exotic but loathsome moth. Shaney started walking. He was nervous, but the streetlamp and the sidewalk and the hedged houses gave him something to believe in at least, the peace that surpasseth all understanding called suburbs. Home, he thought. That extra organ of perception was normally called an overactive imagination, the place where memory and speculation met. At least now he might get some sleep.

He imagined the soft cool feel of the pillow just a moment before he saw it standing in the sidewalk half in dark and half in moonlight. Electric effervescences ran up his stomach, back, and collarbones, stomach clenched and in poured an irritating buzz.

He looked it in the eye, a big mistake.

The animal was a German shepherd straight out of a 1960s stalag-escape film, though more grey and ugly, growling low from its belly up its throat and lowering itself as both diminishment of itself as target and in advance preparation for leap, tear, shake, and kill.

Shaney backed up and tried to remember something, anything. The electric current had faded to an unpleasant afterbuzz, but now his mind was slow. Should he placate or threaten? He tried the latter first, making himself comically large and shouting as best he could given the cracked tones of fear: it produced a predictable snarl and advance, and Shaney almost shit his pants, twice in one night.

"Whoa," he said, reversing tactic, "good doggie." He heard the fear in his voice and knew in his heart the dog could hear and sniff it too.

He wasn't much wrong. The animal looked different now: more like the ragged but beautiful Irish hound, a harrier of the plains. It did not know fear. It was curious about its prey's sudden death wish—sensing a trap. The man had stopped all speculative thought, only saw teeth watering wide and felt the renewed arcing electric current run his body, his heart pounding on an anvil, lungs aching to be filled.

Shaney enacted a primitive dance he never learned the steps to. He feinted left, the animal, which looked more like a mastiff now, shifted easily on its powerful haunches to meet him. Shaney lurched forward, it prepared itself to launch. He hid his face and tried submission, though it riled him (as a dominant species) to bend like this. Maybe the thing knew what he was thinking. Or read him from some index of scents pouring like language from his body, scents incapable of lying. When he looked up again, the dog seemed ridiculously grotesque like a giant poodle gone to seed. He blinked and it was a Borzoi. He blinked and it had turned before his eyes into a snub-nosed pit bull, that most déclassé and evildoing breed, at least according to popular reputation.

This proved to be the fatal tipping point. Shaney turned and ran, screaming out to the sleepy neighborhood for help. Not a light lit.

The creature growled following and glowing. Down a dark street, lavender and rosemary whipping at his feet, they ran and came into a pool of moonlight amplified by a streetlamp burning golden yellow. It became a spotlight for the circling match—human versus animal.

They kept their distance. He screamed, the dog growled. Shaney tried to bisect the imaginary circle and rush past the beast that now, under the mix of harsh and soft lights looked more wolfish than before. Heart thudding, Shaney ran. The Other span and nipped the air quite close to his ear, which completely unnerved the human who stumbled, turning and falling backwards over the curb into a parkway lined with hedge. Then there was a frightening interlude when the animal, now lean like a whippet, came forward yet seemed to be lifted from behind. Then three things came together, and something cried out and Shaney felt pain, something deep inside his body. He stood and wavered and the large lump of gyring fur knocked him on his ass again crashing through the resiny brush where his hand barked against a big enough rock—a rock big enough to swing and do damage.

In his adrenal state he picked it up. But something, not the dog, spun by him like a furred wind wet and electrified. The thing charged (not the dog charged) and bit down on him again, tearing a gash in his palm, forcing Shaney to drop the rock. The mystery thing ran off in a different direction, the unknown thing, but the animal, the obvious dog, came back snarling.

Shaney, pissed off and bleeding and tired of being afraid, bent low, picked up the rock and brained the dog who yelped sadly and fell back. It spun up a second as if jerked on a string. It came at him again, but then slowed and went down, obviously wounded. Shaney closed in and down now, on attack mode, pounding and pounding away at this foe, by compulsion taken over, frenzied. The beast's skull was collapsing like a sponge. Shaney even in spasms of violence guessed that the dog had moved beyond consciousness. There was blood all over. There was soft grass on the dark tract home behind him. He wiped away the red stuff in it and chucked the rock far away into a neighbor's backyard. Then didn't know what he should do. Call out to the neighbors? Whose fucking dog was it? Did it follow him down from the hill country? Or was that the something else? He looked at the dog and felt shame. But self defense. Rationalizing reason.

Breathing low and regular now, he took off but soon noticed that there was still blood as he was walking home. And he was walking home.

He had traveled a block and there was still blood. He wiped again and there was still blood. It wasn't till his third wipe that he realized he was bleeding. The gash was open and wide. He couldn't stop the bleeding with a pinch together, so he pulled a wadded receipt out of his pocket. Another block until he realized it was a sponge of blood, his blood.

He stopped and considered. Shakiness was just around the corner, and home was at least ten blocks down this shady lane. There was no noise behind him. Good. The dog was dead. But he had left evidence behind at the scene of a slaughter, tracks and a sweater.

He kicked off a shoe and took one of his white crew socks off and stretched it tight and wound it around the finger and palm. Good. The killer dog was dead. But he was bleeding and didn't know if he needed to go to an emergency room.

"*Chupacabra*," he said out loud.

He was surprised to find himself standing on his own porch. He had a hard time digging in his pocket for the keys, but they were there. He was sad to note that none of his roommates were awake, part of him was dying to share the crazy events of the last 24 hours. What a difference a day makes, said the commercial based on a once-popular song. Then again, he wasn't sure how he would frame it: the campfire, the sex, meeting the parents, the job offer, the ghost (if that's what it was), and the dog that bit him, the dog that he killed. He went straight to the upstairs bathroom walking through his dark room and locked the door. It took him a whole minute to face up to the wound, breathing hard. Yuck. It was like a tiny open mouth. He thought it was too big to force closed with Band-aids and after all shouldn't he get it checked and get a tetanus shot. Rabies. Oh fuck. He found some peroxide and poured it over the gash, emboldened by his fear of the treatments, the injections in the belly he had heard tell of. He pulled the wound together and strapped a bandage over it too tight. Then another. Then another. It stopped bleeding. He imagined it was healing already on a cellular level. He also imagined rabies germs, or whatever they were outrunning the peroxide, nestling around his heart, lining the arteries that led to his brain. He stumbled back to his room and turned on the light.

The cardigan was lying across the smooth, made bed.

# 6.

Safe, he thought, waking up. Or not, he reconsidered, waking more. Took nothing but memories and left nothing behind except footprints, tireprints, fingerprints, O, and blood. Not at the scene of the. His hand was wounded. After. The waitress witness. To what? Well, maybe he wasn't completely safe. The memories were spreading to include a ghost and, O, blood.

A hissing kitten arched on the dining-room table when he tumbled down for breakfast near ten that day.

"Hello?" he said to the room, at first gentle to not further disturb the cat in front of him. And then louder: "Hello!"

No one answered. Two women lived in the big wood-cabineted house, so, true to stereotype, the place sparkled even during midterm maelstroms and finals frenzies.

Even nightowl Louis, one door down the hall from Shaney, was up and out that day, all the way changed and gone.

The cat, by the way, had adopted the house. First gained pity with forlorn mewing, she somehow finagled treats, which then graduated to cans fetched home from the nearby liquor store, and, finally, got a collar. The whole adaptation process took two maybe three days. Thus integrated, the creature began making the territory its own. Luna they called her long and high, Loooo-na!

"Fuck you," Shaney said after Luna refused both docile and aggressive approaches. Nonetheless, animal followed the man to the refrigerator where human decided to steal a cup of roommate milk to drown hapless granola remains shaken from an old box. He was famished and this might tide him over till his student union chowdown preparatory to teaching section later. And seeing Lila May. His finger and hand, as he lifted the carton to pour, did not hurt, only throbbed slightly like venial sin in an upright person's conscience. And, speaking of sin's wages, he was fearful to examine the animal bite.

First, he wanted news. From upstairs, he brought down his laptop and without spilling cereal connected to the Wifi web mist surrounding the house—login: mycologicalwarrior—clicked on the city's main headline provenderer and found nothing more about the Uncle John slayings. There was leftover burbling about the rock concert death but that was subsumed by a statistical debate about downtown scene crime, up only a fraction of a percent, bragged police chief Ouspensky-Carneros. A longer piece about animal shelter overcrowding and shameful pet desertions got more ink.

Idly glancing out the window, Shaney spied a newspaper languishing in the unkempt grass (A newspaper? Whose? Maybe there for years?). Damn, this granola is good, he thought, though his stomach craved breakfast meats. He went out the door past Luna now busy with some other foe perceptible only to itself. He picked up the paper, which, surprisingly, turned out to be fresh, today's, and opened it to banner headlines: the wanton slaying of a dog not eight blocks away from where he stood. At first it seemed oddly familiar, like an emotional residue from a dream or a

TV show. His own dreams, by the way, had been preoccupied with heaps of lamb and sheep meat offered for the carving; delectable under mounds of mint sauce, a relish he hated during waking hours, but, apparently, esteemed whilst asleep.

Then he remembered the dog attack and his own brutal retaliation. (Should clean the wound, he thought. Don't want to look, he replied.) Then he looked up at the clock and thought he better scamper off to his office since his hours available began in about ten minutes. Shit his car. He'd have to deal with it later parked where it broke down. More money. He had to go. It took him eight minutes to pedal his cruiser bike up to the science building where three unbelievably beautiful women representing splendor, grace, and good cheer stood. One actually winked at him.

Stunned, Shaney crept down the hall toward the grad student warren, his office, found no one in line breathless to discuss DNA strands and aggression. Opening the musty hole, he penned a note, pinned it to the door, and proceeded off to a second breakfast in the steel and glass enclosure where students fed. Walking through the cafeteria lines Shaney was unable to control his appetite—meat, meat, eggs, and another meat heaped themselves on his plastic fake China plate. A mug of coffee filled with Moo Juice (the name of the creamery product on the condiment table) then wolfed the repast while skimming his notes for section.

Someone left an *American-Statesman* on the next table. Shaney scooped it and scoured the columns. Maybe there would be a hint at the police investigations of Uncle John's slaughter: "ongoing" as journalists loved to say. Nothing. Instead, there was a long, passionate piece about the utter depravity displayed by the beastly human who killed a dog with a rock and then ran off leaving a house of loving children not only bereft of their faithful pet, but traumatized by the violence. If such acts are possible, the writer opined, then mass murderers and holocaust and genocide ought be no surprise. Thank you, heartless bastard. It was late last night and this was a morning paper. Nobody would react with such swiftness, he thought, report the crime, write a letter to the editor, and print it so early after. But, as he reread it, he was forced to admit it was the same neighborhood. The crime took place last night. The reaction was now and vehement. Pleading self-defense at this point would be futile. Maybe self-destructive.

The dog-owning children, it turned out, happened to be named Shanely, just a letter away from his own—perhaps related and separated by some Ellis Island error. His folks came through other American membranes, though. His Ardeal, Hungary born father entered after World War II when brain importation from Communist-leaning countries was encouraged by everyone from AT&T to the CIA. His dad was in both of those alphabet soups. The name, which sounded Irish, was assumed to be a degradation of the ancient family of Ceanu. His mother from London, a student nurse who helped Papa not freak after he was dosed with psychedelics at the US Festival in 1980. She redirected him to Erhard Seminar Training.

"Heartless bastard," said a basso profondo from over his shoulder.

"Beg pardon," said Shaney, heart-thundering as he turned his head.

"Hey *profe* not you. The guy who killed that helpless dog," said one of his better section students, whose name, Shaney seemed to remember had something to do with a rock song about genocide.

"I'm not a professor, just a grad student."

"With a giant appetite, grad-ie. Saw you consume many cloven-hoofed animals in the last ten minutes. What happened to your paw?"

Shaney held up his wounded hand, that he honestly had forgotten, since there was no pain. "Really? You've been scoping my intake?" Neil Cortez, thought Shaney. Cortez, Cortez. "Come over just to shame me, Cortez?" The Killer.

"No, dude, to warn you. There's a rumbling around that you're dating this chick in our section and the dean don't like no fraternization. Though it's more like sororitazation, isn't it? Article about it in the student newspaper, you don't watch out."

"About me?" Shaney said, wondering why local newspapers were so tuned into his private shames.

"About you, about ethics and shit."

"I assume you mean Lila May who I ran into at the Oil Can What show."

"Whoa, dude, I heart that band: hella. Didn't know they were there."

"Then how did you know *I* was there with Lila May."

"Facebook, man. Somebody posted it. How was the show?"

"Good until the horrible death," said Shaney approaching annoyance.

"Right on. I get it. Hey, speaking of death by a thousand cuts, are you, wow, yo, going over the DNA midterm today, man?" A beautiful woman passed near them. Neither spoke, though Shaney nodded.

"And speaking of DNA, what about this dog murderer?"

"I'm trying to read it but I keep getting interrupted," said Shaney who didn't mind he wasn't making friends. This was irritating. "Hurt my hand changing a tire on my bicycle. By the way."

"That'll happen. Whatever. Cops want to use the university lab to see if they can separate the dog blood from the human, the strands and shit. Detect the culprit as it were, was, were."

Implications landslided Shaney's mind.

"So much trouble for a dog, you Texans are like PETA on steroids," he said.

"No it's just a science thing, see if they can do it," said Cortez staring at the girl. "DNA, I mean, an experiment."

Shaney, internally panicked, swallowed the big bite of chipotle beef slider.

And then remembered his car stranded, dead, a few blocks from the dog crime scene, which by now seemed the worst massacre of utter brutality and evil ever perpetrated. They were looking for tire tracks and of course the grassy blood could be matched to him. He had never been arrested or under suspicion, so that mitigated the danger. But his car sitting there might get noticed; and there were the tire tracks and his terrible failure to report association with the Uncle John Fire Pit slayings. Heartbeat accelerating, no matter how he tried to apply some calming reason; Lila May was looking like a loose end too, some other voice in him warned. On Facebook. Huh.

Shaney moved past panic, decided it was time he happened to things. "Yep. Gotta make like an amoeba," he said to Cortez.

"A what?" asked the undergrad, puzzled.

"And split?"

"What what?" asked Cortez eyeing the leftovers on the TA's plate. Shaney left the student union fast and worried, mounted his cruiser, and rolled through neighborhoods passing his own house with the shitass cat hissing at him from the porch, back along streets he covered in moonlight with blood, past the attack site now covered with makeshift bouquets and doggy In Memoriams, to his stranded heap sitting in harsh sunlight. He leaned his bike on a fenced hippie house festooned with Buddhist prayer flags, walked back, unlocked said car, entered, put key in ignition, and what the hell, turned it and O! the hum of engagement. He roared it once, threw in his bike, and drove back to school with twenty minutes left until office hours, which he spent shuffling notes wondering at the random nature of his fucked-up luck. The car died three times last night, but rose again today.

But soft, what light. Heading down the long hall to section, he steeled himself to see her. During the hour, he knew, eyes would be upon them and it would be difficult to be distant-seeming; balancing his ardor against Facebook-fed prying minds. He decided to go psychic. Revving up his undermind, he came into the full room blazing on all hailing frequencies, but, to his more-than-chagrin, her usual seat was empty. His disappointment obvious to those tuned to this TA-student hookup-of-the-month.

And she never showed up. He went through the prepared review sometimes stumbling and burbling but better during an aside that touched his own research arena, an effort to convince the world, the scientific establishment at least, that there was no such thing as junk genomic information. (Junk meant genitalia, in those days, too.) When DNA finally came unraveled, he promised the class, the link between animal and human would yield up big leaps in engineering technology-assisted evolution. One of the students suggested that he had seen the *Planet of the Apes* remake once too often. He grinned and said, Dude. Take your stinking paws off me. Now they were his and the kids even clapped for him at the end. He was sad that Lila May was not there to witness such triumph. He was sure she would be in love with him.

He walked out. Now he had time to worry. But then, a cosmic flash! A sudden vision of a note from her in his box. He knew it was there. Somehow.

"Wow," he said out loud walking to his office. "That's what I want."

Louis was passing (by coincidence) down the same hall and came up just as he blurted.

"Talking to yourself?" Louis asked.

And Shaney, laughing, said, "I just realized I'm in love. What do you think of that?"

"Depends."

"Exactly," Shaney answered. "It all always depends. In this case, it depends on blind faith, which is something for an atheist to say. See ya," he laughed running down the hall while Louis passed through doors into the pure white light of a sunny day.

Shaney turned sharp right at the department office door and blasted past the secretary who tried to get his attention. Since his ESP was still on, he caught the vague gesture and registered its importance, though his mission overrode her signal. He was getting a strong beacon of pulsing impulse from the mailroom too. Sure enough, there was a letter from her in his junk-mail-crammed cubby. He growled in satisfaction as he ripped open the scented envelope. "And the winner is…" he thought.

He read the red-ink-penned card sweetly redolent of her slightly evergreen perfume. "Dear John," it read. "Sorry not to make class but an embarrassing thing occurred. Really, it's probably your fault. Let's just say I had been worried about a visitor who was late. After our world voyage yesterday, said visit occurred with vengeance, and I am incapacitated. I get blinding headaches and stuff. TMI? Gross? Who cares? This is my time, and this is what I am like. On a more surprising note, I'm forced to admit I miss you. It's very unwise of me to declare that I think I'm in something here, let's just say, Euphemism, Lila May."

Shaney let out a whoop, though, to be fair, the exclamation came from an involuntary place. She wanted him. Meanwhile, Shaney spied a different note in the same accumulation of dead letters, junk, and lost opportunities, an urgent request to join the dean of the division in his offices ASAP; no appointment necessary. As if on cue, the department secretary appeared in her stunning decollataged blouse.

"Dean wants to see you now please," said Sarah Glastonbury.

"So I see," said Shaney, waggling the memo from his box. "Any idea why?"

"Don't know, sugar, but there are police there, too. What'd you do this time?"

"This time?" he said. This being the first time they ever spoke.

"O as if you didn't know the chit chat concerning you."

"Please enlighten me," he said, hiding his panic, regarding the secretary, who was accustomed to science nerds groveling.

"I want some of them mushrooms you grow," she whispered. "The ones that make the pretty lights spin?"

Now life seemed tight and airless, Shaney had too many uncommitted crimes to count at this point. "I wish I knew what you were talking about," he croaked unconvincing.

"Too bad you need to be like this," she whispered. "A person in my position has many opportunities to lend assistance to struggling grad students: poor, bedraggled, money-grubbing, over-caffeinated, sleep-deprived, angsty, hair suit-wearing, ashenbrowed, kiss-ass grad students. I see and hear things all day long, you know."

He looked at her with new eyes. "I don't grow mushrooms," he said, noting the narrowing of her suddenly cynical eyes. "But I made something with my little chemistry set that makes mushrooms blush."

"Do tell," she said. "Don't worry about the cops. You were here in the lab whenever it was they were looking. Your name is clear."

Shaney felt this beautiful relationship might bloom and jotted down her address. "One square inch of paper will take four people to the moon," he said. "It's in the mail."

"Now skedaddle off to see the dean. Not all news is bad. Oh, and say hidey-hi to Miss Lila May for me." She winked and sent him back to invasion of privacy worries.

# 7.

Shaney saw the hall full of people-are-strange faces *en passant*, worried minds that will never even impinge his. He wondered if this was the way of the world—a universe made up of teases, leading edges, eternal unknowns. They couldn't sense his story either, now that he seemed to be heading towards doom or some other brand of bum closure. He kept his face blank. When he was a kid, riding in his parents' car on the night freeways listening to their chiaroscuro bickering, John worried about the bright headlights gliding by them in opposite direction. He wondered what dramas other cars contained. He would never know, he could never understand; his first taste of utter futility.

Around a hall corner a policeman stood outside the dean's door, talking, making farewell body language movements. Shaney slowed his measured pad through the corridor and decided to cruise past the cop who would not know him, just like Shaney never knew what lived behind passing headlights. He tried to stride past the dean's warren.

"Mr. Shaney," intoned a voice from inside, "is that you?"

Damn. *Someone* knew him. Peering into the surprisingly small office, with its bookcases groaning with dull titles and a Bach harpsichord tinkling from a Bose, he decided to let fate happen.

"Hey." He used the vernacular, trying to deflate any stiffened decorum inside.

"Thought I recognized you. We need you," said the professor.

"That's why I swung by. Didn't want to interrupt your whatever," he mumbled. After an aggressive blocky hesitation, the officer budged, allowing Shaney entrance into what he believed could possibly become *auto da fe*, charges of murder, wanton cruelty, not to mention drug dealing. Surely his college days were ended.

"Thank you, thank you so much for coming, and at such a respectful prompt hour," said the twaddly professor, the dean, whose hair was heaped grey and curly around a flesh dome. Shaney was surprised at the pleasant tone, decided it was irony. "Yes, yes, my boy, as it turns out, for a number of reasons. Are you settled in?" asked Dean Beveritch, fumbling with some papers after shaking hands. Another shape in the corner emerged, a severely un-tailored suit smelling police-y or at least from the world of the superstraight.

"Sure he's great. Found a nice big house to share downtown," said the suit. "Site of the Gleesop disappearance. Found blood there," muttered Brylcreem and Old Spice.

"How would you know where I live?" said Shaney offended by the pry.

The man laughed, as if to say you ain't seen nothin' yet.

"Investigators thought it was menstrual blood, I heard," Shaney added in a blurt, moving over in his chair as if to let the ghost of his dead or missing roommate share this hotseat. He licked his lips.

"Don't be nervous," said Beveritch. "We need your help in a rather delicate, mainly theoretical matter."

"Fuck theory," said the cop.

"Now, Mark, don't," said the dean and turned back to Shaney. "May I present Lieutenant Mark Gospel," he said, "an old friend who sometimes comes here against his own better judgment—to pick our brains." The last phrase ghoulish and slow.

"Fuckin' Ivory Tower."

"So there you have two clichés, don't you know: the potty-mouthed constable expressing his knee-jerk disdain for academia. While, I might add, groveling before us for free information."

"Last time I checked this was a state school," said Gospel, grinning toothy. "Which means we work for the same boss."

"The People, yes," said Beveritch. "You see, Mr. Shaney, the detective and I were Berkeley students back in what they now call The Day. Though most of our radical activity took place under cover of the night, if memory serves."

"If you can remember the sixties you weren't there," snickered the policeman. "Now show him the fucking thing, will ya?"

The dean thrust forth a newspaper, the one in which his canine misadventure was a banner headline. Here it comes, Shaney thought, ready for surrender for some reason. Holding up the newspaper, he suddenly remembered the crying lady, the phantom gliding under full moon across wavering streets. What was that?

"I'd like to get my hands on *that* cocksucking motherfucker," said the police officer.

"Jesus, Mark," said the dean. "Why must you enjoy your freedom of speech so thoroughly?"

"The dog was a horrible mistake," Shaney mumbled. "But self defense."

They looked at him curious, unsure what the joke was.

"Of course, we mean the wolfman, don't you know," said the dean, careful and unsure. "Or, I suppose, the werepersons." Surprisingly, he laughed.

"Yuck it up, Beveritch. Those kids will end up enrolling here and someday fuck up some cute coed and then it'll be you comin' to me."

What they wanted Shaney to read was below the fold, dateline, Austin, a town renowned for its weirdness, the paper reported, where certain high school teens had decided to become werewolves. What followed was coy: a woman staff writer culling from a local television news piece set the unlikely events within the context of kooky trends, cliques, and cohorts: soshes, jocks, goths, hippies and lycanthropes. They wore their hair all "emo" as one disgusted classmate put it and had apparently watched and read far too much from the *Twilight* series, team Jonathan, for sure. They hung tails from their pants and ran through the malls howling on full moon night on binges of shoplifting and elder frightening. Shaney was perplexed, but gradually began to lose the gripping fear that accompanied him into what he assumed was a crucifixion starring him. Now, amazingly, he was being asked to elucidate something evil about someone other. He laughed and said, "Really? You called me in to look at this? Maybe you've confused me with my roommate Sheela, she's taking cultural anthropology. Howls come from her bedroom sometimes, too."

"Read on, Professor Hilarious," said the cop.

Though widely dismissed, there have been a few disquieting incidents, added the reporter, her glib voice suddenly shifting into journalism's shorthand and subjectless sentences. Unnamed reports abounded, though one hysterical mother on the record witnessed her own daughter actually metamorphosing—her word—before her very naked eyes. "Her bones snapped loudly and her back legs extended out, while hair grew on her face amongst her painful screams," said the mother, one Rosa Parkinson. The child, name was withheld a minor, died shortly afterwards, shot in a field by a rancher who mistook her for a marauding animal.

"Aw come on," Shaney said.

"I'm afraid there's more," said the dean. "Go to A12."

The final report after the jump came from a teen who had beheaded a dog. Though authorities were outraged, the teen insisted that the dog was dead already. "I wouldn't kill any animal," Lupe Rodriguez told police. "I wouldn't, like I said. I'd be more likely to hurt a human than a dog any day. And then not really possible. I'm pretty friendly." Apparently she'd butchered the dog, boiled its head, and put the sanitized skull on a pole nearby to ward off other demons.

"You think this is connected to the dog murderer?" Shaney ventured.

"Maybe yes and no," said the cop. "Though that actually never occurred to me."

"I still don't understand what it has to do with me," said John.

"Those drugs you designed," said Dean Beveritch. "There are a lot of rumors going around. People are saying weird things."

Shaney turned cold again; jokes ended.

"We're not here to judge you, son," said Beveritch. "We got fascinating reports from grads who came over from your college where you are a legend, don't you know."

Shaney said nothing.

"You're among friends," the dean reminded him. "The story about the drugs got you past the admittance administrators. We wanted you here *for* the drug. Kind of." He looked at his police pal, who was curiously neutral.

"You admitted me based on doper rumors. What about what I admit? As in nothing. I made the formula and it worked. But if you think some compound I invented turns teenagers into animals?" He hesitated. "I thought only rock and roll did that."

"Kaboom," said Officer Gospel, doing a big rimshot. "The problem is that this this Rosa Parkinson might tell the story different."

"I don't know any Rosa Par…" Then he remembered: Sub Rosa Rosa. He looked around. "Maybe I need a lawyer at this point," said Shaney.

"Don't be ridiculous," said the officer.

"Quite so, Mr. Shaney," said the dean. "If such a thing were necessary, I wouldn't have allowed this conversation to take place without university representation. This falls under the mighty rubric of academic freedom. John, my lad, all we are doing here is looking for the sense of things. Rosa Parkinson was doing a fellowship here last year and she was the one who told tales of you. In science circles such tales don't stay hidden. She's here, my friend. Came from your college to study, dates a professor who told her we were considering you and then she told us all about your reputation. Inadvertently, it won you your post. I saw the hallucinating gal in the paper here, called my pal the foulmouthed cop. She saw children turn into wolves."

"Not on my drugs," said Shaney, but he suspected the whole coincidence was trapping him in something. What?

The cop popped in, "Yeah. There was apparently a bunch of Austin kids one day watching the Teenage Mutant Ninja Turtles and the next day turning into violent monsters with one grown-up who swears they transformed in her presence. I told the dean about this and he called it my motherfucking theory."

"My compound made people hallucinate, nobody ever growled on it," said Shaney.

"There is this thing called bath salts, completely mysterious. Right?" said the dean.

"You know how to make it, right?" asked the cop, hopeful.

The term was meaningless to him—but it reminded him of his murdered mother for some reason. "Honestly, I can't keep up with the kids and their cute-sounding drugs. I just found out that Mollie contains no molybendium."

"I think we're up against a stoned wall," said the cop not quite quipping.

"This is very unfair" said Shaney. "I'm ready to own up to my past, though some of it is founded on rumors." Shit, he just remembered sleeping with Sub Rosa, and it was rather exquisite sex at that. "And if it jeopardizes my status here, I'll still maintain I had a friendly relationship with Rosa Parkinson. But I'm really not aware of anything like lycanthropic side effects or a continuing relationship with the drugtaking subculture."

"Easy," said the dean. "This isn't a test and you're not being chastised or even warned. You are being consulted."

"And you're not accusing me of creating dog murderers? Or murdering the famous dog itself?"

"Like I said, I'll fucking strangle that motherfucker *my*self," said the cop.

"Let me finish. Or any other weird local murders?" He was a little stretched weird at this point.

"Which weird murders?" they asked him in unison.

Shaney looked at them. "Don't you watch the news? The rock concert. This guy Uncle John? Gruesome murders, maybe werewolves."

"O," said the cop. "Was the Uncle John thing gruesome?"

"A mountain man cult and a shocking rock star death, right?" said Dean Beveritch, mock yawning. "Stunning. What will they think of next?"

"Anywho," said the policeman. "What you are saying is that this drug you invented never turned anybody into a bestial monster drawn from legends manufactured in Hollywood before the Second World War, and, further, this Rosa woman was okay last time you saw her."

"Yes. And yes."

"All right, then, my work here is done," said the cop. "But just remember, we'll have our eye on you anytime a teenager does anything weird." He waggled his finger. Then pausing for effect, he chuckled. "Dean Beveritch, please inform your friend here I'm just fuckin' with him."

"Remember, my friend, irony is the enemy of sense," said the dean.

"And, that the true revolutionary should move through the proletariat like a fish through water. That means talking the talk and swimming the swim."

"Whatever," said the dean, feigning youthful vacuousness, "See you at the Elk's Hall Friday. Barbecue."

The cop nodded, collected his uniformed amanuensis, and swam downstream against the current of the college hall amongst nervous-looking men and women of science study.

"I'm not sure what help I was," said Shaney. "But I guess I'll be off too."

"Not so fast," said Beveritch. "And please close the door."

Another reversal, and Shaney foresaw the flux of fate eternally turning back ouroborouslike. How swiftly relief gets drowned in apprehension. Life on Earth. Are other dimensions the same?

"You were very busy this last weekend, Mr. Shaney. Very busy indeed,"

And there's that other shoe, he thought.

"Not so much, sir."

"What happened to your hand, son?"

Shaney held it up for public inspection, wrapped like a mummy with some black color, presumably his own blood, staining the center of the widest swath of gauze. Surprisingly, he had forgotten about it. Whatever pain and throbbing one might have expected had vanished. He remembered the cut, pulled together with butterfly bandages; he didn't want to admit but he knew a scar was left behind. Again the possibility of disease occurred, rabies or some unexpected strain of infection borne on the dead dog's teeth and saliva. Swarming all over him: He turned such thoughts off.

"Picked up a broken beaker. It cut me deep, but the First Aid kit was handy."

"You know we have a university health center. Long as you are here," he said, managing to make the phrase seem ominous, "you're covered for any and all accidents and maladies."

Tremendous silence filled the room. "Very busy indeed," repeated the dean.

"Not sure what you mean," he said, trying hard to separate himself from himself, like when his father used to yell and beat him. Far away, he thought. I will look down on this painful happening and laugh. "For instance?"

"Well, for instance, you managed to make a goddam big impression on the Wulfhardt family. For instance. Spoke to Wulfie himself this morning. Early."

"Oh that."

"Want to explain? We have a professional fund raiser who is shitting purple marbles right now trying to figure out how you did it."

"It wasn't anything," said Shaney. "Funny, really. I ran into his daughter at the rock club, you know the one where the murder took place. She's in the section I teach." Might as well get the bad part out in the air, he thought.

"Go on," said the dean.

"I didn't know who her family was. I just moved here. Anyways," he said, weaving swiftly in the dark through verbal obstacles, "we were both there when the bad thing happened. She was freaked out and we went and had tea. I swear to God, tea."

"I know all of these things," said the dean after a short pregnant pause. "But you did go to a bar with her next, where her parents' people picked her up promptly."

"She sells seashells by the seashore," Shaney said, trying cute.

"It's what happened next that interests me," said Beveritch.

"She left her smart phone at the table and it started talking to me," said Shaney, wildly lost in invention. "The ringtone. It howled and then it laughed. I answered, and it was her father. He invited me up. I went home and brought the phone next morning. She asked me about the homework; I stayed and chatted. They liked me, I guess. I stayed for Sunday dinner. Nice little place."

The dean began laughing uncontrollably, which worried Shaney more than anything previous, more than news reports of the Uncle John slaughter, more than a ghost, the hound of hell, or even the police. The dean's face turned red and he made a kind of choking noise and saliva seemed to be splashing around in his gurgling mouth.

"Sir, are you all right?" Shaney said, half-standing. "Sir?"

Beveritch waved and tried to catch his breath. "Nice," he said. "Little," he continued. "Place," he concluded and ended trailing clouds of chuckle. "Do you have any idea how long most of the university has been waiting to enter that fortress of excess?"

"I found it rather tasteful," he said.

The dean eyed him respectfully it seemed, then resolute. "Well, anyway, I guess your time here is over," said the professor.

"What do you mean, over?" he asked. So it was to be a public execution. He tried thinking of other programs that had accepted him.

Beveritch swiveled his ergonomic office chair towards the dogwood trees seen through the glass. "Coyness is an unanticipated California trait. But I suspect your new life will be full of false modesty, or whatever."

Shaney in measured slow tones, said, "If you were speaking in a foreign tongue right now, I might have a better chance of understanding you."

Beveritch looked relieved. "You honestly don't know that Mr. Wulfhardt has had you pulled out of classes and reassigned to his lab for some biochemical research project?"

"Pulled out of classes?" said Shaney. "You mean I don't get to teach the section anymore? Are you expelling me?"

"No, but you're not going back. I pretty much accepted on your behalf."

"I had no idea who she was, God. There was no hanky-panky. Besides, she could be transferred to another section easily. Accepted?"

"You think this is some sort of sexual harassment issue?" said the dean after considering the dead air around them for a few. "No, you're leaving the whole program and reporting to Wulfhardt Technologies. You are no longer doing pure research here where the equipment comes in hand-me-down parcels from big science labs. You're in the show now. It's what we were training you for in the first place. I like to think I am friends with the Wulfhardts too."

"I'm in what show?"

"Hanky panky?" laughed the dean. "He has some weird animal research project that he has convinced himself needs new blood. Yours. He calls it the Werewolf Study, which is enough of a weird coincidence to pique my wondering when the police just happened to come in with their teenager problem. That's what really made me think of you. Six levels of separation, or whatever they are called."

"I can't teach anymore?"

"Oh for Christ's sake, man. You're just academic fodder in that TA bullshit role. Nobody cares about the goddamned teaching assistant, it's just a way for us to kind of recoup our losses on you. Now, of course, you've become a major asset."

"I have?"

"We let you go work for him because he took a shine to you, and he will help fund us. He even invited me up to the 'nice little place' next week. I hear his wife is very nice too. I believe the figure was somewhere in the neighborhood of one point one million dollars, or as Wulfie the clown put it, eleventy million. He's endowed a chair and this year you are sitting pretty behind it, holding it for the prof we choose to warm it. You are the price we pay for accepting enough money to do more important shit. And working for Wulfie as a grad student will look great on your CV. And if you ever decide to come back to lowly Academia, I guarantee there will be a place gratefully saved for you here. Though why you would pass up a job like he's offering I will never guess. And I think you can be of other uses too."

Shaney wondered. At his tone, as much as at this gift he was about to receive. Not long ago he was celebrating the outside chance of an inside track on after-college employment. Then he was in a pretty shit storm. Now he had a fucking amazing job. Yet Beveritch was using this to some end, a stoat in lanolined garb. "What services can I render for you?"

The dean laughed. "Spook stuff: It would be an opportunity to spy on this man whose enigmatic presence and sporadic funding combine to make the department viable though unstable. People have been running around for years now trying to second guess Wulfhardt's eccentric wishes, or interpret his odd sudden requirements. He once offered a small fortune if the school would concentrate on unearthing neurological findings the Third Reich supposedly made with respect to the kabbal, or mummies, or some such hoohaw. Everybody supposed that Wulfie had been watching Indiana Jones while smoking prairie herb, wacky tobaccy, gannyweed. On another occasion, the family decided to require their university money be employed investigating the link between evolution and progress; Wulfhardt wondered aloud in a meeting why chimps didn't keep spinning off different hominids; perhaps this lurch to humanity was fake given the fact that never happened again. For a science-minded man, he's dumber and more capricious than a jaybird in seed heaven."

"Far out," said Shaney unsure, trying out weird decorum adjustments. "So what's next? I really do enjoy teaching; I'm not kidding, I can serve out two weeks till midterms or whatever. I'm a little lost here."

"That's generous, but not needed. The department will survive, though Professor Borromeo was just in here whining. That tone he takes?"

Shaney giggled. "The kids call him Scooby. You know that, right?"

The dean nodded. "First off, you need to wander over the hill to Wulfhardt Labs. Sooner the better: I'll give you the personnel person's number. Tomorrow okay?" It was in the nature of a demand.

Shaney thought about his own slacker calendar. He had been skating for some time now without plans beyond teaching. He did have a girlfriend, which might necessitate re-scheduling. His roomies planned a vegetarian—or was it vegan?—barbecue. Going up to Wulfie's would get him out of the party prep.

"I'm there," he said.

Professor Lehigh (Lee) Beveritch seemed pleased. He leaned across the desk and said, "Just work hard. Probably don't do drugs up there."

"Okeydoke," said Shaney, whose conscience was preoccupied more with questions regarding the girlfriend. She was the boss's daughter too.

He suddenly realized: It could be all his. He could marry the job and pass the empire onto his own as yet unborn whelp. Besides, what possible information could these ghostly old bureaucrats want? Meanwhile there was some werewolf problem to solve, which sounded like a lovely potential scam. Or maybe it was like that Sigmund Freud Wolf Man, just a funny nickname for a dream of a raw disease.

They parted with a handshake and Shaney padded down the waxed linoleum halls with wings on his rock and roll shoes. He saw himself reflected down as he walked up, corresponding alternate realities that ended on a rubber mat by the door in the hall. He walked back by the mailroom before he remembered his new sweetheart, her note. Should he call, text, or email her? This felt like news he ought to share. (She likely knew but, gee!) Their intensely-formed new intimacy had skipped the usual trial and error aspects of a relationship built on dating as old people put it, hooking up, which sounded so mechanical, but was fraught with the same problems daters had.

He knew not her whims and distastes. He was feeling a little Humphrey Bogart at the moment, so he stopped just outside the brick building and sat down on the brick planter surrounding the chrysanthemums and carnations nodding there and turned his smart phone on.

She didn't answer. Her phone message was Bob Dylan, something, something, Easter, gravity, some hungry women there'll make a mess out of you. And then a long beep.

He choked, suddenly, realizing he was on record, forever. He babbled, hoped she was better, hinted there was news and concluded dorkily. His mind was that transient radio signal haunting the farmlands of Texas. Wanting to make an impression, he couldn't take this bad one back. Then he went back to his business, though wanting to share his good fortune with the world. He thought about calling his parents—well, his father—

and laughed out loud. As if the prison system allowed direct phone calls from your kid. As if he would call the murdering bastard.

# 8.

Leaving campus, Shaney couldn't quite remember getting to school that morning. Hazed and confused. It troubled him yet he walked homeward as if possessed. Then he recalled it all and all of a sudden. The bike left in his rescued car parked in the school lot that died three times, and rose again. Why? Sacred number numerology for a joke crap. Like Odysseus within sight of home he was turned back, except he blew himself back to school to retrieve his car. He got there. He almost died when a police cruiser cruised by. He unlocked the formerly dead heap.

Shaney drove toward home but smelled food. Needed another meal, he felt keen hunger driving by a Tex Mex eatery just outside the campus lot after (impossibly) smelling corn tortillas from within. Parked, brakes screeching.

He entered, sat at the counter, and ordered a big plate of *migas*, beans, rice and consumed bowl after bowl of ranchero sauce with greasy, over-salted chips. He was still hungry when he finished the meal, though. He craved meat. Deeply. They had goat, wow, he ordered it in red sauce, and the waitress looked at him in mild shock. He wanted it now but went into the dingy, bitter-smelling back bathroom to pee. While cautiously washing his hands the bandage flapped partly off, exposing that which he had been afraid to see. To his surprise and shock, the jagged wound was mostly closed, mostly: There was a red line where you might expect swelling over crusted blood. This worried him more than the horror he expected. Somehow he managed to make the tape stick again, hiding the weird miracle from his own doubting eyes.

This worried him. First, and most obvious, it seemed outside of nature. Beyond, perhaps. Last night he thought it was sure to be a scar. Continued at this healing pace, it would be a faint memory tomorrow.

The miraculous strange aspect of this "healing" reminded him of the ghost. He did not believe in such stuff—nothing ever stayed good in this world, things left alone rarely improved. And death swept in to keep the score ever so. Even if the wound was better, inside, rabies, venom, microbes, virii, or small grit from the wolfdog's choppers was now likely sealed inside him and running around like River Ocean circled the ancient world. Microscopic sea serpents, etcetera. His mind felt odd but he left the room, and headed back to his new plate of goat. Chupa me cabras, he thought.

"Douchebag," said the tall dude sitting at the counter as he passed by still regarding his newly-sealed wound.

Shaney stopped. The foul-mouth miscreant was solo and bent over an enchilada with twin strings of yellow cheese connecting the food from his mouth back to the plate it came from. The guy chewed slowly, blinked, and swiveled in his seat to regard Shaney.

Shaney decided to ignore, return to his linoleum-topped, chrome-rimmed table, and the guy at the counter said, "Dick."

Shaney returned to the table and was about to say "pardon me" when the guy waved his hand in his face. "Pleash exshcuse me," he said through a jawfull of tortilla, roasted red pepper gravy, ground beef, in a matrix of Mexican cheddar, call it Velveeta. "I'm so sorry but it's not what you think," he said, swallowing. "Fuck you, fuck you stupid fuckface shit," he added.

"Oh good," said Shaney, "that means that I'm not a douchebag penis?"

"I said 'dick.'"

"What the fuck?" said Shaney squaring for combat and feeling a rumble boil up in his blood a lot harder than expected.

"It's absolutely essential to be accurate regarding my imprecations, douchedick. That is, if I ever hope to trace the structure of my disease some day." He was writing in a notebook. "And I assure you I do, fuckwad," said the man holding out a hand for shaking. Shaney had no idea what now.

"I'll shake your hand outside, asshole," said Shaney not thinking now. "And the rest of you as well."

"I'm sorry," the man said, lowering his hand. "It was my disease speaking, not me, dicklick stupid-ass pussylips." Cringing from an expected blow, he pulled out a business card and held it out for Shaney's perusal. On it, printed in no-nonsense Times Roman 12-point type font, read the legend:

John Ochocinco, Ph. D.
Professor of Linguistics and Communication
University of Texas in Austin
Tourette Syndrome Sufferer

I apologize for any misunderstanding due to my disease.

Shaney was baffled by the formality and the elegance of the solution. Was it real?

"For a long time I wrestled with the shitass idea, the precision of the noun 'sufferer,'" he said nonchalantly filling his mouth with enchilada again, "partly because it seemed too whiny and pat, but also because I don't suffer. Except discomfort and fearful anticipation, fartbreath. It's fucking inconvenient, I admit. Unless, of course, some fuckwad peckerneck beats me up over some unintended shitass utterance. Please, I beg your fucking forgiveness, twat."

Shaney suspected Ochocinco of pulling his leg, but found himself drawn in. "Disease implying victimhood?" he said. "Destroying the line between intention and act. And making the consequences always wrong. Is that not enough to qualify as suffering?"

"What you said. Shit, probably. Suffer the little buggered children unto me? Ah, first let me say I'm pleased as fucking punch you are not an angry asshole, and don't plan to fuck me up and better yet, I can see I am dealing with a first rate shitbird mind, not so common even in this cum-drunk slack-jawed community of faggot scholars," he said. "I actually stole that last bit from a cartoonist."

"You really don't *seem* to be suffering," said Shaney, a bit lost in the layers of reality, wondering if he wasn't just being more than usually patient with yet another Austin weirdo—the streets famously teemed with them—because of his still-basking-in-it good news. "You're fucking articulate, at least."

"There's a line between humorous and sadistic, asshole."

"I just snorted the line, fuck face," said Shaney, now emboldened by his own dizzy disorientation across all moral universes.

"Disease poses many interesting theoretical problems," said Ochocinco, apparently cool. "Meaning, of course, how to theorize about it, not a question of whether or not the problems are real. There is disease as metaphor and language as disease, for instance to mention a couple of bullshit jerk-off popular approaches. But etymology is not vague, fucking-A no, it's Anglo French; disease cut in half to 'dis' and 'ease.' There it only equals that which makes one uncomfortable and my motherfucking condition is clearly that. Discomfortable for everyfuckingone."

Fucking E, thought Shaney, this was a fun sideshow now. This man had a theoretical disease, typical of these humanities pseudoscientists, and not unlike Tourette, cutting everything down to a map of itself.

"But the clinical definition," Ochocinco continued, "—a progressive disorder that can be diagnosed, predicted and even sometimes cured. Then the nature of disease, if we allow it as defined, is determinism.

Antithetical to chaos, but, of course, asshole fuck me, you know that. I often wondered, though, how alcoholism, which seems more like a moral defect than a progressive and predictable sickness can possibly be lumped with, say, bird flu, which is as forward-moving as a wind-up toy."

"My father's an alcoholic," said Shaney. "Meth addict to boot." And a shitass, fuckbird convict too, he thought.

"Well boo fuckin' hoo," said the cunning linguistics professor.

Shaney stirred the bowl of salsa with a despondent chip. If he was waiting for an apology, it never came. The stirred liquid provided a Zeus pool for mortals-watching. Shaney liked not what he saw, the game had soured.

"Anyways," said Ochocinco, also surnamed John, "Tourette's syndrome is not exactly a disease anyways—it's a tic disorder. I'm actually working to promote its status though."

"Wait a minute, your motherfucking license to potty mouth is caused by ticks?" asked Shaney.

A Mexican waitress down the counter looked them over.

"O, you funny peckerneck. By the way, some Cornell fuckwits who study Alzheimer's—also a disease, by the way—for its linguistic shape, its morphemic modes, discovered that dementia-addled greybeards lose straight vocabulary but not the skill set needed to curse. Particularly the so-called F-bombs, which, you may have noticed pepper my discourse liberally."

"The fuck you say," said Shaney, now growing tired of working blue. The waitress looked perturbed.

"That's the spirit," said Ochocinco. "Forget your father and the offense I gave."

"Listen friend," Shaney began, but ceased because Ochocinco raised his hand in a gesture that might have been warning or request for forbearance.

"They think, they're pretty sure, after doing brain scan shit that the words we swear with come from a different part of the brain than the words we use normally to negotiate our lives. They postulate that F-bombs come from the animal brain. It's us barking."

"Howling at the moon," said Shaney remembering Uncle John's campfire and the balls-tightening tingle he got hearing the lone wolf.

"No, barking. Cunt piss fuck shit."

"Sorry," said Shaney. "Sometimes I blurt things out that reflect an unknown, you might say, pathological cause and effect chain."

"Oooh, touché, Brother Motherfucker," said the linguistics professor. Shaney had moved his empty plate over and ordered puffy tacos after polishing the migas and goat. He was still quite hungry and this seemed a harmless indulgence. Irresistible.

Shaney nervously chatted with the diseased man, who commented in subdued imprecations. Ochocinco paid attention without injecting any thoughts beyond mild neutral vulgarities, restraint rare for an academic. Ochocinco pushed back his bushy black hair, screwed closed his shocking blue eyes, and actually listened.

After about eight minutes, though, he had enough. When Shaney seemed about to recite personal history beyond major and birthplace, Ochocinco could no longer contain his impatience, a bouncing knee betrayed him. At that point, however, Shaney decided to plunge, inviting the linguistics professor to the planned vegan barbecue shivaree: grilled vegetation and some band called That Buddhist Moment playing the backyard patio under chili-pepper strung lights. "Ple-ease come," said Shaney, not quite understanding his own fervor.

Ochocinco wrote down the numbers and the address in his smart phone, but kept the phone active partly as a shield against more Shaney talk. He asked if there was anything he could bring and wondered out loud if any of the housemates had taken his classes while he absentmindedly flipped from messages to Facebook and then to his local newsfeed. Shaney was about to say that he doubted any of his roommates had taken linguistics classes but then honestly couldn't remember what they did take. He changed the subject. "I want to go to the famous record store, but truth be told I don't know where it is," Shaney said, apropos of nothing.

"Waterloo," said Ochocinco, staring intently at the little screen. Absorbed. "Pisshouse. Fuck. Shit. Tittyfuck. Pussylips."

"Don't like it there?"

"Kidding me? It's the best record store in the world next to the Amoeba in Hollywood," said the pottymouth prof. "Asshole," he added. "Left on this street out here and about eight blocks toward downtown. Fuckwad."

"Thanks. See you at the barbecue, John." He stood in the doorway to the Mexican restaurant and the sun turned him into an outline.

"Yeah. Well, you're a douchebag," said Ochocinco rubbing his eyes, standing up, shaking his head.

Shaney laughed. Ochocinco did not. "No, he said. "That's not the disease talking. You are a motherfucking guttersnipe. That's you, I would swear." He pointed at his phone, from which Shaney heard a tinny replication of his own voice.

He looked at the phone and it was time to fear again. There was the dog attack of last night unfolding from across the street somehow, filmed by someone.

"You. That's you. You killed that dog. I thought maybe it seemed unlikely but that's your silhouette, I'm sure."

"Which dog?" said Shaney gone ice.

"Oh, come on. Don't look at me like that, innocent eyes. You're the one. So fucked up, you ought to be ashamed," he said.

There was silence. "Says Senor Pottymouth."

"You think I'm bad?" he was whispering now. "My bad language? But you."

Shaney wasn't sure how to respond beyond simple denial. And how should he keep his own mind calm, to think his way out of this wolf of surprise pouncing, yet another happy moment shattered. That's what we always mean when we talk about reality; some fucked up intrusion impinging the bubble where we want to live. The rest is a dream.

"Oh," said Ochocinco. "I can see what you're thinking, I can. I don't want mutual understanding. I want you afraid."

"Cat and mouse," said Shaney.

"You think this is funny?"

"Do I amuse you? Am I a clown?" asked Shaney now unable to stop. He was a quipster when nervous. Laughed nervously when in trouble.

"What you did to that dog is an abomination. What I ought to do is call some cops."

"It's all in your mind," said Shaney, looking bug-eyed and crazy now. Then he turned earnest. "What *are* you going to do? I mean, how *do* you know it was me? It was self-defense, anyways. My word against the dog's." He shrugged. "Barking up the wrong tree. By the way, you haven't cussed in three minutes."

"You're a fuckin' loony," he said.

"Kettle calling the pot," said Shaney.

"Go ahead, dicklick, dig yourself deeper. It's on my fucking phone. Yeah. I know it was you, thought so from the first second I met you."

"I would back down right now, buddy. You have no idea what you're inviting." Shaney said, deep voiced. He had no idea where it came from, that growled threat.

"You gonna beat my fuckin' head in, like the puppy? No. I'm gonna bide my time on you. Give you time to think, monster. I'll come to your party and then decide."

"Oh good," said Shaney oddly relieved. "At least I'll know somebody there. Remember, Wednesday night. Say dinner time? It's a barbecue. Bring your own meat, or no meat. Whatever." He laughed a horrible barking nervous yelp. He threw $40 on the counter and stood up.

Ochocinco regarded him now with unsettled eyes. Shaney backed out the dusty screen door onto the tawdry street. He swaggered—the murderer of monster beasts—and snarled. He saw the windows were greasy and there were dead flies on the sill. His hunger had brought him in past these off-putting things, he missed the omens and clues, but he vowed in the future hunger would only make him more careful—the observant chew, he thought. I'm not even chewish. What has gotten into me, he worried. He felt a gigantic welling in his bowels, which he realized was digestive chemistry turning in a catalyst, a crucible of matter to chemical compounds. These thoughts from a man about to become a paid pure researcher, working for the father of the woman he loved. These were the essentials, the rest was gas.

# 9.

Sunlight rainbowed through suburban sprinkler water and whizzed over mud and weed lawns alike. Above that, dust took flight in breezes gathered into intricate formations only to crashdive bookshelve planks while, at the same moment, splashbits of moisture levitated up and assembled into clouds. Ionic particles flowed too in open currents and collided higher and further. Above that, air left behind, space, mineral, and gas planets most with clustered moons rattled through the emptiness in constant rotation to even out the effect of needling sunlight of an orbiting system stretching six billion miles from Mercury to defrocked Pluto. They will fall too. And O the moons all had light on them.

Our moon was full for one more night.

She was twitchy alone in his bedroom, thinking about her lover but bloated and crampy, rebellious and indecisive at the same time. Louis needed to stay away from it all, yet was drawn by siren calls from all the bodies assembling downtown, he stalked Sixth Street heading towards his storage shed, pretty sure he might not make in time. Then obeyed an urge to go home. Playing fast and loose with safety itself. Meanwhile Wulfhardt in a tower cursed his willful daughter at large on a night to come like this one would be.

Meanwhile, Shaney, evening fluttering towards him, bustled. Proud of his cocky stance against the blackmailing vulgarian, fueled by calories and spices and… there it was the record store, his Waterloo. Nothing calmed him like flipping through discs listening to random sounds the t-shirted, bored employees decided to enrapture wouldbe buyers with.

It was a well-ordered place, light and filled with air. Big windows with Texas sky outside. Flipping through the A section seeking an obscure Aztec Camera EP set him thinking about all the heavy-affect 1980s English bands like Echo and the Bunnymen—better now with every passing year, alarmingly sophisticated pop—lush visionary minor key tunes. "Is it a horrific dream?" they asked. Shaney did not know.

Shaney did know that he still craved food. But he also felt discomfort in the lower tract too. Was he really hungry and poopy at the same time? A deadly spiral? He looked for the public bathroom worried this gas distress might turn into sudden, uncontrolled expulsion. And what kept such accidents from happening all the time, Shaney wondered, why aren't the millions on Earth exploding feces all the time? Statistically speaking. Why doesn't anybody at least talk about these things?

He found the bathroom, used it. Horrifying odor left behind. Emerging, wanting no one to ever go in there, Shaney waltzed down the aisle past Christopher Cross and Dishwalla, heroes in his old college town of Santa Barbara, a nexus of vacuous musicians, beginning with Loggins and Messina, the first perpetrators of soft rock's shameful epoch. He picked up something by Adam Ant—why didn't he do an album called *Adamant*—hoping that cute Indie Rock chick wouldn't see him.

What if asshole Professor Looselips did turn him in for animal abuse? Just his luck, just just as a brass ring appeared? Typical really, the patterns of his good fortune crossing his bad were typical.

The record store speakers filled with Howlin' Wolf. Shaney's feet tapped and his core swayed despite his worries. He recalled images of the stout, stolid bluesman with his white pressed shirt and plain black tie on videos. Can't you hear me when I call? Maybe he would look up this professor with the Mexican numbername and pay him a midnight visit, down on the killing floor. Rip his throat out. Huh.

He laughed. The fantasy went a little too far. Though he *knew* he could never hurt someone on purpose, Shaney began really enjoying the idea. Blood flows down the neck of the Mexican intellectual and the wolf howls. All creatures great and snarl. Self defense. It's okay. He laughed again, seeking balance amidst the hard dark of murderous daydreams in the bright light of the store.

He turned around and abruptly bumped into a young woman. After burbled excuses, he noticed her white-blue eyes seemed lit warmer than admiration. He asked what was she up to this nice morning. Afternoon? Whatever.

"You're funny. You don't remember me."

"Of course I do," he lied.

"My girlfriend is in your section? I came in, gave her the note? You made me read it out loud. It said, 'If I told you you had a beautiful body would you hold it against me?'"

"No, no," he said. "I was such a dog stupid." He wondered what that meant. Twice as alluring close up, the lesbian, and she had some animal perfume, deeper than a shaded forest floor and more floral. Her breasts underneath the soft cotton of her blouse pointed slightly up. Her lips were sensuously thick and he could not keep his eyes from them as they moved with her pink tongue darting in and out between her teeth forming words.

"You're funny," she said. "Smart funny guys are the sexiest. Are you Jewish?" she asked suddenly serious.

"No," Shaney said. "No, I am of Nature's Harmonic Time Cube—in which both word and God are outlawed."

She laughed, nervous.

"I'm sorry," he said. "What's your name? Please remind me, and I'll be any religion you want."

"My name is Maria and yes I'd love to have maybe a drink. This afternoon, evening, you say? By the way, what're you looking for?"

"I'm just looking. But I have office hours today, now," he said, lying and fearful of her directness. He could have her right this moment, and imagined it readily. Scary. "Can I meet you later this week? Maybe lunch?"

She looked at him with deep sorrow in her eyes.

"Okay," she said. "But I won't forget you. I will never forget you." She put her little soft finger on the tip of his nose. He made a snap at it as if to bite. She giggled and it seemed alright again. When she walked away, it was a nice erotic poem. Regret fell on him like base clouds over morning sun.

Just look at those band names, Grizzly Bear, Deerhoof, Sleighbells. Indy rock felt like winter in the Rockies or something. As he marched glumly towards the cash register Fleet Foxes in hand he saw the poster for a concert. The concert. He wanted it. He'd seen Acid Fog, liked their gloomy psychedelia and the girl who sang was an anemic Greta Garbo. Next came Preposition the People, a neo-politico-postpostpunk band a la Gang of Four reborn with smidgens of New Order pop and deconstructed disco. They were breathtaking, demanding that people dance to songs about corporate soullessness, and their anthem "Three Way with the Olsens" summoned him up from the depths as easily as Acid Fog could lie him down.

But they were just the prelude. The headliner was Surly.

Fuckin' A.

Like other legendary underground bands, Fugazzi and The Residents for instance, Surly Bonds made irregular gigs shine with surprise. Their recordings were all live, all fan-created, and all apparently fine with a band of guys nobody knew but everybody remembered when they appeared. Spurious rumors suggested that they had no life other than the collective appearances and were summoned from some underground chamber, though others suggested they were soft cuddly plugged-in programmers and satellite dish installer guys by day then erupted out of their mundane lives becoming rock warriors by night. They arrived separately, plugged into whatever, and shredded the fiber of the universe. Then Surly evanesced back into the unknown until next incarnation.

"Wow," said Shaney looking up at the sign.

"I know, right?" said the bespectacled and be-plaided clerk. "South b-by Southwest."

"Oh yeah," said Shaney. "That's a big deal."

All of the clerks looked at him, two rolled their eyes. Four of six eyes rolled.

"I just moved here—from California," he added, unsure why. If he wished it be a hipness calling card, it fluttered, it failed.

"How much are tickets?" he asked, pointing to the Surly show whiteboard notation in neon Sharpie inks.

"Not for sale yet. But you can b-buy a wristband," he said. "Only $200 now and it gets you into everyth-thing. Though to a show like this you might have to get in line early. Say three day-ays. B-but really dude that's the most fun part of the show, chillin' in line."

"Hobnobbing with your fellow wizards," said a deep-voiced, tall curly-haired brunette behind the counter, who then quickly made herself look entirely noncommittal, ice cold.

Shaney was on this, weighing the expense against his daily bread allotment. Oh, and then, now, maybe he would need two, shit, his "girlfriend," after all. It would be bad form to buy just one himself. Then he remembered: He had a job now. But then he also remembered, he had a blackmailer. But that he batted and buzzed away from his brain.

He felt good about buying it. "I'll take two," he said. "Wristbands."

"Right on," said the clerk. "Though I gotta warn you, the OTRs are playing that same night. Across town, to make it worse."

"The OTRs," said the St. Vincent-looking girl, just in time to prevent him saying something snarky about the all-girl punk band so savage in the 1980s, so legendary in a skinhead boytown. But a reunion of former girl punks? They're either married to retired baseball players or running skeevey thrift stores and tattoo parlors.

"You'd think those girls'd b-be housewives b-by now, b-big mom b-butts, driving ma-minivans," said the guy who was pulling out the wristbands and the paperwork.

"But they're not," said the brunette with the cold fire of resentment in her icy eyes, spoiling for another sexist remark to pounce upon like a housecat eyeing a garden path lizard. Then an odd thing happened: she looked around and saw nobody was watching and unmistakably gave Shaney a slow, horny wink. Electricity hummed in his shoulders and legs.

Shaney thought he must be coming into his own, finally. He chatted nervously saying it was hard to imagine someone preferring any mindless three-chord cacophony over the bruising backbeat and terrible incantations of Surly in their prime, say, "I Remembered Me," or "You'll Freak the Baby" with its obscure allusion to Robin Williamson. That was rock and roll, he said. They both stared at his old school stuff. He privately realized that his salad days had been served up long ago. Then the girl winked again.

A tiny bag with Waterloo on it and a $400 purchase was handed him. He gave card, they returned receipt, and the young woman gave him an extra slip of paper. He knew it had her name and number on it. He said, "I'm John Shaney," and left. She could have gleaned that from his credit card, he realized. He wasn't often smooth.

Soon would be the equinox and spring meant real heat. Meanwhile, he walked to the car under crisp skies, balancing buyer's remorse against the perspective on all the days ahead. The blackmailer did a mental pop up and went into a don't-think-about-it file.

A few blocks from home he passed a taco truck and, goddammit, screeched to a halt, ate a small paper bowl of chile Colorado. It didn't help much and he wanted more but propriety intervened. He drove on. At his front gate he paused and then sighed. Home.

He texted some greeting to Lila. She answered, "It's true you live with the Trinitarians."

"HTF did you know that?" he answered.

"Wait and see," she wrote, the ping arriving immediately.

He walked in and smelled something familiar and disquieting. Something nagged him. What? Just as Shaney was about to analyze the pungent puzzling nasal information a bunch of people hailed him mightily from the kitchen.

"'Bout time you got home," said Charley Flatus the pre-med biology undergrad, who was about to say something else when he was interrupted by Joan Dafinchi, the poet.

"You didn't tell us about Lila May, you dog. Perhaps I should say lucky dog." Despite her avowed lesbian leanings, a boy who hung out at the Trinity abode drunkenly confessed to Shaney he slept with her one drunken night. Frankly, Shaney was intrigued.

"Jesus," he said. "What a fucking small town this is."

"'Specially if you're fucking," said some red-haired frizzy girl whipping up a promising batter near the tiled sink.

"Excuse me?" he said, taking an apple from the communal bowl. My God. He was hungry enough to eat fruit. "Besides we barely are," he giggled. "In fact, I just met her Saturday or Friday or something."

"It's always the quiet ones," said the poet. "I have to tell you something cool I learned in school today."

"Can't wait," said Shaney. The familiar weird smell was drifting around the room like a spirit annoyed.

"But first, tell us," said the unknown red-haired Botticellian cherub. "What's in the bag? What'd you buy me?"

"He's spoken for, darling," said the poet and then wound herself around the ginger, making ambiguity return to life. "As should you be right now, after all I've done."

"I'm making you my famous pizza," she said, huskily. "What more do you want?"

They both broke into high yelping nervous laughter, and honestly wiped tears from their eyes. "No, seriously," said Dafinchi. "What did you buy? An engagement ring?"

"Close," he said, holding up the bracelets.

"Whoa," said Charley, who had been busy with a corkscrew, fucking up a decent bottle of wine by macerating the cork. "Someone's taking someone else to South by Southwest. I thought you just met."

"OTR is playing," said Jean Morrow, the smart roommate's friend, who heretofore had been perched in the corner cutting onions in silence without tears.

Shaney looked at her with annoyance, and just then Louis walked in on his way to the storage shed, aboutface, waved hello goodbye to everyone fresh from his room next to Shaney's, with whom he shared an almost-never-used terrace and porch.

"Pizza later," said the ginger, turning her batter, now dough, out onto a floured board.

"Great," Louis said, "I have some time yet." He re-ascended the wooden creaking way. Everybody laughed. Louis was considered weird but strangely cool.

"So?' asked Shaney wanting to get back to the thing learned, to keep conversation rolling, to keep his eye on the redhead and Joan while Jean trained her sorrowful stare on him. *And* his nose kept telling him something he did not quite know how to interpret.

"Typical man," said the poet. "Wants to know if you can perform domestic skills."

Shaney goggled for a second, then giggled. "No. So. Not sew, a needle pulling thread. Or, I'm in stitches. No, I mean 'So,' what about what you learned in school today? Can you share with the rest of us kids?"

"It's called ethology. Animal behavior class."

"I'm familiar with the terminology," Shaney said.

"Speaking of animal," said Jean. "What did you do to the cat?"

"He's freaked, right?" said somebody else who may or may not have been a roommate.

"Shouldn't you be going upstairs?" asked Flatus, seeming rude, though there was no voice affect indicating hostility.

"It's about some guy named Lorenz," said the poet.

"Oh God, Konrad Lorenz," said Shaney.

"Yeah, I guess he was a repentant Nazi, whatever," she said. "Anyways, he writes about when men and women, when married men and women, fight. And when a man feels like hitting his wife, but overcomes the urge. He feels, righteously, that it was logic that overcame base animalistic desires."

"The kind our friend here should be having," said Flatus, who now appeared to be drunk and, and for all Shaney knew, *was* the whole time.

"But Lorenz says that this supposition is completely wrong."

"Like Konrad was about the Nazis." Shaney was passing glib now.

She ignored this. "In fact, it's a triumph of instinct. Human reason allows him to beat his mate, even though it impedes, no, thwarts the drive to reproduce, to protect his own breeding stock. But instinct prevails. When men don't hit women it's because our strong animal patterns triumph over our so-called liberating free will. It feels like rational thought but it comes from more ancient forces. Who knows what other things we do that seem reasonable but in fact are bred in the bone?" She looked triumphant. "Though Konnie thinks humans are doomed by the civilizations they create."

"Logic choppers rule the town," murmured the poet, whose eyes shined on our hero. "Lorenz is fairly well discredited, nowadays."

"Yeah but it makes you think," said Joan.

"It makes me think that he's crazy to stay down here," said Flatus. "With her waiting."

"Yeah, what's up with that?" asked the ginger. "Are you playing her cool, Mr. Cool?"

"He's paying proper respect to his roommates before he retires to his palace of love," laughed the poet and they all broke into their girlish nervous laugh again.

"What the fuck are you talking about?" asked Shaney at the tap pouring water into the half glass of wine he had cadged, to rinse out its corked taste.

"Lila May? Upstairs presumably waiting in your room?" said drunk Flatus. "Presumably in a flimsy burnoose."

Shaney looked at them. "Wait. What you are saying is that Lila May Wulfhardt is waiting for me in my room? And has been all this fucking time? Why didn't somebody tell me this?"

"We thought you knew, man."

"Yeah," said the smart roommate. "How else do you think we knew about you two?"

"Ootdleetoodleedoo," said Flatus.

"The internet?" Shaney said.

"Panopticon," said the poet.

"Jesus Christ, the whole time I'm fucking, oh, Jesus Christ. Well, okay," He realized as he bolted up the stairs what his nose had been saying to him. Her perfume and her body odor were borne upon the microbreezes of this sublunary world, ten parts to a billion, yet they had ricocheted off his nerve-endings and caromed around all the receptors lighting lights like a pinball machine. Yet his own rational self ignored it, misunderstood; absorbed in the crosstalk of all the other sexy stimuli washed against the one message he ought to have heeded. He exulted though. She had found him out and invaded his lair as if it were hers. Like lovers; which now, he supposed, they were.

With a soulful bounding leap he popped open his own door and found the room mystically enchanted. A dim blue light caused by moving the bedlamp over nearer the old plastic alarm clock suffused the room and there was a princess of honey hair snuggled underneath his cotton sheets. He stood, mouth open as whispering breeze crossed his face from the open windows and a smell of sandalwood musk and roses drifted around visiting corners of the room, filling up his breathing-loud nose. Was he panting?

"Hi buddy," she murmured from underneath a parting veil of drowsy sleep.

"Is that what I am?" he asked, surprised at the soft tones of his own voice. He wondered how clean the sheets might be.

"You know what you are," she said and gestured, slipping a bare arm out to indicate space beside her. He leaned against the snapping-closed door. "I'm inviting you into your own bed," she said.

"God, where are my manners," he asked. "I would be honored, thank you."

"My pleasure. I hope. Well, one mustn't presume and besides…"

"I'm so sorry I didn't come up earlier. Those dolts downstairs didn't even tell me you were here."

"Oh, I suspect this kind of thing happens all the time," she giggled, yawned, and stretched luxuriously enough to make his heart shudder with sexual pain.

"No," he said, moving onto the bed after losing his shoes, "It does not. And even if it did, this would be the greatest."

"You're not mad then, I take it?" she said after they kissed and she moved him over enough to roll back the sheets and he saw her long limbs and was lost to it.

"I'm happy," he said. "I'm so happy."

"Ooh, one thing," she said, breaking off the proceedings with a finger on his chin separating them.

"No, please."

"Yes, you have to know. I'm, well, I sort of hinted in my note, which I hope you got."

He thought and remembered. "Mmm?"

"I'm having my period. Started after you left?"

He wondered what that could possibly mean. They were safe, for one.

"My grandmother told me only an animal will make love to a woman when she's riding the, you know. And oh. Oh, please, yes. That. Uh-huh. Wait. A towel is a good idea. I guess, well, I guess that means you're an animal."

He growled softly.

"Goodie," she said.

# 10.

How painful it was to hear them. He was waiting for homemade pizza, but instead he was treated to the unmistakable sound of Lila May and his stupid STEM roomie making loud love. Oh yes, he knew it was her, maybe not at first, but then he heard the woman saying, "Honey" like she used to say in his ears. In Louis Lamel's ears. Shaney said something in the halls about falling in love? But it couldn't be Lila. The coincidence was scary.

The yowling and hissing and endlessly agreeing with each other, yes, yes, as all human language was reduced to affirmatives. Yes, I will, oh yes. Paging Molly Bloom. Buzzes through a kazoo of drywall, spackle, and paint reached his pricking ears. Passed also through the travertine-cladded air ducts, looped out and around the terrace, echoed from the stone barbecue and reentered Lamel's window as high fidelity sensurround. There was no mistaking her. He has the woman I've wanted since first I saw her at the Village Green preschool and kindergarten, Lamel thought.

Back then, his family was part of her family's clique, though his parents thought the Wulfies were almost monsters. In Texas, money is calling card enough for society and who cares if it's made by plundering earth's bowels, running animals to the slaughter, or biomedical research. Lamel's parents hinted something might be wrong with the Wulfhardt ways, though. Too hightoned and lowbrowed at the same time: Living in a town named after one's recent ancestors seemed declasse. As if owning the air and ground were substitutes for nobility.

Lila and Louis were in private school together, her face always turned from his when he smiled friendly. She was brilliant and enshrined, too busy for the likes of wee smelly boys who approached her with dead birds and amphibians, horny toads. She frowned a lot after she came back from a long stay in a hospital, after her famous horse riding riding accident. He said, "What's wrong?" one day when she was sad. She looked at him with surprise and said, "How dare you."

And then one day he was asleep in his room, naptime over a book, and a knock woke him from a rich dream. His mother asked him come into the kitchen where, lo and behold, Lila May and her mother sat. The moms were chatting, lipstick on the Marlboro Menthols burning in the plastic ashtrays, the waffle iron open. His mother said take Lila outside to see the swingset that your huffingpuffing father built.

Everybody thought they were babies playing with toys. But one look into her imploring eyes, he knew he needed to whirl her away. Save her. They walked out to his sister's plastic giant dollhouse and played doctor and nurse until horrified mothers found them a-stew in golden mutual admirations. Henceforth banished from each other's company, which only made their friendship sweeter, they re-met in high school in the library closet and resumed the game's better version, or, as she used to say, in the Biblical sense.

She went away to many colleges. He stuck to Texas. When Texas played A&M they reunioned, found a way back to the high school and sin, always.

She only turned against him when he told her to. After their tragic trip to Mexico and the change. She wouldn't believe. O tears in her eyes, when she wanted him to stand up to her father. Her parents *were* monsters. Now he was one too.

Listening to the roars of love, he rolled over, and, speaking of monsters, almost screamed. An animal with phosphorescent eyes stared from the bottom of his bed. Shit. It was the stupid-ass cat who disapproved of Shaney so vociferously last week, now observing him and groaning. Not a purr. Watching him hypnotized, curious, Mr. Dennis Dinkykins had a vivid face even as the dim light of the streetlamp filtered through dusty curtains; eyes, complex and striated as a kaleidoscope, fractaled into a map of crazy that threatened to draw Louis down. He jumped up quickly grappling puss-puss and opened the door. Mr. D. hissed horribly and broke back into Louis's room, his closet. Louis checked his watch and had to run. Got dressed, it was later than he thought. The shed was smart escape if he made it. He left the house, crossed the highway as dark shadows shrugged into the willows lining Waterloo Park. There flitted among the white trunks strange lights, moths, and stray ideas, his among others, a community of forgotten notions. And then the moon, beloved. Not a thin worn out moon, but the beach quartz radiating light of scary love.

He ran for the shed. Apparently, he ran into the guy who knew Shaney at the Uncle John party. Gangster Lean, don't be thankful for what you got. Was Louis not Lupus killed the stutterer.

# 11.

Shaney woke up hungry from dreams of a bounteous feast: a large segment of beef, flaking apart and dripping with a dark sauce of sweet unctuousness, studded with long-simmered prunes and miniscule cloves thrust into orange skins floating. Next to it, in a steaming bowl, a thick-kernelled pilaf, rice slowly cooked plump with stocks and small-diced onions and peppers sprinkled with parsley and cilantro and more dried fruits. Around that in a sumptuous web were fresh and cooked vegetables. A bowl of fruit sparkled to one side and the *piece de resistance*, a chafing dish of plump ground-meat-and-shellfish-stuffed dumplings awash in salty sauce. He reached his hands out and promptly woke up.

"Jesus," he said.

"Now John," she answered thick with sleep, and suddenly Texan. "We are too sinful already to add blaspheming." They looked at each other and he giggled.

"I'm unbelievably hungry," he said. "I just dreamed about it."

Hands down by his waist, she said, "Indeed."

He crossed his eyes comically and said, hungry and she said, "Eat ye therefore," and he wondered at *her* blaspheming. After a long reiteration of the night before, they rolled apart with his stomach growling in earnest.

"Now that does worry me," she said. "Let's dine down on the avenue."

"Gilley's is closer," he said.

"Stop being a tourist, sugar."

As she rolled towards him she suddenly stopped. "Eeew, what's this?" she asked, reaching across her sublime breasts and pulling a bandage out of the sheets.

"Must've fell off in the tumble," said Shaney grabbing the offending blood-spotted thing, and holding up with the bitten hand. There was no wound, scar; nary a scratch.

"Is this a joke?" she asked also considering the spot he now considered with something like horror. "I didn't feel it on you last night."

What could this mean? he wondered, but faked. "Guess it's healed."

"I didn't even get to kiss it," she said, kissing it, then opening her mouth wide to pretend bite. He yelped and jumped out of bed. "The better to taste you with," she said in an other-worldly voice, not so Texan. He pulled the bedcover over his nakedness, a little fearful in fact, though it was the hand-self-healed mystery that weirded him. By this time, she had gotten up on her haunches and snarled.

"You should run," she said. And he did, dashing into the attached bathroom, closed the door, and as he whizzed like a waterfall his heart was pounding: the hand again, which was earthworm white from the bandaging, but showed nothing more than a scratch where the deep gash was. Microbes inside? Rabies and whatnot? She began scratching the door.

"Me too," she said. I gotta go too."

He started the shower and unlocked the door. She was dressed.

"What about breakfast?" he said.

"What about class?" she said. "Don't want the young professor to get on my shit in section today."

He regarded her again. Then he remembered he had forgotten.

"O. You don't know about that," he said, drawing another untold tale from the thick anthology of stuff he kept from her: the dog, the blackmailer, and the ghost or whatever. But this he decided to share as the water ran. He told her about the dean and his new job.

She looked at him closely and said, "That's interesting." She did not really look happy. "When do you start?" she asked.

"I'm going to call today and go up there whenever," he said.

"I *will* have breakfast," she said. "Fuck biology."

Then she pulled down her pants and sat down on the toilet without an ounce of self-consciousness. He cocked his head, surprised.

"What a you starin' at?" she asked like a dockworker.

"Beauty and the beast?" he said, pointing to them in the mirror steaming.

"The quicker I become a real girl to you, the better," she said.

Breakfast was silent, mostly because Lila May sat astonished at the shovelfuls of food he kept heaping in. On Shaney's end, it felt like restraint. She suggested they discuss her father who could be a demanding taskmaster.

"He's not demonic," she said. "Just driven. He has drives." He brought an awe-inspiring amount of food together in one glum act of mastication—a chomp if you will.

"Go up there, talk. But don't take the job until *we* talk."

Shaney looked at her with abstracted eyes, thinking about her lips but unsure what it was they needed to talk about.

"We'll talk," he said and discovered the toast on his plate with sudden joy.

His arrogant eating habits aside, Lila May found his lack of curiosity worrying. Should she worry so early? Usually it took longer in the arc of lovermakings.

Back to the house empty now save the cat hissing as Shaney's scent entered. Lila and he sat on his unmade bed, and then fell back on the pillows. Her hair smelled sour but also an incense of spring flowers and far behind that, musk. He kept staring at the phone and finally he fished the phone number out of his yesterday jeans and called.

She left, promising later. He was expecting a secretary but got the man himself.

"This is Hindemann," said the voice expressed through the electromagnet end of a connection bled through both wires and radio waves in space. It sounded like a voice from a German submarine movie.

"Uh, hello, uh, hello," said Shaney, bewildered by the unknown ahead.

"Yes, can I help you?"

"Oh, um, sure, this is John Shaney," he said.

"At last you call," replied the man. "Ve had almost giffen up."

"Um, I'm sorry sir. I just found out about the um, the um…"

"Chob," he said.

"Right," replied Shaney. "I just found out yesterday."

"Und you are hesitant?"

"No, sir, no. Not at all. But I guess. This all came so suddenly."

"Dots what she said," said Hindemann with a low chuckle. "Oh, I'm sorry, you know how engineers are. Why don't you come see me und we can discuss your terms und get you started in the lab. Soon I think. How about right now?"

"I'm in Austin," said Shaney, who wondered what engineers were like. "It might take me a few minutes."

"I'll leave the front door open. Come up for late lunch. Ve haff the most exquisite cafeteria, I'll treat you."

"I'm pretty hungry," said Shaney fresh from breakfast, but famished again. "I'll come right up."

He gave Shaney simple, efficient directions to the lab. Turned out he drove the same route he took Saturday night. The drive was quite different from Saturday night's anxious haul, though. The sun played along the edges of his vision, glancing though the season's roadside green, and the sky was thin blue with high stretched-out candy strato-cumulus clouds, not far from outer space, Shaney decided. A silver jet traced contrails along the horizon—cotton from petrochemicals.

John Shaney had never really had a girlfriend before, though he had, as the kids say, hooked up. He didn't know what Lila might think of him charging off. Maybe not her approval, but Lila May's scent went with him and it was intoxicating stuff. He developed an uncomfortable erection driving towards her father's factory, plant, lab, whatever. He wondered if he would see Papa Wulfie and if the scent would leave him by then. He lost the hard-on.

Good thing because the parking lot appeared suddenly and he found the visitor's slot right away and hopped out wondering why he wasn't nervous right now as he went into the building that well might launch his life's work.

The secretary slash receptionist was expecting him but bade him wait on a bench-like moderne couch propped up beside a brush-metal table on which were carelessly scattered magazines that might tempt practitioners of the chemical arts and sciences. There was a *People* Magazine there, too, just in case. It had an article about the upcoming South by Southwest fest and Shaney was sorely tempted to read it but feared some eye was watching now, expecting him to peruse technical journals to follow the latest debate on bio-enzymes and rhysomic catalysts. Also there? A philosophical literary journal with a themed issue on "becoming animal." He was curious but he had a film studies roommate who left journals lying around with titles like "The Three Stooges Sucking Seed: A Homoerotic and Lacanian Investigation of Power." Shaney hated writing that used bullshit jargon like "posit" and "interrogate" instead of "place" or "question." This is the "pause it" before they "interrogate" me, he thought.

The door popped open softly changing the chamber's atmosphere.

"Aw, at last," said Hindemann, introducing himself. "Our chenius comes to us."

Shaney blushed, and put forth hand and some self-defacing comment that Hindemann dismissed while pumping with clammy grip.

"Please, excuse," said the personnel man. "I've just been helping stir a batch of dogwood extract which one of our men claims can be turned into a reasonable facsimile of schnapps. It's not all work und no play here," he said raising eyebrows.

Shaney, wondering what ostensibly well-paid technicians and scientists needed fake schnapps for, thought better than to ask. He cracked up as if he got the joke, though. The German led him through the door and down the corridor.

Hindemann's office had nothing to reward the eyes in it. There were photographs of some woods outside a brick city, but they were less than nondescript and nowhere near bad enough to amuse. His desk was neat with a family photograph and on a deskmat centered were a pile of papers, which Hindemann pretended to regard.

Shaney waited, suspecting this was some kind of test, but thought mostly about the lunch he had been promised, for which, on cue, his stomach began a distant sound of thunder roll. If he noticed, Hindemann didn't respond.

Finally they both said "well" at the same second and then laughed identically, each slapping a knee, but not each other's.

"I suppose you have some questions," said the personnel director.

"No doubt," said Shaney, then swallowed against the ridiculousness of his own response. "Let's start with the obvious."

"Good idea."

"Well, the, what is the job and how much…"

"Does it pay?"

"Umm, yeah."

"We were thinking somewhere around this," he responded and handed a sheet of paper with a long row of numbers.

At first Shaney was confused by the list, but when it translated the salary into high five figures he lurched. His eyes goggled.

"I knew it," said the personnel man. "I told them it was nowhere near enough." He quickly handed over another sheet with a far greater sum on it, somewhere upwards of six figures, and sat back looking worried.

Again, Shaney's reaction was shock and again Hindemann mistook it for scorn, handing him a third piece of paper, though sputtering something about being sorry this was final, times being what they are and still Hindemann looked flustered and prepared for the worst.

"It's fine," whispered Shaney, hoarse, fearing also his lack of strategy might become apparent. He had never dreamed such princely wages might be his someday. Now they apparently were.

"Ach," said the German, muttering in mother tongue. Then, redfaced, he pushed a package of benefits, stock options, and other related corporate materials and boons toward the young man and bade him examine all at his leisure.

"Great, this is all great. But I still have a bigger problem," said Shaney, emboldened.

"What?" asked Hindemann horrified.

"I don't know what I'm being hired to do," he said.

"Vy, resurch," said the man across from him. "Vut you usually do. You don't think we actually want you to perform some kind of function, like a technician or a staff person. You are the talent. Of course, ven and if you discover somesing that will change the vurld, ve vill own a lartch portion of it. Dot's what we do," he chuckled.

Shaney said he understood, though he didn't. Long pause. They looked at each other. He knew what he wanted to say, and waited for the older man who regarded him puzzled.

"Lunch?" Shaney finally said. "Celebrate?"

The older man looked at him through narrow eyes and said, "One might imagine that one would want to see his lapratory before eating," he said.

One might imagine wrong, thought Shaney who could smell the tang of pork slow-cooking two floors and the entire length of the building away. "But of course," he said, crestfallen. He felt like some kind of drug-addled man now who must maintain the veneer of civilized behavior, before getting a hit. "Lead on," he said.

Hindemann looked deeply relieved.

The lab they stood in was furbished generic with beige walls and mauve settees thrown in to perhaps humanize the beaker-and-bunsen-burner-dominated environment. Closer inspection proved the first impression true. It was all about high tech equipment and little designer flourishes like a mini-bar and an espresso machine in the corner next to the sprecto-oscilloscope-anonometer-spinny thing. On the wall was an enigmatic German Expressionist woodcut that seemed to be a portrait of, of all people, Herman Hesse.

There were manuals and textbooks on a little shelf. Shaney couldn't help but laugh.

"You caught ze little ruse," said Hindemann.

Shaney ran his fingers along the spines of a series of tracts bearing on biochemical metamorphosis experiments conducted in recent years relying heavily on propositions drawn from evolutionary psychologists who want to explain our behaviors in terms of animal glands and behavior patterns picked up on the road to civilized salvation.

"Whatever I want to work on," he said.

"Ov course," said Hindemann, chuckling under his words. "If zat verk happens to parallel the vested interests of your benefactor…"

"Boss," said Shaney, thinking, father of my girlfriend, though the terms seemed antiquated or at best inadequate after the savage raptures of the previous evening.

"Then of course it vud be vut you call a vin-vin circumstance.

"Vunderful," said Shaney. "Can't wait to get started."

"But not on an empty stomach," said Hindemann who seemed to pick up and drop his own Teutonic tones at will.

"Amen," said Shaney. "Did I mention I was famished?"

The Wulfhardt Enterprises cafeteria brimmed with life. Besides lively servers there, it had flowers, vegetables, fruits, fowl, seafood, groundfood, and ground food. There were dumplings stuffed with ground meat like his dream and striped with a hoisin sauce reduction. He heaped a plate of noodles served with medallions of pork tenderloin in cream mustard sauce, with a sprinkling of tarragon and flecks of chive and dill. He also had a heaping helping of brussels sprouts in a butter-lime sauce. Shaney finished it almost without breathing and had his eye on the dessert table when Wulfie entered surrounded by lab coats and Brooks Brothers. He breezed by the table then stopped abruptly. When Hindemann nodded, Wulfie dashed over and held Shaney's hand and fork in two of his.

"You won't regret this," he said.

"I hope you won't," said Shaney, carefully lodging the half-masticated into the corner of his mouth to ensure no foodstuff erupt onto his new boss. He remembered guiltily about not conferring with Lila May. He felt perhaps he could relax about all that other stuff, the food now coursing through his veins as sugar and raising optimism's levels.

"Let's talk at the end of next week," said the boss.

"I'll look forward to it," said Shaney.

"Start today," said Wulfhardt. "Work till five."

Shaney was surprised at the boss's bossy tone but felt it impossible to consider otherwise—resistance was futile.

# 12.

After lunch, Hindemann abandoned him and Shaney wandered halls searching for his lab. It was some kind of grid, no doubt, but the doors were all equally green and the few that were opened afforded duplicate views of the usual science accoutrements. He felt a little tickle of panic sweat form on his lower back when he rounded a corner and saw a worker fidgeting with a nameplate over a door. He stood there watching.

"It's for the new kid," he said.

"*C'est moi,*" said Shaney, feeling clever and relieved. What part of his life was luck, fate, chance, divine intervention?

"*Moi,*" said the worker echolalic. Shaney decided since he didn't know what the game was, never mind the rules, fuck off and walk into the office, which was now heaped with equipment he began cataloguing and putting away. He felt foolish and didn't know what he would do with the next four hours of his first working day. Much less his whole new life. Then he hit on the brilliant idea of simulating some more of his signature molecule.

It, his molecule, was a variation of the indole ring familiar to hallucinogen studies, more specifically a six-membered benzene ring fused to a five-membered ring containing nitrogen. Its genius was its adaptability and its close resemblance to the serotonin molecule, which easily permeated the fatty barriers around neuro-transmitters and once stealthily there was able to lock on to those transmitters easily, sending what some scientists considered false signals. Other pioneers of the psychedelic experience suggested that it opened the mind to what actually was out there. The similarity of hallucinations suggests both theories at once. Maybe the chemical sends predictable false pictures, or, more interestingly, opened all and sundry to the One. Either way, it was an instantaneous adaptation—host creature attains visionary status or becomes holy fool, often thought to be one and the same by broad consensus, or whatever.

The mushroom itself from which the molecule derived was taxonomically placed in the agaric family, based on its spores and morphology. Shaney was obsessed with the idea of taxonomies, because, like speculation about the visions themselves, the arguments of classification spun and reversed themselves constantly, no matter what scientists might say to the contrary. The last argument about psilocybin mushrooms was decided in a dispute over the mushroom's bluing or non-bluing clades (family) membership by the Nomenclature Committee for Fungi of the International Botanical Congress. The two mushrooms now belonged to two different clades, though the druggy molecule within both remained the same. In cynical moods, Shaney decided to fall in love with this kind of nonsense passing itself off as precise science. Especially so, because mushrooms constituted their own kingdom. Not animal, not vegetable, but fungi, a thing whose primary function seemed to be dissolving the other two big kingdoms before and after death. Decomposing was obvious. Before death, mushrooms helped animals to see outside themselves better.

Shaney goosed the benzene ring and found an attachment that made it look prettier, accessorizing the fusion. Then, quite by accident, found out that the high it produced made hardened criminals weep for docile joy. Not that he knew any hardened criminals; though he was at one point partying with some future young Republicans.

If it did something else thought Shaney about the goners around the fire at Uncle John's, was it his fault? Did he accidentally make the teen wolves?

By the time he finished requisitioning the chemicals needed over the inter-office mail network, he looked up and was shocked to see it was after five. He had straightened some things and left little rubble piles in other places. He had personalized the sterile space. His phone buzzed away on the Formica top, slide-dancing to the side. Who the hell? he wondered. Then, before even picking it up, he knew.

"Don't be mad at me," he said to the air near his cellular phone's speak spot.

"Why sugar? Are you in the arms of another?"

"Another what?" he asked. She didn't laugh. "No. But I disobeyed you. I took the job with your father without talking it over. He kind of made me."

She was silent.

"You are mad."

"No, mainly I'm surprised. Most boys do what I tell them, so this is a surprise and I'm not sure what to make of it."

"Admire my decisiveness."

"Good cafeteria, huh?"

"Jeeze," he said. "I'm sure hungry. Want to meet me for dinner at one of the taco trucks on Congress Street?"

"No, sugar. Time for you to admire *my* decisiveness. Go get yourself some food and come on over to the library before it gets too dark. I don't want to walk home alone."

"An hour hence," he said.

"Make it two and a half. I actually need to study. Even though I'll be thinking about you most of the time. Disobedient boy."

"Myself whispers in your ear."

"No. Yourself howls in my mind. Maybe a punishment would be in order. A spanking, huh, maybe?"

Shaney blushed and she could hear him doing it.

"Oh, maybe yes? Let's try that," he said. "It could work."

He walked out to the parking lot, didn't have to punch a clock. Nobody was in the lot, but a lot of cars were. Lights lit around the building: Daylight Wasting Time had not yet begun. He looked out into an empty field and shivered. He was still hard too.

Thus his new jam began: a week of awkward work adjustment followed by nights of blissful exploration. At work, he would breeze into the building early—well, early for him being somewhere around nine—and stare at a computer screen for half an hour then follow his nose down to the cafeteria, eat, drink buckets of coffee, and finally settle into some sort of tentative groove a half hour before lunch cravings assailed him. He ate voluminously an expanding diet then returned, did emails and web surfs, and then resumed whatever balking experiment he had undertaken the day before only to realize self-consciously around closing time that it was near pointless vanity. He had turned out the giant batch of super-hallucinogenic liquid and began re-titrating it to see if he could make it more concentrated. Work was all second thoughts, worries that his useless impostorness would soon be discovered. Someone must be keeping tabs on his progress, connecting the pointless dots of his supply orders. Truly, it was random activity, yet he soldiered on.

She had a towngown pad in the spacious Las Zorras apartments not far from campus, once an exotic site, and wanted him to meet her there more nights than not, for a kind of getting to know you pre-honeymoon. She usually was there waiting but slipped him a key on the second day making no big deal noises about it, her showing up late while he waited, watched the TV (his roommates didn't own one), or snooped through her desk and closet for little unknown truths.

Truth was, she always surprised him. As a lover, she was never the same each time. The first time she took him around the world, he was dazzled and glowing afterwards, somewhere beyond sexual satisfaction and a great workout. She laughed as he stared at her naked body, her nipples alerted and covered with fluids. "When she was good," she whispered catching her breath, "she was very very bad." But her non-bedroom self was equally rambunctious. She bought pretty things impulsively, from art to books to art books to posters for her nice apartment walls. "You don't need money," she would say, eyes scrunched. "You just write checks."

Yet he often forgot she was a rich man's daughter, partly because she worked so hard, but also because she played hard too on both sides of the tracks. In the weeks to come he learned her. She went where she chose, bars and soirees, and took him with if she deemed it handy. Or not when she just wanted something like girlfriends or art openings. Shaney did not often care which. He had a bit of work to do. Shaney did not understand the canvases and collages with baby doll parts protruding but he had to admit the mannered artists were fun in conversations. And Lila always was. Conversing with her elders, or straight people, or those in some kind of authority, Lila May squared her shoulders and dropped an octave, understanding and complimentary, but she excelled at sending strangers home with a goofy observation of some magical nature. Part enchantress. She told the man taking tickets at the Alamo theater one night that he was the Gatekeeper of Electric Shadows. Next time he saw her, he said, "Bing Bing and Ling Ling are waiting in theater four."

Shaney was lost in the references but didn't mind all these men staring at his girlfriend.

I mean, she declared him her boyfriend. But he must have harbored doubts. So many ex-suitors. In his listless hours left alone in her sweet apartment, smelling live perfume and a pervase semell of curry powder, he searched her private places until he found the letter. He shouldn't have read it but that's what made it so engrossing. From a boyfriend majoring in psychology. Dear Lila, it said, this is all your fault. Accused her of playing a game he called Monsters. One that grownups play with children alternately frightening and amusing them into helpless laughter, boo! a bit like no contact tickling. "You do that to men, I've watched you. Then you did it to me. Came on like a gangbuster. Disappeared and then boo! You are back for more with your lover/child frightened and overjoyed out of his wits. I won't let it happen to me," he said. Loser, Shaney thought.

"I don't mind it," he said one night when she came home late in hiccups. "Being your latchkey boyfriend."

"Whatevs," she said. But she was actually glad. It made her feel safer to come home to someone there but undemanding. Plus Lila liked him for sex, a lot. This suited him perfectly, because his newly expanded appetite had changed its focus from gluttony to lust. Since starting his nine-to-five job, he was almost always horny, as if someone rubbed sandpaper on his skin and left it tender to the touch of an easy breeze. His eyes popped at the sight of female anything. Earlobe or knee dimple equally had alarming influences on his flow of thoughts and perceptions and exasperating urges overcame him like narcotic rushes. (Maybe it was the neon lights in the office, not being full spectrum incandescent elicited such brutal lust onset.) One early morning in the cafeteria, he caught himself eye-bulging at the sight of the bared arm of a worker dolloping freshly scrambled golden yellow eggs into a chafing dish. Following up the arm, he realized the blond-haired server was a scraggly-bearded boy. He was not gay, he reminded himself.

Even in depths of late-afternoon absorption, stray thoughts of long limbs between white sheets would shiver his mathematical computations to bits. Without thinking, he ground his loins against the corners of his bench as he measured liquids and twice he had to call off work to retreat to his lockable private bathroom blissfully equipped with hand lotion and copious toilet paper. It was all he could do to keep himself from calling out in these moments of impure imagination. His memory began working in a peculiar fashion: The scents of women he had known— there had been a few—floated into the room like spectral presences with memories attached. Nobody was there when this happened. Perfume, sexual smell, even the sour sweat of one particularly nubile athlete chick from California, suddenly leaped up as real in-the-moment sensations, vivified with all the power of a prophet's vision, nasal hallucinations.

Then there was the girl who ran the machine shop. Veronica Wipes was her full name on the company email directory but Jesus he didn't believe it. Jesus. He didn't believe her, either. Muscular tanned legs over big leather work boots with frilly socks. Up above them short floral dresses foamed about her knees like a fabric cloud. She always winked at him. One day, he ran off into his bathroom after her deep voice asked him why boys had to have such rough hands. He said I dunno. Just to make me happy, I guess, she sighed out a breath scented with Sen Sen. Maybe it was Good and Plenty on her breath, her thick soft lips and gruff sweet voice.

Thus the job was where real wantmaking got started and Lila May profited okay by his keened edge come home. She took him into her arms and laughed with pure happiness to see how quick and ardent he came to full attention. They sometimes made it to the bedroom.


Commuting was the worst aspect of his new life, and he learned to hate it in that first week. His kitchen-to-classroom grad student trek of seven minutes seemed a distant picnic memory. The road to Wulfhardt labs was desolate even by Texas standards. Tumbleweeds provided the sole entertainment and Shaney had too much time to think driving there and nudging home and into Austin traffic. He remembered things. Like Uncle John's place. The dirt road up to the site of forgotten slaughter was just a turning twist of dirt off the highway. Exiting the freeway, he drove past the cul de sac where the dog attack took place—an event which newspapers were still trumpeting as blight upon the civic soul. And then there was the shortcut. He dared not even remember that. The spectral form, the crying voice, the proof that a disembodied world might exist—was that the right word, exist?—was like a wound. But computer maps said it cut a third of an hour off the trip, and it was daylight.

Thursday he decided to chance it. With a potential blackmailer hovering and the meeting on Friday with Lila's dad to come not to mention the Saturday BBQ, with Ochocinco's demands, a lot was on his mind. He left work though thinking only of her. She had this way of breathing sibilant into his ear *she* thought was *so* funny. "My semester started sassy," she would wolf-whisper, "but certain circumstances insisted on a stasis, a caesura if you insist." He got wood thinking about it. Like now. And on top of these memories, as he tried to leave, Veronica asked him if he thought he saw something in her eye and he went in close. She put her hands on his hips while he looked. She had a disturbing aura.

Hurry home. So, in a rush to see his girl, he took the turn-off, *that* turn off.

It was far more beautiful than he could have imagined. It wound sharply up through regions and lines of vegetation, quickly becoming pine. It was unexpected, and the woods, he guessed, got dusted with snow in the dead of winter, which was only a few weeks ago, and, coming around one bend he spied a white patch bound in shadows, confirming: encrusted with thrown pebbles, yet it shone through like crystals. The sky was bluer and more comforting compared to the dusty pale above the desert below.

He came along the ridge gripped by memories again. This was the place where the uncanny thing revealed itself, sure. He slowed his car down without thinking about it. It seemed so tame now, the landscape. There were log cabins that, on closer look, revealed themselves as public restrooms facaded with half-rolls of fake pine. All around it growing up were sapling pines and derelict cones, full and half moons of rust-colored plant trash, life renewable. It was a park, a rest stop.

And amongst those scrub (actual) pines was a bench quite close to the road. And on that bench sat a woman. And on that woman's face sat a somehow familiar-sad smile, under raven tresses, he mused. (There were ravens in the trees, too.)

Shit. He knew the pale face. And on it was this memory of beauty, though where and when he first encountered it was shrouded in some psychological fog. He sent out a little cool-guy wave, hands barely off the wheel. The woman looked at him with wistfulness and certain hunger. He gulped.

After two more bends and a bit down the road he realized: that it was Lila May's mother alone on the bench. It froze his thoughts. Then he doubted; it was just another kind of apparition, he was now sure that this place played with his mind, showing him things he wanted subconsciously to see, fuckin' A. Well that's interesting, that's really fucking interesting. I want to see her.

He saw the mother in the daughter's face that night. Even while rolling around he saw her and wondered what kind of neurosis or perversion, subspecies of incest, or whatever flower in the taxonomy of obsessions this hallucinatory desire represented. He couldn't offer himself a clue, not even in dreams.

Which, by the way, were becoming progressively more colorful and full and architectural. Houses he forgot his family had habitated; neighbor lairs and schoolrooms from long before his parents' years of amok. The room he found his mother in. When Thursday midnight changed to Friday he just happened to be watching the clock, the little glow-fingered plug-in alarm clock next to her bed. It swept over straight up change of day and no bells rang. He had spent the night before, but insisted on going home early hours to sleep alone and wash and change into fresher clothes than those he had there. She thought it was cute and told him: nervous to meet Daddy about the job. All the same, she warned him, Father could be an adult dose of weird.

"Thanks for sugar-coating it," he said.

"Just be yourself," she giggled. "And more. My father responds to self-confidence. He's American."

Shaney was too worried to fake a stable persona, but he rehearsed a few boastful remarks, just in case. He walked home that early morning dark and quieter than he ever remembered. He could hear his pulse sounding hollow in his neck. Nothing came out of the bushes, though. When he got home, he lived through a series of drunken roommate catcalls and went up to his musty room and peeled back the sheets and got in and slept down in the depths of luxurious emptiness, his limbs unwound to dark.

When he got to work, the place was almost abandoned. For a moment, he wondered if it wasn't Saturday. People began trickling in, a sheepish woman from across the hall gave him a little wave. She had a smudge on her forehead, At lunch, Shaney thought he might engage in small talk ask about how long it was to Easter or something and he did and one of the techs, how should I know? Shaney retreated feeling foolish and timid. After two hours alternating equations and wall-staring, he wondered if the boss had forgotten him. There had been no notes or emails. Good. He could slip away to weekend free. When he got up to get a coffee, he almost knocked over Hindemann's patchouli-scented assistant, who said whoa. "He will be expecting you at 4 p.m. sharp, hon," said the clerk. "Come early."

Shaney meant to keep his eye on the clock, but he went spinning down into the splicing places of molecules imagining he could see them in a micro. Looking up he almost yelped. Veronica Wipes was in the room smiling and flexing her brow in a spastic wink. He was about to consider some crazy proposition when he saw the clock: 3:54. Shit, he thought. Pushing past her murmuring and wondering how she got in the closed door room ran down the hall. And yet, anxiety's tidal pull took him down as if into sleep, a dreamy drug feeling. The halls were empty and the way was straight and sterile. He had memorized the long path earlier but he got lost then suddenly smelled the perfume of Wulfie's assistant, and stopped outside her door. It opened as if triggered psychically.

"Scientists," she said, shaking her head.

He supposed that's what he was. The assistant was dragging him down the hall.

And all of a sudden Shaney felt actually drugged. He was swimming a tick behind reality. Bemused, even. Wow, man. Searching his memory through a gauze darkly, he wondered how such a state might have transpired. Perhaps, like Hoffman the famous Sandoz "scientist" who discovered LSD, he had ingested some accidental compound through air. Maybe psychosomatic. He felt supremely objective, unworried yet fastened onto detail like a minimalist artist. She stopped them outside the boss's suite. She looked rather patronizing and gave him shirt inside belted trousers tuck. Trousers. He wondered if this would constitute sexual harassment. She was hot, he suddenly realized, her breasts huge and he enjoyed her smell as well. Wow, he thought, and suppressed a giggle. Maintain, dude, he told himself.

"Cool your jets," she said.

Shaney nodded, finding the waiting experience to be bizarre. It had been mere days since his academic career ended but it might as well have been a century. He didn't miss it but his sense of order was swirling in the corporate science world for no other reason than that somebody was bellowing behind a door. Deans don't really do that. He took a deep breath and hoped hard for something normal to happen. He heard laughter. He calmed down for a few seconds. Thanks, he told his central nervous system. His hand twitched oddly. His will bent the anger into cheer.

"Our shining star, our rookie acquisition," said Wulfhardt when access was granted, half-rising from behind his monstrous desk, indicating a seat, a motion which Shaney mistook for the outstretched paw of a handshake. He awkwardly withdrew it and plopping sat staring at the stubble-lines of his own silver grey corduroys.

"Find everything you need?" asked Wulfie, like a store clerk. "Everybody helping?"

Shaney turned his gaze at the retreating assistant and smiled broadly. "Your staff has been awesome at every turn," he said, noting her nod, she approved his glib unctuousness, for sure.

"Splendid," said Wulfie. "Now let's get down to whatever the fuck it is you think you're doing here."

"Sir," said he, fearful. "Is there a problem?"

Wulfhardt stared at the ghost space of his assistant. "Of course there's a fucking problem. Why do you think we brought you here?"

"We, sir?" said Shaney.

"My board of directors, the talent-minders at your college and me. We. Neither royal nor editorial, but a conjugation of responsibility for your fate," Wulfhardt said pointing one fat digit straight at him. Motes were whirling, phrases and images too on a breeze symphonic with the carried songs of everything. He was beginning mild hallucinations. Awkward. Shaney shook his head and cleared his throat. "I spent this week orienting myself to the lab and its possibilities."

"And drawbacks?"

"None detected so far, sir," Shaney laughed, offkey.

"Bullshit," he said. "And again I say bullshit."

Shaney's head seemed flurried now, as if inside a glass and water paperweight snowing particles.

"Number one," interrupted Lionel. "I know for a fact that the labs need a great deal of improvement and, well, number two, you have done far more than orient yourself. Your chemical orders told the whole story, man."

Shaney *knew* his diddling was observed and his number was up. They were onto him and he felt especially vulnerable with a test tube back in his quarters loaded with some white fluffy new drug, enough concentrated power to take down the whole city.

"It was brilliant and you know it," continued Wulfhardt. "I wasn't even sure you had surmised my problem, my fucking problem. But you started in with the ergot formula—though I should tell you we've rejected that, the historicity is off. But you know we were thinking European monsters, the old colonial imperative. How did you know, lad? Though, I did allude to the monster in our first conversation." He looked at Shaney and made a gesture, come on, now, out with it.

"The were-werewolf problem?" Shaney asked.

"A clever boy, an upright boy. Worthy of my daughter's attentions too I would say."

"Maybe it would be a good idea to keep her out of this," said Shaney with an underlying snarl that surprised even him.

"My boy," said Wulfhardt, "I'll pretend I didn't hear you set any fucking terms."

"Fine, Mr. Wulfhardt," he replied. "Long as you leave Lila May, as I said, out."

The older man steamed, swiveled his big chair, and looked out the window onto a graceless parking lot rimmed with scraggly hyacinth plants. When he whirled back he was beaming. "Suppose you want to hear about the lycanthropes."

"I'm all ears," said the young man eyebeams a-fizz, moods swinging inside like monkeys in a cage. He knuckled his eye and something behind it like a shower of sparks fell from an open short circuit inside. Panting, he leaned forward. Ghost bones shone behind his boss's face.

"You know this state has played host to shape-shifting monsters since before the arrival of the so-called white man."

"So-called," echoed Shaney.

"You likely know about the Yaqui Indians, and this disreputable California intellectual Carlos Castaneda, right?"

"No," he said, murmuring.

"Well, perhaps that's for the best this stuff doesn't seem even tantalizing anymore. They were all the rage back when you were born. Anyways, his books discussed a tribe of Indians habitually using peyote and jimson weed taught themselves to transmute into animals—chiefly wolves, then crows. *Scheiss* like that."

"I-I-Ice," he said locked into another echolalic attack. This mysteriously-ingested drug was weird.

"Agreed, frightening," said the unaware Wulfhardt. "To make the ridiculous story short, the Yaqui tribe after many displacements from Mexico and Arizona, sent a small tendril-like offshoot to a city called Presidio on the border of Texas and Mexico, a place marked by numerous mythological associations—images of conjunction, crucifix legends, the town itself was once known as Junta, which you may know means together, a mélange, a blending. Then fiction mixed into science by Castaneda himself, and his books brought a pack of young wannabe mystics seeking some sort of philosopher's stone in the desert amongst the alkaloids of hemp and mescal."

"You're making this shit up," thought Shaney, abandoning any hope that Wulfhardt might come to some point in this story. "Mescaline?" he said, helpless to the rewiring of his speaking mind now in progress. "Wannabe?"

"I know, your interest lies in the mushroom. But there are other factors too. Wolf legends more macabre precede all this hippie shit. By the way, I think they succeeded. The post-hippies could turn themselves into animals at will, with effort. But something else as well."

"Chupacabra," said S., starting to pull together the weave of his loom.

"You've been reading up. I would be impressed with your surmise if the damn thing wasn't a drive-in movie monster nowadays. But no, the Mexican demon doesn't appear here. There is an Acadian strain, however, which far fewer folk appreciate."

"Fuh-fuh-fuh," said Shaney.

"I don't mind the *occasional* imprecation, my boy, when warranted, go ahead. What the fuck, huh? Yes, when French Canadians entered the state via Louisiana, they brought their own version, the fuckin' *loup garou*, the skinwalkers. Turns out, the French Canadian myths included a lovely Catholic strain of soul-selling to the Prince of Darkness in exchange for the right to morph at will into animal form. I would likely sell my soul, that which I don't have, for such power."

While listening, Shaney began perversely remembering his new woman, the one he loved. Unbidden, except maybe that her father was sitting across from him, Shaney's brain began running vivid videos of her limbs, then in sensurround, her lips applied to various sensitive body areas, and then gathering into a psychic knot, an internal Imax huge image of her, Lila May Wulfhardt assembling like a hologram, opaque yet see-through, lips moving to articulate her wonder and reassurance, then pouting, she demanded he phone her soon as the meeting was over. "So, like the city Presidio, the entire state finds itself a nesting place for the wolf-fucking-man and his mate, wolfette." The old man chuckled now. Knitting and unknitting his illustrating fingers.

"You're not joking, sir?" Shaney then started visualizing another Wulfhardt woman, and this vision hit him hard. Gwendolyn.

"No. The reason it's not funny is because people believed. Besides, the state has a number of reasons for its own bad conscience boogeymen. Its history since the Alamo has provided others with plenty of reasons to disparage us."

Shaney was getting over his hallucinatory moment, but struggled to keep up. "The president's uh death, Dallas."

Wulfhardt looked at him with surprise, like it never had occurred to him. "No, boy. I meant the Bush presidencies, offset by the Lyndon Johnson legacies." The Lila image turned less opaque, more diaphanous. "But there are other reasons too," said Wulfhardt. "My own people, if you will. There were the camps."

"The camps." He thought, oh no, the automatic joke about Germans, "Zis iss a new camp, zere vill be no eshcape," he thought now and found himself repressing a giggle.

"You know about the camps? Think it's funny?"

Shaney flashed a hoping-for-help look, a please in his gaze. "No, sir," he said.

"It was real, I remember it, and it haunts me. Outside of Austin, where German POWs were kept. Probably you don't know. A lot of people don't. There were eighty thousand World War II prisoners kept in Texas, most of them German, most captured after the invasion of Africa. The camps held about three thousand soldiers each and many of the interred considered Texas the most exciting adventure in their lives. Among them, it was rumored, were Nazi scientists who had performed experiments of the eugenicist pseudo-sciences popular in the Third Reich. Jews and gypsies and homosexuals were their guinea pigs. One scientist got let out of the camp by the CIA to teach at your college. He was a drug experimenter like yourself."

"Please," said Shaney, nervous about the implications. "I have no idea where this is going. No idea what all of this has to do with psychedelic drugs or werewolves. I really don't." The hour was latening, besides, and his urge to call his girl was crowding out all other thoughts.

"Neither do I," he said. "Stop looking at the clock. Am I keeping you from something else? But really, I have no idea what these drugs mean either. I assume you were drug tested before you came to work here. I mean, what are you saying? Drugs?"

"The kids in Austin. This werewolf thing you seem to be heading towards has something to do with drugs. I can only assume the movie *Altered States* got under your skin in the 1980s. I mean, what?" said Shaney self-conscious of his own aggressiveness, brought on by what, he wondered.

"Please, calm yourself, Mr. Shaney. I assure you I know nothing about anything you are saying."

Shaney took a deep breath. The whirling began pleasantly again. "Really? Then please tell me: What about monsters?"

"Ask around, my friend. People will tell you there is a werewolf problem in this town. I'm just giving it a folklore, rumor-based origin. What I want to know is whether it has any scientific basis. Is there maybe a syndrome that turns normal people into wolfen. Then a drug might help. Maybe the drug is the problem. I don't know."

"Oh," said Shaney. "You don't think it could be a disorder, like schizophrenia or a weirdo disease like Tourette's or lupus."

"Maybe. Are you interested?"

"Utterly. Can you get me a fer sure infected person?"

"I knew it would be genius inviting you here to work," he said. "I'll show you something Monday. Meanwhile, this," he said, handing Shaney an envelope, which the young man took gingerly.

"It's not poisoned, no worries. Your paycheck, my boy," said Wulfhardt. "I like to hand them out personally."

"Thank you, sir."

"No, I thank you," he said and warmly shook the hand of the man who was fucking his daughter. And more, and worse, and very soon.

# 13.

Papa Wulfhardt drove home silent, worried and went into the private hospital wing of the big house. Two cars were gone from his huge garage. Wulfie put his key in the elevator, stepped in, and rode down a few hundred feet. His private assistant met him with deep concern. The asset has terminated itself, he said. Wulfhardt sighed.

An hour earlier, Shaney stood outside, after the meeting, after running back to his office lab, throwing on his black hoodie, and grabbing the keys to his hybrid, laughter rumbling up from his gut. It was the clean joy of relief, that sudden release from long, wearing worries. He felt celebrations were demanded, then remembered the BBQ would be a-raging at home. Nice.

Then he opened up his envelope just before sitting in his car and his bowels went wow. Big four figures for just a half week's work after taxes and a handsome payout to his insurance and something called a retirement fund. Hell, he was in his twenties. Shaney was pretty sure his father never made money like that, even before his depredations were exposed. Wow. He wondered if the bank would even be able to cash a motherfucker like this. Then he laughed at his own naiveté, and decided to get used to his new life: Shit, after paying rent, student loans, and whatever for utilities he had over $900 to play around with—and that was just one week's pay. And, he hadn't done shit except make drugs he could easily dump for a coupla grand as well. He was on his way to mogul-dom.

The car whispered to life and he headed out of the parking lot determined to take the scary shortcut home, sailing among fluffy clouds in the distance, and he would be coming into his new favorite city just as the streetlights began to glimmer with passion and hope. For passion, he hoped. He remembered to call Lila May and his buzzed state allowed him to. But when he grabbed the phone a sudden onset of popo-paranoia occurred and he dropped the cellphone into his lap.

The shortcut was at the next turnoff and he wanted to pay attention but Shaney's unloosed mind skipped larkishly from celebrations to close calls to problems of cellular biochemistry, a topic he ought to brush up before next week. But such issues as membrane transport, receptor mechanisms, and cytoskeletal functions whirled around and only made him realize with a pang of half regret this odd buzz was declining, the rush no longer felt. He wanted to stay high. All of it was beyond his choice, though.

Bolstered by the night ahead, real money in his hands and soon to be in his pockets provided him a chance to look smugly down upon his impoverished roommates. This he relished and it surprised him.

This was an arching road, and it was difficult not to think about loftiness when the very sky around the car seemed to be thinning and thinning blue—that color just before the black of surrounding space. He thought about a car that might travel such distances: oxygen. Then there would be a nothing. The zero around everything with crisp icy emptiness inside. Not that he was thinking about death, but more he considered the zero before his life began.

Some scientist had recently revealed that any photograph of black space sufficiently enlarged would reveal myriad nests of sparkling stars, and he wondered for the millionth time how traveling through the cosmos as God or superhero might really feel, bending and bursting the bubble of law that dictates none shall pass the speed of light. Somehow he would someday travel like the *2001* Dave bathing in psychedelic nebulae.

He would be the zero then, stretched out to infinity. The universe wrapped around.

Again he reached the spot where the oaks turned to pine and he remembered his fear and his vision. His ghost.

He drove past the rest stop. There was the woman again, the one who was not unlike the mother of his girlfriend. This time her head was down in folded arms as if ready to play Heads-Up-Seven-Up on a picnic table. Outer space cold surrounded him when he knew (somehow don't ask how) she was sobbing into those folded arms. He knew he would stop and stop her sobbing and stop he did. It really couldn't be helped though he half thought it wasn't a grand idea.

And it was true. First thing he heard, hiking the weedy dirt path from the parking lot was *loud* crying. A chill passed through him; his specter's voice had returned. As he broke into the clearing, Lila May's mother on the bench put her head up and showed her ravaged red eyes. She saw him and put her hand tight onto her mouth.

"Mrs. Wulfhardt?" Shaney croaked.

"You know me?" she asked, mortified and amazed.

"John Shaney," he said. "Lila May's friend. Had dinner the other night."

She appraised him and began crying again.

"O no," he said. "There there."

He sat down close, very close. She turned her head, embarrassed. Shaney reached across the table and plucked from a package of plastic-wrapped Kleenexes she had, a gallant's move. After a few hollow-sounding there-theres, he asked if she wanted to talk. Little creature comforts had their effect. Mrs. Wulfhardt reached across the table to a clear plastic glass half-full of *pinot grigio*, a little condensation on the window-y wall of it, clearly proving it still cold. Shaney could see a plastic cooler at her feet, which he doubted not, held the bottle that the wine came from. She glugged it down and said, where are my manners? Reaching over, she almost tipped, though Shaney said he was fine and she said but she wasn't.

"Mrs. Wulfhardt," said Shaney about to stumble into some sort of maybe-you-shouldn't discussion, when she interrupted.

"Gwen," she said, having deftly poured two glasses of wine and handing one to the younger man. She raised hers. He felt inclined to demur but a deeper impulse rolled up him. He picked up the flimsy cup and knocked it gently against hers. Cheers, happy days.

She giggled but then her face returned to sorrow and self-pity. "He's probably doing the same, the same with some little cutlet on a spit from the college," she hissed. "Wouldn't you imagine?"

Shaney was embarrassed now. "If we are talking about your husband, I have to say the answer is probably no," he said, gathering strength from her wide eyes. "I just walked out of a meeting with him," he said. More like half an hour since Shaney left Wulfie. God, he might have an office fling. Maybe Veronica Wipes?

"My husband? I wish he was the problem," she said. "A case of simple marital infidelity wouldn't require all this. I could probably take on a lover under his nose in my own home," she said, giggling. "I bet he has."

Shaney was confused.

"Funny thing is," she said, helpful, "you probably know *my* problem. The cause of my sorrow." On that note she drank like a soap opera star. "Beveritch," she said and hiccupped matter-of-fact.

"No thanks, my glass is still full."

She laughed. "Not beverage." And then she started crying in earnest, falling onto his neck breathing wet. "No," she bubbled between pained sobs. "The dean, Dean Beveritch. He's the one who broke my heart," she said lifting the glass, spastically pouring some wine over both of them. He grabbed a napkin and began to daub it hard and awkwardly and she began to cry voluminously and hard sitting on the hard bench. She pulled him into her wet grasp.

Something else was hard by now. Shame.

She began in a high-pitched voice (somehow not whiny) to enumerate the occasions when the dean, who she never failed to refer to as the dean, abandoned her in her moment of need.

"He led me on," she said. "Do you know how much that hurts a woman? We're not like you boys who can turn it on and off at some emotional spigot."

Actually, Shaney had had girlfriends who seemed perfectly capable of being in love and then boop! not in love, changing without regret. One in particular, he remembered, then… Jesus! Mrs. Wulfhardt, that is, Gwen, curled long fingers around his waist and pulled him close to her wine-fuming mouth as tears slid down her face making slippery roads of her cheeks. Shaney lost the power to discern her words and was now engulfed in a cloud of perfume, wine, and now was ridiculously hard. His back on its own volition gave a little lurch forward to put his penis more conveniently within her reach. She held still: some sort of scanning device. She began to stand up, forming apologies and grateful words for the company and comfort he was lavishing on her. She sort of said something about how lucky her daughter had been to find him, which was a turn-off. But then she sat down and buried her face in his neck where tears slid and his nose found the nebulous perfume again rising on heat convection waves from what seemed an oven below. It was unbelievably sexual.

"But really I have to go," she said slurping down the rest of her wine.

"Maybe it's not such a good idea you drive," he said as they began standing up from the park table and bench legs entangled throwing him belly to belly against her. She froze. Oh, Jesus, he thought, now she knows what a little fucking pervert I am.

There was no attempt to be polite or ignore. "Seriously?" she said. Her eyes narrowed and then expanded and he felt the tide of hallucination pouring up his cortex again. "For me?" she asked. There was a pulse at her forehead and her eyes went in and out. "Aren't you the flatterer?" His hand had been near her arm and he pulled it away, eyes wide as if fearful of a blow.

Instead she reached over, took his hand, and put it on her back. Diver ready over the pool, her eyes soft focused. Instead of pulling away, she moved closer and there was considerable heat in her exhales. She kissed him and then again. "Gwen," he said and if he meant it to be a reproof that wasn't the way it came out.

He had no idea what to say next, but she made talk unnecessary, pulling him to her so her down jacket was crushed into his cotton plaid shirt and her hands ran up around the back of his neck as her mouth opened for their third kiss, his stiff breathing predicated by autonomic reflexes and hormonal rush.

Her mouth was cavernous with areas of heat and cold. It had an interesting tang, this mouth, comprised of afternoon wine and breath coming from below in the bellows of her past. Breakfast, chewing gum, toothpaste and something wicked and exciting wafted into his mouth from hers. Meanwhile her tongue had begun a sinister but sweet dance. The kiss broke and they both were panting. She said, "God," and took her hands up under his shirt pressing almost into his flesh. The kiss resumed.

Shaney wasn't so much powerless to resist as he was overwhelmed in the wake. She pulled him to the brink, his body did the rest. He broke the kiss again and half-supposed he was going to say something like, this is crazy, but, instead moved his lips into the place in her neck below her ears and above the collarbone. She said, "Now."

She pulled and pushed him loin to loin, backed off and then locked onto his lips while her small, cold-ish fingers slipped down into his pants via the gap in his belt in the back. Then slowly it came around the corner and found him hard in the soft cold. He gasped and put his hand on her breast and the rest was a tidal wave. She began to pull his pants down right there at the bench, in the darkening park, then thought better of it. "Come here," she said, panting, and took his hand dragged him stoned on the sexual rush of it all staggering, but not far.

What privacy did she think she would gain dragging him over to a little clump of iceplant and throwing him down on top of it? She crawled on top of him. The succulents had a surprising amount of give and he rolled over on her, and by now her blouse was open, her bra had parted to reveal a small perfect breast which he took into his mouth, a vampire for her love.

Meanwhile, she had his pants down somehow and her hand on his penis, pulling it harder than one might have thought wise. The roughness of the act passed through her and into his nerves, somehow, too, though. He snarled a little as he took her full breast into his mouth and arched his back—no mean feat with her holding tight—and yanked down her pants. He could smell her immediately and that made matters much more compelling. Urgent. There was no turning back, no consideration of time, place, or appropriateness of mate. Hah. He was lost in the act, more lost than ever before or after it, this was complete immersion of self first into self, primal version, and then into her, primal other. Or maybe she wasn't other. Not at that moment. Maybe nothing was. She guided him into her and it was a furnace not unlike the pleasures of kissing her mouth, vastly open and yet tightly fit.

And she came unglued. Just the presence of his erect self turned her loose to the elements, and she clawed him through his shirt. Luckily through thick cloth because her nails lacquered expertly by the Vietnamese girl Tran were sharp and strong. And he might have borne such a scrape forever. Oops, she reached under and he *was* marked. He didn't give a fuck, though, when she began an unbelievable crescendo of inchoate chants and then an orgasm so loud that ravens and crows in the trees around them launched and wheeled out wondering. Awe and fear departed, Shaney acquiesced to the power of the feeling he helped create and began his own exclamatory release. He never made a noise during sex except this time and this time he called out. And then collapsed with her on top.

Their breath commingled as their wide-open mouths lay next to each other. Neither could have stood up at this moment, so spent in tearing, grasping, and blissful frictions, so tender a moment opened before them, desert flower, rare and likely doomed. They became still in the moment's presence as real grace made do with them. He took her hand up to his mouth and kissed and then took the fingers into his lips. She whispered something about love to him. He was beyond any critical evaluations. They were happy.

Harsh light of a passing car leaked back into their brains and reactivated the need for at least some decorum. Spread-eagled and half-naked, they were too close to the road in waning daylight. So satisfied, they pulled their own clothes apart from a balled up whole and toward the postcoital separation of their bodies. It was not shame. Instead, they began handing each other items and helping each other on and over shoulders and up buttons and zippers—mostly he to her—with a sudden intimacy and tenderness. Wordless, he walked her to her beautiful old Thunderbird and kissed her deep into the nape of her neck and she giggled. "Should I?" he asked, knowing the answer and she smiled sad knowing the question. What he didn't say: "call you." It was all about futility ahead and happiness about to be left in the past forever.

She revved up the car, apparently undrunk now. Her window was down and he twined his fingers in hers. She pulled some scissors from the glove compartment and he straightened. She bent down and he heard a noise snip. She came up smiling. She handed him something very soft. Her hair, a lock. She wove it into an Un-Gordian knot. He didn't know what to say, because it also looked like Lila's hair. Then she spoke. "Make her stay home, my home, on the full moon," she said.

"Okay?" he answered. She meant Lila May, he knew that.

"All I ask," she said. Considering the depth of her feeling expressed, not to mention the aftermath of intimacy, the bond their transgression had formed in that lovely flurry, it seemed a small request, a promise weird but easily kept. "You stay home too," she said.

He would not keep it when the time came though.

She drove off and his happiness waned as the distance spread. This was impossible, ridiculous, but he might be in love with Lila May's mother.

# 14.

Wulfie looked at all the blood in dismay. How is it possible, he asked the assistant. The cell was drenched and there was black around the edges of the red pools.

"He chewed it away, his wrist," came the reply.

"I've never heard such a thing. Does this happen sometimes, ever?"

"Teeth are sharp. There isn't a lot of resistance, tough tendons, but the artery is there. Where there is a will, there is a way."

Wulfhardt thought about imprisonment and free will for a second. Survival and death wish. Camping overnight at Fort Da, I would say.

"We can't report it." Wulfie looked at the blond man and realized the only witness stood in front of him, silent. Two people can keep a secret, Wulfhardt thought, if one of them is dead.

Meanwhile, Shaney was ravenous again. He stopped the hybrid en route home and rummaged around for the can of nuts he kept handy. Empty. He looked at the car clock and realized he was late for his roommates' soiree. On his phone he found a text from Lila May. Guilt he brushed aside, Gwen's spell remained unbroken. He worried what it would be like to see his girlfriend. She would be late, very late, said Lila's message. Please don't be mad. Shaney was intoxicated with relief.

It was time to get home, time to shower off the day. His outdoor enactment of *The Graduate* in reverse. He thought about Gwen, her cavernous mouth and her breath: every tinct in it he could remember. He was actually getting excited again. The way of the world, the human condition. To be haunted by what you can't want. Also, he felt tenderly towards her.

Change the subject. He was ornery hungry now. It had passed from idea to a yawning, growling need. He saw a truck stop near the bottom of the pass, a place of chili dogs and tamales microwaved, gas station tacos. His growling stomach said, fuck yes.

He ordered two dogs and three carnitas on small tortillas laughing at the notion of a vegan barbecue, a funnier oxymoron than jumbo shrimp or anticipated serendipity. He wolfed the food down and smeared the greasy red off his lips with a couple squares of paper towel offered free to valued customers. He was feeling lower, meaner, and happier.

He headed home knowing he was late but ready for no prep work and a big entrance. He thought about his hoveled student roomies now from the vantage point of the fat check in his pocket. He no longer *needed* to share their space. Hell, he could magnanimously pick up the month's rent. Then, maybe the poet would be so turned on by the gesture she would take him into her shrine-like frangipani-scented boudoir and they could scansion some trochees, or whatever. His imagination switch was flipped. He chuckled lower and meaner now. He was a bastard for what he did. He allowed that. Rather than feel sorry for himself, however—or Lila May, for that matter—he was already building his cocoon of tough guy hide harder. His stomach growled for more food, and his mind was ready for almost any eventuality, Bring it on. Even when he remembered that the asshole professor was coming too. Inconvenient but not insurmountable, this blackmail worry. Maybe there was a way to put Ochocinco's threat aside without spilling blood or incurring guilt… just figure it out, the tough guy inside him said. Can't live with him, can't shoot him. Poison? He didn't think he could actually.

He found a place to park and hefted the twelve pack he bought at the rest stop out of the backseat. Through the chain link fence he saw the cat lighting away out of the corner of his eyes. Then he brushed open the front door and came face-to-face with a real Texan.

"Hey. I'm John," Shaney said holding out a dry hand.

"Name is John, too, name of John McGilvray, at your service, me. Everybody calls me Texas," I said, taking the hand in mine. Warm.

Shaney smiled at me, the man seated in the tiny foyer before the living room on a wooden crate with a battered Martin guitar in my arms—strumming it, natch—rested on my blue jeans rolled and frayed over brown, beautifully scuffed yet elegant Tony Lamas. "You here for the bash?" I asked, causing my chin to jerk towards the tinkling laughter and chatter over icy cups.

"Indeed I am," said Shaney back at me. "You?"

"Ahm proudly attached to the poet who lives beneath the stairs, I believe she's goin' 'round tellin' folks ahm a diamond in the rough, a kahnd of sagebrush Dylan Thomas, ah believe is the proper epitaph she has prematurely laid on me. Though I rightly prefer the poetry of William Butler Yeats who I studied in my three seasons in hell, Texas UT? You got any connections here?"

"Texas gone to Texas, ay? Oh, I live here. Upstairs."

"In the previously alive girl's room? Yessir. I heard you was some kind of legendary chemist of the entheogenic persuasion. But then ah also heard you was a biological research type. Well?"

"Which is it, you wonder." Shaney laughed, this guy seemed fun. "I plead guilty to both."

"We all a little guilty in the ahs of the Lord," Texas sang with a voice that opened in deep registers like a lost growl ascending to unlikely trills. "You hear the one about the guy goes into the doctor who says I got good news and bad news, and the guy says give me the good, and doc says they gonna name the disease after you."

Shaney said, "What's the bad news?"

"Aw you just tryin' to be regular folks. They ain't no bad news since Jesus washed us in his blood. Is it true you got a job up in Werewolf, Texas?"

"Where wolf? I mean, what?"

"You know, old man Wulfhardt's labs. Oh, shit. I remember you now, you the one runnin' around with Lila May? Oh shit again, I made that sound bad, din't I."

"Yeah, but I suspect I've got it comin.' Why do you call it that? Werewolf?"

"He din't give you the lecture yet?"

"Matter of fact, he did, today. But how do you know all this stuff? You're more like Lowell Thomas than Dylan."

"Ahm gonna pertend ah don't understand that reference so's not to spoil my country-cred. Of course, I as an English major once dedicated to the study of Anglo-Irish modernist writers once worked up there, too, you know, after I dropped out still owing my perfesser an *explication de texte* or two. Just a cafeteria cowboy back in those days, but Wulfie used to come in ever' day and drink my cappuccinos and eat Austin Bakery brioche and tell me his wild tales of wolfen neur-oo-sis." He paused. "Also, I was in love with the lovely Lila myself, but you gonna hear that a lot before you die. From other forlorn boys."

It gave Shaney pause. He wondered out loud, "Think this wolfman stuff is a form of insane obsession?"

"Oh give him some credit. Course he is obsessed, but he's got this idea that whatever breeds the notion of Texan singularity into us also creates the urge to push it past the fulcrum point of social compromise. Totem and taboo shit, ya know?"

Now and all of a sudden, Shaney felt seriously lost. "No, I guess I don't know" was what he wanted to say but the sight of this smug strumming street poet, this prairie proselytizer stuck in his maw. "Yup," is what he actually said, then hazarded an ambiguity. "He's pushing my envelope towards me."

"He thinks that the distances of Texas created a breed of humanimals who want more of everything because they are surrounded by nearly nothing. Raised on cactus and beef, they long to slake their thirst and call it barbecue. Soon they begin to develop a very fake sense of bonding, like, we are Texans, but what they really mean is Texas made us. Only wolves live so split between pack and sullen hunt. That's what he would say."

Now Shaney's eyes were popping. This cowpoke is smarter than me, he thought. And loves Lila. He suddenly longed for the conversation of plain folk, or, failing that, loopy grad students, a self-beleaguering breed he now felt comfortable with. "Well, nice to meet you, but I better check in," he said.

"Ya'll come back. I'll be playin' here all week," said me, name of Texas, then broke into a shockingly beautiful rendition of John Prine's "Angel from Montgomery."

Shaney headed toward the kitchen expecting solace, or at least greetings. Fat chance.

There was a bottle of Beam on the kitchen counter. Shaney plunked his twelve-pack down next to it and reached up into the closet for a tiny shot glass that he knew was there. Pulling it down, he found himself reprimanded by his roommate Ron. "Make yourself at home."

"Okay, I will," said Shaney, oblivious to the implication of Ron's sarcastic tone.

"I mean I know it's a party and shit, but really? You just rummage around the cabinets like you own the place?"

"That's my cousin down from Seven Limbs," said a young man to a young woman drifting by the kitchen on their way to some other party locale.

Now Shaney was indeed perplexed. "Are you pulling my leg, Ron? And why?" A thick-eyed hippie-looking blonde chick looked on and nodded in complicity with the proceedings, though on whose side she was remained unclear.

"Far out, man," she said.

"I know you, dude?" asked Ron. "Cause I don't appreciate you barging in and grabbing shit like it's yours."

"Right on," said the girl.

"It *is* mine, Ron. My shot glass though I assumed that a bottle o' whiskey at a party at my house is fair game. Fuck," said Shaney, some gorge rising within.

"Who the fuck?" said Ron as the poet walked into the room. "This guy used to live here or some shit?" he asked her.

"Chill, chill, dear-heart. This is a party. People share things at a party," said the poet.

"Excuse me," Shaney said, now getting angry. Maybe he wasn't the most enthusiastic roomie. He paid his rent.

The poet raised a trembling thin digit to her lips and winked at Shaney. "Why don't you go make sure the barbecue is right, Ron, honey, and I'll figure this out?"

He looked belligerent but temporarily pacified and rumbled out to the back yard, which Shaney could see was dominated by a big fire and little twinkling colored lights.

"Please don't be offended, he took something, we're not sure what it is, please don't be offended. Seems like it only affected his short-term memory. Only remembers the older roomies. Short term is all. He couldn't even remember why this party was happening, and it was his idea."

"He took something."

"There's a pipe in his room, and, actually, we wanted you to check it out."

"Me."

"You are the biochemist with some reputation for psychotropic condiments. No?"

Shaney laughed, guessed he had that coming. Sighed. "Show me," he said. The poet took him by the hand and led him to the staircase, and as they walked up it, she leaned on him. Her surprisingly well-muscled skin pressed through the double layer barriers of their clothes, and he felt each point of fabric-coated contact like fire. He was about to be turned on again. Really? He thought. His stomach rumbled too.

"You got to try the mushroom burgers," she said. "Portobello soaked in raspberry vinegar and garlic."

"Can't wait," said Shaney, lying. When they reached Ron's door, she leaned upon him more insistently and laid a wet kiss on his cheek. "You are such a dear."

More like a wolf, he said.

O she said and laughed at his halfwit retort and took the occasion to squeeze his arm. He leaned into her to show he was not afraid. She kind of moaned. They walked into the room and there on the low bedstand was a small metal pot pipe turned on its side with some white powder spilled around it.

"What is this?" she said, and though he thought she was talking about the substance, he realized her hand was rubbing on his penis through his yielding jeans. He yelped, she laughed. She ran her fingers back and forth back and forth and hummed. He arched his back at first surprised then forward as it commanded him. He swooped in and then stopped. He kicked the door backwards.

"Please?" she said. "It's been a long time, um, with, a, um…"

Before he could suggest "man?" she, smiling like all wickedness, kissed him hard, and he gave back. *Her* mouth was like a regular mouth and he had a vision of its red insides, his tongue found her teeth and licked along the sharp ridges. He saw them as a range of sharp mountains. She laughed low, walked over, and locked the door. She pulled him so close then pushed him onto the bed and climbed onboard laughing softly as he looked up. "There's something about you tonight. It isn't just me." The poet mumbled something that sounded like grace before meals, then reached down and sweetly pulled his stiffened junk from his loosened pants. After a few deft movements and a seraphic dance against him in silky clothes, she went down hungrily on him. If he was surprised, he had no time to register, or object had there been an objection.

"Mmm," she said coming up for air. "You naughty boy, already at it, by the taste of things. Nice. So that's what she tastes like. My Lila May now." But it was her smell, Gwen's, faint and sweet, and surprising, constituted a turn on for the fluid poet. This must be *his* day. And every dog does get one. Syllogism, accent on the final two syllables. He was a dog. Therefore…

As she went to work, his excitement turned into an unexpected fantasy. He thought about Gwendolyn in the room with him, not this salubrious woman or even Lila. The slight guilt he felt served only as a seasoning to his pleasures which were becoming pointed, and fast. His head fell back and he heard the motor cars, the buses, and the airliners roaring outside. He began to cooperate fully with her then, his mind both far away and here, his blood carrying messages he enjoyed but could not understand, all promising a new day dawning bright. His heart leaped out and his lungs began to catch fire, and so it went. So he came. Then she stopped and stood abruptly, slinked up to the door, checking the lock.

"My turn," she said in a high voice and hiked up her little skirt and pulled down her cotton briefs, bringing her fragrance to his face on the bed. She smiled, said something he did not hear. It was a fine idea, he thought, seemed delicious. But as she drew near enough to lick, fate intervened in the form of a jealous lesbian lover.

"Caroline?" said a muted voice outside the door.

"Ssh!" she mimed, finger over her lips, and pulling back the proffered treasure.

"Honey?" said the desperate one, music from another room, the hall actually.

The poet made a sour face and put her hands over her mouth and his. He took the opportunity to move in closer to her. He didn't care. He wanted to make her happy, too. He was hungry for her, strangely hungry.

"I know you're up here and it's breaking my heart," said the woman outside. Shaney supposed it was the hippie girl, but he didn't know for sure. After a silence, a slump.

"Bitch," whispered the poet, pulled away and up her panties. She kissed Shaney with her tongue in his mouth and whispered. "Remember what you owe me," she said.

"Anytime," he said, post-coital, cool, God's gift to women of all ages. She leaped as light-footed as a doe from the bed, pushed the window open and swung out of it and onto a nearby oak branch noiseless. She held her place for a second smiling and dropped like a marmoset, a cat, presumably landing light on her toes. Presumably, she had done this thing before. After a few seconds, Shaney closed the window.

He felt distinctly as if he had large wide furry ears pinned back with pleasure. Smiling, he turned his attention remembering the tipped-over pipe and the white powder around it. He crouched, then stuck his index finger idly into the pile of white dust and brought it to his lips, removing a grain and rolling it around his palette, tasting the bitterness and hoping things might go numb. Not coke, he decided sadly. What the hell, he thought. Stuck his finger in his right nostril and inhaled sharply.

Sledgehammer time.

The left side of his head went numb and he lolled back against the bed dazed. And then Shaney stayed that way for an indeterminate period. He was locked in a psychic position, eyes fixed on the woven rose in his roommate's cheap rug. His heart slowed to a sluggish chug and the world around the carpet flower disappeared. Vast weaves of particles passed through him with impunity like the Northern skies that shimmer in curtains of spectra. He did not see them, he felt the particles passing, and each did to his central nervous system what rubber mallets do to golden cymbals. It was funny but he couldn't quite laugh, and then he dreamed. There were animals on the edges of a plain with red eyes aglow.

He came to after a brief eon twenty minutes with his head in a dense patch of fog. He tried to speak and found no voice, nor could he force his toes to wiggle. He then slipped back. He saw a movie and a dream based on the movie.

Then he came up again and it was all fine, shrugged off like nothing. It occurred to him that at any time in his spell or trip or whatever Ron the owner of the room might have returned to reclaim it, and find him compromised in a lot of the damning situations that had transpired in the meantime.

Shaney bobbed up, remembered that he must take a shower to remove the evidence of his earlier sins and unlocked the door and padded down the hall. A much louder party now reached his ears. He had been gone 45 minutes, and, oddly, part of him wanted to go down to see if there were any cute girls. He smiled wolfishly and waggishly down to his room, locked his own door, and took some hot water naked whilst croaking out a popular song from the latest Man Man CD, a paean to some sort of take on "Engwish Bwudd," though his ability to summon precise lyrics was fuzzed up.

Toweling off, he found immense luxury, the dead cells of his body left exposing roseate flesh up to the world. In his room he carefully selected only cotton garb to swaddle his redeemed self. Now he felt an inner glow he had earned, and he headed down the dusty steps to show it off. What was the drug on the table, would he be called on his neighbors to identify it. There were really no symptoms, or, whatever, effects, but was there ever a drug so strong without side-effects? A miracle like his hand or the ghost. The ghost and Gwen. He was sure taking this all in stride. Maybe that was his sin. A fervent lack of wonder.

The place was reeling and boiling with rapturous words and laughter. One would not expect a diet of mushrooms, quinoa, and assorted veg could produce such Rabelaisian heights and depths, but maybe Shaney had the wrong idea all this time about vegan pantywaists. He was smitten immediately too, by the sight of so many healthy-limbed women gathered around the goat-bearded grad boys who accumulate in university programs. He wandered through a klatsch of film theorists debating the rhetoric of fictive tropes when seen through the prism of queer theory. One of the thinner hair-picking women asked Shaney point blank if he knew why men loved *The Three Stooges*. He said it had something to do with queer theory and she sighed agreeing.

"If at first you don't succeed, suck and suck until you do suck seed," said a familiar voice from behind them doing a creditable Curly. It was roommate Ron. Apparently back from the dead. He said hey man to Shaney as if nothing had happened. Over in the corner was a clutch of real professors, unmistakable in their obliviousness. A professor is someone who talks in someone else's sleep, said the poet. Shaney was pretty sure these lanky gibbous monkeys were not from the science side of things, and, therefore, huge bores at home.

"The secret uniting all religions is the backwards glance," said one parchment-skinned white man with wire-rims and a combover. "They all ask us to retreat from the rung we currently occupy on the evolutionary ladder. Jesus wants us to become as little children, the Buddha thinks we'd be best in an amorphous state before we began desiring, better yet, before we can define our needs, and Mohammed insists on surrender of the ego. Step down, retreat, go back. I yearn for a religion that asks us to step forward into the cosmic grandeur of the mind, to *embrace* progress, everything, not only to humble oneself."

"Dianetics. Ya owe it to yaself," said some wag, chuckling, parodying a once-extant commercial for the cult.

"That's because they don't understand anything paradoxical, fuckwits. Their assbreath logic language is simple declarative crap though the universe moves in great shitbird bursts of oxymoron," whispered Ochocinco hoarsely and leaning on Shaney's ear. "The universe explodes to create in every direction, while humans cling to hunger and horniness. These pissant motherfuckers live day by day to get full professorships publishing poppycocksucking double talk that has fuckall to do with the way people live their buttfucking momentary lives. Squeezed bloody from our mother's twats, wading into air, needing, and producing crap only to end up in this asinine argument. What's wrong with the deity?" He paused. "Howyadoing fucking dogkiller?"

Shaney's skin prickled, his buzz was spent. Shaney stumbled backwards and a beautiful young writing professor with golden shawl tied around her hips caught him.

"Whoa, there. Walk much? Where'd you get those big feet?"

He mumbled, "Longfellows," and said "The better to dance with you?" She nodded dismissal to the flirt. Meanwhile the ogre had disappeared.

He was alone in the crowd. These moments happen. He heard someone laughing and he heard an expression of denial. He saw strangers and they did not move or make space to let him in. He heard gossip and remixed Grizzly Bear songs, the great American band of his time, playing outside by the firepit.

He was about to go thence and give himself up to this music when Louis walked in. There was still time. They caught each other's eyes and he caught something unintended in Louis's.

"Hey stranger," Shaney said. "You know any of these people?"

Louis Lamel laughed. "Yes and so do you. These are the best minds of our time."

"Don't ever change, you. Watch out for Ron, he's bent on some new drug that the kids are all clambering for. Clamoring?"

"Something you made?"

"God, I do have a reputation."

"Would you be pissed off if I told you that that's how you got voted into the house?"

"Yes. So I guess I should bring down a sheet of the compound and pass it out. For a psychedelic, it makes a fine party drug. Besides, I'd like to get that fuckin' asshole professor over there stoned into a hospital somewhere."

"Ochocinco. He's a dick. I'd be careful around him, though. I wouldn't want him not on my side," Lamel said unaware of the blackmail threat the little weasel posed.

Just then some drunk bumped Shaney into the little clutch of professors, a solar system temporarily in the gravitational sway of one Lud Sphlinz a hip sociologist of truly wide erudition. He could cite theories all afternoon, yet somehow managed to avoid quagmires. That most rare of all creatures, the elegant and original pedant.

"You sir," he said.

"Me sir?'"

"I want to discuss the properties of this elixir you are famous for."

"Jesus Christ," Shaney said. "There is no point in pretending anymore is there? I was let into this town on almost every level because I have a drug that makes people entirely happy for hours without much of a hangover and without any anxiety obvious in the experience. That's all."

All three of the shaggy heads lolled a bit at this.

"You want to try some?" he asked. Lamel declined but the professors seemed truly game. Once were hippies. Without a word they all headed up the stairs. Lamel followed in the wake, opening his own door to seek the troubled cat. Shaney made them wait in the hall and they were tittering like children. Inside he pulled down the Oxford English Dictionary that sat so otherwise useless on a brick and board bookcase—its best utility hiding things—and opened to the phrase *ego death*. There were twenty sheets of paper, each soaked with about 50 hits of the compound, which Shaney refused to name except in secret to himself.

He took out two sheets and grabbed a pair of scissors from the shelf. Out in the hall he handed each of the greybeards a square and each was sworn to silence.

"My boy, you now have as much on us as we on you," said Sphlinz.

He sliced up about 30 more squares and handed them over. "Distribute it as you see fit. But give that little dickhead Ochocinco four, please."

They all grinned, happily co-conspiring. Ochocinco apparently was pariah to these brain geeks too. When Shaney saw that gleam in their eyes, he gave them another sheet and a pair of scissors.

"None for you, lad?"

He looked wistfully, but thought only of his trap. "Don't think it works for me anymore," he murmured though he wondered about the incapacitating stuff in Ron's room. Maybe the buzz was back, as a hangover. The drug was stupid numbness first but the aftereffect was happiness.

At the bottom of the stairs a little argument had broken out between some poststructuralist explicators and a New Historian, who seemed all the more antique because he kept insisting that texts could not possibly be insulated from the lives of the men and women who created them. The others looked at his quaint-ass self with patronizing smirks. Shaney was reeling with hunger at this point and actually pushed his way outside to find food, or barring that, mushroom burgers, but discovered only drunks quarreling over which one of them had the bigger course load and the strictest committee and the toughest topic for research papers.

Shaney knew these people too well. Lost in self-pity, moaning about how busy they were any time you asked. Remaining always on the outer edge of real community in real towns, they got respect from each other but none from parents and friends who weren't academics themselves, who laughed when they complained about grading papers. Try roofing. They rarely married outside the cult. Too often, their children turned on them.

The moon was on the horizon, a black margin formed by the wooden fence. It rode up, damaged down one quarter, but seemed prepared to be whole again. Shaney felt some kinship with the cycles and seasons here, so different than Southern California's moon swimming lost in desert and sea surfaces. Here moonglow exploded out on land baked under craven sunlight. He was impressed with these landlocked souls, wondering how they came to terms with such imprisoning glares. They clung to the rare darknesses that came. He decided to try same.

He poured a stiff drink of tequila and let it burn down. There was an old dry-sucked lime and he brought it to his own lips kissing, tasting the residue of his forbears, taking in more germs to do battle with any plague waiting to rise in him from his bite wound. Gone but unforgotten. He patted the paycheck in his pocket, thin paper thick with representation of riches, like the moon headed into fulfillments. He had been a very bad boy. The liquor and the lime encouraged bigger transgressions soon.

When he came back in the back door, she came in through the front. He saw her seeing him, but she was whirled away into a sea of greetings. His girlfriend was the most popular woman in town. It made him proud. He needed to see her, but his way forward was blocked. Ron, in fact acknowledging him, grabbing him, dragging him into the temporary clan. "Dude," said Ron, obviously back from his mind-meld (and suddenly Shaney realized he was no longer buzzing either on the powder or the jolts of alcohol he'd just consumed.)

"Dude," Ron repeated.

"Yo," said Shaney, adhering to customary call and response.

"You hear they added the Squeakies?"

"Ron, there is no part of that sentence I can either understand or make response to at this point in time."

The others laughed.

"The OTR show, man. The one you bought the bracelets for at South by Southwest, you lucky dog. I'll go with you, man, you need a pretty date. I'll be your punk rock arm candy man."

"Ron," said Shaney, "though your generous offer is nearly impossible to resist, may I remind you I'm not going to the OTR show. I bought the band to get into Surly, as you may remember. I love Surly, who are playing on exactly the same night at the same hour... I'm sort of a fan of the Squeakies though, now that I recall."

Another early 1980s girl punk band—there were a few—the band was named either after a Manson follower or the lead singer Janie Jetson's alarmingly pretty but piercing tones, employed during a great and cataclysmic career centered around the "Fuck Me, Fuck You" parody of Lionel Richie, though they went onto a short wacky collaboration with Beat wife-murderer William Burroughs, and then, famously found oblivion from the half-moon hole of a hypodermic needle.

"I'll go to the Squeakies," said Ochocinco who was suddenly in Shaney's face. "I son of a bitch eat pussy," he added.

"You two know each other?" asked the poet, his half-life-lover, who had sidled up to the group simultaneously. Most likely because Ochocinco, though an asshole, had a job as referee for an arts journal which the poet hoped to crack someday.

"He's part of a fuckhole research project I began a few weeks ago," said the professor whose eyes were ablaze at the moment. Shaney thought he knew why, hoped he knew. Hardly anyone ever maintained on a big dose of his shit. Not with dignity. They tended to go down into waves of transporting ecstasy, roll on the ground, haunted by pleasure. Shaney couldn't wait.

Ochocinco said, "I said, I would like to go and I'm pretty sure Mr. Shaney Dicklick would like to take me with him. Buttfuck."

"Going somewhere, honey?" asked Lila May who'd finally pushed her way through throngs of friends to wrap herself lightly around Shaney with a sweet, swift kiss. She didn't see Louis at first.

"Gotta say, the professor here is blowing my surprise to you, honey," said Shaney cooler than one might suppose.

"Ooh, I love blown surprises. Surprise me right now."

"In front of everyone? Well, okay," said Shaney staring the maleficent doctor in the eyes. "For our anniversary I bought us passes to this little festival you guys got goin' here, South by Southwest, heard of it?"

"Somewhere."

"Yeah, well, I thought you might want to join me at the Surly show. Preposition the People are opening."

"Goodie," she said jumping a little. "Anniversary?"

"Wouldn't you rather see OTR, dude?" said Ron looking on in disbelief.

"I'm not buying into this punk rock revival stuff," she said, worming her way deeper into Shaney's heart. "When's the show?"

"Three weeks Friday, my dear," said Shaney now truly emboldened as he watched Ochocinco grabbing his stomach bathed in torrential sweat. Yes, he thought. The megadose is taking effect. Nobody would pin this on him, since his colleagues, the hirsute social scientists, would have to admit their own role in administering it. "We've been together a week, give or take," he said. "One month by then."

"Have to go without me honey," said Lila May softly, shocking Shaney.

"Huh?" he said, vague.

"Full moon," she said. "Don't think you should go either, tell you the truth, my wild love. Not with that bite on your hand and that innocent cast of your mind."

# 15.

Assign the turning-point a time and place. Say it was the vegan barbecue and revel in the irony, werewolves and vegans. You need to begin somewhere when you tell a story somewhat wild, y'all; same with a joke, but the turning point ought to be delivered straight. Fast. A guy walks into the doctor's office. Skip the important details about what he has or checking in with his insurance first, making the appointment. Start at the midpoint, says Aristotle. Another way is to leave out bits in the middle. Aristotle never said this, exaggerate the unexpected right there in the middle. Guy goes to the doctor for a checkup. Doctor says you have to stop masturbating. Guy says why? Because I'm trying to give you a check-up.

At that precise moment in the party Louis appeared to her.

Lila May Wulfhardt whose eyes were cold blue rimmed with dark almost black to differentiate it from the clear white—no one stared long into her eyes without sacrificing portions of will. How she must have manipulated her parents like those *Children of the Damned* glaring heat and ice into the air and after crossing space to sink weak earth eyes. I was smitten so long ago. I was merely ruined for other women forever, that's all.

"Hi," Louis Lamel said.

Her smile lines melted then resumed a half-look of remembrance acknowledging everything at once, including the utter desolation of love lost. Because big Austin is a small town after all they were bound to meet.

"Hey is what the kids say. Hey. You're here," she murmured. "It's so nice to see you here. How is it that you are here with me and here?" She touched his arm softly.

"I live *here*," Lamel said. "Didn't you know? Didn't my illustrious housemate your new flame mention me?" He smiled trying for the right voice, urging the right look from haunted eyes.

"Wait," said Shaney, suddenly there. "You two are friends. You know each other, let me guess?"

"Acquaintances," Louis said, shrugging. "Or whatever."

"Don't, darling," said Lila May turning to John Shaney esquire. "We were an item back in the day, John. And we're still good friends. I hope."

"Still good friends," Louis echoed.

"Oh," said Shaney, balancing jealousy against a bad conscience, that included his earlier semi-incestuous delight, not to mention his very recent blow job.

Her eyes made a sad smile and asked Louis to show her where and how vegetarian hamburgers were grilled outside. Vegan, Louis reminded. Shaney was about to interrupt when she squeezed his hand and sent him a psychic blow that backed him off. Simultaneously all conversation in the room stopped. He stepped back and was seized upon by one of the hoary professors.

"You know her?" asked the aging academic.

"My girlfriend," said John.

"Her father is your boss then," said another blunt prof, downwind from the situation. "Nice."

Seemed like Shaney's personal bio was hive knowledge, which might have made him mad if he wasn't wondering at the same time what Louis Lamel was up to with his lady love in the outback.

"Nazis, you know," said one of the oaf-profs.

"Nonsense," said the first, older colleague. "Big donor to the humanities as well as the sciences. More liberal than a rhesus monkey, I hear."

"No not him," said dorkus professoricus. "The grandparents, German SS captured in Africa, scientists, Jew-haters, tried to prove the link between North African blacks and the apes was more direct, pop Darwinism with racist agenda, mandated by *der Fuerher*. Escaped from Texas POW camps. Brought in by the CIA and obsessed with foxes or something, marmosets, badgers, whatnot."

"Wolves," said Shaney. "Everybody knows it is wolves."

"Well, of course, young man, of course wolves," said the first scientist. "Werewolves, because they are Wulfhardt and this is Texas. If you hang with that family and you want to keep your job, you better get interested in werewolves too."

"Because this is Texas," said his chum, whom Shaney realized was tripping, staring upon the colors of his own subtle tweed coat.

These guys are fucking crazy and I gave them drugs, he thought.

Meanwhile out on the patio with Lila May, who held a glass of red wine in her hands and draped herself along the backyard fence like Guinevere in the royal court of Arthur, Louis was making conversation.

"Guy walks into a bar with a piece of pavement under his arm. Bartender says want a drink?" said Louis.

"Yeah and one for the road," she said, her shoulders miming laughter. "How are you, really?"

"The same, no improvement."

"I had no idea," she said. "About you living here. He and I meet here. Sleep. Here."

"I could sense you. Let's just say, if you drove by in a car, I would sense you. So yes, but what was I supposed to do, move? You can't believe what I went through to get the room in the first place. Murder, actually."

"Oh," she said. "That was you?"

"Funny and intuitive. But is it me?"

"I don't know, Old Flame," she said. She never believed him, his delusion, her daddy.

"I swear I want to die. I don't know what stays my hand," he said.

"I don't want you to," she said. "Does that help? For what it's worth I still love you."


"You ever wonder about that fucking five-pointed star you see everywhere?" asked the older of the two professors, bearing down on Shaney. "On all the shops downtown."

"Now, now, Claude," said the bearded one.

"Oh hush up, Stanley. Like it's some big secret."

"The Lone Star," said Shaney. "Texas. Everywhere."

"I'm serious. You ever wonder what the Lone Star is all about?" continued the older of the two. "Wondered since it was *so many* stars one can see above the non-fruited plains of this expansive desert country. Why one star, lone among the myriad."

"Because you stood alone against Mexico?"

"That's one guess. Some people say it was the so-called long expedition of 1819, others say, as you just did, it expressed the desire to achieve independence from Mexico's Two-Star Flag, though I've never been able to find that one in any real historical account. Conversely, some people believe it expresses the wishes of the people to be included in the newly forming republic, America, which one hundred years later, they were quite happy to see dissolved. Confederates, remember? Though not obstinately so, Sam Houston didn't want to join."

"Back to the star, Claude."

"It's not politics, or it's identity politics. It's real intention is a declaration. The star on every store says, I am human, not a shapeshifter. Do business with me."

"It's more like *L'homme* star, you mean," said Claude Sorkazy. "I am a man, it says, a Texas Man. Decidedly not a manwolf. The French wolf down from the Cajun country that most affected the shopkeepers here all the way up to the mid 20th century. The *Loup Garou* come down from Acadia and Maine to Louisiana along the Mississippi river with the trappers and in galleons, later on motorcycles spreading here with the open range of vulnerable cows and cowboys. And then the Mexican Wolf came up too. The shapechangers came from everywhere and mingled with the men and women here. The star was demarcation," he said.

"Chupacabra," said Shaney.

"Very good, lad. So they, the shopkeepers who didn't want to let them in, had to build themselves a warning system, like blood over the lintel for the Angel of Death."

"That's just silly," said Stanley Brandled, professor of semantics.

"But the Lone Star is ultimately a mystery. It's one of those well-quoted ideas that has no basis in fact, that has no meaning, like "Play it again, Sam," in Casablanca, which nobody says. I'd like to get out of these wet clothes and into a dry martini. No one ever found a source for that, either. We all agree on its vague poetic truth, goddammit. Lone Star shining above."

"Which," said the semantics professor. "Is still the most important kind of truth."

"No," said Shaney, "science is."

Both of the professors laughed. "They're so cute when they get their first lab coats."


"And what about that fucking guy?" Louis outside with Lila said, pointing to Shaney whose bobbling head could be seen through the foggy kitchen window. His heart was beating hard as always around her. Does he love you?"

"That part doesn't matter so much and you know it. Like Jane says, I want them if they want me. Ohmigod! Were you in the club?" asked Lila May.

"That drummer leered at you."

"That was enough?" she asked.

"Apparently. *He* had a hair trigger where you are involved. Listen, I'll leave."

"I didn't think the bond was still that strong," she said.

"Delicately put. That drummer leered at you. *He* saw it somehow. That's all it took."

"Is there more I don't know about *him*?"

"I can make *him* leave town, if you want. Though that would contradict the whole Keep Austin Weird movement, wouldn't it?" Louis laughed one sharp bark.

"What about my father? He promised to help you, I mean, *him*."

"Can we not talk about it? No."

They both knew what Lila's father was also capable of.

Shaney was still framed in the window, his head cocked back and laughing.

"You have to admit he's cute," said Lila.

"I don't have to admit anything. He's a way out, though. Maybe he'll help your papa. He'll help me get rid of *him*. That's what you are thinking?"

She sighed. "Such a lot of pronouns. He, she, it. Stay," she said.

"If I could, I'd never budge from your side."

"I'm… right now I want you then. Stay."

"That does it," he said. "Gotta go."

"God damn you, too," Lila May said, tears jeweling eyelashes. She grabbed Louis who got drawn into a whirlpool of an embrace that made him shudder and need to go somewhere else.


"I thought being a professor meant you embraced that sort of thing."

"What sort of thing, Mr. Shaney?"

"Truth."

"Truth," said Brandled, "is bullshit negotiable. Not science. It really means that which is hidden and then revealed. Not some flaming standard. Absolute Platonic Truth," he intoned. "Logic isn't truth, it's just the supposed path to a fact. That's absolute, facticity, but even then, not very concrete and true. By that T word most people mean mathematic truth something by and large ignored by the public. Math observations are frequently repressed. Tell me, boy. What was the first year of the new millennium we not so long ago celebrated? What year did the parties take place?"

Shaney got it, "Okay, 2000, though that was really not the last year of the old millennium. Mathematically speaking. It should have been 2001."

"Bingo," said the prof. "And the first day of the week is mathematically Sunday, not Monday, and the Earth revolves, the sun never rises. Yet we go to work on Monday and watch sunsets, never earthflops. Science is an insular world, most human don't experience it, cos it's boring to folks."

"Fuck mathematics," said Brandled, who waddled away from the little circle, allowing Ochocinco an opening. He begged a momentary indulgence, and buttonholed Shaney who obviously did not welcome the intrusion. Super-stoned Ochocinco seemed on his last legs. The angry fix would send him out into the howling streets soon.

"I like the idea. Camouflage mindfuck. You know, that was not the disease speaking."

"What the fuck *are* you talking about?" said Shaney. "With all due respect."

"I also like the idea of drug inscribed on paper, so we fly into the universe of psychedelia on a genre, a purer artifice. Each drug is a genre. Your barbiturates and opiates are tragedy, fall, as are your stimulants like speed and cocaine a kind of comedy, rise. This stuff is a romance novel, precursor of epic poetry."

"I wish I could speak nonsense so eloquently," said Shaney. "And look at you, all not using the signature pottymouth?"

"Shut your fucking mouth, dog-killer," said Ochocinco loud enough to stop banter around him. "You will meet me at the Surly show and take me into it. I've always wanted to go to South by Southwest and my meager professorial earnings preclude it. My town, you know, I was born here and yet I'm too poor to enjoy its best-known tourist experience. You'll take me. Then we'll start negotiating. I think you tried to poison me tonight, but, you must know that, like Mithradates, I live on a steady diet of poison."

"Name your poison then, obscure Greek king, and shut up," said Shaney through clenched teeth. He could see Lila May alone on the moon-painted patio outside.

"Surly night is the name of the price."

"So a date is what you want, big fella?"

"Fuck you if you don't come. There is video." He turned and left abruptly, past the real Texan, who shrugged and mouthed the word "Asshole" plain as speech.

The other two profs closed ranks. "There are unsavory people all around this town, you know. His reputation for weirdness is earned."

"We were interrupted," said Shaney breathing hard but calming fast. "What is the Lone Star and what does it stand for? Something in French?"

"Italian and English and Spanish."

"The Lone Star, the one you see everywhere you go? A warning to the wolves?"

"No, foolish boy. Wolves can't read. It's a pentagram, put there to designate the presence of men, not monsters."


She came in the back door and made a beeline for the front. Shaney excused himself and planned a neat intervention.

"At last alone?" she said, with something in her eyes perhaps red from smoking dope or the fire, she hugged him. "Mmm-hmm, you smell good."

Shaney straightened with a sharp pang of guilty fear and then remembered. "I came home stinky from work and got in a long shower. Got something else too."

"Is this a dirty joke?"

"No. I got a fat paycheck from your father. I'm already spending it. Find us a little cottage, pick out the cars we'll drive. Cute together cars, like a Beemer and a, a, another Beemer, huh?"

"My, imaginative."

He felt weird, then, remembering what kind of money she came from. The kind that made it easy for her father to give him a fat paycheck almost on a whim.

"Don't listen to me," she said. "I love it when you dream out loud. But I'd love it even more if we were dreaming together. This party…"

"Where were you going?" he said.

"Oh, honey, not leaving. I just want to get a sweater from the car. But, well, maybe, we can take a turn through the crowd."

"A royal processional."

"Then sneak upstairs and lock the door." She had a touch of evil in her thinking. Shaney was fine with that.

At the door they ran into Texas, (me, folks) plucking and singing that Jimmie Dale Gilmore song, you know, the one about Dallas being a death wish in a rich man's eyes.

"Ma'am," I said tipping my big hat.

"Oh, John," she said (meaning me). "At least go talk to my father. Or his secretary. She liked you. Please. They want you back."

"Yes, ma'am. If it makes you happy."

"I've told you a million times, my happiness is a lost cause, long as I see the way you get treated in this town."

"But I'm from your town, if'n you remember."

She bent over and kissed Texas on the cheek. He looked guilty but I felt temporarily happy. Shaney believed he had wandered into a ritual harder to understand than the Catholic mass in Latin. He never questioned the kiss, but turned and asked if the asshole professor had left.

"He was pretty fucked up," said Texas to Shaney. "You do that?"

"Wish I could take credit, but he was born that way."

Lila May looked tired and sad. "I'm going to get my sweater," she said directly to Shaney. "Wait here. John, tell him about the time we met at the zoo."

They watched her swish her way down the path. "You know who Nasrudin is?" John asked Shaney, eyes wide.

Shaney said no.

"Don't matter. One day Nasrudin was walking down the street when a bunch of soldiers came up behind him. He got scared and ran into a graveyard and jumped into an open grave to hide. The soldiers got worried'n followed him. They found him there all huddled in the dust and one of them said, what're you doin? Nasrudin said, a better question is this, pointin' at the fella, Why are you there and why'm I here?"

Then laughing raucously which ended in a phlegmy smoker's cough.

Lila May returned and was about to re-enter the party when her cellphone began buzzing like lashed-together bumblebees. She picked it up and turned on a light to read the text, inscribed in light. "Oh, no."

"What?" said Shaney, thinking only of a bedroom visit cancelled. Believe it or not he was very horny. Reluctantly she showed it to him. "Mother sick. Come home."

"Mother dying," she said.

"What?'" said Shaney now surrounded by all the dark universe. "What do you mean. I just saw, I mean your mother, at dinner the other night."

"I never told you but my mother is sick, she has a rare form of something hits her hard sometimes. Doctors think she's faking it and sometimes she just drinks herself into and way past stuportown. Sometimes she disappears. My father used to think she had a lover," she laughed, slow, sad. "Sugar, I have to go."

Shaney was turmoil inside. "I'll go with you."

"No. Why would you do that? I'll call you if I need you. My mother has her own wing at home. It's almost nice, like a hospital. But it's a family thing, a tribe, a pack."

Part of him was offended. They were already walking out to her car.

"Night Lila. Say hey to Gwen," said John from behind.

"Sure will, honey," she said over her shoulder then turned to Shaney. "You're a darling to offer and I'm an inconsiderate bitch to refuse," she said. "But this'll blow over. Keep warm thoughts about me and I'll sneak into your sheets when you wake up, I betcha."

"It's a nice fantasy," Shaney said, "but I won't be able to sleep now."

"Oh sure you will, surrounded by the voices of your party friends and right into dreams about me."

"I'll worry about your mother," said Shaney, his dark heart beating.

"I'll tell her you said that," she said. "It'll help her get better right away."

# 16.

Monday, thought-tormented, Shaney drove up to Wulfhardt—back to work. The weekend went without Lila returning. He had wanted her. Also, he worried her mother who was sick might say something in feverish delirium. So many tribulations. What good things were there to think about? I think therefore I am in trouble, he thought.

Saturday and Sunday had careened downhill from Friday's buzzy rush. Forlorn then wretched then spent. He tried to remember good stuff like money, for instance. He had graduated into worldly success without trying, or, actually, graduating. But it wasn't as comforting as he imagined. And his girlfriend? Beautiful but gone missing, missed. And worse he could hardly remember her without guilt bombs going off about his outrageous breach. Make it worse? Shaney couldn't stop thinking about how good

Gwen was, sex on the patch of park land, his girlfriend's mother; his boss's wife. Such spontaneity must create wakes of destruction, he supposed, yet he wanted her again with succulents.

And then, the remote complications, the suspicious deaths that might come home to roost on him like ghost chickens. He kinda believed in karma. Though he hadn't done any of them there murders, had he? But then. The dog and Ochocinco with his evidence of crime against dogkind. Self defense most foul. Around and around he went, changing moods like a jukebox in a home for the manic depressive.

He tried to stop thought by concentrating on the driving Monday morning. And then, just before the crest of the hill, the first part of The Discovery came to him.

Finding it when his mind went blank. The telescope shows hidden stars. The obviousness, it felt like, duh.

Can Something Transfigure into Something Else, provoked by times and, hah, phases of the moon? Patterns of migrationlike. Seasonal styampedes. Cicadas. On the job, he looked at the science. What had come before? He spent two more and then three weekdays girlfriendless, though she texted with mother updates and requests for patience, but he didn't really care. The right path had definitely opened. Asked a microbiologist down the hall whether anything in the cellular world died and then came back to life altered, or, produced asexual offspring after death, like a Phoenix from ashes. Just wondering, he said. The microbiologist laughed and said no. Though, he said, now that I think of it, there was a widespread belief that certain cells, called enveloped viruses, like furious rabies, insert themselves into host cells which then die but come back to produce the virus particles from within the envelope, becoming, I suppose, he said, like a zombie or a ghost, come back from what? Death? Undeath?

"Furious rabies," said Shaney with dull surprise.

"My field of specialty investigation in college actually. Makes people hydrophobic, weirdly enough; also makes people do violent things."

"Like a wolf," muttered Shaney. "Afraid of water?"

"Exactly," said the professor looking like he had been tricked into an admission.

Then another thing; the newspaper story.

It came with the packet Lionel promised—a lot of formulas with bios of researchers. Datelined Miami. The headline was eloquent old journalism: "Witness says naked attacker ate man's face." There was no byline, but on this pre-apocalypse day of Our Lord, Tuesday May 2, 2012, the copy in a thrilling one sentence paragraph read: "THE ASSOCIATED PRESS: A witness says a naked man chewing on the face of another naked man on a downtown highway ramp kept eating and growled at a police officer who fatally shot him to make him stop."

The story continued: "A bicyclist named Larry Vega had chanced upon the scene and told a television station that told the newspaper reporter, 'The guy was like, tearing him to pieces with his mouth, so I told him, "Get off,"' Vega said. 'The guy was just eating the other guy away, like, ripping his skin.'"

The news story sent Shaney to the internet, which sent him to a rash of other reports cojoined to speculations, finally leading to a drug which Shaney had heard of somewhere where?—bath salts. A college corridor, lunch at a little Mexican café. Where? What seemed most incongruously surreal about that was his mother, Shaney's mother, he kept thinking, when she wanted to say bullshit, often said, "bath salts," as euphemism. Now he remembered Dean Beveritch's office, bath salts, and why he thought about his mother then. She also bathed in it, too, which further confused the boy and dizzied the man. The basilisk was made of basalt. He spent an afternoon in his office in the gathering weirdness of his girlfriend worries trying to track down the exact formula of bath salts, which turned out to be just another designer variation on the now boring conjunction of amphetamines and mescaline. Been there, done that.

Each day after the first revelation, the drugs and the rabies, he was alone working and thus lost all other worries. She came back. She wanted him to wait for her at home while she went out to an opening. Wait in bed, she said. He said fine. He occasionally worried that Gwen, sick and fevered, might let slip a mumble or two on their roadside transgression, but that faded to background too. Meanwhile, Lila May kept sending him assertions of faith, hope, and love by texts. But the strongest of these was love. She came home and then she went out, but meanwhile he was onto some sort of phantasm.

In this way, possessed by the work and half-abandoned by his girl, two weeks passed. Shaney was a model employee. His appetites, so strong a few days ago, subsided, though his energy did not. He barely slept, and rarely came home or to Lila's, before ten at night.

He plodded methodically through the literature, then came another on-the-way-to-work revelation. He had become obsessed (without hardly thinking) with the cycles of nature. He did not know why. Tides, and the fact that nobody really understands why they happen. Things like water, which feeds the plants that become grapes that supply the raw materials for wine, that left out over time becomes vinegar; that makes itself after long passages of time (the avenger) back into water. Then he began thinking about cycles in the mind, such as those posed by neuron-blockers and additives like his drugs, de Bruijn cycles for neural decoding and synaptic vesicle cycles and that led him, as he drove back thinking mildly about his mom-and-daughter lovers, to the idea of peptide cycles as used by body builders in the illegal world of dosing. All of these things are not connected, he thought, unthinkingly. But it felt like they were and his mind was the glue—some synaptic logic only his mind knew. Maybe he was fighting a bug, he thought. There was something else and he heard himself give a giant sniffle, wet and trailing phlegm that he swallowed, creating a horrible cycle within, something starting up the ecosystem, something alive. But his mind began playing on a theme and before he knew it he had driven past his offramp but arrived at a remote idea of how he could possibly induce werewolfism in a lab rat, or, maybe better, a stray dog. He laughed at his own furiously rabid chain of thought. Not bwahaha, but aha!

Next day, he again drove past the turnoff for Werewolf, Texas as he always called it now. It was a Eureka this time. Exchange could be made by the viruses that are, after all, considered to be animal, vegetable, or something else. The virii die and come back as a ghost of themselves. Vinegar to water to wine. Man to wolf to man, which, after all, must be on the evolutionary chain to this now.

He turned the car around, wended his way back to the lab, and practically jumped out while it was rolling, shirt hanging out. He went straight to his office, opened his computer, started writing down notes. He could barely keep up with his own mental dictation of (as if from above) the cause of the chain of being to being metamorphosis on a cellular level. He made a few mistakes but couldn't stop. Then he opened into the internet to type an equation onto a website that remembered to see if his work might be anticipated elsewhere. Everything the cloud suggested was inane drivel compared to his inspiration.

"Furious rabies," he said out loud and then chuckled as a whole new slew of mathematical ideas began unspooling. The computer gave little beepy sounds, which he thought might be the world of science contacting him with congratulations, as he unlocked with whirling fingers the tumblers of IT. But it wasn't applause accompanying his end run to fame, it was an email from the boss with links to web sites that depicted human transformations—it was the story of the face-eating man, coming back to him from the stupid boss, his lover's husband, his girlfriend's daddy. It was fucking irritating. The email contained more, including more faux literary drivel including a Wikipedia entry on the Beast of Gevaudan. He knew the truth, he was pretty sure, and it wasn't legend and it wasn't drugs. He thought about germs then circled back to his big three-part revelation.

He called the boss to get an appointment. He got a machine that seemed to be phasing in and out like psychedelic music. He left a message. Then he worried. *I think I have the answer, though the question is swirling away.*

He went numbly to the breakroom for coffee and stale bagel, but there was a loaf of brioche on a cutting board with a little sign that read: *Eat Me*. Okay, he thought, *with fine normalcies to guide me, I just might make it with a colliding pool table of ideas inside.*

His skin was flush, and he began to realize not with excitement. He soon had to admit he was running a low grade temperature, though no other real flu symptoms. Lila May had still not returned calls today and he was half-sure of the worst from her department. The work at hand, the poetry of his new idea was pressing him yet he wanted her company. No he didn't. Yes he did. Maybe he could send flowers to Lila's mother and maybe that would flush the daughter out.

He went home and found her not in his bed, and his flu or whatever came on like a potent drug in gangbuster mode. His temperature spiked and he was trembling when he finally went between the sheets.

The next day dawned on him headachy and joint raw, but with energy back. The Idea trumped the influenza. For some odd reason peace had been made with the stupid cat who once hated him—it now occupied the foot of *his* bed. He tried to push it off, but the cat looked at him with devotion and hunkered down. Taking three aspirin, a bottle of orange juice, and a little food, enough to coat his stomach, he drove up the hill wishing only to discuss the breakthrough with Wulfhardt. He pulled over at one point, walked around the rear of the car and vomited. His motivation remained strong though. Back into the car with the moon hanging above the morning blue he drove wicked far to the lab.

It killed him not to have anyone with whom he might share his discovery. He wasn't sure. Like a musician who invents a melody and then wonders if he hadn't stolen it, the Idea seemed to belong to the wide world first. He began to feel alone and then more alone. As he wandered the blank halls past door after door of closed labs he wished for some sign or clue as to what actually went on in this facility. Lacking imagination, he imagined everybody else was doing nothing too. All living high on the promise shown in classrooms long ago, from whence they were harvested as was he.

He went back into the lab and turned on his computer. The local area network with its usual *esprit de corps* announcements, birthday lunch for Selma in personnel and another silver ring found by the machinists' locker room. I have a bag of avocados in the break room, help yourself. It said that Mr. W. wouldn't be in today and that our prayers and best wishes should go out to his wife and daughter. A card is coming around, it said. No more news than that. The halls beckoned him out.

Once wandering, he sought Wulfhardt's secretary and found she had left her desk but could be found "at lunch on campus," a note said, and went. The breakroom was a clamoring locus of unrest. A number of people were gathered and chattering with curiosity over why there were so many police asking questions. Everybody got quiet when Shaney walked in. Conversation stopped dead after his throat-clearing query about the boss and scheduling some time was met with frank frosted murmurs all around.

"Mr. Wulfhardt is still, um, busy at the hospital," said the secretary.

Shaney caved and said, "I'm being ridiculous. I just hoped things had gotten better, what with all the…"

He didn't finish because he was interrupted by a stubby researcher in a greasy lab coat who asked what he thought about the police.

"Me?" said Shaney. "Why does my opinion on police matter?"

"I just thought you being the focus of this attention. I mean, I'm just wondering what it is they want to know about you."

"Yeah," said another labcoat. "What gives?" The room was torn between embarrassment and curiosity and reluctantly leaned forward.

"Listen" said Shaney. "I'm sure I don't know what you're talking about. Perhaps there's some mistake. Police?"

"Aw come on," said one portly colleague.

"This seems a little violating," said Shaney, stumbling backwards. "What did the cops say?"

Wulfie's secretary intervened, saying it was likely some kind of security matter that Mr. W. had initiated. Happened all the time. The others clammed up and Shaney was not so much mollified as caught up in a web of weirdness.

Just then a distant howl.

"Yay," said the secretary. "The roach coach is here."

"'Bout time, said the porcine inquisitor. "Let us know when you don't feel violated." Everybody laughed, surging out as a herd, re-addressing their regular debate over the comparative value of chili verde vs. carnitas. Even though the cafeteria was great, a lunch truck was the event of the season at Wulfie Labs.

One pretty girl asked Shaney if he wanted to join them. "It's surprisingly good, the *coche de la cucaracha*," she giggled and winked and ran.

He walked to his own lab and was immediately re-swallowed up in the Idea. It could work with some work he thought and brought open his computer and started playing with the terms doing math while compiling a list of tools and ingredients he might need. And a lab rat, he thought, or a dog. A dog would make more sense. He wrote an email wondering if experimentation on dogs was ethically permitted and under what parameters he might be allowed to procure, house, and inject one in the name of the Idea. He made that into a joke, he thought, though emails are so often emotionless and irony-proof like Northern Californians and 1970s feminists.

"You should be ashamed," said Lila May from over his shoulder.

He jumped. "Jesus," he said, shaking as she apologized and moved in to kiss him, her man of shame. She held a single rose.

"Why?" he said. "I mean, ashamed for what?"

"Sending roses to my mother long before you even consider sending them to me," she said. "You darling man."

He winced and found a way to gracefully erase, he thought, the message he was composing, though instead he sent it.

"Fan mail from some flounder?" she asked, clearly well versed in the Rocky and Bullwinkle universe. Another plus. "Listen, honey," she said, "I can only stay a few minutes, and I'm so sorry I haven't answered messages today. We've all been so worried. Mother was bit by a feral cat, the doctors think, but I think it was just drinking this time, my mother's collapse but with her, um, condition it's impossible to know. Anything under the sun will set her off."

"Or the moon?" said Shaney.

"I can see you're already too close to Daddy," she said.

"He's very generous. I don't know…"

"Don't, darling. You have no idea where he's leading you. But listen. What I am about to ask you must swear to do."

"We're already going steady," he said.

"Thought that was established. You aren't cheating already are you?" she said, striking him with the rose. He winced. Heavy hammers fell inside.

"I thought not," she said and took his hand and led it through space to her breast. "Swear to me you will not leave your house this weekend—

Thursday, Friday, Saturday, Sunday to be safe. Swear on my heart," she said and pulled him close to her and began rubbing up and down on him. He took over. She reached down and found him, grasping the whole package through his thin pants. She was all over his mouth with her mouth and her other hand coaxed him up through the thin fabric of his khaki work slacks. "Promise me and then lock the door," she said.

He went for the hall door, she went for the bathroom door, popped it open, hopped up on its wide counter and hitched herself forward so access was unimpeded. Indeed it was perfect and he slid aside her white cotton and she gasped because he was already all the way in her. And she was already far too excited to allow any holding back and though he hoped they could come together it wasn't like he was going to slow down or hold back either. And then he thought about *her*.

You know. Her. Lying on the iceplant by the road giving it up.

Gwen.

Rotten that he was thinking about this girl's mother at this moment. Despicable. It was a hard turn on too. He wanted to call her name, Gwen. He felt his lips form the word as he looked at Lila May's beautiful face. He moved in close so as not to see. The daughter did not smell the same as the mother. He could vividly remember Gwen and how she tasted, too. For some reason Lila caught fire at that moment then and then it all came and went. Ah. He was a melted pool. The sweat that formed in patterns on their skin looked silvery in the harsh bathroom light. She was exhaling like a runner and looked flagged if not destroyed by the contact. He was clear now, guilty but sure of himself.

He loved her.

Gwen, that is.

It wasn't even alarming though it was going to be a hard thing to pull off. Perhaps the best idea was maintain as is until… what?

Lila May was telling him how much she missed him while she hopped down, pulling up her pretty panties in one smooth move. She kissed him and said something indistinguishable from a moan. But she was talking, he realized. "Promise me not to go out on Thursday or Friday night. The concert, don't go, or Saturday. The third day's often the worst. The concert, don't go," she said repetitive. "Make yourself safe."

"What? The cops were here asking questions about me," he said, hoping to change the subject. The liaison with Ochocinco, he had an idea. He had had another Idea.

"I know, dear. The police. It was about that Sunday, that day when you came over. Something happened. But you were with me. They came to us too."

Shaney was puzzled. "Surely you mean Saturday," he said, thinking about Uncle John.

"No," she said, "they were quite clear. It happened Sunday night, an incident, they said it was too terrible to discuss. Daddy said you dined with us. And don't call me Shirley. I said, you drove home early in the evening. Wasn't it early early? Daddy told them you were alright. That made them happy, I think."

"Alright?"

"Daddy likes you. 'Alright' means golden. By the by, when my momma opened her eyes and saw your flowers, she started crying. You lovely lovely man."

"She'll get better, then?" he asked.

"All because of you," she said. "I gotta go, sugar. Promise me you won't go."

"Why? You know I'm not out with anybody…"

"Except that horrid man nobody likes. But that's not the point, who. Please ask your roommate."

"Your ex," said Shaney.

"He'll maybe protect you, if you need it, my ex. Best thing though is not to need it. Stay home. Lock the doors. Sometimes that actually helps."

"Helps what?"

"Ward off this whole Austin curse or whatever."

"Aw-woo," said Shaney, though the sound seemed to grow resonant and huge inside him. He stood straight just as she moved in to hug and kiss him, awkward. She backed away. "Sugar, you're burning up!"

"It's nothing," he said. "And it was all about you."

She took his hand then and curiously looked where he had been bitten by the now dead dog. "You're sick. If you don't go home, I'll go tell Daddy's secretary to send you. I repeat. You're burning up."

"I say it's you, my lamb."

"Your what? Good God, have I been compared to livestock? Go home, stay there, lovely man."

She backed out and he felt his own forehead, perhaps she was right, he could work at home after sending in this email—it was gone. Fuck. And he almost jumped when his laptop pinged to let him know some message had come in, but then winced hard when he saw the email was from Ochocinco. Sometimes it was difficult to maintain faith in a universe of random happenstance, shitty things all seemed to be connected.

"Don't forget our date," it read. "Friday night a half hour early. I want to get right up on the stage to see them. We'll buzz past the line with your passes, my friend. And we can discuss your future then. See below."

Beneath it in a box was an email video, black on grey. He clicked the arrow and from the amorphous shapes emerged two shadowy creatures, one upright, one on all fours. The camera zoomed in on the face of the hominid. It was him. The dog's presence was more like a black-stranded cloud surging around, a wave of dirty fog. He fell back and the dog, representing penumbrous doom, filled in the space. What happened next was going to be the final blow, but the video ended.

The computer pinged again. "We know how this will play on YouTube. To the end, gruesome." The computer played the Kinks' "Death of a Clown." Shaney felt haunted.

He tried miserably to get back to his Idea. His fever percolated through the day and was still radiating when he got into his car to go home. He turned on the radio and drove, though. He needed to take the shortcut and the radio began telling him about the winding stairs that led to the surface of the sour plain of existence known as Austin where Vestal Virgins danced. And how in this darkling plain gems emerged That is, busy elves, pointed of ear and full of fear and pointed values, too, like integers and the musical loci brought them to the surface.

Somebody phoned in and asked what would be the best jewel amongst the assembled crown and, unlikeliest of all, the voice from the radio of solemn sleep said, OTR, but stay on the road and Shaney swerved off the shoulder and the caller asked him if he was crazy. The best show would be overshadowed by the full moon and all the wolfen bands that would play out in the park, beginning with a reconstituted Steppenwolf lineup, then the Howlin' Wolf Tribute Band followed by Peter Wolf and Wolf Parade. Shaney found himself bouncing on the shoulder again.

"You must go see Surly, whose best song, "Wolf Whistle," was dedicated to Mozart."

"There was a lot of music and then there was Mozart, then there was a lot of music and there was the Beatles," said the caller who was called Ochocinco. "Fuckin' A," he added laughing, fuck, shit, cunt.

"I don't like the Beatles," said the other voice.

Then Shaney was home and stumbled in the door and found his room where the cat lay on his bed and barely moved when he turned back the sheets and collapsed. Sailing into the bounding night.

# 17.

He got up once on Thursday, all morning in bed, and made his way into the kitchen, which was empty. He was warm last night and he was cold and at one point he was drenched and felt better for an hour. He knew he smelled sour and was hungry and thirsty. His hands shook from weakness and his legs were rubbery. He tried to eat, but fell over leaning for the milk. He stumbled back into bed rather quickly. Afraid. Somewhere in there he got scared about not waking up, so he made himself rise. He went out into the living room afternoon and saw the poet sitting there, crying. She looked up and asked if he was okay.

"I don't think so," said Shaney and almost fell over reaching for the newspaper. "What about you?"

Next thing he knew she had him in his car. She said, I heard a joke about a circus fire. It was intense, she said.

He laughed politely.

"Okay, now I know you're sick."

"Where we going?" asked Shaney. "Why were you crying?"

"I'm a poet. I always think I'm going to die. I'm taking you to Student Health. You're still enrolled, I checked online. It'll be free."

"I have money," said Shaney.

"How nice for you," she said. "What do you have?"

"Besides money? Rabies?" he asked the world. "Furious rabies. Chupacabra."

"The bats," she said. "I knew it, they're everywhere. Sooner or later somebody will die. Like me."

"Lived here three months, haven't met one bat yet," he said, remembering the night and the swarm over the moon like a Universal horror film.

"Then how?" she asked.

He held up his hand and it made him dizzy as he was about to explain the anomaly of his wound, then he pointed over to the side of the road. The world spun for every action there is a reaction, simply. He lurched the arm into a broader gesture. She got it, parked suddenly and as he pushed himself out the door and began heaving nothing, she was already there somehow with her arms around him, tenderly.

Meanwhile, near the University, Lila May was wrapping up her day visit with her mother. The sun angled into the yellowy room, casting a necrotic tinge into the corner behind the bed. Its aura transmuted her beautiful mother into a strange kind of morbid sage. Lila May broached the subject of the flowers Shaney sent. He loves me, her mother said. He loves my role in the family doom, she muttered, though he doesn't get it yet. There you go again, Lila said. Why doom? Why must everything trend to sad endings? The universe may be winding down, but some things improve. Homely girls like me turn into small wonders, Lila laughed, and children practicing scales burst into song. Her mother smiled and said yes, of course.

Lila caught a glimpse of herself in the open bathroom window framed in black shade. She looked good in tragedy, which this might become but was not yet, she reminded herself. Outside the hospital room it was green, billowing, blossoming, windblown upwards green with brown birds flying short weaving arcs in and out of foliage, the trees, deciduous, full of water unlike the surrounding desert lands. As she cocked her ear to hear Mama murmuring, her mother distinctly said that John Shaney was the love of her life. Lila May wanted to know what was more random, the arcing birds or the meandering thoughts of her drunken visionary mother.

She left and stepped outside. Little yellow flowers seemed to lean towards each other huddled and closing by the setting sun outside in the wind. The random and the willed, thought Lila.


At the other end of this same medical complex, Shaney was being led into the student health reception room looking like Death's son-in-law.

Sybil Fracturite, the nurse, took one look at him and decided to intervene. This person might be bearing some student-ghetto-bred plague, and ought to be isolated before he turned into monstrous blood-splattering man like in that book about African membrane-devouring microorganisms. Dude. She deftly brought Shaney inside, separating him from the poet who felt miffed at being doc-blocked, cut down in the midst of ministrations. Which reminded the poet of another recent visit to this same place Her girlfriend (the moaning one from the hall at the vegan barbecue) who suffered a scary overdose on some blotter-drug: that one ended lamely since her moaning lover decided to enjoy the drug, riding into the wee hours babbling stuff the poet could only guess at, in rhapsodies she could only imagine, along with the mysterious source of the stuff. Guess from whom.

Nurse Fracturite put Shaney on a gurney in a curtained alcove and waved a thermometer near his brow. It didn't blow up cartoon style, but it rose fearfully quick and high. She scrubbed and put on gloves, and donned a white paper mask whose entire purpose seemed to be medical since its warp and woof certainly could not filter poisoned smoke much less microscopic pathogens. All the same…

Meanwhile, Lila May was about to make an unusual rash decision. Standing on the top of the pure white cement steps leading to and from the downtown hospital wing that bore up under her family name, she decided to go not to either her apartment or her family home but to Shaney's place and throw herself at him.

Not checking up, mind you. Just, it would be fun. She wanted to be straight before she defied Papa's rules for the first time. Not about throwing herself at some boy, that is. About the night when the full moon gilds the desert land.

"The doctor will see you in a second," said the masked nurse whose garb didn't plus young Shaney at all, he assuming she was observing some typical protocol because of some other danger lurking somewhere elsewhere in the halls. He was happy to be in the arms of some institution meant to watch over him. He thought about his own mother and laughed, she never would. Shaney guessed he'd have to call in sick for the Surly rendezvous and ensuant blackmail.

The doctor promised actually arrived, after talking to the nurse at her admitting station where he eyed the poet through capacious double glass windows on the waiting area. The poet gingerly reciprocated the gaze, wondering if this experience might make a good sonnet, unrhymed and raggedly unmetrical. The doctor thought, she could be mine, while discussing Shaney with the masked nurse. Doctor smiled at poet and headed back.

Her father was often here. She thought about calling to prepare him for the betrayal as she crossed through morning air and white cement, and then carefully treaded into the tufted grass. Spring always seemed near on campus somehow no matter what season it was. Little white lawn flowers, white-rimmed around yellow like sunnyside eggs small as baby's breath, but there were also long lupine out by the roadside, budding promise as she pulled from the car lot and past med center environs toward Shaney's place. She tried to call John on his Bluetooth, but it picked up with his comic message, "Please leave an electro-magnetic representation of your voice inscribed upon the digital disk provided by my phone carrier, which shall be retrieved, analyzed, and addressed for potential response with habitual regularity by me, the entity creating this vocal simulacrum you currently perceive at early convenience. Or not. Thanks, kids."

The downtown billboards were full with "Texas Welcomes You" messages for arriving visitors, that horde descending from the music and the film business worlds for South by Southwest. Smaller signs proclaimed the bands Lila May's friends preferred. Locals hoping for exposure, fame, triumph, exploitation, disappointment, and with any luck drug rehab. Some signs made her laugh. "Welcome to Austin, now fuck off" being the best among them. "Keep Austin Weird Supports the Wolfsbane Helpline" caught her attention then her breath caught just around the corner from John's house. She stopped the eggshell blue Audi, pulled out a silver pen, and sat there in her car. The residences were arched over with thickening canopies of trees. (In dark boluses of leaf slept the famous Austin bats and inside them were microbes of healing and destroying grace.) Lila May looked up and wondered how soon trees bloomed, the dogwood and the hyacinth the reflection on the safety glass overwebbing her. The world seemed horrifyingly knit together, and her skin was goosebumped by her blasty air conditioning.

The sun pours in like butterscotch, thought Shaney. Bet the poet out there never wrote anything like that good old Joni Mitchell song, the one his dead hippie mom always liked. It was warm by the window, but he was worried. What would happen if Lila May found out? What if it was rabies, what would I tell the doctor how I got them? And what of the legendary treatment, giant needles in your abdomen? His head lolled back upon the bed and his nose ran. In the middle of all this, I get a sniffle. Butterscotch snot. The doctor came in. A woman. He wondered what she might say first, like, how are we doing?

"How are we doing?" she asked.

"Don't know," he said. "Got a fever, pretty delirious, oh, that's an exaggeration, been sleeping though. Two days."

"Good, bed rest is good." She was busy with the fingers at his throat, the eye close to his eye, and then the bland-flat taste of the wooden spatula applied to tongue and the little light in the ears. "You'll probably need some more," she said.

"You know what it is?"

"I'm afraid it's a virus," she said.

"This virus have a name?" he snuffled, knowing women hated that. Blow your nose.

"Indeed it does, whatever's Latin for common cold," she said. "Think you need a hankie and a blow. Old school: Rhinovirus, Corona too."

"Wait, now wait," he said. "The sniffles just started. I've been having all kinds of weird symptoms for a few days. And the sleep."

"Okay," she said. "Maybe it's a slight misnomer, common cold. It's a motherfucker cold," she said. "I'll admit. But it's no reason to feel disappointment. I'll take a swab and a test just in case I'm wrong," she said. "But a cold is a virus, and the virus is the most powerful of all the foes we face."

He looked at her.

She giggled then resumed professional. "No really, Lord Virus, I call him. Even the Conquering Worm must bow before Lord Virus, an evil harrower who mutates and adapts to everything we throw at Him. You know, we cured polio, wiped it out. But the common cold is our ancient foe and will probably stand against us when people sport jet packs and Walt Disney is revived from ice."

He looked at her with wonder. She was witty and a doctor and he was a little smitten. (He smited easily.) She had blue eyes whose irises were encircled with blue lines and she had magnificent breasts. He was all ardor, though she saw him as a slab of meat needing repair. But he looked nice in the window bright sun pouring in.

"Need me to write you a note for classes?" she asked. "Get you out coupla days—you can watch *Game of Thrones* on your laptop in bed, drink chicken soup."

"No, thank you," he said, and almost forgot he was here on a fake student ID. "Grad student," he said, recovering. "Sections. Mice. Running data and stuff." He wondered why he was lying so hard.

She looked at him with more interest. "Pre-med?"

"Clinical, drug designing."

"Maybe you can get a job with Wulfhardt when you graduate, pretty cushy," she said. "Least that's what I hear. Don't be so disappointed, it was good you came in and it was nice to meet you." She looked at the chart, "John Shaney," she said in a fake mechanical computer robot voice. "Besides, the tests might prove you have something extra cool like rabies," she said. "Though ebola seems more likely."

Furious rabies, he thought, chupacabra.


Lila May opened the little gate and wandered up the path, knocked at the door and pushed it from half-open to yawning wide. The stairs had teeth, excrescences, stalagmites of aura. She said yoo-hoo, like you do, self-conscious and ready to laugh at yourself if detected. But nobody answered.

She had come this far and decided it was alright to invade the room where they made love. It was the top of the stairs and there was definitely something that filtered in and out of the wallpaper, drifting across, blown on an unfelt wind. She pushed open the door and saw the tiger cat curled in the heart of the bed. It looked up and was at peace. She looked around. The trashcan had a few tissues wadded in it and the room had a slightly sour smell of sweaty sleep. On the desk a piece of paper had one word written on it: Gwen with a question mark. She began a letter to him on the next page of blank paper.

"Somebody told me you were working at home. Naughty boy. Well, maybe you're up at the lab and I just missed you. Please don't be angry about me standing you up for the concert. I know you think this whole family thing is crazy, but there are more thingies in heaven and in Austin than your philosophy can dream about, or whatever. I will wait for you at home. Come over to the house when the show ends if you can. Yes, I know you will go and I'll live with my fears, but, then, who doesn't? Mother asked for you again. Father, and this will make you laugh, seems to be getting jealous. If I thought like him, I might be too. Don't worry, though, he will do as I say. Love, Me."

She got up and walked next door to Louis's room. He was there reading *Steppenwolf.*

Louis said, "What are you doing here? Run, Go back to Wulfhardt." Something came drifting out of the wall and tried to catch the utterance but it was too late.

"What about you?" she asked.

"I'm heading for shelter now," he lied.

"Do you need a ride?"


The poet came in but saw disappointment on Shaney's face. She *was* a terrible poet but a good observer, though she misunderstood his sadness.

"What is it?" she said hovering over him. Now she had a drama to inhabit.

"It's nothing," Shaney answered.

She was blown away by his sexy stoicism. It must be really bad. "What will you do?"

He apologized. "No, I'm sorry, I mean it. It's really nothing. A cold."

She looked confused and then cheated.

"What," she said. "A cold? What bullshit."

"I know, right?"

She looked through him at nobility fled and drama dudded.

"A bad cold, though they took a swab to test it, just in case. She said, a *motherfucker* of a cold," he laughed a hyena sound.

"She," she said, looking through the window at the auburn-haired fox of a doc. "She said that. I like the doctor," she laughed and punched his arm. "Well, better luck next time you contract a malady. Here's to real disease," she said, lifting the bottle of spring water they brought to mollify the stay.

"I'm so embarrassed, I really."

"Forget about it, I was the one insisted. Hell, let's celebrate. Ever been up to the Salt Lick? No, well, I think it's feed a cold starve a fever and we're gonna stuff the hell out of those microbes with some Texas Bor-ba-cue," she said, exaggerating the accent.

"Virus," he said. "Virii."

They hopped into his car, she drove southwest toward the city of Driftwood, him protesting at first then falling into a stupor as the road hummed underneath her overheated car with grrl rock on the stereo, Sleater-Kinney giving way to Aimee Mann. He was soporificized and didn't notice when Lila May, still conjuring nice thoughts about him, drove by in the slow lane passing fast on nimble wheels of her Audi Fox blasting The Master Makes Margarita, a respectable local postpunk band with a beat and lyrics about the moon's irresponsible eye.

The poet saw it in the late afternoon horizon, light that wouldn't wait to come out, thinly slicing up into the old blue; shining with desires and their dire consequences. They pulled into the wide sand parking lot. Shaney walked into the sunlit room, a ranch-style restaurant with large wooden tables and a patio outside. There was green light and smoke, which mostly vented up the roof leaving behind a woodsy aura and curling wisps of fat. Everyone shone with carnal glee. Children were pulling apart large juice-laden sections of stringy brisket. Some smeared with sauce, but many devouring it dry and sighing deeply at the flavors. They ordered. Shaney's hunger returned with a vengeance. His unaccountable disappointment disappeared and he knew, as he quaffed the first beer he allowed himself, tipping it against the poet's hand and glass, that he should celebrate the fact that the dog's bite was in vain. "Not in veins," he said aloud, his rabies chased away.

"Pardon me, darlin'?" she said, her eyes sweeping to see who might be there, who might see her, the part-time heterosexual, with a nice piece of ass at her table. He was, too, this Shaney. Blond, narrow enough at the stomach to set off his well-developed haunches, promising a thrust and lift, but his forearms were his most seductive parts, broad and strong. He was handsome in a California lifeguard way, retouche nose peeling. His eyes, dazzled her from the first. He was oblivious, twirling patterns on his paper napkin with his finger, imagining what might come next. He did sort of owe it to her. You know. And a bloody good meat meal was nice too. He would treat and then he would at home too.

They devoured the meal moments after it arrived. Big greasy pork sausages tinged with garlic. The brisket had smoke, pepper, paprika, and was that onion salt? It went down, chased by cabbage slaw and gulps of fizzing delicious beer. He was happy and he turned to her and said let's go home.

"You mean dot dot dot?" she asked.

"Does your door have a lock on it? I don't know anybody named Dorothy. Dot-dot. I don't think we're in Kansas anymore."

She nodded and he smiled, ready.


Lila had left Trinity house earlier begging Louis to quit the obsession, crying. See a doctor. But Louis would not. He knew what he was and there was no cure.

And then the Thursday full moon rose. He felt it.

It entered over the shoulder and stabbed into his dimming eyes in a mirror, knifing.

Relentless hunger for all our daily needs magnified passed before his eyes with lusts mixed and folded in. Misplaced angry lusts.

Then a spasm turned his stomach, acid bile forced up the throat and savage, bitter burning washed over the tonsils and the voice box, a wet flame. A lot of pain, body doubled over. A poison that the organs attempted to deal with repelled but then accepted the same as a crucible accepted the wax and the matchtip, brutal alchemy with arms writhing.

Skin blossomed hair. Smells spread in the air; pore-dust and sebaceous oils gone bitter-stale with time slurped outward as the follicles wormed out hair, now turned to fur that itched and burned. He shuddered with some violence and little blood stains shook out everywhere. His tongue widened and spread, longing to lick that blood away. All away.

First big wave of metamorphosis and Louis disappeared. Was now the creature, lurched out as the bones redoubled in density and twisted and broke and reformed. Throat burned from bile rasps as breath crossed its scorched surface, burning scraped and stretched larynx. Pause for effect. Gather strength by looking straight into the moonbeams. Then all erupted again as hands contracted to fangs and the forearm foreshortened as the collarbone expanded and the haunches developed itchy, catastrophic strength. Gone, Louis Lamel, the wolf is your mind now.

Who knows what happened next. His eyes attuned to other spectrums and his nose broadened to a wider range of heat and information. A beating heart full of blood. Then final eruptions as the spinal column like a fantail whipped. Now there was no now.

He needed the open space and he got up, dizzy at first and then stretching and then a spasmodic shake sent more blood out. Domesticated animals smelled him and ran to cover. They wanted to be indoors and beneath the bed. He clumped to the window and inhaled. He glided down into night air. *His* howl cut through suburbs and entered rooms of little children at play, whose round eyes peered at the forbidding dark-filling windows.

Shaney was in the car now warm but it was a nestled warmth rather than skittish fever. She had music on and was breathing in a shallow way, hoping for the same thing he was hoping for but wondering how she could get rid of him fast enough afterwards in case her girlfriend showed up. What the hey, who gives a shit, she giggled, knowing that doing the wrong thing brought pleasures sweeter and more enduring. The better to eat you up, she thought. She shook her head and decided that this next phase of her life was over, the moon now rising.

Back home, they both furtively checked the horizon; he for Lila, she for her other her. Halfway upstairs though she turned on him and pinned him to the wall. God, he was warm and hot looking too. Through his half-clean jeans she felt him.

His roommate's door was wide open and the room was a mess, torn sheets, whatever. He closed the door, peeled off into his room and there was the note on the bed. "Love, me." She was gone and he was free, free to pay his debt, to explore a night of nights, though the fever maybe was beginning to return with aches and sniffle flowing more than small daubs from the hankie could stanch.

He walked in on her putting a silk bathrobe over her white shoulders and whiter bra. He glimpsed the tops of her breasts. She said, want a drink?

He said, we'll be alone tonight.

If she didn't understand exactly, she took it to mean it would be alright for him to relax. She wanted a drink now even more.

"I've got whisky in the larder downstairs. Good for a cold."

"I'll go get it."

"No, sugar, I'll take care of you, fetch your medicine."

"The better to care for your dot dot dot."

She laughed, threw some clothes back on and slid out the door, wondering what would happen next. Her phone went off and it was a text. It was *her*. As she reached back into the closet she rejoiced to read her paramour complain that a night out of town had become a necessity due to some silly snafu involved in getting SXSW coffee house, the lesbian coffee house, accommodations.

Her foolish heart soon sank, though, realizing that her hidden bottle of Beam Rye was gone, purloined, no doubt a victim of the tofu barbecue.

"Always the way," she thought, the poet. "The way of the world is elation cut by catastrophe, in the midst of life, farce."

Sticking her head in the door, she saw Shaney self-consciously perched on the edge of her bed. "Honey pie?" she said.

He turned around wondering if she was making fun of him. "I'm gonna run to the liquor store, someone drank my bottle dry."

She had doffed the robe and thrown on a sweatshirt in such a few seconds he couldn't keep up. "Don't do it for me," he said, and then realized she had put at least three beers away from the tin pail of Mexican lagers they automatically brought to the table at Salt Lick. Guess maybe he should've driven.

Remembering his own infirmity, his silent battle with Lord Virus, he felt a little weird. "I'll make the run," he said.

"Nonsense, you bundle up against the cold and save some energy. Be back in a New York minute," she said. He gave her a comical salute. He wondered what the hell that phrase meant. Is time faster or slower in the city of Manhattan? Laying back on her thick white bedspread self-conscious about his shoes he kicked them off, dirty socks, he felt uncommitted and uncomfortable now. Couldn't pull the plug though. He thought about Gwen. He did this for fairness' sake, of course, though it was not fair to his Lila. And as millions of untrue hearts had argued before it had not much to do with her. It had nothing to do with her.

# 18.

The backyard fence had a missing-tooth gap, all leaned-over wood heaped and angled away by roommates who made this transit on commando booze runs sometimes very late at night and often inebriate. The roommate-approved shortcut took two blocks off the walk from home to the little liquor store on a path through an abandoned yard and a sneak past two abandoned houses Janus-facing two streets, overgrown with apple trees and wrecked engine blocks sprouting wheatlike weeds. In below shrub-worlds of dusty fruit and lost toys *he* waited, knowing the end to every sentence. This was what *he* loved. Love beyond thought, the end. Of safety and surprise. *He* loved the end.

She was debating, internally. Composing. Those fucking drunken fish that drank my drink. Though, to be fair, it was a party. On the other hand, the bottle was tucked away behind stacks of stale crackers, canned bamboo shoots and half-empty boxes of baking soda and baking powder, all dusted with webs of spidery mites.

She came out on the front yard of the shortcut to a street empty except for the television shadow-puppet lights in windows showing across crabgrass and elms. She thought she heard a noise and turned around. A woman is never safe, but then she remembered her self-defense classes: rah rah ree, kick him in the knee.

At the end of the street was a confluence of neon and rushing car lamps waving brightness back towards her emerging face, killing the memory of the dark suburb left behind. She made the liquor store in record time, her watch said two minutes and a half. The store had an automatic door, swing open fast then re-seal itself because the summer heat coming soon would need to be locked out hermetically. Inside was the smell of dust, candy, and the pissy vinegar reek of spilled beer and wine, someone had dropped a sixer and they were still mopping in a corner with the yellow sign that said caution, *piso mojado*. She smiled at the rockabilly chick and the dilapidated hippie with his absurd starched white shirt under bib overalls—his hair pony to her pigs. He said, "y'all," but never finished the sentence, because female clerk put her two fingers on his mouth and fetched down the quart of rye without saying a word but winking solemnly at the poet, who felt a tiny tug of guilt entering an establishment that might not know your name, but sho'nuff knew your brew.

The poet nodded and pulled out the Japanese crane wallet with her I.D. and small stack of credit cards. She snapped down the one that her daddy didn't pay and wondered a little blankly how soon it would be that the stipend and the fellowship checks hit the bank. Oh, next week, she realized though she entertained a poetic second knowing that the future, even when scheduled, was not assured. "Much obliged," she said, trying to sound cool and ironic old timey.

Again the hippie tried to say samething, but got the same hand over mouth treatment from the pretty pudgy clerk with whom he slept. The poet reentered the night, which was full of eyes.

She thought about the room in which the two clerks played out their little psychodrama. Flash: a play? The one she meant to write? Talk about unity of place. Call it *Counterpards*, then she thought of that movie *Clerks* and wasn't that filmed in Austin? No that was *Slackers*, but she got all those hipster flicks jumbled.

With the door swung closed behind her, she felt funny and free. She was going home to him and he would be good for a night of pleasure and then kick him out the door because, well, he already had a girlfriend, but, well, might come in handy from time to time, men are so easy, count only on the recurrence of the horndog.

The street ahead was a bit forbidding, darkened windows like disapproval as she passed into night, but she kept anxieties at bay with literary thought. Some kind of haiku about night and hauntings, a simple thing she could write down in the few minutes while she poured them both a drink and before she pulled his pants off.

Something moved outside her cone of sight but not of hearing.

How did she know? Simple. All other sounds around her froze: ambient tree whispers, insect screes and buzzes and nightbird moans. Wait, quiet because it was early spring and ergo not much raucous turmoil in the trees. Oh good first line. Early spring and not much raucous turmoil near the trees. Or in. Follow it with something from inside: I sense false danger in the season, the season I misread. Doesn't scan or even cadence. I sense a sound that moves over street noise like a silencing bubble. Good, though true. It was too quiet and true.

She toed the edge of the abandoned house's ragged front lawn, crossed the property line. She looked at her phone where time and light were kept. She went to flick on that light but something came out of the darkness, huge and black, something right next to her and batted the phone away, far away, down the street. "Oh shit," she said. She felt a scream forming in her then let it out.

It was *him*, coming across the way from the house behind her in a rush, pent and then exploded, waiting her return in the bitter-smelling evergreen hedge overgrown and filled underneath with trash, webs, and nests. The smells had deadened *him* but he was equipped for this now and knew he must get her off the street. It worked ridiculously well. She moved into the property, not back to the store. *He* ran her into the dark.

She was afraid and that inflamed *him*. She ran repeating her cloacal mantra, oh shit, oh shit, oh shit. As she reached the side of the house hoping for cover she decided that it would be better to calm down and hide inside but, oh shit, in the first place, what is it? No hard tread behind but she heard a scissoring of the air, a sinister breeze, like it was a movie camera panning around her.

She jumped up on a door stoop. The abandoned house had fucking locked doors. She looked into the deepness around and saw nothing, so she made a sprint to where a little patio was. Behind her, she heard a bigger breath and something pushed her forward, her muscles banded and her bowels almost burst. She started to trip over her own steps, stumble, recover, stumble, fall, she fell forward across the patio vaguely aware that the skin of her knees was tearing open from the scrape. So much for a soft slink into bed with Shaney, she thought absurdly. Yearned for normal sin.

"Shit," she said, the doors were locked and the windows mirrored the deepness, jumped up again and panicky unthinking ran for the bushes as the moon soon came sweeping over her like a spotlight and a fast cloud above moved west, branches sparsely knit over the blank yard with leaf embroidery. But these moving focal points offered no view of her attacker, and she listened and then sprang simultaneously into a thudding fire-heated skin and breath—a clumsy head-on tackle. She was unlucky, though. Their *pas de deux* may have sent the culprit tumbling clumsily toward the fence giving her time to recover, but she now remembered that she felt a razor graze her arm *en passant*. She gasped and reached down now but that limb lay numb, she moved, symbolically brushing away the pain that now came up, but her hand came up too drenched in her own blood. Blind fear and panicky adrenaline ran through her and made her run. She ran an escape pattern: out and then back to shelter, the old house. She heard a snarl behind her and leaped up to a tiny kitchen window that miraculously gave as she pushed at it, window imploding glass and screen though as she flew over it, she dragged her own belly across a raw shard and felt another sharpened tear go down her stockingless leg.

She had forgotten propriety and civilized discourse much less the promised roll in the hay with Shaney accompanied by gulps of happy burning Jim Beam. She began to take stock of her surroundings in quick surveillance. Face to face with dark and trash spotted on floorspots where the lights beamed in through dirty windows. And then it hit her. Some horrible festering smell wafting up from beneath the hardwood floorboards. The house reeked of death.

It was sulfury like bad eggs, but much much worse. Shit, she thought. But this was not excrement. The odor was unmistakably decomposing tissue and liquids turned to microbial stew, an awful odiferous signal that implied diseases in every breath, though to a carrion-feeder it was probably ambrosia. Fuck, she thought, shit.

Her assailant had not made an audible move since she'd made shelter in this horrid-smelling asylum. What was he? It? She thought about her arm and staggered forward into a patch of windowing moon. It was really fucking bad, blood was sheeting out of a long scratch and she decided to tend to this first, ripping off her tiny skirt and with the pumped-up will of the victim, tore it into sheets and as she crouched in panties, little blouse, and blood-drenched arm, she fashioned a way of binding the numbed arm that may not prevent eventual scarring—she had already decided that the worst was over and wondered where she had chucked the bottle of rye—she felt better until she saw her leg in the square of white light. God, she thought. Shit.

It might be an artery. Her jaw started to tingle and thoughts seemed to wink out like streetlights as day dawned. There was only a small strip left of the skirt and maybe, she insanely thought, she would need it to mop up the trail she left across the room. It was a black trail, but she knew what it was. She began to shiver and as she did, something (large, shadowy) passed across the window.

"Help," she asked of the evening outside and of the families in houses bent into the tube, engrossed.

"Save me," she whispered now to Shaney waiting in her bed. She sent her thoughts out through the wires of human conductivity that didn't exist, though scent of blood and fear messages might, but she sent a signal wave beating up and down like powdered dry wings across night's dull slate. She was in full delusion, a blessed reprieve.

Shaney might have received the distress frequency (if there was such a thing) had he not succumbed five minutes earlier to deep sleep at the precise time poet breached automatic door and spied Tweedle Dee and Tweedle Dum clerks flirting in front of the bottles, implicitly imagining a long unmolested and creative life leaving a legacy of insightful and unforgettable verse, not to mention the payback head from Shaney, who lumbered through the darkness into dreams where all women were one, the one he would be ready to love (poet), the one who waited at home for him (Lila May), and Gwen in the wing set up for her brooding drugged-out convalescence. All of them thought of Shaney's exposure to the wolf and worried about blood. One of them was unraveling.

Death was waiting outside the poet's temporary haven. She sang. Come early spring without the sound of raucous turmoil in the trees. I sensed false danger bind my wounds, misreading his empathy. That might be okay? Why rhyme? She felt a little lulled now. Her moods went swaying like spinning plates. Now she was very sleepy, thought she might rest, she felt safe and her nose had somehow compensated for the horrible rankness coming from the floorboards. This wasn't bad.

Shaney started up from a half-dream, his muscles had suddenly clenched and he had stumbled over a step in the dark in a dream, the imperfection of even his own dream-state, randomly reacting, the butterfly effect.

Meanwhile outside the abandoned house *he* prowled silently, his fine-tuned nose offended, if that's the right word, by the smell of a dozen rats dead in the basement, killed by a developer who planned early next week to come in and look at the property again after poisoning. He had left the poison, tiny blue cubes, not remotely dreaming how many would die in a kind of vermin genocide, pregnant animals shrieking for a sip of water, a terrible thirst which the poison made unslakeable. Whatever…

Meanwhile, the poet was blood deprived daydreaming about a rescue from her boyfriend and the warm bed of an ambulance.

"Don't worry," the beautiful doctor said. "It's just a motherfucking cold and I have just the remedy for you," she said leaning over, the top two buttons of her soft cotton blouse open to the heaving halfdomes whose heat activated an expensive musky perfume from Paris.

Oh, shit, she thought. I'm still here, the smell of putrid decay stirred up by a dry wind from below. She stood, though it was not a good idea. She clumsily tied her blouse now around the knee socket where the wound was flowing. She saw nothing out in the darkness and decided her assailant had run for it. She was woman, she was invincible. Wow, what about that poem: The dry trees dying in the raucous wind. Or something. She limped over to the door.

Her strength barely held her and her hand at first could not turn the knob, which, she realized, was simply locked with a latch. Turn that and the air rushed in chasing the horrible stench back. Maybe she threw up, she could taste the sour dairy ending edge of it in her mouth, something was drying on her face, though perhaps that was blood. She would sure scare the first person she saw. There in the glowing moonlight tilted on a crazy axis was her bottle of rye. It would taste extra good right now, though it might not be good for her, settle her nerves anyway.

When she stepped down on the crab and weedy grass, he was next to her. Not gone, after all. Tremendously muscled with eyes as blue as Nordic ice. She said goodbye to the world and made inchoate sounds as he tore her stomach open and began feasting on inner organs, unwinding and winding up in them, tearing apart and savoring the small bits only animals knew.

The arterial slash usually accomplished all. *He* didn't drink blood, *he* didn't really like the flesh taste of human, the kill was important and the only way he "knew" to make sure was this devouring and tearing which, in her shock, became the prelude to a darkness that obliterated time, poetry, and even her fondest memory of her father opening the door on summer morning to the tree house he had built just for her to sway away summer with curious birds. Unendurable pain tore everything away, her last minutes strangled by fear and then, passing out, the part of her she thought of as herself extinguished for eternity.

He knew the moment that happened but was unmoved by the something that passes into the air. *He* never saw the sigh of consciousness, the slough off of identity.

He rolled into the bushes when a car started down the street, likely lost, made a three-way turn, stopped to examine its GPS reading with windows rolled down. He thought about another kill. Like a stray old caribou this car was. As the tough guys liked to romanticize what he did as "thinning out the pack."

He washed himself. Licking and cleaning and then inside he felt that tug. He felt it tickling in his throat and the deep part of his abdominal muscle sheath, a howl that signaled his ownership of murder.

Shaney heard it in his sleep and started awake. He looked at the clock. The poet was not back from the grocery store or liquor store or wherever. He got up and passed through the ghastly cloud of unknown stuff, the nebula of death that now had doubled in the hall. He didn't register it, the scientist.

Shaney went to the bathroom. He took the medicine he had wrested from the almost unwilling doctor, something tincted with codeine, yay. Aspirin, water, cough syrup. Which room should he return to now if the other roommates came in, what would they think? He thought he ought to go out into the night and seek her out. It seemed chivalrous, so he wrapped up in a hoodie left by the door. He walked out barefoot into the early spring night. He could hear the sound of rock and roll coming from some venue. It was cold and a shiver started up him from the floor to the tips of his hair. The other one stopped miles away. The codeine kicked in quick.

*He* could smell Shaney on the nearby streets, so he went to see. But the young, sick man now drugged went back in the house and up the stairs, leaving a note for her "wake me." He went into his room, shaking almost violently, now chilled with visions of disconnected dreads. Then sleep rolled.

# 19.

Always alone in the first and last moments of each day, heading in or out of dreams, everybody, lost in welters of thought, maybe, but always alone. In bed, alone, even if some pretty someone else has arms wrapped around. John Shaney woke up in his bed alone. Day dawned, not much brighter than the last hours of last night, the full moon having made its transit, exit stage left, if one was facing a certain way from Sixth Avenue's South by Southwest din, super dark just before this soft morning and alone.

Shaney awoke and Lila May awoke, but the poet would never awake scattered to a few clumps of brush, and her final howling pains, her final fearful denial were all lost too. The club district had passed from crazy loud to straggling shrieks and cheers then blurring to bed. Morning found most folk tamed by hangovers some remembering shrieks and howls. One person, returning from her exurban excursions went looking for her lover and on her sweetheart's bedroom door found only words "wake me," assuming they were sly words left for her, smiles, dull music in her ears. But the handwriting looked weird and she wasn't in her room. Who wake whom from what?

Shaney awoke and Lila May awoke and she reached for her cell phone and called him and he was not quite innocent but alone in his own bed feeling relieved to hear her voice. Having not found occasion to sin, though it was still unclear why, he was faithful by default of a terrible happenstance. Of that, he was more or less innocent, but that was a big word, innocent.

She decided to let him into the fold. She had played monster for far too long. Okay. It was her habit, find a boyfriend, ah, boo. Lose a boyfriend, a terrorized boyfriend. Some psych major (not a real boyfriend) wrote her a letter describing the game. To her. Maybe she should show the letter to John, she thought not knowing it didn't matter. We play monsters with children. Shaney was in the boyfriend club if she was doing this, playing monsters with him proved it. Only one other made it so far, and turned out to be a wolf. Turned into a monster.

Day heat streamed through the windows just a taste of what the scorching summer would bring, but endurable now. The metal walls had been rolled down in her house and the hospital wing had not reported any calamity, so she felt safe inviting him into what was formerly exclusive.

"You were out when I came by," she purred.

"At the health center," he replied, voice made distractingly sexy by phlegm's presence in vocal chords. He remembered it now, the terrifying push, he pushed the professor out the door where wild creatures snarled. He killed the pottymouth man, but dreaming.

"Sugar pie?"

"It's just a cold," he said laughing at her sweet concern, déjà vu, "the cute doctor said it was just a cold but she took a swab to make double sure."

"Glad you didn't come visit Mother then," she said.

"Oh that's nice, ashamed of me already." Of course, he was alert now. Confused too. He loved the woman; this was the girl. Plus, he wanted to kill someone. In his sleep.

"No, sugar, Mother is immensely susceptible—a bit hypochondriac, but also the kind who catches bugs all the time just to prove herself."

He caught himself hoping for a dark thing on a mountain road with her mother. It felt like delight, he stretched.

"I suppose with your bad cold you don't want to come up here tonight after the show?" She made a humming interrogative noise.

"Will he let me in, your father?"

She was silent. "I didn't want you to work for him. I want you to be safe. Up here. Safe. He'll do what I ask." She looked around at the big window un-shuttered now but the grounds were fenced and the motion detectors were off but would go on again soon as darkness re-arrived. "I'll ask Daddy though. Are you going to work?"

He remembered now it was still Friday. Tonight was Ochocinco, who he wanted to murder, and the concert. He had to avoid all this, exposure, blackmail and who knows what else. Shaney had to murder Ochocinco. He'd watched enough TV crime to know.

He said, honestly, "I don't know when or how I feel about work."

"Take your temperature," she said, sultry advice from a distant vixen.

"There's noise downstairs," he said, and, indeed, someone was hollering his own name. "Imma go see. Want me to call you back?"

"No worries, dearest. I'll call after Daddy breakfast."

He hated that phrase, No worries. "Okay, miss you."

She cooed something, the phone died. Then yelling came up the stairs. Shaney opened his door and the poet's girlfriend stood there staring, glaring. "Wake me"? The note was facing him in his handwriting, she held it up on the landing above the stairs.

He told her a version of truth. Student Health, they ate and she asked if he wanted a drink, sweat out the cold. She offered to fetch a whisky. He waited in the living room but it was too hard to. He crawled off to bed. Surely she is passed out, in there. O, he suddenly realized what they weren't saying.

O she never came back?

The girlfriend looked less pugnacious and more concerned. Which store did she go to? He guessed the neighborhood. Her car was still here. Did she take the secret way? If she did it was a secret, he quipped and nobody chuckled. Then the whole house was on the front porch looking wistful, remembering Lana, the first roommate who went missing. Someone looked at the doormat for blood.

Shaney was feeling self-conscious, vulnerable, and weak. He didn't want to say too much but had he said enough, and he still felt shaky. It would be crass to go out in the kitchen and cook some oatmeal and eat it in front of everybody but his whole being was crying for it, food, and his vision was wavering into tunnels so he did what he usually did in situations like this, pulled out his phone, looked at the time, and said I've gotta fly.

"Aren't you worried about her?" said the mousey roomie, holding a copy of Seybold's short stories to her breast like some kind of shield.

"Of course," he said. "But I have to be at a section."

This lie bought him everything via the shared sense of collegial responsibility. Most grad students of the world would drag themselves out of narcotic stupors or even orgiastic sex to make section or the class they T.A.ed in; it was the modicum of order they respected. It was so sacrosanct that no one even remembered that Shaney had quit school two weeks ago. They automatically bowed. He skipped upstairs, grabbed his keys, and drove off toward the Tex Mex joint where he first met Ochocinco. To eat and plot a professor's timely death.

# 20.

In Wulfhardt, Lionel was just sitting down to eggs benedict and thinking about black people. He wasn't quite sure why there were no African Americans in his company. He never asked the human resource department if black candidates for employment were ignored, failed to impress in interviews, or were ruthlessly discriminated against. But there were none. His security team could use a black man with a black belt. He wondered at the many changing faces of racism. Maybe it wasn't worth thinking about.

Shaney did not own a kill weapon, not even a camp knife. He devoured the bowl of chips and thanked his stars he had ordered before the place filled up with out-of-towners. There were music biz folk (black clothes and shades), Hollywood (black clothes and black baseball caps), and hungover gay party dude drug dealers (black Hawaiian shirts). By the time the steaming *migas* arrived, he realized he couldn't do any crime. Sure, he had killed that dog, which was how this all began but that was hot blood. This was cold. He could maybe use that concentrated dose again and think of some way to slip it in the blackmailer's mouth. Ochocinco might succumb to a monster version of a heroic dose, dose the blackmailer again, but a thousand times worse, and when the doc went loopy in the club, alone, Shaney could steal his phone, delete the video. Ochocinco would still be alive, technically. It lacked the moral heft of a real murder, the karmic debt was reduced, he guessed. Shaney scraped the plate, burped cilantro, and headed home, which he hoped was sorted out, roommate-wise. He should move out to his own place, he thought. He stopped and deposited his check in the bank ATM, remembered to call in sick, which he wasn't feeling anymore, and suddenly felt calm, he thought.

Out on the streets, SXSW posters had gone OOC.

The signs for Surly and Preposition the People show were prime among the surreal streetcorner posters. Shaney was intimidated. Some big show starring Grizzly Bear and Panda Bear, avant gardists from the Republic of Brooklyn rode the telephone poles and liquor store windows with references to full moon partying. His momentary calm was gone. If he concentrated the concentrated doses?

He went home pulled out the already-strong bottle, consulted some deep web drug source his father showed him, set up his mini-lab and began titrating and funneling and distilling. The final product was so scary strong that Shaney held it with tweezers, poured it into a Visine bottle with an eyedropper, and wrapped it in tin foil, skin contact would likely be enough to change blackmailer into drooling heap. What he wanted. Who said his blood wasn't cold?

A ruckus began belowstairs. Shaney moved his chemistry set to the side of the big oak table in his room on top of the cosmic swirl of its grain. He washed his hands and walked down the stairs through the lonesome spirits of the dead. He looked down. A blue uniform stood, surrounded by a gaggle. One of them said, "Behold the man."

"Ah," said the cop and reaching back making come hence signals to a plainclothes.

"Mr. John Shaney?" said the bug-eyed detective.

"That's me," he said, wondering about a town where cops come in and out of your life with such blasé frequency. "What can I do for you?"

"We don't know yet. You seem to be the last person that saw her," said the officer a young Turkish-American named Ahmedjianian. "Your roommate, Joan Dafinchi." In the policeman's hand Shaney saw the note he wrote.

"She's dead," said Shaney, and realized how stupid it was to say so.

"We think it's her," said the police, looking keenly up at Shaney.

"What does that mean?"

"Sorry. We found a body in the bushes of the house behind," he said, pointing roughly towards the backyard and beyond. "It's very bad. There isn't enough to identify."

Shaney gasped at the image. How and why? This was a very rough town. And then he thought, it was murder, and it was on him again. At the very least he was a monstrous jinx, or the city was a jinx for him. Which? "She was wearing shorts and a pair of red kicks," he said.

"Probably her then," said the policeman after a long regard and a pause. "Again, I'm sorry."

Shaney looked at him. What was he supposed to do here? He was sorry too in an abstract way, but he was also frightened. His unpaid sex debt would remain unpaid through eternity. Among his flock of deaths, including dogs, mountain hippies, and rock drummers she was the most real—intimate. But there was no order, no evolutionary scale, was there? He might end up a suspect half a dozen times by the end of next week. Though. In truth, these cops don't think much, this one is too clumsy for that kind of craft. Cops, like most people, go with feelings.

And yet, Shaney thought, I was actually planning a murder upstairs. He was not quite innocent and not yet damned.

"Were you 'seeing her'?" the detective asked.

"Did we hook up?" said Shaney numbly. "I think that's what she wanted, but I have a girlfriend," he said. "Lila May Wulfhardt," he said.

The cop closed his notebook. He squinted and turned around, saying thanks, stay reachable we may have questions and Shaney felt he was living in a television show. He went back up the stairs and considered calling Lila May but decided to take a nap instead. He was still a little sick. He slept through horrifying images, laid there as they piled dust of graveyards and slime of sewers over him. The poet offered him a drink and said that he still owed her. He said fine and woke to a thumping bass line outside. Far away music. The clock dial told him he had 40 minutes to make his assignation with the man he wanted dead. He checked for the tin foil package. He walked out, looked down the hall at the dead poet's room open and crammed with flowers now. He resolved to end the threat one way or another. Ochocinco had better be there. Shaney felt the change was due now.

Through the streets Shaney saw the precursors, all skin-headed and tatted from arm to scalpline. Ink as if the boys' own veins had opened in hideous tacky illustrative bloom. Mostly it was hard-edged stuff, though. One t-shirted Chicano kid had blue wings up his biceps. Another wore the rippling images of the inferno, Dantean souls lost like refugees from a homefront catastrophe inflamed. The boys all looked like they had done time rather than squandered it, all prisoners' hardened muscles and shoes without laces, the better not to not hang themselves. The teardrop tattoo ubiquitous with its melancholy ambiguity (self pity or warning) dripped from every eye, all inked blue like blood before it meets the air outside. The mood they set was doom.

He felt himself cross into that other dimension not of sight and sound, but of prickly misgiving. Everything here conspired to tilt the world onto an axis of unexpected acts. He saw the people in lines forming before nightclubs as foolish flocks, sheeves, sheaths, and sheep of abundant gullibility brought together by hoodied harvesters. Every upturned face was ripe for a cheat; every bouncer seemed poised looking for juicy prospects. Even the squad cars sliding by felt like carnivores on slavering watch for prey.

He passed Congress and Sixth and headed east. Patron herds thickened there, street life vagabonds drifted upon all, strays who preyed on strays, though at that level of feeding it was hard to tell victim from ravaged— everyone become leftovers.

Shaney felt strange; recalled the night when he saw the ghost followed by the hell dog. He felt trapped in a distinctly dreamlike state, one could never control from within. The sense of a world no longer random, but with tables turned—he was the dream the world was having.

When he got to the club his heart fell. The people-with-passes line was around the block. Looking at the door and the cinderblock walls of the venue he reckoned surely he was not destined to enter therein. And, how could he commit murder outside the club? He felt that fat chance had broken with him. He stopped at the end of the line. A loose confederation of acquaintances passed. He nodded.

"What did you do to her, monster?" one of them said.

"Hush, that's him? He's pretty cute," said another.

"Fuck you, murderer," said some unknown person walking by. The pretty woman in front of Shaney in line turned around and looked him up and down. He shrugged.

"Drunkards?" he said.

"No. I don't think so," she said. "Besides, I awready got one of my own."

"Pardon?" he asked and she hiccupped loudly and turned around where her boyfriend said sheeit and howdied Shaney with a whisky offering; a world of safety and affection. He made Shaney drink from a flask. Then Shaney's stomach grumbled in ominous rolls.

# 21.

Up in Wulfhardt the shutters were rolling down. Lila May looked wistfully out on the garden, she always wondered if the wolfman and his wolfwomen wandered through those yellow roses, if they snagged their fur on them. She was a child again at this moment and she was afraid. Not of the silly circumstances that united her to her father's obsession—this was all easily endured for love of him and all the fine things he provided her. She had rebelled after high school, sure, but he gradually convinced her the best way for all was her at home when the cycle began. His superstition was real, she reckoned, because the cause of fear was always the home. Anyone can turn into a monster, look at me, thought Lila. Her boyfriends would testify, no one is immune. Daddy ought to fear what was already inside the Wulfie fortress. Gwen, back from the downtown hospital, was re-ensconced in her home medical wing. The household went to cheer her.

Lila walked down the long hall filled with art her mother collected from Los Angeles artists like Ed Ruscha, Billy Al Bengston, and John Baldessari—regular guests at the house who regularly drank up everything then left behind some souvenir. Gwen believed that all culture headed west towards the end. Lila May entered the hospital chamber, which always reminded her of the final rooms in *2001: A Space Odyssey*, sterile but beautiful. Her mother stirred, looking drowsily drugged, and murmured hello.

"How's our boyfriend?" said Gwen, bringing needle, tube, and hand to her mouth.

"Papa's good," said Lila May, and on cue Papa himself glided in.

"No, our *boyfriend*," she said stressing the word with scorn attached. "John, darling John, thrusting, sweating, passionate John."

"Mama, you're not making any sense," said Lila May regarding her father, whose face betrayed nothing.

"Oh, aren't I? Why hasn't he come up to visit? Your father's jealousy?"

"Nonsense, Mama. There's no reason for Daddy to be jealous. John asked if he could come see you."

"He did?" she asked breathlessly struggling to get up. "Why isn't he here?"

"It's a full moon, darling," said her father with a deep resigned voice. "We'll bring him up when morning comes."

She looked around and started laughing. The laughter went too long; Its echoes filled the art-filled halls with shame.

Lila May walked away, down the hall to her room, embarrassed. She nearly always was embarrassed by her parents and their antique buried resentments.

You could see it in family snapshots, Mother and Father crowded away from each other, half smiling. Rebellious pouty Lila smiled wide and got spoiling hands applied: Disneyland trips, ballet camp, and a sweet composition wheel skateboard not to mention her famous horse. Still Lila May's dreams raced in front of her like Russian Wolfhounds prancing. Getting what you want in life takes talent. Lila May did so with earnest grace and ingratiating need. Her voice soothed the fine line between whining and quest for salvation. The horse was her best work.

Shenanigans was the only real love of her life. Twelve years old, she had him in a corral up in the corner of the property among crazy eucalyptus trees. He nickered and chomped when she ran home daily to curry, pick, and feed the beast. She called her horse Nanny for short and rode him on the sloping trails of the mesa to the south and, when she found out what a bounding, disciplined ride he was, Lila May pleaded to learn the steeple-chase. Daddy said yes.

It was on a leap that Lila May met the great reckoning. The horse reared up, flew, and then caught on a hitch of air maybe or fence or maybe even Lila May's own doubts. When the horse came down upon her the pain and shock to her backbone was so intense she passed out. Months of agony melted her pre-adolescence. Drugged bed rest, surgery, and therapy, which, at that time was inquisitional. She got mostly better, but Nanny did not survive.

Lila cried all the time at nothing. Sister Dymphna, an eighth grade grammar school nun, spent one rainy afternoon lunch period alone explaining the universal inevitability of death to her. Animals do not have souls like we do, said the nun. They just die. Lila hit Sister Dymphna hard in the stomach, then got thrown out of Catholic school. That's how Lila met Louis. They had one year together and then high school where she had time to think and suffer. And change. High school was different—drugs mixed with obsessions. Pot with pottery, coke with reading—a lot of bleak stuff, from the lesser beats to *Bleak House*—Duke Ellington records and Vicodin stolen from her mother, the films of Robert Bresson on espresso, and finally the Austin band scene ingesting any- and everything. But she was never quite wasted. She turned her whole body towards the acquisition of learning, cultivated mentors. She made other people smile easy into laughing conversation. She did not disappoint ever. She went off to Sarah Lawrence as an art student but was not apt. She came home to Austin pursuing varied disciplines as a scatterbrained dilettante then followed the family trade. Something about John Shaney felt predestined to fulfill her.

But the day passed, and Shaney never came.

She got bored studying and played with her computer clicking in a quest towards the concert she was missing, and then found a feed from that very venue, someone with a little telephone camera filming the show with a scrawl that told precisely the amount of moments before the bands would take the stage. Apparently, the doors hadn't opened yet and the live cam was from some techie guy who volunteered security and went rogue one man film crew for the people who couldn't be there. In fifteen minutes Preposition the People would play. She went into the bathroom to brush her teeth and came back to see if her boyfriend would appear on cam.

Meanwhile the moon. It raced up from the black hills surrounding Lila May's valley, full over Wulfhardt.

Outside the venue, John Shaney lost patience. What if he didn't come? What would that prove or disprove about Shaney's newfound willingness to, well, kill? Shaney was pretty sure that the drug taken in such a high dosage could prove lethal affecting motor centers, some involuntary functions, the snake brain. It would wind a snake around the brain. Insane in the membrane, he thought, and giggled. Someone nudged him from behind, he turned around irritated and there he was—Ochocinco in the murderable flesh.

"Looking forward to the show," he said. "You little smegma. Forget about me?"

At that moment the line lurched forward with surprising force. One only needed to show a bracelet here, and the doorway yawned and swallowed this line whole. Meanwhile, some altercation had broken out amongst the ticketholder queue awaiting authentication by electronic gun. Shaney got a glimpse of the bar inside and already it looked packed. He smelled it too: beer and beer puke and body sweat from people who made clubgoing an avocation. He felt queasy. He had been sick enough to go to the hospital a few hours ago, after all. He also remembered someone he knew was dead, found near an abandoned house. And he planned to murder a fellow human, right now, for expediency. He felt sickly strange and all of a sudden sweaty.

The moon rose over the lowslung restaurant across the street into burnt orange skies. The crowd now jerked forward and pushed Shaney into a press of human flesh, and Ochocinco, to whom he had given a badge, was now nowhere near. How can I murder you if you just go away?

A spasm of crowd mechanics lurched him forward again, and once inside Shaney was crowd-moved toward the dead center of the hall. It was not where he wanted to be, now surrounded by folk with this strange sensation building in him steadily, bad smells contracted his gut. He looked around. His intended victim was nowhere visible, and he was pressed tight in a scrum. Flesh pressed against the flesh and plaid shirts of boys and waifish girls met his t-shirt and sweater. Then he shifted and found himself in the middle of a young professionals pack.

Music thumped overhead and Shaney felt dizzy first, then absorbed in sensations made by other people. Contact high. At one point in his beamy dreaming, a beautiful young woman backed into him and giggled into his face and just then yup puppies started grousing about some intern who had been hired because he was osculating derriere as one of them put it then said hello to the young girl who humphed a bit and moved away. Looked at him like he was spent nutrient expelled from a membrane.

Shaney felt something welling up. It didn't feel right. It felt like some interior part had been given a hot poker then passed haltingly and then spastically down and around his guts. He could almost visualize it. He began to sweat profusely. Then a brief remission, then a sharp stick pointed in two directions, also passed down. Then, as revelation he knew he had to take an alarmingly sudden and, by the feel of it, massive dump. And he was stuck in the middle of a crowd.

Shaney glimpsed another beautiful girl, who looked at him and then away shyly. Then his gut wrenched him again and the sweat pooled in the small of his back. He was trying with a failing combination of deep breaths and tightened ass to hold on—he was losing the battle and started at first to nudge and then push his way out. It was now approaching emergency and the sweat became a precursor of the embarrassment he would feel taking the only public shit he had ever heard of. He pushed his way through, clenching, the sea of faces separated and he made it out. Something tiny and burning came rolling down from what was presumably his butthole's green room.

It was horrifying. He could smell his own anxiety. Then, agony of agonies, he farted, and feared it would contain solid matter. It didn't.

But as he stopped to pass through another reluctant-to-part crowd, a dainty pretty girl smelt what he dealt and the girl crinkled her cute nose, registered disgust. He waddled around the last clump of souls until he saw a bouncer and asked him where the restrooms were. The guy looked at him as if the question was infradig then jerked his head towards the patio. Shaney ran, forsook all pride, out where the first blast of fresh air and the promise of commode facilities allowed for another small pebble of poop to roll down the chute.

Gross. He was now heading in a loping roll toward a door that said Men praying it wasn't occupied, knowing it was.

There were three hulking presences in the crapper, looking for all the world like quarterbacks from an Ivy league school. They leaned on the wall and they reconnoitered him. For a second, Shaney's bowels retracted, the emergency seemed gone.

"So the professor said, we live in a state of nature no matter where we are," said the curly-haired brute preliminarily scouting his nose with a finger.

"He never lived in Albuquerque," said the prep with the pink cardigan.

"I mean in the chain of being, there being no God and all," he answered, satisfied with easy pickings.

"God has left us alone in the forest formerly known as a garden?" asked the second bro with deep concern.

What was it about the Texas kids? wondered Shaney briefly before pushing his way past one of them to an apparent open stall. It had to be now. But the sight that greeted him was disgusting on a level that would gag seasoned bus station janitors. Bodily functions smeared like nutty paste from a toilet seat onto a wall, a Hokusai wave of shit.

"Anyways," said the first goon, who looked in the stall and shared the vista without comment. "Anyways, he asked the class if they were environmentalists, if they were hip to the hippies, I mean, your mom, he says."

"Mine were Albeganasians, who preached a gospel of truth through the demiurge Lucifer," said the thin third pardner.

"Dude. Go back to the seminary."

"Anyways, the hippies," said the most loutish lout. "Do you not wish to use the facilities?" he asked Shaney, laughing. The other stall was closed, locked, and Shaney was sure the loss of his load would be sudden and precipitous and horrible. He was sweating.

"Yeah, so the hippies believed that humans are natural. The Romantic Movement intersected by the Existentialists. Nature precedes existence precedes essence, like. No God, no more Cartesian opposites. We're all from nature."

"They bake sedse, dose hibbies and your brofessor," said his fat friend blowing his nose and shaking his head as Shaney stumbled forth. "Dature brecedes feces," he said letting go with a fart and a snort.

Shaney's need overwhelmed his nicer reflexes and he closed the door on himself in the loathsome, grappled down his pants, and "owned" the chamber of bodily waste—his first reflex was the gag, which, if followed to its logical terminus would have added vomit to the shit that fanned out around the pot. But his loosening bowels trumped all vile stuff surrounding. Kadoom plop flume.

"Once more into the shitty breach, dear comrades," said the biggie lout. "But nature's opposite is always called artifice and artifice can be superfine like Michelangelo or it sometimes menaces the environment. Like ozone or Mutagen. The big beautiful city that makes movies also makes smog. But there can be no artifice if all is nature."

"Oil is natural yet it menaces the environment. Oil Can What."

"I know, right?" said skinny, just as Shaney let loose another half pint of dismaying stuff.

"Oh, dude," said one of the louts, whose knowledge of the world was suddenly informed by senses, not ideas.

"Leave us leave now," said the first. "But let me leave all of *you* with this. If we are Nature's creatures as the hippies attest, then everything we do is natural and should not be judged by the selfsame hippies who denigrate polluters of nature. We are it."

"And this fucking dude is the summa of nature before the archangels invented pride."

Shaney kept thinking, I wish I could be alone on this planet. Inside the stall, the cascade of odors, garlicky, fermented, like a strong meatloaf that died and then took over all atmospheres, one part per million could kill a herd of bison in Montana. The horrid-smelling effluvia left John Shaney in a sweating state first and then an embarrassed state as coda.

But that was followed by a mini satori. Relief was an inadequate word. Even while sitting there stuff still on the wall of the stall, he felt cosmically better. He flushed and flushed again. The smell lessened, leaving him only his own sweet relief and sweat smell. He exited alone and pale from stall to overlit room, splashed water on his face, plucked raggy bits of paper from the dispenser to dry his sodden hands. Brought into peace now that the poison was gone, his thought processes turned very clear. He tromped out into the patio and face to face with Ochocinco.

"Thought you ditched me," said the blackmailer. "Pussyfaced prickeating crapsandwich."

"What's your fucking problem," said Shaney, now cool. "I got you in the fucking door, didn't I? Now you want me to hold your hand and dance with you? Fuck off." Shaney's whole body was vibrating at this point.

"You haven't heard the last of me," said Ochocinco who turned around just in time to see *him* come over the fence. The foulmouthed professor stepped back, went redfaced. "Your upturn on the wheel is about to fuck off," someone behind them said in a croaking tone with a full moon as his witness.

"Whatever," said Shaney, sidemouthing to Ochocinco and oblivious of the now present wonder. "Why don't you go run to your mommie with the shitass pictures you have of me. I bet your whole academic career hinges on some sort of equivalent grift, asshole," he said, pushing the scrawny professor back, two arms to Ochocinco's chest. Ochocinco fell back too easy and yelped like a little girl. Shaney turned around and said, "What the fuck."

*He* hit the ground with knees bent like you are supposed to do though it did not seem like training was involved. It was *his* face that commanded attention, the brown fur brushed back straight, the eyes as human as possible though you had the sense they did not see anything the same ways humans see them. (There was neither pity nor vilification anywhere there.) The nose, *his* nose, was broad though ending in a black-moist snout through which hot breath was rushing both ways. And that left the mouth half open with thin lips curling back from teeth long and sharp.

*He* had a white shirt, a rather dressy white shirt over the upper moiety of *his* manimal form. The forearms ripped it up the sides like fruit bursting and fur rolled out over the material in a rather attractive contrast. Likewise *his* pants, the material ripped up the legs, now bent even further as he crouched and paced in a semi-circle stalking. He seemed completely uninterested in Shaney and began corralling the professor by little half-arc rushes and two-step retreats. Inside some music had started and Shaney in his terrified stupor felt oddly that the pursuit was in tune to that music, a dance. The creature was lithe. This is probably what killed the poet, he thought. It was beast, he thought, killed beauty and then suddenly the creature rushed forward pitilessly tearing at Ochocinco's leg, tearing the tendons behind his knee and the man collapsed sobbing as the beast reared back when suddenly a bouncer came out on the patio and said, "Aw Jesus, not again. Get outta here you kids." Shaney was vibrating inside his head, his signal was fluxing, he was faint. Again? Kids?

The bouncer fell back into the club and tried to close the door but fled when the creature, the werewolf, let out a bloodcurdling howl that froze everybody for a half mile around. And repeat. Was it announcing the end of something? Shaney looked on for the moment helpless as the wolf rushed forward and began to tear away chunks of the professor's clothes and perhaps flesh too. Ochocinco gurgled in his fear and pissed himself, though he helped himself for a moment by throwing his arms up, which caused the werewolf to retreat and weigh options.

"Chupacabra," thought Shaney and stepped forward just as the wolf re-descended on the victim. The garden stake along the wall came away in Shaney's hand as he began shrieking, "Stop, stop," and beating on the wolf's white shirt and raising blood from the rough hide of the beast.

*He* looked up interrupted from the shaking of his prey between gleaming teeth. The manbeast had Ochocinco by the shoulder, trying to whip-snap the professorial neck. Ochocinco was goggle-eyed and drooling. Where was all his famous cursing? Shaney watched the attack as if in slow motion. The werewolf's broad hairy hand swept Shaney and his weapon away.

Ochocinco sobbed and dragged himself backwards trailing a red blood plume on the patio's red brick—so much blood. He held his arm out over his face and said no, no, as if warding off a dog or a fate. But then the wolf attacked again, going for the throat. The professor twisted himself and the creature came up throwing Ochocinco ass over head into a corner.

Shaney jumped up again just as the club door burst open and a trio of bouncers, behemoth creatures, followed by a cadre of clubgoers came out into the air yelling. They went quiet though when the wolf leaped through the air and reattained his stunned meal. Shaney was mad now that his own prey had been snatched; the wolfthing was doing Shaney's work for him. It didn't seem right.

Crazed, Shaney stood, took what was left of the tomato cage (or whatever) and began thrashing the beast around his back and pantsed-up hindside again. A wacky melee began with Ochocinco limp-slinking off and then running towards the door. Others had found weapons; brooms and fire extinguishers and small wooden chairs that they started using in unison on the werewolf, who, noting his meal's imminent departure, swung around and taking the glancing and hard blows came at Shaney who backed up into the corner as Ochocinco went into the club trailing gore. The wolf looked up at Shaney and suddenly they were looking into each other's eyes. Shaney said, "What?" out loud and shook his head to clear his vision and saw the Saint Christopher hanging from the matted fur neck. The wolf also shook his head, snapped in John's general direction, and ran off.

Before he left, the wolf sliced a young man across the belly with his fangs. The boy died of shock, fright, and blood loss an hour later.

# 22.

Shaney became something like a hero during that hour.

Realizing a trap, *he* scanned for an opening, pushed through the Emergency Exit outside set off an alarm crouched and snarled out of the patio.

Inside, the unwitting band took the stage. There followed a long wail of something, guitar feedback, maybe, wolfen warble, perhaps.

Dazed and chaotic thoughts haunted the porch. Shaney looked at the wounded boy but he couldn't. Blood flowed away from his stomach despite the ministrations of one of the bouncers. Shaney went over to the fallen professor. Another bouncer was there but the professor was dead, or nearly so.

"You were awesome, dude," said the muscly interloper who clearly knew something about dressing field wounds and was busily ripping his own black t-shirt into strips to become bandages and a tourniquet. Shaney felt the shakes come on as the adrenaline withdrew and his old human all too human self reemerged. A red dressed woman was ogle-eyeing him.

"Awesome," repeated the now bare-chested man ministering.

"It was nothing," said Shaney, guessing some primitive mystery scared off the beast, not a brave beating with gardening stays. A theory was germinating in his mind, though. Saint Christopher. Another theory, and another prolonged scream came from inside.

"Here hold this," said the bouncer with his black rag on the red wound with Shaney's hand now saving his foe's neck, red everywhere, the blood of the professor who had finally stopped swearing.

"By the way, you drop these?" asked the bouncer. It was the Visine bottle wrapped in tinfoil: Shaney's murder weapon plan apparently fallen out of his pants.

"I don't want to know, man," said the bouncer dude whose job it was to keep drugs and death out of the nightclub. "Whatever floats your boat. Fucking brave."

Another scream came from inside: music starting up. Meanwhile sirens grew in night air through the starry and streetlit night, blooms of horrid acknowledgement that police brutality had been called in against criminal brutality. Inside the scream was the opening band's vocalist. Preposition the People's Simon Torquay. He had no interest in tragedy surrounding, that's what makes self-absorbed rockers great.

A medical team swarmed the professor, so Shaney stood up, pocketed the tinfoil superhit and went into the club where the band was shuffling a groove. They played "The Old Gypsy Amen," that postpunk anthem:

> The way you walk
> is thorny though
> No fault of your own
> Thorny thorny
> But as rain blue
> Enters the soil
> And as the river grown

Thorny thorny
Enters the sea
So tears run to
Predestined ends
for you and me Amen


Shaney shook his head at the strangeness that seemed familiar. He felt sick again, though, and found another bathroom not ten yards from where he was 20 minutes ago. A lot had happened. He went in the bathroom, sparkly clean, and had himself a normal piss, then vomited with extreme prejudice. Mollified feelings followed again. The blue sea of the toilet flowed.

He washed himself, but was soon surrounded by new people in the loo who recognized him for vanquishing the foe.

"That guy was fuckin' weird," said one, washing his hands. "Huh?"

"What guy" asked Shaney, genuinely perplexed.

"That Halloween guy you fought out there."

"Excuse me," said Shaney. "You mean the werewolf?"

"Whatever," said the loose limbed one. "Though I thought the costume was pretty unconvincing. That guy was fucked amok, right? Fuckin' A."

"That wasn't a guy," said Shaney.

"No shit? Talk about trans? Gender fluid, wolfperson. You were awesome, dude. Though now I think of it, I am chagrined that was a chick."

Shaney said, "You're kidding, right?"

"No man. Even if it is politically correct."

"That was a werewolf, friend. A werewolf."

The guy looked at Shaney and left and Shaney followed him into the gathering chaos.

Ochocinco passed on a gurney. Somebody was pointing at Shaney and a small delegation of ambulance attendants and a cop came over, but Shaney headed in a semi-circle around the floor. Behind someone was unmistakably hailing him, but he was pretending obliviousness; mostly, he wanted to step out the door and to lose the drug in case the cop decided to search him. He came around a corner where there was a merch table and flung the little wad of foil out into a row of chairs, free. He headed for the door when the tiny entourage caught up with him.

"Excuse me, sir," said the attendant.

Shaney asked what.

"We just want to make sure you're alright," he said as the policeman circled around him obstacling Shaney's possible exit. He didn't like it. He was starting to feel trapped. Flight or fight boiled in his veins and he wanted to leave.

He pushed pass the cop who grabbed him by the arm. "Excuse me?" he said.

"We just want to ask you a few questions," said the cop who was pulling him back. "Make sure you're not hurt."

"I'm fine," said Shaney, who began to identify exits, to find the fabulous egress.

"That was a brave thing you did, protecting that guy," said the cop. "Know him?"

"Yeah," said Shaney matter of fact. "Matter of fact we came together. Name is Ochocinco, a professor."

"Great," said the cop. "What's his first name?"

Shaney honestly didn't know. "I honestly don't know," he said.

"Came to the show together, you don't know his first name." Over in the corner someone was holding up a piece of foil, it might be *the* foil, showing it to a bunch of guys. Shaney was worried now. "That's a crime?"

"Most people in Texas know everybody's first two names. Last names not so much. His name is Jimmy Ray," said the bouncer pointing to the cop. "I just met him."

"Listen I'd like to see, um, Ochocinco. They take him outside?"

The attendant began feeling Shaney over. "Just looking for scratches," he said as Shaney pushed him away. The band was chanting "Thorny, thorny, thorny."

The guy holding the tinfoil started screaming and a bunch of people moved over there, while the cop's attention was distracted, Shaney slipped out the door to a different melee.

There were ambulances, city and otherwise. Considerable argument was going on between two drivers, leaned up against conveyances that read Wulfhardt Enterprises. Shaney knew the lab did medical work but never expected human services too. He thought about Gwen, then, in the private wing of a hospital or some such thing. He asked the Wulfie drivers where the first victim was, which drew blank stares. Just then a newsreporter came bounding up to Shaney and breathlessly asked if he would like to do an interview on camera for the nightly news live crew. "Why me?" asked Shaney, fearing the answer.

"You kidding?" replied breathless beauty. "They say you were the hero of the hour."

Shaney was looking around desperately, Ochocinco must be gone. "How many ambulances have left?" he asked the newscaster distractedly.

"None. They just arrived."

"So what happened to the guy I was, um, helping?"

"The guy whose life you saved?" replied the broadcaster of trim coif and high cheekbones, the kind of skin the camera loves. "A professor, I think."

"That's the one. Wait, I didn't save him. The creature killed him."

"Well, then somebody's cussing up a storm over there in the ambulance. We can't turn a camera on him. This is family exploitation news."

"Where is he?"

The reporter pointed over to the far car and Shaney pushed past the rapt surrounders and saw an ambulance driver next to an empty gurney on which blood was soaking.

"I don't know how but that dude's gone," said the attendant, pointing to the ripped apart straps used to hold down crazy drunks and TCP ODs before their Mr. Toad's Wild Ride to the hospital, where most human lives begin and end.

"Someone took him."

"No, man, he tore his way out of the bed and ran off into the night. Had to go. And when you gotta go."

"Impossible. His throat was ripped open. His arm was shredded."

"That's what I woulda said, but this guy just hauled ass out into the night. I chased him, but like I said, the man is gone."

"Are you getting all of this?" the reporter said to her crew, a gang of gangly interns from the UT film department.

Shaney looked up, saw he was being interviewed, "I never said it was okay."

The newscaster looked seriously worried now. "I, hey, don't get mad, man. I won't broadcast this if you'll do an interview."

"Hey, there's the hero of the hour," said the dour bouncer from inside now wrapped up in a sweat and hoodie against the sudden chill of the early spring air. A crowd of kids surged around him. "I heard you fucked him up good with a tomato cage," said one hot little coed, a tomato herself, and the crew turned immediately from Shaney to the petite chick speaking shit.

Glad to be off-camera, Shaney jumped when his cellphone trilled like a hyena though he would have sworn he had turned it off.

Lila May spoke in a voice reduced to tin tones. "I'm looking at you," she said.

Shaney swept the crowd.

"You're on television, honey. Live at Five Crew. You're cute and a hero too I hear."

"I can't believe they shot me. I told them not to… Ochocinco is gone," Shaney said jumbling all his anguishes together.

"What, sweetie? You were shot and your drink is gone? You had a drink and shot? Listen Daddy wants to…"

"You believe me now?" asked a gruff voice over the phone, a voice like doom. "A werewolf problem."

Shaney doubted nearly every aspect of reality by now. Some supernatural power had taken control of the universe. He knew but didn't know. "Who is this?"

Wulfie had snatched the mobile from Lila. "Your boss. You know, your girlfriend's father," said Lionel in a voice like a cheap imitation of James Earl Jones, all Luke-I-am-your-father and shit through a kazoo. "What's this about you being shot? I'll send a car."

"Listen," said Shaney, who now saw the camera pointed at him and the cute newscaster pointing too. "There's already a bunch of ambulances here with your name on them. What's up with that?"

Lila May had grabbed her phone back. "Daddy's ambulance will take you. Where were you shot? It doesn't show."

"Shot. By the television camera."

"Oh." For a second she seemed disappointed. "Oh. Okay then, his car will be there. Take you away. He says don't talk to the news team. Why do they call them that? Yay team, go!"

"Tell him to find Ochocinco, who was cut from ear to ear, but ran away," said Shaney now talking on television after camera and reporter moved in on him. He was suddenly angrier than he could possibly account for, mad at the world. "He's probably already a wolfman, I guess."

"Somebody, or a wounded wolf ran away?" said the reporter. "Get this. We have a report that the first victim's name is Ochocinco, like the professor."

"Like the halfback," said one of the camera guys.

"The victim, apparently with mortal wounds, has left the scene. Excuse me, sir, your name please?"

Just then, the man with the tin foil package in his hand came screaming down the street, tearing apart from his attendants and an officer. When he saw Shaney he screamed a high-pitched keen pointed at him and was promptly wrestled to the ground still wailing.

"Can you please tell me what you saw in there?" said the reporter.

"You're joking?" said Shaney.

"No sir, it's pretty confusing. Somebody claimed a wild animal went all amok. Maybe one of the bands brought it in. What did you see, sir?"

"Shaney," he said, defying the Wulfhardt code right now. Fuck the job. "John Shaney is my name and I saw my roommate who now has become a werewolf. I saw a wolfman attack."

The camera man went silent. Someone in the studio managed to superimpose Shaney's name as Lon Shaney, werewolf-slayer, it said, electronic graphics. It made him seem wrathful, deific, and foolish at the same time but who knows anything about human hearts when the media frames events in hollow clichés and brainless speculations? The camera moved to a herd of onlookers surrounding the ambulances, jumping and howling for a glimpse of blood. A bunch of teens, dressed stupidly like

Universal monsters in cheap grocery store Halloween costumes cruised by too, yelling lusty catcalls. One girl mummy poked her head between Shaney and the camera and growled, "Hi Mom" and promptly lifted bandages and flashed her round tits.

A black car pulled up and a driver got out and took Shaney firmly by the arm. "Mr. Wulfhardt needs you up at the lab, sir," he said. "He also told me to say they grabbed your professor with a net."

There was a buzzing in Shaney's hand a bumble bee early for the spring, but it turned out it was a phone offered by the driver to Shaney who, numb, lifted said buzzing device to his lips.

"Yeah," he said.

A voice said never mind put the driver on. Shaney was beyond reason now. The driver leaned into it, head crooked for instructions, said yes, sir; skillfully guided one confused public hero into the car with the classic arm cupped over his head to prevent him smacking his melon. He handed Shaney back the phone, which was now dead. Meanwhile a policeman, spotting Shaney in the backseat of the car, started to holler but the black windows of the car rolled up and the car glided away from all that chaos. When Shaney looked back, the cop was standing helpless in the middle of the street.

Like a police cruiser, the car had no inside handles. He was trapped. Shaney knocked on the window a few times and tried to use his phone but it wasn't getting any service out here. He wasn't finding it difficult to relax, though. The backseat was leathern and cushiony and climate control led toward dreaminess. Dreams were near.

He wondered all of a sudden why Lila May was in his psychobiology class. She wanted to be a botanist. Maybe she was interested in psychoactive plants. Loco weed Texas tree-hugger and leafsmoker? Shaney doubted it. They never did any Austin drugs together. He started to muse about Texas and yellow roses and bluebonnets, and then remembered their specific taxonomy from that memorizing class he had to take O years ago, bluebonnet, genus Lupinus, and, O, motherfucker!

Maybe the phone didn't work, but WiFi was fine. Lupinus: of the wolf. So named no one knows why but maybe because it ate up all the nutrients of the soil. No, stupid. Lupinus mutabilis. Changing wolf, or something such? Ancient Romans ate the plant's beans. Romulus and Remus meets Little Latin Lupe Lu. Everything's better with bluebonnets on it. He was loopy. The coupe had soothing air. Set the climate control to super chill.

They took the road up to the haunted cutoff that Lila May suggested, though, of course, from the opposite direction, which Shaney had rarely been able to find from this end. He thought about Gwen and that got something going in him. Or maybe it was a response to the Eureka! Moment, a molecule detection erection, realizing this was all the con he needed to bend old Wulfie with if it came up. Investigating Lupinus Mutabilis. The solution was beneath your nose the whole time.

In dark, the car passed the clump of iceplant trysting place, he was now running backwards in spacetime through his first night and day with Lila May in the grand house, stopping here twice where he had seen the crying ghost and made love with the crying woman. By glum guess he intuited that bedding with either of the Wulfhardt women this night was not likely to transpire. He would be separated from them, he premonished.

He banged again on the window, but the man was indifferent. He tried screaming and he even fantasized for a minute how he might try to turn himself into a wolf. After all, it was him that had been bitten. It was his wound that had healed. Without the chemicals. He who had considered murder, he had changed with the full moon, he never even considered such a thing as murder like that before, though, on the other fang, he had been the one who came to the rescue of his wolf's now hapful victim.

Coming down the hill to the town of Wulfhardt, in the car with the Wulfhardt logo on it and into the back driveway of the house of Wulfhardt, Shaney suddenly got the last link he needed to his formula. It didn't make any sense that he hadn't seen it before. Lupinus mutabilis. It was of a random nature. It was terribly obvious. All of it always is from silver bullets to Dumbo feathers. It didn't make any sense that nobody saw it before and he suddenly couldn't wait to get on a computer and make sure that the pathology wasn't registered, that the synthesis had never been made. It was embedded in Robert Louis Stevenson and Stephen King.

The mind is never imprisoned in a body like the intellectuals say. It *is* the body. Like artifice *is* nature like the hippies say, now where did he hear that? The transformation only had to take place in the mind first, the rest would be easy given the juice of Changing Wolf Flowers. He might make Wulfie believe it long enough to save his job.

When the gates swung open electronically there were bright lights. A coterie there poised to greet them, though neither Lila May nor her father joined it. A team of men in hospital uniforms took him out and up and asked him to sit in a wheelchair. Shaney said, no thank you. I'm afraid we have to insist said one rather large man who took Shaney by both arms and started to tip him backwards. Shaney yelped and even pushed back awkwardly but it was him against iron. The man, who smelled like stale cigarettes, had him in the upper hand and with the superior cool mind. Still Shaney resisted but then the insect stung him from behind and he said what the fuck, and the others laughed *at* not *with* him.

# 23.

It was a nice bed after all and he was talking to a very pretty woman, though it bothered him somewhat to be bound down to it. The nurse murmured comfort. Then disappeared.

Then it was the middle of the night, and the sweet nurse became the deep comfort of dark. But his bladder was howling at him. He dimly remembered a bathroom with a swath of something foul pasted across it. He yelled but no one came. Then he was asleep dreaming of peeing. He pissed himself—hadn't done that since when it burned his skin but he slipped back to sleep once again.

In sunlight, he was clean with new slacks and the smell that greeted him was like Listerine, Dial soap, Crest toothpaste, and Right Guard deodorant crossed. He wondered if he was free and tried to get up. It was easy. He felt great, actually. There was a plate of food under a plastic warmer. There was a bathroom attached but no windows.

There was a newspaper tucked under the dish. That was thoughtful. The coffee in a carafe was nice and strong and the food was delicious, and he unfolded the newspaper to a picture of himself. Heroic Man Fights Off Dog Attack, it read and he thought that like most media accounts of anything there were equal parts truth and mistaken conjecture in it. That a man fought an animal, that much was true. But false as well. Shaney never believed in ghosts or wolfmen before he moved to Austin. It might have been his mistake. Another story was about surprising violence widespread or spreading out onto the streets during this festival, which had become one of the defining events of Weird, Texas. Pages later, Shaney read a review of the Surly show—which happened despite an unexplained animal attack and police intervention. Then the show began. No further mention of the pottymouth professor mauled to death but skipping away into the evening half light. The reviewer thought the show was better than the Mabuwie and Bowery Ballroom classics.

Shaney wished he had seen the show and wondered what happened to his expensive wristband. He imagined he would never get Ochocinco's band back either and would have to explain that to Lila May, who, he suddenly remembered, lived a few yards away. Then he remembered his formula for directed hallucinations into flesh, the bluebonnets and the sad virus. The id and the superego, he thought. It was just nature and nurture. He could coax them both together and apart. He thought about fairies and absinthe, predictable patterns like the so-called Persian rug seen by eaters of hashish. De Quincey, I would add, with his vast expansion of time and space derived from the ingestion of opium. Certain substances create very specific visions. He wanted a computer to set down these ideas before they left. And his phone was missing.

Feeling good anyway, he went into the cool-tiled bathroom equipped with a shower and all other toileting accoutrements with his own clothes folded neat and smelling clean in a corner. His wallet was there and he looked inside it and saw himself, a California driver, staring back. There neatly wadded was the wrist ribbon that would get him into the South by Southwest. He supposed he was clean but got under hot water naked as a purge, then shaved his ragged whisker bristle and remembered the howl and the long run down the primeval lane toward a kill waiting in a meadow and decided he was remembering that American wolfman movie from the 1980s. Then he heard in his mind's ear the Zevon song. His hair was perfect.

Shaney decided on a whim to try the door.

It opened easily.

The hall was bright with pouring sun. At the hall's end wide windows opened into a courtyard. He thought of patients, people soaking up rehab sunshine, whatever vitamins solar rays provide. What are vitamins? He the scientist didn't actually know. The same way he didn't know how CDs worked. He cartoon imagined an alphabet of nutrients found in sweet tart Fred Flintstone-shaped molecules: a taxonomy of virtuous antagonists standing opposed to the animal array of bugs, horrors that brought in diseases, like Lord Virus. Riding corpuscles of white.

He walked toward the light and found another open door and in it saw a woman with a clear mask over her face and wires run into her skin and a suffusing light surrounding her considerable beauty. Like a fairy princess on a bed displayed in a sleeping enchantment, she lay ginger-tressed and somber. Then he realized it was Gwen.

Now Shaney *was* bewitched. He walked forward and saw the wasting thinness and satiny white pallor of her hand transfixed with a needle putting in some clear liquid, possible refreshment, certainly drugged. Her breathing seemed regular, though, and a monitoring screen moved jagged teeth-shaped spikes deliberately across its green half-lit screen, measuring what? The heart's output of ampered current? The spasming messages it gave as it pushed fluids around a hungry system? She woke with a start.

"My lamb?" she said with a wonder and a sweetness he had never heard in a lover's voice before. "You finally came for me?"

Shaney was struck dumb by the unanticipated vision.

"Why don't you say anything, my love? Is this a dream?"

"No," said Shaney. "I'm a prisoner here, too," he said, though it felt true and melodramatic at the same time.

"What are you talking about? Who is a prisoner?"

"You're bound down to the table," he said, seeing a strap across her stomach.

"I am?" she said and easily removed the strap from across her. "Oh this," she said. "Sometimes at night for my own protection I must be fastened in. You know, I'm not well. I told you that, dear, didn't I? Before we made out in the succulents. That was nice," she said, sighing and perhaps unconsciously lifting her hips a little from the table. "When will we be lovers again? When?" She was now a little agitated.

"You're married," he said. "Your husband is, well, this is his house."

"Didn't stop you out in the park, did it dear lamb," she said. "Man in a state of nature is naturally horny. Woman too," she said jiggling now.

Again, he didn't know what to say and began to fear the intrusion of either Wulfie or Lila May. He tried to think of a way to back out of this gracefully. Realized with a horrid start that it was not possible.

"Just go into the chest of drawers over there," she said. "Get my clothes, my lamb, my rescuer. Do you have a car here?"

"No, I…"

"Doesn't matter, there are twenty in the garage and I know where all the keys are. We won't take his favorite. How will you let Lila May down, though? This is very awkward, my sweetheart. You know, this might drive a weaker woman crazy. Where are you going?" she said. "Get over here right now."

As Shaney began to back out of the room, he ran into a body standing, muscled, solid.

"Here's my husband now," she said.

"Hush, my darling. You'll disturb our visitor," he said walking over to the machine that stood under the bag that led liquid straight to her veins. He punched a button. Shaney saw her body again with a sharp perverse pang of desire. She was old, okay, but so beautiful and now by some strange mechanism he felt he could feel her touch, the way exactly he had fit inside of her. Snug. Blissfully connected. Wulfhardt pushed a button again and Gwen protested, trying to get up and Wulfie interceded.

"Help me, please," he said to Shaney and they both held the churning woman for a few electrifying moments of absolute panic—Shaney almost went blind with fear—and then she slacked back onto the bed.

"My two best fucks," she said, gesturing vaguely but unmistakably to the air between them. "Save me, please."

Shaney had a problem looking Wulfhardt in the eye as he emerged from the room where an attendant also suddenly appeared assuaging the woman who was now making inchoate sounds. But he reminded himself that he hadn't exactly been invited in—it was something more like a skulk.

"You found your clothes, you feel much better," said Lionel Wulfhardt.

"What the fuck," said Shaney.

"Please, somebody must have told you I hate vulgarity."

It worked for a second and then Shaney who worked for the man said, "What fucking right do you have…"

"I wasn't letting you into my house with even the off-chance you had been bitten. Your fight with my assistants only bore out the suspected truth."

"What are you talking about? I fought the wolf at the club."

"And apparently won. That was the very source of my suspicion. And, as I said, it turned out I was right."

"You didn't say anything of the sort."

"You turned last night," he said. "I knew it."

Shaney looked at him. "What are you saying?"

"It was weird, though," he said. "I admit. We had the room bugged, surveilled, on camera. It didn't happen until you were deep under and then it didn't actually go full term. Weird. But you had the metamorphosis. I'm surprised you didn't dream a bit of it. You swear you did not know this?"

"All I remember is a very sweet nurse talking to me."

"There is no sweet nurse in my employ. We left you alone to see what would happen. There's film though I would say it's a bit unclear."

Shaney remembered a nurse like a dream of a movie. "This isn't happening," he said. "And even if it was true it doesn't make sense. Why set me free now?"

They were walking down another corridor past the mid-century chic modernist furniture, the Warhol soupcans, and Hockney swimming pools on the wall. His host gestured around them. "Sunlight all around us. You are many hours from being dangerous to anyone."

They reached the breakfast nook where two brilliantly orange mimosas awaited them. "What about your wife?"

"Interesting that you didn't ask me about my daughter," he said. Shaney was in the middle of a cartoon archetypal drama: Oedipus on acid.

Orange juice met his lips with an aftertaste of surprisingly cheap sparkling wine accumulating grossly sweet in his throat.

Lila May was standing there. This was a family that liked to appear, like ghosts.

He didn't know what to say, but his boss blurted out, "See who came to visit?"

Shaney was genuinely frozen, without any aid from instinct, herd behavior, or even reason to guide him.

"He was just asking about your mother," said Wulfie as Lila May came forward and tenderly took Shaney into her lithe, soft arms wrapped in a feather-weight soft wool sweater. A cloud enwrapped a dream.

"Told you how considerate he was, Daddy."

"Oh he's an emotional man. I was just explaining. Mrs. Wulfhardt, Gwen, suffers from something no doctor so far understands. She has spells, and, combined with a very unfortunate penchant for drinking and painkiller drugs, she finds herself taken by the pixies, as the Australians say."

"Demons," said Lila May.

"Semantics are unnecessary; though I believe you may be right. Mr. Shaney here is like family, now, didn't you say?"

"Don't call him mister. He is part of this mad scientist family?"

"Young lady you presume too much. Remember you live on my largesse." His voice was a self parody.

"This is my house," she said in basso profondo, playing along. "And when you live here it's by my rules." She reached for Shaney's drink and drained it. Shaney had no idea which way to look, which voice to use if he had to speak.

"That's the right idea, but you don't need to go so low, strong enough content. What do you think about all of this, Mr. Shaney?"

"I don't know, except to say I figured out an answer to your problem."

Wulfhardt startled. "What?"

"I need to go home and get my computer, I made some notes and I have to check some papers and some math but I think the answer to your problem lies more in superficial treatment than in any cure. Plus I think I found a pharmacological culprit."

"I'm listening."

"It's always bothered me when health food people complain about medicine that treats the symptoms instead of the disease. To most people, if they thought about it, the symptoms *are* the disease. Who would care if you had a cold if you weren't sneezing and coughing, right?"

"Life is too short for philosophy. Tell me your solution."

"Besides," he said, ignoring him. "They do it all the time in therapy nowadays right, don't they nowadays? We get sad or grieving or find it hard to talk to others and they pop some Prozac in us."

"My, so cynical," said Lila May.

"No, he's right," said her father holding up his hand. "But what you're saying then is the metamorphosis can be controlled at the skin level," he said.

"At a language level, or a kind of epistemology, it's maybe all in the lycanthrope's head, some concrete form of neurotic visual charges. It's real, or it's a collective nightmare. It doesn't matter. But I'm certain that this whole syndrome or whatever has to pass through the skull to get to the body. And that's the only place I know where to work, anyways." Shaney was bullshitting so fast he forgot the bluebells. What the hell.

"The hallucinogens. Some plant-based chemical."

"No. I think a virus," he said, now resolutely swung offtrack. "Its viral work is on the brain, the reptilian, the Chupacabrian brain. It has to be directed, but then it could probably be modified. Whole time, I started thinking about the legends too. All the stuff that came and went, the wolfsbane, the dogwort, but they weren't there to prevent you from being eaten by either the wolf or his curse. Only one thing protected you. Only one thing killed the wolf."

"A silver bullet?" Wulfhardt said. Sarcastically.

"A magic silver bullet," said Shaney, not quite unserious. "Turns out silver needs certain poisons to be refined. Certain poisons also ameliorate a high, too, the hippies say. LSD gets more intense you add a little arsenic, supposedly. I think silver additives absorbed into the blood can poison and it becomes a matter for renal systems to clear."

"But this isn't all in the mind of some shared hallucination," said Wulfie, like he was trying halfheartedly to convince himself.

"Wee-you, wee-you," said Lila May.

"It is a kind of epistemology, isn't it? Just think about some of the more common druggie hallucinations, like patterns and follow-ups people taking acid and mushrooms and the like have. We can't tell for sure, can we? But it seems like we're all seeing the same thing; it's just the language is difficult. You can't describe the ineffable nature of a high, but everybody wants to go to the light and see the walls flap around and it actually seems like it's a shared experience. And then there's pink elephants on parade and blue fairies…"

"Absinthe makes the heart grow fonder," muttered Dad. "I'm not going to follow you if you are taking me into some kind of how do we know that the color we call orange is the same for all people who say they see orange. I'm not."

"Daddy believes that people turn into wolves and kill people."

"So do I now. But I'm saying it's all in the head and can be controlled like depression or a bad trip." Shaney remembered the werewolf movie that was and was not his dream last night. "I'm saying, erase the hallucination. Bring the vision to a predictable place and then extinguish it, like Thorazine kills LSD. Do away with the wolf video inside the wolfpeople."

Shaney beamed. Meanwhile Lila May was getting kind of hot for him; he was full of bullshit but a lot smarter than she ever thought. She knew he was cute and smelled nice the first moment they met. Now she knew more.

"And you have a formula?" said Papa.

It crossed Shaney's mind that the virus that carried the theoretical infectious self-hallucination, a moveable neurosis convincing us we are wolfen, call it insanity gone viral, could be a form of insanity, an illusion. This was actually his final genius leap though now he was lost making mental formula revisions wondering if formulae could make the new ideas presentable to the boss.

"I hope you don't think I would be wasting your time, sir, if I hadn't a good inkling. But I need my computer."

"There are many computers lying idle here," Wulfie said.

Shaney was up, his moment. "I keep mine standalone for fear of hacking grad students."

"I'll send a car," said Wulfhardt.

"Not without me in it," said Shaney nodding furiously, sorry that Gwen was off the table, so to speak, but at least he had an escape route, improvised. Once he was away…

Wulfhardt promised a driver in 20 minutes and flew off in the direction of Gwen's ward and Lila May took advantage of the departure to retrieve Shaney to her soft den. The light was almost blinding there, and she had her tongue in his mouth. Then she jumped up and straddled him, laughing.

"I think there's probably something scary about you," she said.

"This from the daughter of the man who all but accused me of sleeping with his wife. And here we are now. I'm scarier than *you're* used to?"

"Did you?" she asked, then broke down into laughing tears.

"There," he said. "There. I never…"

This was way weird. She didn't stop but he seemed remote somewhere in the middle, she took him out and let him finish in her hand and soon he realized they were on the bed tears running into their kissing mouths, and not much later he said sorry. She said it was me, I did it. He said I was a wolf. What if I made a baby wolf, what if I made my baby a wolf. She rolled away, breathing hard. And she just looked at him.

"Okay," he said knowing there was no way to stop this and thinking about Gwen. This was really too weird. "I'm sorry," he said again.

She lifted her hand to cover his eyes gently and said, "It's okay. Sooner or later, every man has the problem," she said.

He guessed it was a good cover. He couldn't and she wouldn't be mad. It was supposed to be ego-deflating, but it made things easier. The ego and the wolf. Shaney cared less, the more he thought about it. If he was a man who had an animal inside but didn't want to that was moral. But he came. She popped off the bed and disappeared into her bathroom. Meanwhile, he stared up at the sunlight playing on her wood beamed ceiling.

"Will you come back?" she asked. He got up off the bed, she pulled off the sheets.

"Like I want to, but don't you think he'll just isolate me again? Nah. I better go. You come to me."

"He won't let me out till the full moon's over."

"Someday tell me about your grandfather, okay?"

"No," she said. "That's not going to happen. He used to tickle me."

The buzzer on the intercom went off, good timing. "He's already heading for the front door," she said back to the kazoo-like voice that announced the ride's immanent departure. "Come back," she said, watching them in the big flat screen's yawning ghost reflections. She gave him a concert t-shirt, Wolf Patrol, one of her favorites.

As he hustled down the wide stairs and across the empty two-story-high living room with its piano, he wondered about her mother more, and crossed into the blinding late-noon light and hopped into the backseat of a big Lincoln, black as the desert around them was white. As he got in the car Lila May stared from the stoop, she waved. She went inside. And saw her father.

Her father, inside looking out the window said, "epistemology," and snickered. "Read it on Reddit. Accent on the piss." It was all too easy, the world of men, thought brainy Lionel. That boy really is working for me now. In the car, Shaney thought about Gwen calling him lamb. He was proud to be her lamb heading off through the desert and into the city.

# 24.

Or at least into the suburban side of town, which driver and passenger traversed in blinding bends of time. The outdoors blurred, the passage of Texas space, made Shaney dizzy. So he read his telephone and then flipped on the little television screen and watched the news, wondering why reports of violence did not begin with him and the werewolf he conquered. Or why it didn't deal with the bleeding neck of Ochocinco. One report alluded to the pre-concert mayhem, the worst since that Oil Can What show a month ago. Some smarmy editorial blamed a negative effect that the burgeoning festival might have on young people today, and wondered if the music and movie business might not be the real source of all this violence. Cut to some hippie-ish indie kid in a record store who echoed the sentiment. Corporations were coopting youth culture with unrest and violence, he drawled in the international blurred tongue of potsmokers, though the scraggle-bearded youth added that music ought to have charms to soothe beasts just as the Lincoln stopped and they were in front of Shaney's house.

"Jesus, you're good," Shaney said to Chuy the driver who grunted back acknowledgement.

Shaney bolted for his door, went in easy, did not stop and say hello, fearful of roommate impediments. Maybe this was his house too but he wasn't so sure of his standing. The cat met him halfway up the stairs with a nuzzling run from wet nose tip to flared tail. Shaney could see a ghost at the top of the stairs, but he was oddly sure that the ghost could not see him.

In the hallway he felt a strange qualm. He heard a loud horn honk. He was looking down at the poet's door, half-opened as if the room itself expected her back. It wouldn't ever happen, Shaney thought. He opened his own door and there in the musty light was the laptop with its ideas inside. When he looked in the closet for something warm to wear he felt the air prickle his neck. When he turned around with Louis Lamel standing there he almost wet his pants. "Jesus."

"Crazy, right?" Lamel said between hoarse pants, gulping too. "Let's get out of here."

"What the fuck are you talking about?" Shaney answered folding up the computer and using it as a kind of shield. "That's the same St. Christopher medal. You're a fucking…"

"We're going for a hike," Lamel said, "Those shoes will do."

"I've got a driver waiting for me down there."

"I took him out."

"What do you mean?"

"Well, I don't think he's dead, but he's not walking home on his own volition tonight. I'll take you out too, if you don't go with me," said Lamel, calm.

Shaney was afraid and Lamel loved that. But he couldn't hurt Shaney, he knew. Or strongly suspected. Lamel grabbed Shaney's phone and threw it down the hall.

"I'll scream for help," Shaney said. "I'm not embarrassed to scream, you know."

"Actually, I was going to praise you for your bravery, but, really, now that I mention it, was your bravery fucked things up."

"I did."

Down the stairs now one arm on an elbow. "You interfered and now that asshole fucker shit is on the loose."

"Ochocinco," he said. "Nice impression. Well, you tore his throat open."

Lamel laughed. "There was a lot of blood, there always is. But his carotid artery was not breached or even much neck immolation. Not for want of trying, though. Tell me something. That guy's an asshole. Why did you fight? I heard what happened. Don't actually remember this stuff."

Shaney looked a little blank. "I don't know. He was blackmailing me. Shuddawuddacudda let him die, but I couldn't. Didn't think about it."

"A dog you can murder. Real threat and you go noble."

Shaney was perplexed. "The dog," he said again trying to make sense.

"Well, I guessed you guessed that was me, him, that night a month ago. It was actually a dog at first. He attacked, I showed up. The other I. I guess. I assume, I, *he*, was there to protect you. Remember? Probably seemed like two animals, and suddenly you were winning? I must have convinced the dog with force. But in the mixup I clipped you. Accidentally. Then you went berserk. That was you. That was bad."

"You know," said Shaney trying to slow them down. They'd made Congress Avenue by then, moving at a good clip. Still a few blocks to the river that flowed away from the civic center. "You know there's an element of surprise and surrealism about this. You were there to help me?"

"Protect," Lamel said. "There's a difference. You belong to Lila May, and I belong to her as well. It's not easy to understand, but it's rigid hardwire, you might say."

"Where're we going?" Shaney asked. "I'm a little lost. What if I refuse?"

"I need you to see something. Plus I hate you. So hurting is an option."

Shaney was quiet at that. They moved at a clip that winded him. They reached the river at an overpass bridge where, tucked into a corner, led a path down between pavement and empty lot.

"After you," said Lamel. "Don't worry, I won't bite, ha."

Shaney tumbled and Lamel felt a pang. His pathetic physical specimen-ness, he thought, him sleeping with *her*. Oh, I could smell her on him, but in full moon I could pick her out in a full football stadium.

"Let's try again, why did you interfere? I had him and now he's loose."

"I don't know why. Something just took over," said Shaney unafraid.

"It's going to be very bad tonight. He's turned many by now. Matter of fact, I'm not even sure when the moon comes up, so maybe we won't have to wait till night to see. Maybe it'll start in fifteen minutes. Ochocinco loose, a new wolf. And more. Half of downtown will be dead or turned by midnight. Mark my words. Maybe a hundred wolves. Everything Wulfhardt fears will come true."

"I wish I knew what you were saying about Wulfhardt, dude," said Shaney like they were bros arguing over beer pong rules.

"By the way, I think I have a cure," added Shaney.

"O," Lamel answered and ushered him across the well trod runner's path into a small briary north of the river where a grove of pepper trees bent with some earthly burden. Here the river chugged industriously. Lamel liked it because animals came down to it. Beautiful, this river created green places in desert, like imagination in an American mind.

The land was chirping around them. When Shaney saw the thing on the ground he responded with a sound like someone slugged in the gut. Oh, he said, uh.

He bent over.

"Don't touch it," Lamel said. "Bats are the most virulent animals nature suffered to crawl across the floor of, um, itself."

"What's wrong? Why are they outside in the sun? Don't they usually fly around by night?"

"Wulfhardt Labs, this is what happens." The creatures struggled and spasmed, leathern wings wrapped around like dried parchment.

"What's going on here?"

"This is nothing. Over there."

A few yards later there were four or five and once your eyes got used to the shade a number more to make it a dozen. A plane covered in wild thyme and ragweed was littered with hundreds of grounded black bats, some dead, others suffering in not-so-silent agonies. Their radar sounds were pathos. "This is what happens when you meddle with Mother Nature, friend. This is how the calculations of scientists play out when met with all the complicated machinations of this mother planet."

"Please stop talking like a B movie preacher."

"Oh, fuck you if you think this is some dismissible aspect of my melodramatic side. This is the direct consequence of just one of Wulfhardt's crazy fucking obsessions. Before this whole stupid werewolf paranoia hit him it was vampire bats. Of course, that was easy. Obvious because Austin is famous for its flights of bats launching themselves out into the crepuscule for food. He was sure that the old stories of undead bloodsucking were folkloric remains from the germ-bearing creatures that swarmed the night. Bats got blamed for a coupla recent pandemics, if you remember. You know, there used to be storms of them flying over that little town that bears his name. So he hired a kid from the university to look into it. Get rid of the Wulfhardt bats. Whatever poison he found worked. Now they lay here starving to death. You are looking at the end of bats."

"Oh come on, 'crepescule'?" said Shaney.

Lamel glared at Shaney. What a little piece of shit he was. Lamel could kill him so easily, he thought, if only he could.

"I mean, Wulfhardt couldn't be *too* crazy." Shaney was looking at Lamel, sensing the distance. "He's rich and he owns everything in town. In fact was gonna ask you about the ambulances with his name on them. What is that really?"

Shaney guessed then what was what. "Look," he sputtered. "You don't have to answer me and I guess I appreciate you taking me out here and warning me about his stuff, right?" he said babbling now. "A nod is as good as a wink, though this, well, this is a head jerk fer sure."

Lamel ground his teeth. He was not innocent, yet he was not willing to seek power over his own primitive drives.

"You're going to kill me," Shaney said.

"Don't you get it?" Lamel answered. "I fucking can't. God knows I want to. Try to understand this. It's the herd. You belong to her and she belongs to me. It's simple and irrevocable. I, *he*, could have taken you out four times and *he* didn't: The nightclub, Uncle John's, the dog, and the other nightclub. Plus there's another wolf, you know. I think I protected you from her at Uncle John's."

"Her," said Shaney, confused at first then resolved. "That's not it and you know it."

"What are you talking about?"

Now he was cocksure. "It has nothing to do with Lila May or some den bullshit. Or some shewolf you just made up," he said though Shaney did remember the boys at Uncle John's calling the howling wolf a girl. "It's something about me, man, me. You, *he*, came at me in the nightclub after you took out Ochocinco and then you, like, bounced off. Like a force field or some shit."

"Because you're Lila May's mate."

Shaney shuffled his feet and nudged one of the dying bats with a leather shoe. "Hah. Okay, dude, listen. You, *he*, can't kill me because I am *him*. It. Whatever. Wulfie locked me in a hospital room and watched me on a monitor last night. He said I started to turn but stopped. At first, I didn't believe it."

Lamel sat down on a dusty boulder on the edge of the field of death. "I thought there was something. Of course, I nicked you."

"Yeah and my hand healed completely next day. That's weird, man."

"But why *didn't* you turn?"

"Want to hear my theory? I think my body just fought it off. Because I think it's a virus, see?"

"Not a curse."

"Take time to think about this like a scientist. You know I'm right. If *he* doesn't kill you, *he* leaves something in your blood, maybe his saliva. You become *him* in one gestating month."

"Or not. Because it's not a curse."

"It's the only way to explain why I got a mild case. But I fucking went to the hospital, and my fucking hand healed. And Wulfie said I almost turned.'"

"Whatever is in your blood is the cure. The asymptomatic wolf."

"Huh. Plan B." Shaney looked like it honestly hadn't occurred to him. "Wow, something already in my blood, fuck my old ideas."

"Okay, I'll bite. What was Plan A?"

"Silver," he said. "No, don't laugh. It's got something to do with colloidal poisoning. And, plus, this legendary link between the myths and the truths. But now I can isolate whatever's in my blood and make an inoculant, or whatever. Why are you laughing?"

"Really? Silver?" What a fucking maroon. Silver has nothing to do with the legends."

"What do you mean? Chupacabra," said Shaney.

"Curt Siodmak, born in Dresden like the Wulfhardt clan, died in Three Rivers, California, made his mark in Hollywood, though. Wrote the 1941 movie, *The Wolf Man*, among many others. He came up with the silver bullet, man. He said it in his biography. One day on the lot. Silver. It's elegant bullshit, though, I'll give you that."

"You know, I saw those movies, too. I downloaded the famous one you're talking about. I wanted a laugh. In the opening scenes, a hand opens a book of ancient lore, which has to do with the so-called medical definition of wolf man."

He stopped, Lamel urged him forward on their walk. Thought maybe I shouldn't let him die. "Pray, what did the book of ancient lore, also written by Curt, have to say?"

"In the movie opening, the book on the screen claims it's a mental condition. It doesn't mention anything about actually turning into a bad dog. The opening makes a clear case it's a psychosis, used by murderous men to distance themselves from what they do. You call the werewolf in you I."

"Bullshit," Lamel said. "But also Bingo."

Over to the side of the powdery dust trail they could see the mountaintop and the river. They saw the silvery edge of it ascendant. "That's the way back," Lamel said, pointing at a trail down below heading at a perpendicular to the waterside. "I'm leaving you here."

"No, you're not," Shaney said. "You have to protect me."

"You know, Shaney, before I was a werewolf, I was a Roman Catholic."

"I was a Presbyterian," Shaney said, trying to be cool.

"Listen to me, asshole. The Catholics have this thing about sins of commission versus sins of omission. You can go to Hell for things you don't do, which if you think about it is exceedingly scrupulous," Lamel said.

Shaney laughed, "I know."

"Shut up. This is my committable omission sin. I'm going to abandon you here. That's why we came out so far. Fuck the bats and fuck Wulfhardt. I just wanted you out here because there's another wolf. I'm afraid of her and she's been seen in these hills and beyond. No, shut your mouth and listen. I hate you and I hate the way Lila looks at you. For all these reasons I am about to not do something and my Catholic half is going to Hell. I won't go to confession, I'll die and be judged. It's a lot cleaner that way. I don't think *he* can be punished for all the murders he's committed. The part of me facing damnation is going to jog off in that direction and swim across the river right there. Oh, I can do it, even without changing I get really fucking strong. Across the river, I won't be able to hear or smell you and I will turn into *him* and *he* will likely head for town. That's what I suggest you do, go back the way you came, starting now. And now just look at that." He pointed at the moon rising.

"She," said Shaney. "The wolf near Uncle John's."

There was the moon like a beautiful hallucination, the thin silvery edge of the shining moon breaking the ridge before dark might start to descend. "Yeah, like Uncle John's. You know, you are pretty smart."

"And I'm the cure."

"And despite what I say to Lila, I don't want to be cured. I want to live forever."

Herkyjerk Lamel started down the hill bracing himself for waters ahead.

Shaney screamed his name, "Get your ass back here."

The wolfman laughed and headed into the river, stripping.

Shaney estimated his return along trails back to the river bridge about 20 minutes. This meant when he reached the edge of town, the moon would be an inch clear above the sage crest of the desert foothill. That pockmarked satellite favored by sailors and farmhands would be beautiful tonight.

Not for Shaney.

The path grew deeper shadows. Evening was haze and high clouds and light winds. Ring-necked doves filled surrounding trees and mourning doves too. They bubbled sad airs. From some nearby aviary came peacock and peahen screams sounding like threnodies for damned souls, or maybe just plain old woe. He heard the first long, low howl when he spotted the running track. *Her?* He was walking into the killing floor.

Best to have a goal. Try for the house, grab the phone and computer, and see if he could make it to his car, lam it to Wulfhardt. He couldn't remember after minutes of panicky reflection broken by another howl from the south just where his car was. His hard shoes, now blanketed in dust, hit the aggregate pavement. He was flying over the river path. He saw a globulous bee and a hummingbird of more slender girth behind it rise at the same time from the waters as if in greeting. Onward. He seemed not to tire or be winded. He would make the road in five minutes at this clip. Then straight up the middle of Congress Street to Seventh and home. He couldn't call Lila, they wouldn't let him in this late, maybe he would be safest at SXSW, mingling in crowds.

Would he have been safer staying in Wulfhardt? Perhaps tied down on a hospital bed wasn't so bad. He'd have access in the morning to both his lovers and work on the cure. And then the howls began. All around him. He might have heard screams, too. Blood pumped. The bellows of his lungs fanned that blood. There were honks in the distance and then he heard sirens ranging every which way. Some mode of perception, a new sense, seemed to be working. The city as soundscape became more real and internalized. He heard reports, gun sounds bouncing back to him like sonar curves in a submarine. He "saw" visions of street blocks with figures running far away. A scream resolved itself into a node of visual representation somewhere near, like musical notation. His newfound sensory mechanism bloomed widescreen to meet the widespread cacophonies. His joints hurt as if they were stretched out on a torture rack.

He sweated and he panted now and traversed the road. He was at the bridge but didn't remember climbing up. But here he was sniffing north east west south; news, he could see a line of cars stopped above, empty, driverless. He felt a rush then heard a swelling scream come from Sixth Street, approximately.

Suddenly it was night all around him, he felt the pain in his joints subside but then his stomach contracted and he bent over and threw up something yellow and horrible-tasting. It was so sudden he felt no initial shame but caught himself apologizing and to nobody afterwards. He looked around then up. To his mortification, he saw people at the tinted windows of a twelve-story hotel looking down at him.

"I'm sorry," he shouted foolishly. They couldn't hear and weren't listening, but they were pointing and gesturing up the road and as Shaney made his way up to the summit of a small grass hill, he saw the State Capitol building and a stream of people running away from it screaming like Japanese monster movie extras.

Up on the street and indeed, those cars *were* empty. What brought them to this stalemate, snag, jam, he wondered. People streaming not into town for South by Southwest, but out and angry: North by Northwest. Mad. Another stream now ran by him silently, not gesticulating but pie-faced, ashen. Another series of screams a few blocks away and then howls up around the city, which he now read like a three dimensional map he knew. Smellscapes too, he thought. Fee Foo Fum. Fie it.

Shaney took an unexpected variance from up Congress Street when the next group of screaming citizens gestured him away. "Behind us," said the face of a tall, balding, and intelligent-looking man dressed in nice slacks and a white shirt. In truth, the crowd's panic transferred into Shaney. There. He saw one. It was coming at him, looking balled-up and intensely dangerous with fury or whatever bursting from it each time its limbs exploded out and the fur came forward galloping. Shaney ran, peeled off from the major thoroughfare that paralleled the river and tore sideways through town.

Then he saw *it*. In front of a liquor store he had never noticed before with a chain link fence that went nowhere but ended in a pole. On the pole was a man impaled, blood everywhere. And something else. The body should have been dead, but it wasn't. It was struggling and writhing upon a bloody pin and changing. Under the dark this horribly mutilated body leaked life while its arms began to grow hair and its face made cracking sounds as nose and mouth turned to snout and fang. The inefficiently murdered were coming back as civilization's scourge. This was really happening. But in the end, seconds later, the impaling pole did too much damage. The wolf died halfway through its origin of species recital. Shaney was sad somehow. But another series of screams coming from afar and moving nearer pushed him off.

A jog through suburban neighborhoods made him feel safer. He hadn't heard anything for a bit and wondered where he was going. Away from something, yes, but towards what? And then he came upon the Volkswagen sedan, doors opened in the street. Maybe somebody abandoned it. He heard sirens converging somewhere a long distance away. He thought about stealing the car. Shaney came around to the passenger door and saw the family strewn around the front- and backseat. The man who had been driving was opened up at the throat, but the child to his right got it a lot worse. In the back, there was a mother and probably a daughter, there was hair of honey-blonde color everywhere, a lot of hair in clumps. There was blood too. So much blood.

God, he thought. Death was now his byproduct, his fucking legacy to Austin. Come drummer, campfire stooges, Ochocinco, to this, he saw himself reflected in the turned car rearview mirror: his offspring, his red progeny. Maybe the family was watching television half an hour ago, the child giggling, then saw a commercial for pizza, got a truly joyful itch, a wild hair if you will, that they realized they could scratch. Maybe dad groused but was swayed by mom and kids to open his wallet and reach for the keys. They piled in telling jokes and riffing on the family's tease-able memories and then as they were about to close the clunky car door, they were slaughtered by some ancient curse or viral eruption that came via Shaney. His jinx bequeathal to this family on their way to pizza followed by bible study group, caught offguard by a monster, broken on the wheel of hunger and chance.

Five blocks away from his own neighborhood, Shaney stumbled on a rifle on the dark ground. Beyond it a dogman kneeled over an open corpse from which it tore gobbets. Blood ran. Shaney picked up the gun with care. The dog/wolf/creature turned his eyes to him. Shaney's heart was thudding and he thought about raising the rifle and then he thought oh fuck me and ran. The wolf kept eating.

Down the street with the big gun in his hand he heard the painful high keening of hurt dogs. Where were they? He encountered another group of humans but they did awkward social distancing, the contract had been suspended, made no eye contact, instinctively threw up their hands. Shaney thought, in deference to the chaos? And then remembered the rifle in his arms. Would it do him any good? Why was he holding on to it? He heard more screams of pain and fear as the passing group passed.

He went out in the street and started hollering. He wanted to howl out his frustrations. Behind him came a snarling. He whirled and saw the beast bounding up to him.

Shaney felt a jolt inside like never before. Like a drug's rush (he once spent an evening smoking cocaine and still tingled remembering the ringing in his ears and the jolt of well-being gained with each big delicious hit) but this was stronger. He leapt to one side without consideration for where he might land, which turned out to be the door wall of a blue Datsun. He picked up and ran Hightailed it over a cinderblock fence, across a backyard of white quartz stone and cacti and out onto another street and then turned back. Hoping to allay the beast he thought perhaps his scent would pull it, but when he jumped back over the wall there was the blood-flecked mouth waiting for him.

Shaney went down against an SUV, sliding along the smooth wall and tearing a scratch across his back on the chromium strip. He felt it now, and looked up to the moon for help. Perhaps he could will himself into the metamorphosis. Yes. Something bloomed at the end of his spine and some weak signal began to rise. The snapping beast came to a halt, smelled his back blood. Shaney lifted the rifle and the beast kept moving forward with his head cocked. At this point, the wolf looked more like a German Shepherd with his canted expression, his eyes like carefully crafted jewels, kaleidoscopic with visions of predation dancing. Shaney lifted the rifle and shot it in the bridge of its snout and beautiful eyes. The wolf sighed and went down.

John Shaney got up, a man, and looked at the gun and looked at his hands, which were very human. It was night and the cursed cursing moon was beautiful like the wolves' eyes and Shaney loved the forces that left him high like this. The chemical jolt ran its course and his heart thudded with pleasure in touch with a brand new set of emotions; unexpected gratification.

Up ahead he saw a surprising array of lights and incongruous sounds; happy squeals and laughter, loud lights, and bright chatter. He had overshot his own neighborhood running in numbed-out mode and was now near Sixth Street, the amoral hub of South by Southwest. He slouched up the street and broke through a throng of already-drunk revelers who seemed unaware of the Apocalypse taking place behind their backs, outside this bright zone.

"Hey, alright, Daniel Boone," said one young dude standing there. Shaney realized he might actually look weird with a rifle and a smile on his blood-splattered face. Wolf blood he thought, also contagious? He wiped with his bare hand and lowered the rifle, tried to look casual.

The street was thronged, though early in the evening, and most of the party-goers were of the aging touristy persuasion, trying to catch a thrill though the real action wouldn't start until later when the moon, now overhead, went down over the other mountains, in the meridians of desert haunts and ancient mixed grass prairie beginnings.

He heard sirens coming from the direction he came from, but he heard blaring music coming from up the street where he was heading. It was singing and something like:

I hope wherever you are
I hope there is some Austin
In you tonight


A phalanx of 30-year-olds in pancake makeup with lacquer-sprayed bedhead hairdos came holding guitars as if parodying Shaney's rifle stance. He realized the robotic-looking boys were crews traveling around an orchestrated mob. Inside it, lights shone on a kid with thick faux-nerdy glasses lip-synching like crazy to the blaring song about the party that is Austin. Shaney thought about his benighted father singing about Woodstock in the shower, not long before he killed Shaney's mother.

He was heading right into the blue-tinged cone of street lights and reflections off impossibly white kids marching toward him. Somebody yelled, "Cut cut cut." Shaney first registered the phrase as a violent command and then recalled its filmworld meaning.

"Who's the guy with the fucking rifle and what's his blocking?" said Orin Feeple, the AD on the set who had just usurped the stoned-out nominal director currently trying to get into the pants worn low by the cute intern from Emory. A commercial from the Independent Movie Channel, the film meant to reflect the spontaneous weirdness of Austin's signature fest, all of which Shaney sussed in a glance. Trucks and ostentatious aluminum boxes spray-painted with the youth-courting cable channel's logo reminded him of home where his television-dominated family-room glowed by the light of whispery Prius commercials.

He stalked away numb and wondering what Cassandra price he'd pay for warning everyone about nearby werewolves. At the very least, he figured, the rifle would be taken away—yet his conscience fluttered at the prospect of so many dying. Yelling wolf seemed bizarre till he remembered the torn scalps of the children, the blood. Then he saw the wolf—there—down a side street stalking up on two legs, blue pants torn a soft growl and a tipped snout clearly headed in his direction. He choked on a scream. Someone else screamed for him on that dark street and Shaney hustled his way into the crowd and marched into the arms of the dead poet.

There she was, his would be lover, the one he owed oral sex to and wished to repay, truth be told. The woman widely reported by police as dead stood breathing dressed in white, eschewing her usual inky coat. Tears were near Shaney started misting with relief and held his arms out offering an embrace. He thanked God aloud.

The "poet" stepped back, awkward. She was surrounded by Shaney's sullen roommates in protective phalanx yet all were agog at the sight of him armed with rifle. He called her by name.

"Whoa, dude, you got it wrong," said ubiquitous party monster Ron. "This is her twin sister, dude, here for the funeral, man, which is Tuesday at the house."

Ron walked towards Shaney oblivious at first to the weapon and the blood on Shaney's face. "Haven't seen you much, man."

Ron turned toward his roomies in a huddling pack now. "He was close to your sister," he said to mimic woman. "Roomed next door, in fact. More importantly, he was the last one to see her, well…"

"Shut up, Ron," said the poet's girlfriend, who was also there. "What's with the fucking artillery?"

"Werewolf," said Shaney, finding his voice. Neither ghost nor resurrection sister would faze the hunter, though a vision of ghostly pentagram shadows on her face and the roommates did give pause. A chain of five-pointers stretched across the crowd. Wolves are coming, he thought, you all die. But didn't speak. He gazed as the hallucination became more focused and the pentagrams danced. He was too embarrassed to save people! Weird.

"What're you on, man? Can I get some?" said Ron, chuckling at the gawping Shaney.

"Werewolf. Your sister was killed by a werewolf," Shaney said turning to the eerie resemblance dressed opposite.

"Jesus Christ," said the poet's twin, named Gudrun, a baker by trade. "My sister sure knew how to pick 'em. Boogie-boogie," she said waggling her hands in mocking fashion. Such frigidity was unexpected, Shaney thought and then grew angry as he saw a chain of Texas stars on string pass above them light up. The shadows on the faces, an accident on top of a TV display. Thus the pentagrams.

"Fuck you," he said to them all. "I'm tired of this shit. All of you, go die."

Lisa Lykes, the cute one, stepped forward. "Please. Chill. Can't someone stop trying to compete for Chief Griever? He was your sister's lover."

"Bullshit, man," said the lesbian. "We were married."

"Oh, please," said Lisa, adamant before false-righteousness. "Like you weren't fucking every cooze in sight. You were hitting on me in a bar when your wife was dying in that vacant lot."

"She was very real," said Shaney horrified by such talk. The vacant lot while he was waiting to go down on her in accordance to love's duty's call. "She was really nice," he added inadequately.

"She used to make these fuckin great waffles on mornings we ditched school," said Ron dreamily.

"What about you, John?" said the cute one, turned lethal in the hypocritic mists. "Was she your hetero squeeze-toy?"

"When I was sick she took me to the health center and then we went to The Salt Lick." He was strangely calm and then he looked down the street and saw the flash of fur, or maybe not. Some screams came from that direction.

"Amen," said Lisa. "So what're you fighting about?"

"Apparently wolfmen," muttered Gudrun.

"I so want to see a werewolf," said Ron, staring at the back of his own hand over which a Texas star shadow danced.

"Come with me, then," said Shaney, turning sadistic in the idle banter, tired of fiddling while Austin bled. "I'll show you one right now."

"Meet you on the flip side, homies," said Ron acting on what Star Trek captains call impulse drive. Shaney wanted to get away and Ron had a key to the house.

"Later," they all said under their breath, Lisa turned around, though, and called back wistfully, "Come to the funeral party on Tuesday," she said and (unbelievably) gave Shaney a wink. Shaney still spooked looked on in growing bemusement, the group heading to a nearby club that didn't have a line but, Shaney happily noted, was shielded over by a giant pentagram, Lone Star, whatever.

"Dude, what is it you got?" said Ron, looking on. "Speaking of which That blotter shit you have is solemn truth, can I score more of that, hmmm?"

"Yeah, Ron, you can. I'll show you a werewolf too. Just walk me to the house, okay? I'll set you up with a few hundred hits."

"Dude."

He followed. Shaney meant the offer too. They ran promptly into professor Beveritch, the Dean, and alongside him in tow was a leggy woman Shaney was sure he had seen in at least two of his lecture classes. She smiled at him then looked down at the strewn ground.

"Mr. Shaney, I presume," said the dean. Nervous drunk Ron looked leering-obvious.

"Beveritch's bitch," Ron whispered to Shaney. "Dean, uh, hi," he said aloud.

"You know Ms. Trinckable?" said the hoary academic enjoying his svelte companion in the mild night air of celebrative city life. "Don't you have a report due to me like this week; your semester progress or something?"

"I'm no longer a grad student, sir. I thought you would know that," said Shaney, perplexed.

"No, I don't know that. Nobody thought to tell me. What are you doing instead of pursuing your great gift?"

"Sir, this is confusing. I'm sure you know I'm at Wulfhardt laboratories. Since you set up the meeting and, and, stuff."

"Studying what?" he said. "Working on what?"

"Um, werewolves," said Shaney.

"We're gonna go fuckin' see one," said Ron leering intensely at the young woman wide-eyed. "Want to come?"

She took this opportunity to grab Beveritch's tweedy arm and snuggle close for protection. "We'll be late," she said. "Tickets for the Iceberg Heads," she said. The band was the blandest of acts possible on that SXSW day.

"A second," said the dean, raising a halting hand. "What're you saying?" the dean asked into Shaney's space. "Werewolves?" asked the dean.

"Maybe that's what the rifle is all about?" said blondie.

"Listen, Shaney," he said, "I don't know what's going on there. But I want you to consider coming back. Pure research is much more rewarding in the long run and even though I've never made that kind of money, there are intangible benefits."

Shaney looked at the beautiful woman who looked back at him with unexplained fire.

Then the prof laughed. "Just fucking with you. Talk at the college is that you are making things happen for Wulfie."

"Talk," said Shaney. "Things." Chupacabra, he thought.

"Yes. Buzz."

"Speaking of buzz, he's giving me 100 hits to walk him to the house," said Ron who seemed somehow to be getting more fucked up by the minute even though not physically imbibing. "A-woo, werewolves of London," sang Ron. "His hair was perfect," he added.

"I'm taking him home," said Shaney.

"Call me," said the professor. "I still want some sort of report."

"Nice to meet you," said the woman. She winked at Shaney.

"Come on man, I gotta pee," said Ron. "We're off to be the whizzers, the wonderful whizzes of Aus. Tin. Get it?"

"Whatevs," Shaney said. He had no idea what might happen next in his life.

"I know, right?" Ron added. "What will pee will be."

"I lost my keys," said John.

"There's always a key under the tree. The Bodhi Tree key."

Shaney was about to ask what that meant realizing they were about seven blocks from the house when the world became fabulously spread apart. SXSW music mixed with the thrumming bass of a lowrider gliding by and a long La Cucaracha horn blowing. Lights twinkled. The sea of faces gave way to a dark spot swimming with purple outside the pool of street light and pine smell filled Shaney's nose. Something big rushed by brushing Ron, who said "What the fuck," in a loud voice and then began bubbling.

"I know, right?" Shaney said repeating the tired mantra of the age, but froze looking over. Ron's face was ripped across the right side and a large flap of scalp was hanging over his eye which appeared to be gone along with his ear. He fell back and then stumbled forward. "What the fuck," Ron repeated softly repeating again the bubbling gurgle. Shaney fell further back, too, his stomach now lifting up its own contents in an offering to the streets, which the dusty indifferent road accepted.

Home, he thought, wiping off his mouth, I need room. He looked up and the wolf was upon his roommate who had been so pleasantly stoned just moments ago. Ripped, thought Shaney, who was now freaking out so bad that his limbs were tingling. His heart, he thought, how much can his heart take? And then the wolf was joined by a smaller wolf, which Shaney had a terrible feeling about. Was that a ripped red raincoat on its back and he remembered the child in the back of the car. The bigger wolf turned viciously on the smaller wolf and then from the corner of its great big eyes spotted Shaney staring stupidly back, in awe.

Shaney ran and wondered if the rest of his life was to be flight. He felt the tingle become a mild pain and began to wonder if his death at the hands of a beast was any more preferable than being torn apart by his own heart's fingers, heart attacked. His legs lost any shred of weariness and his hands began to scoop air as he ran. He could see the channel between the houses and knew the streets as if they were labeled. He could sense behind him the presence of three animals running and when he stropped suddenly tearing the ground apart—how did he get so strong—the three whizzed past him. He lit out between the houses and heard the clucking of a hen and felt the breathing of a fat opossum on a white branch redolent of Hawthorne bloom.

The creatures had caught up with him as he crashed into a hedge. His face was scraped and he tumbled ass over knees into a meadowy backyard full of tragic gnomes. The young ones raced forward and then screamed in pain, admonished from behind by teeth and the two of them slunk off behind the big wolf with what great ears he had and Shaney knew at once from the ripped place along its throat that this was what was left or maybe the enhanced version of Ochocinco ready for anything now—ready for revenge.

As Shaney backed up on his back crawling with his limbs he felt himself clenched into a muscle. "Fuck you pussy shitfaced fuckwit," he taunted, but the wolf was not particularly into irony. This was to be different from flight and he was ready for it somewhere in his new system of sensory knowledge. Remembering the gun, the rifle, the weapon in his hand. Shaney held it up and steady into the eye of the beast if not its belly. The wolf began a sure advance and Shaney saw a silvery strand of saliva flow beautifully from his jawline. For me, he thought, wow. Fuck it, I want to live, he thought and pulled the trigger just as the smaller beast leaped in front of the two of them, took the bullet, which passed through its heaving furry side, squealed like a child and landed bleeding on Shaney. The larger wolf had run back into a hedge of citrus and the lights in the house came on, when Shaney was prepared to stand up and be an embarrassed backyard intruder. He had never shot anything before this night, now two, and there on the lawn was a human child. The gun went off again and Shaney left the vicinity, though he had no idea where or how.

Behind him was death. In front of him was safety, life—he was going to save himself, he thought, wondering how many more bullets this rifle might hold. He crossed into a little suburban street near a liquor store with cop car lights down at the end of it. He raised his hand and then got a glimpse from the side, a rushing creature came close and then squealed in the colored lights.

"Halt," said the cops. "Throw down the fucking gun."

It was a long way, reasoned Shaney, then decided to trot off. One of the cops fired into the air and another asked what the hell he was doing. He scrambled up a sidewalk and was heading for the house nearby when the bullet glanced him, hard. He was blown against the wall of the house, the same house, deserted, the poet's last false refuge.

America, he thought.

Now, in a changing second, death was in front of him, his life behind; the reversal sudden and complete. It is always like this probably. It wasn't his whole life, but it was visual and filled with regret, it brought his knees up to a fetal curl. He heard everything around him as he scrunched against the wall. Crickets grinding legs; the resounding joys of Sixth Street, pretty far away; classic rock coming from a kitchen radio. The song about the crossroads and falling on your knees.

Shaney picked up the cold rifle from the dew-kissed ground stumbled from what had been done to him and all he had seen. Fuck rationality from now on. Yeah. He took off for home. The cops must have been bewildered and then he heard them screaming.

He found the back patio and he found the door still locked crap and found the key under the bodhi tree, a stupid potted plant near the back door. There was a sign about the funeral for the poet on the counter. He thought he probably should not go—then he thought he better. He was bleeding all over.

Up in his room, though, he felt good. Outside there were sirens and screams and the sound of music even on the streets protected by the pentagram, the lone star state of mind. He grabbed his gauze again and went looking in his roommate's room for bigger bandages. He found a sanitary napkin. There was more blood even though he put a towel over the wound. He found his laptop and his toothbrush and a pair of clean underwear. He went to the mirror and washed off the spots of blood. Disinfected it ouch. Locked the doors for a few moments and lay down not caring what his mind or his self might turn into. Every night we give up logic, rational thought, and the veneer of morality. In dreams, he sang, a candy-colored clown tiptoes to sprinkle stardust.

Woke to the bedclothes thrown about, blood on his sheets and in the towel. Fuck it. He threw the sheets and the towels inside a pillowcase. He snuck a peak at the bullet wound. Gone. Natch. This is my blood that shall be given to all. His roommates were silent or sleeping or gone. Checked his pockets and headed out on the streets. There was the limousine with the driver gone. He decided not to worry. Deep down in his pockets were the keys to his car. There all the time. There up the street was the vehicle. He was out of here. He would find Lila May and her mom, make them his wives, and would save the world from its scourge with the strange fix of his own blood dried on his dirty sheets.

# 25.

Picking up the morning newspaper at the diner outside Wulfhardt, with the waitress practically in his lap outloud wishing he would have not been such a stranger, offering her phone number and if she knew he was coming she would've baked a cake, laughing, telling him what time she got off, case he was wondering, and meanwhile Shaney was perplexed 'cos the Austin paper on the chair next to his table had no apocalyptic news, crazy, and the internet on his phone had nada mucho neither, silence of the lambs, he thought.

He surmised the SXSW publicists got to the newspapers to under-report a slaughter, a debacle, endgame for humanity, though they did run a missing persons blurb about a family car found dripping with gore, apparent victims of a tragic hit and run incident, but bodies gone and no reports from hospitals busy with the usual violent crime endemic to a rock and roll pop culture festival.

In a part two headline, the columnist proposed: Bath Salts Epidemic Hits SXSW Crowd, subhead: Violent Frenzy By Outsiders Critically Injures Scores of Locals: Dressed like animals, read the lede, imitating recent horror film, cinematic violence and on and on; bath salts meant bullshit.

The rest of the paper was full of foreign death. The United States had egg on its face because some soldier deployed in Iraq had gone on a civilian killing spree. Meanwhile, the moon was falling off the full and tonight the tourists will caravan home.

He paid, tipped the pretty girl, got in his car, drove to the now familiar place, but automatic gate wouldn't open and some rough voice told him to chill a sec and he edged his car up though he wouldn't be warmly welcomed he guessed.

More importantly, though, he knew what to do now. The blood in the pillowcase.

He fell asleep waiting but was shaken awake by the bodyguards, scared but then remembered he had good news; the good news was in the backseat.

One big guy stood him up, took his keys rudely and the other took him by the crook of an elbow and brought him back to the kitchen and towards the same glass of fortified orange juice left 24 hours ago by the looks of it then left.

Shaney decided to go see his girlfriend and as he sauntered out into the living room with its two storeys high of family portraiture, he heard a crying coming from the lofty heights. La Llorona. A hand tapped him from behind and he jumped. Turned around and he could see that Wulfhardt *pere* was pissed.

"You made psychedelic drugs in my lab?"

Shaney regarded him with uncertainty and then refresh-buttoned his mind. "Shut the fuck up," he said.

Wulfhardt, impressed, did so.

"I found the cure," said the younger man. "I am the cure. And the light and the way, saith me." He realized now how tired he was how lightheaded from all he had seen and heard, but knew he had to press on. He had slept through the hours of the wolf in his car outside the restaurant. He wanted some distance from the killing fields and now here he was babbling to jaunty Wulfhardt. His side was healed. He was a wolf. The experiment was over; he knew all he needed to know.

The older man had a feeble grasp of the words. "What you are saying, then, is that you believe me. Werewolfery in Texas."

"And I found a way to defeat them. Are you even listening?"

"There's more than one?" said Wulfhardt plunged into a sullen and sudden brown study.

"Yeah, but it doesn't matter. You were right about me. I'm one of them. But then again, I'm not. Two wolfmen, I mean wolfpeople attacked me. Make it three. None of them could go through with it. Have you ever read Conrad Lawrence? Their instincts forbade them to kill one of their own. If you could figure out how and why to take someone into the curse but short-circuit it, you have the antidote, inoculation. I'm living proof that the disease can be fought. Hell, I'm living proof of everything." Babbling.

Wulfhardt quietly digested it all. "And we're stuck with theories, and more tests, and more fucking interns…"

"I hate to interrupt but, no. It's in me, the antigen or whatever. I need to go to the laboratory and draw my blood. I want to look at what is floating around in there. How the wolf that bit me changed my blood."

"You were bitten and you hung around my daughter."

"Didn't I say for you to fuck off? I didn't know." Shaney started thinking this was all starting to speed up like a runaway train, with engineer Wulfie McMoron at the wheel.

"I'm going to drive down to the lab right now," Shaney repeated. "I want to analyze. But first I want to see Lila May."

"Out of the fucking question," said Wulfie, colder than punctuation marks. "We have a hospital here and I can take you to the lab. Let's get the blood here now and maybe some other kinds of samples. I'll get the doctor and the technician. Get down to the medical wing. And by the way, steer clear of my wife too. I know you fucked her. We'll go down together."

"I didn't," he said.

"More likely she fucked you, I know. I'll have my revenge, don't worry. And for my daughter. If she ever found out. Either way you are staying real close. But not with either of them."

Shaney speechless feared this scary development and the voice his boss was using. Everything changes and suddenly Wulfhardt was guiding him, telling him to sit in the infirmary's small kitchen and left Captain Beefcake to watch him.

Me and my big mouth, thought poor John. He wanted out now that the tide had turned, would rather take his chances with the wolf in the open valley of the river. They sat for 15 unbearable minutes. Then a tech came in a white coat and took Shaney's dark red blood with a suction needle thingie, then a quick swab from the inside of John's cheek. The crisp attendant gave Shaney a wink. They handed him a beaker, pointed to the toilet.

People who would do any crazy thing Wulfie wanted. They said alright attaboy and then started teasing him. One of the lugs stood up and walked back to fetch Wulfie. His motioning blue eyes sent Shaney back into the room. He paced and thought hard. My father's mansion has many rooms, he thought. He straightened up, tucked in, opened the door, and started walking down the hall, calling for Gwen only to be physically seized from behind.

"What's up," he said.

"You win," said Wulfhardt suddenly there. "Off to the lab."

He wondered about his future now, the fate of his cushy job and giant paycheck seemed sealed against him.

"Ve'll take you in the limo," said Wulfie's personal secretary Hindemann, here to handle the termination, S. guessed. "But you won't need to drive, dot's for fucking sure."

All the big guys laughed. There was a noise in the hall and a little confusion—Shaney thought he heard *her*. He wasn't losing his job, more likely his life. This could be the last time, he thought. Gwen. He fought. Tried to bite. Was overpowered. The beefy guy slid Shaney, corduroys shrieking against upholstery, into the car then crowded in too. The door shut them into a tinted cocoon. The car slid down streets smoothing out rock, gravel, and cracked onramps leveled by the car's butterglide suspension. If this was doom, it was the cushioned kind, thought Shaney. Pulled up and guess what? Behind the lab, and there's the other smaller lab.

"Let's hustle," said a particularly fat-marbled guy moving up close to him. Down a corridor, getting narrower and narrower, and as the walls closed in the group speed increased till he felt himself compelled as if to a killing floor, which turned out to be a dark room that smelled like his father's garage shop, old oil on dusty pavement with grace notes of exhaust. These are the last things I will ever experience, he thought, and his legs went suddenly rubbery. The beefy guy caught him and asked if he was okay.

"Okay?" Shaney croaked. "No."

"Whatsa matter, friend?" asked the heartless goon with adamantine arms.

"Where will you throw my body?" he asked.

"Your what? Whattayou sayin'?"

"After he's through with me, where will you assholes bury me?" Shaney had a vision of a maimed corpse alone, him.

"Wow. I thought the Wulfhardts were the only nuts here, but you seem quite insane to match." He crossed his yes and twiddled his index finger in the air. "It's *fun* to be cuckoo," he added in cartoon voice.

Shaney wanted to bolt but let himself be moved indoors. He was walking towards his death. Why don't the condemned suffer heart attacks, he wondered, at the last walk to their end? Inside, he was taken by other hands. On a television screen hooked to the microscope his own blood danced with rhythms drawn from the circadian, Brownian, and tidal impeti. There rods and exes danced among moving and oscillating membranes of the cellular life that we once called paramecium. People would point and get excited; Shaney didn't know any of them except they seemed far more knowledgeable than he.

Maybe he wasn't so disposable, he realized. The first blood would wear out, no doubt, before they found whatever it was they were looking for. He would be a donor. Maybe get a cell or a nice apartment. Give some blood. Three hots and a cot, meanwhile. Adaptation is what we do. Meanwhile he had to pee. And he wandered out the door and down the hall and found the men's room and saw himself in the hall of mirrors made by the facing sinks lined up in the lavatory of the laboratory where groups of men might wash their hands and stare across at themselves and infinity, receding into the shrinking end of eternity discussing sports or some compound that forms a catalyst and converts the world to pure sparks of time—maybe ignite the world. The lathery soap around his hand evoked an actual memory of his sixth grade visit to the toilet alone sudden calmed reflections beyond the intricacy of classroom games. He wondered if it meant anything that this memory would come now or if all was a shower of randomness.

He returned and they seemed to have never missed him. He might have walked away from this imprisonment. The scientists looked dissatisfied.

"Whatever it is, the pathogen is not obvious," said one senior fellow who addressed Wulfie.

"What is it that you described to me?"

Shaney said, "Huh?"

"That wolf attacked you and what happened?"

"It opened a force field, he spun out howling, screaming in fear or something. Whatever."

"Anthropomorphizing, likely," said the senior fellow. "Wish I could have seen it."

"We could duplicate the operation easy enough," said Wulfhardt. "We have to wait a month, though. We'll send our werewolf after him, see if it repeats."

"You own a werewolf?" asked Shaney.

"Easy squeezy," said the thugee dude. "I just followed him till the moon went down. He ate a lot and I shot him up with a thorazine dart. And then he went to sleep like a baby. Want to see him?"

Wulfie shrugged. They stood up. Mr. Lug grabbed Shaney and walked down the hall to an exit. The door opened to another hall. Wulfie ran a card through a security machine and a vast James Bond room lit clack

clack clack. "I've got calls to make," said Wulfie in robot voice and turned around to leave.

Down into the vast hall Shaney saw a glass cube. Inside it the Mexican man, the professor, Ochocinco. He was crying.

"Tell him to shut his fucking mouth," said the larger thug. A henchling jogged down to quiet the professor who wasn't cussing now. The thug screamed at Ochocinco.

"Now now," said Wulfhardt returning and pocketing his phone. "I coulda done that myself. Remember. He's a person. Until the next full moon. Drawing his blood regularly? Feeding him?"

The big thug nodded.

"Shaney? Is that you? Help me?" said Doctor Pottymouth.

"I'm in the same thicket you are," said Shaney.

Wulfhardt answered in terse voice. "You and that monster belong to science now. Real science. Not the polite university kind. And if you want to live you will cooperate I want you to draw a lot more blood right now. Much as you safely can."

They headed back up to an elevator and sat in a bureaucratic office. That made the whole thing seem worse. They'd left the hall of horrors for a meeting. But there was a shout down the hall. It was Wulfie's secretary assistant calling Shaney's name.

"I was not to be disturbed," said the old man.

"John Shaney," said another voice from down the darkness. Outside the door of banal furnishings.

A throat cleared and there they were, the boss's secretary with three of Austin's finest. "John Shaney," he repeated.

The secretary pointed at John.

"I'm Shaney, officer," he said aloud then stepped forward as two uniforms approached with handcuffs.

"John Shaney you are under arrest," said the biggest cop and began to recite the Miranda mantra. "Do you understand these rights?"

"Yes, I do, but what's the beef?" Shaney said giggling now. Escape. He laughed.

"John Shaney you are under arrest for a felony charge of animal cruelty," he said. "Lobo's law," said the cop.

"Loco's law," said his partner. "You killed a fucking labradoodle, laughing boy, and we got it on tape."

"He also was planning to kill some more dogs too," said the sniffy secretary.

# 26.

The free phone call wasn't working out for him. His mother was dead, stabbed to pieces a couple of years or so ago by his methhead father currently somewhere in jail. He had this vague memory that his father's time was served in Texas, maybe they could be cellmates. You stabbed my mother's face? Yeah. 'Sides that, how you doin?

He called his girlfriend first but hung up before it rung. He felt terrible and guilty, but tried the Trinity House. They never picked up or called back. Later he found out one of the roommates had filed a complaint alleging possible abuse of that hissyfit cat. The watch captain had made notations in a computer file that pooped up the info when (fuckshitpiss) Ochocinco sent the video—bingo, two strikes. En route to the hoosegow one Veronica Wipes of the Wulfhardt lab called the station to report that

Shaney once requested puppies for experiments. Delivered, sealed, and signed his fate was. Some pop cop psychologists claim that the burgeoning personality of a sociopath will often first be detected by the maiming of pets. Besides, Texas liked putting people in jail.

Now that he escaped Wulfhardt's clutching claws, and though ignorant of most of the treachery against him, Shaney began to fear what that jail time actually might mean. Icy cold, zombie afternoons wandering over numbed old cement floors, endless days adrift like a phantom staring out he would stare through the moral pall that hung over violent folk. For him it would be something like a revisit to his stifled childhood. And then memories. Haunting the old haunts, the ghost pains come home.

His heart was thudding. Nothing softening here, this floor was a petrified stormcloud subducting life itself. The sheriff led him by the arm out of booking procedures and into a holding tank brimming with people itching their own skins off making druggy talk from terse lips below red eyes. Many arrests were made at SXSW revelries. Some of these folk might have come from the Surly show, some might be turned, surmised Shaney.

No one asked what he was in for. Even mean people harbor sympathy for the plight of pets and other so-called dumb animals. Would they hesitate to hate him, the accused canicide? Truth was, funny thing was, a lot more human death surrounded him, stuff he was more responsible for, so maybe he had some bad K coming. Overdue for society's plucking hand. He held down the cell's corner trying to look invisible but tough.

His biggest fear was getting bailed out by his boss.

She decided to attend the funeral for the dead poet at the Trinity House, "a celebration of life," that bulwark phrase used nowadays to usurp a person's right to be honestly grieved. Maybe she wanted closure, another cliché thrust in the path of honest suffering. Technically, there were two losses, though. Ron's whereabouts were unknown but suspect though some believed he just "ran off with an Austin ho." Or maybe Lila wanted to find her own fate somewhere. Her father turned on her. Her boyfriend was in jail for animal abuse. Course, he claimed to be innocent despite the viral video.

On the day of the poet's memoriam she showed up alone. It was two weeks before the epidemic and half a year before the weather slipped away from us. On the warm, warm day, they were all in the backyard under flowering trellises that would die in the coming summer. We know that humans can adapt to anything. Lila was human, therefore....

Anyway, she showed up and it was hot outside but inside cool. She went through the front door. (The jamb represents fate.) The party was in the back, the sign said: The celebration of life. In the haunted living room she yoo-hooed but it was a high and anemic hale and it produced nothing but self-consciousness. She crossed into the kitchen over polished hardwood floors that creaked with her passing. She meandered through memories accumulated around the kitchen arch into a room that afternoon sun lit. She watched the folks outside sopping up PBRs and IPAs and talking RIPs loud with the bravado of youth and booze. Bubbling small talk. She overheard two earnest boys on the porch: Police hint it might be a long time solving the mystery of the poet's death due to the thoroughly baffling animal tracks around her mutilated corpse. She learned this, and Lila May shivered in the cool room thinking of the poet's last moments then moved on to the upbeat funeral.

He hadn't returned her calls in three days, she said to those who dared to ask. She knew jail was tough, fraught with the thing she feared most, lack of free movement. People there thought she should leave him there. Lila was sorry for the poet. She wondered if the room was open. For rent.

There was a table and there were muffins and she ate two of them and thought they tasted weirdly spiced. She passed between two cliques on her way to the wine. It was next to impossible to move around the roadhog fat professor (some unyoung were there too) who was loudly discussing, believe it or not, the eschatology of narration in Luke's Gospels as a Gay Apocalypse, which he kept referring to as a conflation of the eagle and the lightning bolt. The willowy, ashen students surrounding him seemed one part zombie and two parts recording devices set on playback to respond with phrases they were programmed to like. Like "ideology," "trauma theory," and "Enlightenment Project," phrases murmured internally with titanic force that precluded argument, much less actual understanding.

Another nodding professor nearby had become famous describing the ontologies of overhead observation, spy cameras in satellites, space spooks and space ghosts, a corruption of film studies. The satellite eye had put a footprint on all of the earth she said in a metaphor salad.

One of the bland students brought up the possibility of a satellite stopping the wolf attacks in the city.

"I thought it was teenagers," said someone.

"She once wrote a poem about being the mother of nothing except a dumb fate," the professor said indicating a picture of the poet. The poet's sister passed by rolling eyes.

"It's the oedipal myth all over us again," said one dirty-blond-grey stubbled old man holding court.

"Please no, Bruno," said an even older man coming up behind him and bumping up against his ass in provocative buttfuck simulation.

"Just another myth about man's unsuccessful negotiation up from the happiness of animal life," he said, "into the half-achieved odyssey toward angel envy. It's also all about the nightmare of technology."

"Here we go," said the swishy partner sloshing wine and words.

"Who asked the riddle?" said greybeard of his rapt attenders.

"The sphinx," said one of the grad students who should have known better.

"Precisely, the composite animal, a man face but the body of a lion, meant to imply the only possible way towards wisdom was combining the two natures. Always religions want to take us backwards and the Greeks worshipped animals and trees. Revered. Iconic, you kids would say. And what was the riddle?"

"Four legs in the morning, two legs in the afternoon, and three legs at night," said Lila. "Human beings."

"Yes, the ancient poet's anticipation of the Darwinian answer. Where do we come from? Four legs. Where are we going? Two. From days when we crawled on all fours, then find ourselves erect."

"Speak for yourself," said the bonhomie man. "Eee-rect yourself."

"And then technology is the flourish, the third state. We invent tools to take us where we will go. We evolve to two legs and then conquer infirmity by brandishing the true sword of the angel that threw us from the garden, the rod that parted the Red Seas. A rod to brandish over the other apes, employed to take us into the cosmos."

"Into the cosmos with Mr. Kubrick," said the professor's fool. "The jawbone and the space station. The waltz. O our imperfections save us, homo habilis needs technology. Tools. "

"I prefer homo ee-rectus," said his friend slinking his hand around his friend's broad shoulders. "My man has tools too."

"But tragedy ensues. Since he is no longer bound by rigorous animal kingdom codes he must kill his father and must copulate his mother, then pluck out his own eyes and hobble into the future. Discuss."

"The ancient Greeks in the time of Homer invented the discus," said one classics postgrad girl, scanning but seeking laughing affirmation she spotted Lila. The girl gasped and said, "You've got a ton of gall showing up here. Word is, you all took John Shaney away before we could beat the shit out of him ourselves," she said.

"What do you mean, you all?" said Lila.

The others tried to calm this drunken funeral-goer, but she turned harder against Lila. "O that's just the way we talk in the south, but seriously, what is up with that shit?" she asked. A more sober woman suggested Lila leave. Which was ironic since normally her presence would make a party's reputation.

Lila backed out of the weirdo clique. Obviously John didn't kill the poet. Did he? Turning she went into the house, and spied a photo of John pinned to a dartboard. What did it mean? She went up to their bedroom on three legs using the banister as tech support to steady her weary tread up to the old trysting spot. She hid behind the door, maybe wishing John or Louis was there to save her. She wanted away from such horrible people and had the room to herself. She stood there shaking and confused at first. She wanted to leave but wanted to stay. Gradually, as she watched the window gather rainbows in its edge she thought she might be going crazy then realized in a blinding wave of revelation that the muffin she had eaten was likely an edible. Oh well. That explained the shaky walk. Speaking of the oedipal, she thought about Professor Exlax downstairs and his homo friend and that curse and that riddle of his that went around and around in her mind and her father and she thought of Grandpa the Nazi doctor who used to tickle her for so long she peed, what he wanted was wrong, demonstrably. Go against nature, this room grows hot. That pot's got paraquat. Her imagined father replied: It thickens the plot. Before she knew it she was wandering free dancing with the wisp that came out of the hall room, the cat.

No one to say meow, kitties
Meow

She sang that song that John liked. Animal something. Not "The House of the Rising Sun" Animals. Not a "soul whose intentions are good" Animals. Collective, the Animal Collective, the creatures are comrades.

Her Papa thought that the cowboy was a wolfkiller. The cowboy named Texas who once was a promising researcher till he started drinking. That one went crazy. Papa wanted to study Texas' theories. The transfiguration of organs, he studied the apostasy no apoptosis of cells when killing a cancer, like Grandpa's, something to do with the creation of an amphibian. Something to do with teenage acne. A ghost of a cell might be left behind and then be manipulated. Reanimated. He made it work on a hamster, which was almost funny, he said. Nobody knows how he did it though because Texas disappeared into a bottle and then a room full of guitars.

John was a wolfkiller and she guessed a dog killer. Mother must be saved.

She went soft rummaging through the stuff in his room, John's room, and for a moment found happiness remembering. She hugged some plaid stuff that hung askew in his closet where a cat slept. There was a clutter of souvenirs on the table: bar napkins and movie stubs. Memories. The night they watched *Brave* twice. The monthly anniversary at Stubbs. Only one month. Hair? A locket of? Mine? Woven into a fetish? She never gave him it. The rape of the lock. My heart a tress. She found a list he made and she was on it "to call." But not at the top. Still, there. There there. Just before VapoRub to buy and Jim Beam to swill. Oh well, boys, she thought. Put head on pillow and smelled his sour left behind sweat.

His phone was ringing somewhere, muffled. She knew the ringtones, Tchaikovsky Peter and. She couldn't find it but it kept ringing so she tore the room apart, bedclothes on the floor. Then she saw it in the little alcove, the shrine they had made to the Texas Lone Star, he loved it. The phone was in a bag with drugs. She reached in picked up the phone vaguely recognized the number said yes in a hoarse voice. Hoping to find him.

"John, Darling," said her mother. "I was so worried about you. When are you coming back for me? I miss you so much darling darling. What happened?"

John Darling, Lila thought, wasn't that the eldest child among Wendy's lost boys? She was numbed. The voice repeated the pet name.

"Hello, Mother," she said. She wasn't stoned anymore. She heard a well-defined gasp and then the phone went dead.

This wasn't happening. My darling darling and it was her. Gwen calling John, her cell number plain on the "recents." Looking down the list; over and over mixed in with others and hers. Her number and mine. Mother said my darling darling and it sure seemed like reality. Her number and her mother's. She bent over the trash can and threw up everything she had eaten for the last eleven hours.

Okay maybe she was still stoned. Maybe she was having a heart attack or some shit like that. Meowkitties. She said, When are you coming back for me? He's somewhere else now. In strange straights.

Lila thought about Oedipus. Fuck my mother and kill my father further. And what about me? What walks on four legs? Dog. I used to think men were dogs, said a female comedian she knew, and then I realized they're not that faithful. She washed her face in the inside bathroom and tears washed the washed face and she threw up again. She patted herself on the towel.

Outside again she found it impossible to breathe, she was whitefaced in the reflecting window. On the tabletop outside were tequila and a shot glass. There was also kahlua and cream. She made a tiny drink of one third each ingredient. Be brave, she thought. Brave bull. She drank seven more, licking her lips and feeling a little better after six. Delicious. She had one more. Her stomach was warm now and her fingers felt cozy.

Find a way to walk and mingle a respectful moment then run home. Wait. Which home? Apartment, can never return, Mama's neither. She goggled, her pale head held high, and she approached the grad student cohorts. They were stoned now too. All civilization is stoned and don't know anything. Doesn't? She was trying to get up the nerve to interrogate but the crowd was not paying attention to her righteous glares. They were mesmerized by a drawling rap performed by none other than Texas who she knew in a Biblical sense not so long ago. Who she was just thinking about. He winked. Remember? He was at that other party when she was armlinked to John. That seemed a distant memory but was just a month ago. Texas was John as well. John Toad. He winked at her. She was proud of her buzzed self for remembering. She wandered back to the drink table and had two more. It settled her stomach and she thought about her mother, being her mother, up under her boyfriend. She had one more.

Texas's song was funny. It was his contention, articulately drawled, that there was not any real gravity, in fact, the earth sucked. She did a cowgirl whoop and then put the back of her hand toward her mouth. He winked at her again. She walked backwards and had one more one. This was how you treat trauma goddammit.

And then Texas John the Revelator began to talk about Townes Van Zandt's "Waiting 'Round to Die," which brought Lila May into his rich sway again. Maybe the heartbreak of a cockblocking mother could disappear inside live music with THC and Tiny Brave Bulls to help. Maybe Texas would become a bore again. He wouldn't fuck Gwen, though.

The crowd swirled away from him when he broke off. He asked her what happened to her nice boyfriend who used to live here and she shrugged and said you have no idea.

Someone put on Howlin' Wolf's "Down on the Killin' Floor" and then jump-skidded the needle to "Smokestack Lightning." John Texas asked her to dance. She allowed it. He held her with a surprisingly light touch. Precise in his scuffed Tony Lamas, he used stabby little steps that rocked with the downbeat and he had more than three moves. Her head whirled anew from the dope and drink that had transformed her trauma into a surprisingly soothing comeback landing. She hardly knew anything and barely knew her own self this moment but she really wanted more than a dance. He said, here we are. She felt loose, she felt left and right for his right and left. The boy was laughing inside. He always won over these smart girls easy. He didn't even worry why.

They played Arcade Fire, a stupid OTR song about rape and rape culture and then somebody put on the Holy Modal Rounders, the werewolf crying in the moonlight.

And Lila got scared. How did these college children know this song? "Nobody, nobody knows my pain." Why would they play it now? Louis for sure. Her fucked up psychotic wolfboy grammar school boyfriend. Some of them turned around and looked up to Shaney's window. Or was it the conspicuously absent Louis's?

"You want to dog this cat and go to a shivaree?" said Texas to Lila's ear, soft.

"A what?" said Lila May wondering where John went to with her mother and when and why she didn't know about it.

"It's a singing and drinking and fightin' thing," he said.

"How does one dress for such an affair?" she said, half-remembering the joke to which he referred. "I want you to take me to a real party, yes," she said aloud and people around went suddenly quiet. The faux pas went right loud, as Texas might have said.

"You," said the lesbian lover suddenly pointing across the newly-formed circle at Lila May. "After all your boyfriend did this to this house? That's what we think."

"You have a boyfriend?" said Texas.

"Yeah," she said. "I did. I haven't heard from him since Friday night, or maybe it was Saturday ago. Everybody's so secretive. What did he do? Guilty till proven innocent?" Besides fuck my mother, she thought.

"Oh, nothing," said the lesbian, under the weight of 13 Lone Star beers and an Adderall hit. "Probably murdered my girlfriend." She was on her way to clobber Lila May when half a dozen pairs of hands grabbed her.

"Please," said Lila May, leaning into the stiff khaki of the cowboy's shirt. "Oh. I didn't know. I'm sorry, I'll leave."

"Good, bitch," said the feisty former girlfriend of the poet. Current girlfriend of the former poet?

Texas said, "And he's in jail? And you said you'd go to the shivaree with me?"

She said yes. She pushed past the bewildered Texas and walked through the whispering living room and out the screen door and into the suburban tranquility of Austin, Texas.

She was stoned again. Every element of the outdoor world seemed carefully assembled by a symphonic composer of stuff. She didn't know the world and she didn't want to know it right now. She missed John Shaney and wondered why every boy she loved made derelictions of decency such a priority. She wept to see the peaceful little rocks on the walkway, pavement and plant life standing there perfectly ordered mute witnesses to her melodrama. The thirsty dust of Austin. She looked out from the porch and decided boyfriend or no, she would abandon herself some decency too. Back to Texas again for a while. She knew he knew she would too. As Townes would say, princess where you plan to turn to?

They called his name at the exact point when three hooded-eyed hoods were noticing Shaney and sauntering towards him. The cops told him he was going to the county lockup since the tidal wave of South by Southwest arrests had filled the city's tamer tanks, and that his roommates hadn't called and that maybe he could try them again after he was facilitated awaiting arraignment which would come early Monday morning. There were no clocks and they had taken his phone away so Shaney could only guess where he was in the solar cycle. Surprise. The sun was blazing down when they walked him in his dayglow orange overalls and yellow plastic handcuff ties across an enclosed driveway, to a bad bus ride where fear began to ooze up seriously from the upholstery. Crossing into the greyness of the sweat-smelling jail that held the redolences of all justifiable fears and horrible vices, Shaney felt his stomach flip over itself.

Smelled like cumin, overboiled onions, urine, and dirt, the inside stench woke him to a fullblown dread. It was motherfucking real now.

When he was arrested, he thought only and about liberation from Lionel's laboratory, supposing bail or even escape might present itself though there was that odd moment at the lab where he felt a death wish creep, something Freud said sexual glands wanted, pathways to annihilation, odd pheromones on dry winds running the arid spaces of rural rhythms back to animal, Shaney guessed and then thought better. Retreat from Fort Da.

Now he kept thinking this wasn't happening. Okay, it sounds trite, but it was impossible to grasp and weird enough to seem like a dream. A monstrous dream. Then reality impinged.

When the slammer doors swung open, guards with inhuman faces began demanding his attention and cooperation on pain of pain.

"What's this pussyface in for?"

"Dude. He killed an animal."

"What the fuck?"

"I know, right?"

"No, I'm serious. I had a hamburger for lunch. They pop me for killin' a cow?"

"It's ironic isn't it?" said Shaney.

"Shut your fuckin' mouth, pussyface. This guy killed a puppy dog."

"Fucking animal abuser," said the one whose forehead lumped out like some mannequin of missing link ancestors. The one who looked like Moe Howard only beefy said out loud, "Fucking killed a housepet."

"Jesus, takes all kinds."

"I suppose it doesn't make any difference if I say I am innocent," he said, then realized how death-wishy he really was. "That it was self defense."

After they finished punching his stomach and exhausting the foul synonyms for homosexual, they put him in the showers laughing, issued a new uniform, investigated his body cavities with rough fingers inside prophylactic gloves giggling and drew him out of the privacy of the antechamber and into the main bolgia of hell. The bad background smell now seemed to be compounded with fermenting sewage.

"Jesus," said the black bowl haircut. "What kind of swill they serve for lunch?"

"Pipes backed up again," replied the hominid.

Shaney's stomach hurt and his mind was drifting upward to the ceiling, but the guards took him down, down stairs that led to a steamier level, with empty halls. They closed the door to the hall and led him to the laundry room where they took turns for ten minutes with a hank of filthy towel stuffed up his mouth.

He moved into a dim place semi-permanently that lasted somewhere subterranean all the rest of his life. They said he would pay worse if he spoke of this, though, later he found out that everybody knew. It was an accepted part of environmental adaptation, like initiation. While it was happening, he prayed that the monster inside him could respond. But it didn't come.

Body odors bloomed out inside a world completely devoid of any feminine graces—flowers and citrus and incense were miles away. He limped. The guards pushed him forward and bounced him a bit. Now he was feeling it, the constant vulnerability of existing in time. Wait long enough and all the comforts of home and privilege yield to this. Pain waits like death does. His stomach filled with a dread poisonous cramp. He doubled over and began to puke. Ready for it again, they laughed and said remind them to send for the janitor. They went back up the stairs to what seemed like a main room.

He walked out looking up into three stories of layered cages and a waning light trickling down through slats and breaks and dusty-mote emptiness. It was architecturally stunning, like cathedrals of old, high iron and pebbled glass letting in slant light like discovery or revelation, a monument to the most fervent desires of the people who exercised power to ape that other power they believed lived above them forever. In this part of the world it was crazy pride. Justice was for a sacred system: rule of law, they called it, but it was better than that. The cage in America was the kernel. Liberty mattered but security more. The poor, the sinful, and the colored must be tamed for the system to work. Shaney would eventually prosper here, got a friend to send some of his blotter in a letter. He bartered it away. The guards were beaten by Shaney's new friends a month later and then six short months later Wulfhardt's company worked his release. The puny monster in his blood was gone—chased away like a horrible dream. But its legacy was the cure and the Wulfhardt scientists made many fortunes during the wolf epidemic, And Shaney got used to using a toilet seat in front of everyone. He looked out and saw the pattern of bars, light, and shadows, falling light, long solid against the stale and filmy air. He looked down between his pale limbs into the ivory bowl of the toilet. There was blood swirled against the porcelained steel like a rose patch in snow seen from far above.

# 27.

Moons and moons after Shaney launched the Austin werewolf epidemic, Lila called Louis Lamel out to the old Zilker Gardens to meet in the cool of the evening at the dinosaur grove between Butterfly Trail and the roses.

Louis was surprised after so much time. "Why at this particular juncture?" he asked, wondering what had changed. "Why now?"

"Imma save you," she said and laughed her spooky girl laugh. "And before I do, we'll walk to the Moon Tower together. Like back in the day."

Next call, she invited the formerly incarcerated John Shaney to come, too. Half hour later. She had a nice surprise for him, as well, but didn't tell Louis that or even that she called her onetime lover. Didn't tell him a couple things.

She also didn't invite her husband out there.

Me, that is. Texas. The man she married on the rebound after all the misadventures in Austin leading up to this here shapeshifting apocalypse pandemic. I got no invite. She didn't talk to me much anymore, though she was living upstairs from me at the Trinity House, as I mentioned at the outset of this book. We, Lila and I, took it over after her dad went to jail for kidnapping and murder. By that time, living in the big Wulfie house seemed like a pitstop on a house of horrors tour. Lila gave Veronica Wipes the Wulfhardt lab to run, though her father preferred the German dude.

I found out about Lila's little park and garden party the way I always did, eavesdropping while I drank beer and wrote music. She talked on the telephone with the speaker on. Disembodied voices drifted through the air ducts, couldn't hear who, only: Meet me at the park. Sound traveled in phantom drifts through Trinity.

Maybe we lived precariously at the moment, but you know what they say about paradigms. Shift happens. I mean, she wasn't walking out on me if I could help it. I planned to follow my wife—protect her from the newborn terrors of an Austin night, including other men.

When she got there, Lila May took out her gun. The bullets weren't silver, but silvered.

Okay, I imagine some of this, as I said before, but I also had a long talk with the Shaneys after I died and came back. You heard me right. And Louis corroborated when he had presence of mind after some coercion. My Space Ghost.

She moved the gun to her big brown leather purse. Then she helped Gwen out of the car after carefully unfolding her wheelchair. She walked (rolled) past boys and girls playing hopscotch, Red Rover, and Pig Pig, past the redfaced hot dog man selling skinless franks to fat customers, smiles across their multihued faces. A lazy wind inched foam around calalilies. The Ornithomimus statue looked bent and beaten, our dinosaur frozen midstomp where garden plaques name edible plants, and poisonous too. A mere ninety degrees today and Zilker humped up familiar in hillocks. Hot but cooling off. The climate noticeably changed by then, you realize.

Louis found her sitting by the dinosaur. Then he saw Gwen and thought: This might be awkward. Walked forward smiling, upbeat, though. Faces we show the world. She's going to think "old" when she sees me, he thought. His saggy jawline reflected in a car window earlier. He wondered if his "other him" was older, too. Is his snout flecked with grey? Are wolf years like dog years or does monster immortality preclude aging?

She was hiding her eyes behind sunglasses.

"Hi," she said. "Or as we say in the Lone Star State, Hey."

Hey he said. They hugged and she cried for a number of valid reasons.

"Honey," Louis said. "There, there. Hello, Mrs. Wulfhardt." Louis used to feel guilty just looking at Gwen in the early days, walking porn, he called her, and he was warm for her form that eve as well. We all were. Small with a lush hourglass form, deep brownblack eyes that sparked at men. He had another guilty feeling that night, something to do with his altered ego. Snuck a peek at her palm, just in case.

She looked away. "Where is he?" Gwen asked.

Lila May sighed. Salt tears rolling from behind large fashionable sunglasses. There, there, Louis repeated. There.

"Gotta say, I don't feel altogether right about… this," Lila May said between big air-gulps. "This whole thing. I have good intentions, though." She pointed at her mother who was staring intently at the sky.

"When?" asked Gwen.

"I should have written you a long time ago, I should have wrote," said Lila.

"You were busy, took another route."

"Maybe a bit too rote," she laughed. "I did miss you. I miss a lot of things."

"I'm sorry about your father," Louis said, trying too hard. "Sorry."

She smiled. "You and Daddy," she said. "Surprise. He's still in jail, maybe forever. His experiments over. People are suing, as you might imagine." Did she pat the purse then where the gun did lie?

Back in the day, her father didn't mind Louis though the rich man laughed at Lila's then boyfriend's low-paying itinerant teaching gigs; myths for the misbegotten, he used to say. Louis mocked Wulfie's science nerds. Gwen was more wary of Louis, because he tried so hard not to stare at her on the rare occasions when their paths crossed in the enormous house of Wulfhardt. But she was often bedridden back then, drunk, Louis assumed.

They stood and took up stumbling tear-eyed along to the trail to the Moon Tower and away from the dinosaurs. Lila walked remembering the plants with signs in the garden that I (Texas) took her to before we married. The plants with names you could use in a song.

"Congratulations," Louis said. "You got married."

Lila touched his face, caressed rough beard stubble. "My father hired him back after he quit, you know. He rehired him because he claimed a cure for what you have. After John was arrested, before Daddy was." Her voice trailed away.

"What cure ideas did the well-educated cowboy have?"

"Had to do with teenagers and frogs and metamorphosis that begins in a cellular process or something. Apotheosis, no. Apoptosis, good word, huh? He mansplained it to me. The death of cells that leaves a ghost. Inviting new cells to cooperate, how the tadpole turns to the frog. All the changes that occur during metamorphosis, including losing the tadpole tail. The tail told to disappear all stimulated by a teeny increase of thyroid hormone in the blood. It was more important than multiplying and dividing cells; it included death and replacement. Turns out, it made John's ideas better."

"John? The dog abuser? And what happened to Tex? Where is he right now?"

"Where is John?" asked Gwen.

"Mama? Hush I told you. O, Texas, we separated, though he still lives here. I mean there, your old house, the Trinity. It's weird, it's in between. Louis, I just couldn't do it. I said, 'I can't do this anymore.' Now I'm ghosting him. Now. Don't return calls half the time. My husband married a ghost. I played monsters with him, like with you. But I invited you out here in the meadow tonight to ask a favor," she said. "And to do you a bigger one. Got excited seeing you."

"I need the bathroom," he said, clumsy from birth.

They were halfway to the Moon Tower walking through the dying trees to the public lavatory before dark, and the park was suddenly uninhabited. Her hand through his arm she leaned lightly as always. He was pushing Gwen, who was peering around. It had been a long time. Lila probably checked the gun again. And, meanwhile, the ghosted husband (I, me) was driving through Austin to confront Lila in the BO-Tankic Gardens. Zilker. Drove fast down Lamar and over the bridge, right turn on Riverside Drive. Screeching wheels.

Louis sat in the dark toilet, remembering where he lost her. Where *he* was ghosted. Pyramid hotel in a Cancun room that held volumes of sunlight. Sugar sand beaches lapped by amniotic waters, but in the midst of lobster buffet her father's creepy factotums appeared. Next thing he knew Lila was shaking the white sand off her painted toes, packing to fly back on the family jet. In tears. Her mother was sick, they said. Her mother was always sick. Louis Lamel stayed on at her insistence, but turned angry, revenging himself on the mini bar that Wulfie paid along with hotel bill and tickets home. One morning a knock at the door. "We have a large party coming in late Sunday night and will not be able to renew your room again," the concierge said in very smooth English. "Perhaps I can help you get one in downtown Cancun." Louis did not recall any extensions then panicked about his ticket home. Tried to make a phone call but Spanish inadequate and they kept transferring him. Sick to his stomach and hungover with shakes discovered his flight left an hour ago. Opened the minibar and down to use the internet, find travel agent, but America was dead to commerce.

He stood alone in the humid evening near the hotel's outdoor buffet, ate lobster and beans and inhaled beers. The moon was out and the evening going indigo and two women skipping toward the rubber tree jungle said O come, follow us into the wilderness woods the jungle forest the trees. Inside a snake hung from a low log with its head up. In the evening full moonlight it hissed off into the clearing path through the balsam pear and the beadvine, the butterfly pea, the chewstick, the dodder, the white clematis, and the moldy bread and cheese. Leading him past a half a black cat, dead. Omens. Below its shoulders an outspilling of noodle tubes, viscera, large pipes and small.

He felt the wolf before he saw it, in a jungle, past the edge of civilization where Mayans once trudged. They believed that each embodies a god or an animal, the chu'nel. Bent over on its haunches with the cat rump in its hands and mouth buried in the meat and silky black fur. Blood streamed its long mouth. This one bent over looked like a Goya Lobombre. Channeling the chu'nel. Came as bikini girls reentered the humid dell. It slashed him, they screamed, it turned to run away but was scared off by gardeners who also followed the girls.

Meanwhile back from the toilet in the park, the women awaited him in the dying park.

"Take off your sunglasses, please, I want to see you," Louis asked.

"No," she replied.

"I thought you came here to save me."

"Yes," she said and thought about the gun again.

"What favor?"

Meanwhile: I found the park, as the dark was due. Didn't see her car. Then I drove past the dinosaurs, towards the dry river, around the darkening gardens but there were no cars on Lady Bird Drive either looking for Lila, my monster ghost.

"I need a friend to stand by me," she said. "I need you. I mean, to protect me. And Mama."

"Me. To scare somebody? You mean, when I turn?" He was angry then. "It doesn't work like that."

"No, dear. Just someone to watch over me."

"Thinking I'm too old for you now," Louis laughed self-conscious. "Even the wolf is old. But we will do as you command. By moonlight."

"Never too old for the moon in the clouds above," she said. Then: "Wait a minute," she said. "It's a full moon?" She looked around, the park, her mother. Disingenuous heart.

"O God," she said. "I have to go." She pointed, the rising moonglow on the mountain's serrated edge, and his back itched and he probably felt follicles blooming or something. Light hovered in clouds.

"Why?"

She looked at Louis. "I timed all of this wrong. Full moon? We have what, thirty minutes?"

"Why worry? You're always safe," he chuckled, confident.

"You can control it."

"Don't make me laugh. I barely control myself *now*," Louis said. "You're safe by dint of the den's laws. You are mine were mine and instincts prevent me hurting you." This theory he derived from some half-remembered party talk. Some ethologist named Lawrence something. Besides, he had snuck a peek both their palms. No pentagrams. No kill them tonight.

She said, sad, "A long time ago, honey. We were an item. Is that a powerful force anymore? For you?"

"No need to be sadistic about it." The clouds were up higher and the moon came touching them and got covered.

"Check Mother's straps will you?"

"Jesus, Lila, she's bound tighter than Houdini's yoga pants. What's the deal?"

Lila clutched her bag close still wearing those big sunglasses, the better to not see him with. The moon was edging up. "Keep her safe and us too." Gwen shook her head. "What are you thinking about, my dear?"

"Mexico," he said. "What else? Where would we be without your father stepping in?"

They patched him up fresh from the Mexican jungle: blood everywhere. They knew the "wolf," a crazy man, said the concierge while the workers started rosaries. It wasn't a man, he said. Apologies, nostrums, even a bruja visited. They offered another week on the house but some gringo appeared and arranged a flight home. He took Louis to a little infirmary on the warehouse end of Cancun. Needles and drugs. He woke on a jet, then a hospital in Texas suffering booze withdrawals, Montezuma's Revenge, and fever. Three days then home. The bills covered by anonymous benefactor. Wulfhardt manse returned no phone calls. She was gone, meanwhile, all his scars disappeared, and the stitches fell off. That was weird. One night he smelled estrogenous derivatives walking home. Alone in the girl's cute studio he saw the moon nose up around the bottom of her dusty windowsill and heard snarling and woke with a bloodstained shirt in a park, a bloodstained blouse in his hands. Picture in the paper the girl murdered. When he tried to turn himself in he threw up uncontrollably till he stopped thinking about it. He went up to see Lila. Saw Gwen instead, front door as the moon rose. More bloody hands in the mornings to come. Gwen never made the newspapers, so maybe he didn't. Learned to rent a storage space, line it with rubber and mattresses, and lock himself in. The wolf had no idea how to work a lock, even one that Louis knew the combination to.

"You and Daddy," said Lila May Wulfhardt.

Meanwhile me parking while singing an angry Townes song. Taking it on the hoof, so to speak. Turnstiled, junkpiled, and railroaded too.

"Are you going to ask *me* what *I* am thinking about?" she asked. They stopped just outside the light of the Moon Tower coming on.

"I know what you were thinking," Louis said. They were walking away from Gwen, who was rocking in the fading light.

"Oh really. Well, *you*, mostly. I was thinking I missed you calling me like you used to, even when we broke up, even after we saw each other at John's party," she said, nervous. "I was wondering if you finally forgot me."

"Fair enough," he laughed. "But that's not it."

She looked away. "Anyways. I liked that boy, John," she said. "Listen," said Lila considering her words, "I know how bad this sounds, but, please, did you turn John Shaney in?"

At first, Louis thought she meant, *turn* him as in Werewolf him, which he never. O, she meant did he give Shaney to the cops.

"No," Louis said, offended. "Probably it was that creep Ochocinco."

"You mean the dead man? The performance artist who pretended to be a professor with Tourette's syndrome? The one who stole a football player's name? I agree he was annoying. All performance artists are. All Art as Prank bullshit. Urinals, soup cans, wrapped buildings, and beyond. He might have been a grifter, but a snitch? Besides Ochocinco was killed at the Surly concert by a Bath Salts freak," she said.

"No. By me, by him, I mean, the wolf. After your father let him go. *He* killed him a month or two later, lost track. You don't remember?"

"O yeah," she said obviously not remembering. "The truth is important," she said and opened her bag, saw the silvery handle of the gun. "But don't avoid the issue. What was I really thinking, Mr. Psychic?"

"Shenanigans," Louis said. "That's what you're thinking."

She pulled out an already diminished Wild Turkey pint from her purse clunked next to the gun and took a swig, offering it to Louis who shook his head. She kept the gun hid. "How did you know?" she asked.

The evening was losing the soft pink all around them, the bushes and the smaller foliage packed densely here at the heart of green inside the spreading desert. Lila's feet kicked nervously back and forth. They both feared what was to come out of the transforming dusk.

"All you ever think about."


Neither knew that I was not so far away. I read the labels on the plants and tried to make a song. And then the lurking paid off. Was sure I saw them hand in hand, I raced around them through another path I knew, got ahead and waited. Not so long. Careless laughter. I pounced out and people screamed. Just as I was about to grab the man's thin shirt, I saw it wasn't Louis and Lila. The citizen pulled out a gun, an experience folks from Texas know. I turned tail and ran. The shot rang out as I plunged into snaggled dead plants by a dry creek. Hid in a big old drain pipe on the culvert. The couple ran in an opposite direction, hoping they killed the pouncer.


Lila May thought she heard a backfire. "Okay, when I'm scared I always think about Shenanigans," she said.

"Must be frequently frightened," Louis mumbled.

"I loved that horse. He jumped everything I aimed him at and it felt like we were flying together. You yawning? Am I keeping you up?" she asked.

"You told me this story a million times."

"You don't have to be a dick about it," she said. She took a big drink.

"I am a dick. And worse, an old one," Louis said, sniffing the air. Thought he heard gunshot, not backfire. Moon edge now over the hilltop horizon and he was not turning. Maybe he was getting too too old. Clouds over the skyline's ridge. Lila was meandering and drinking.

A ways away, foolish and chagrined, I crawled out from the spider webs and dust of the pipe, headed to the dry lake then swung back past succulents, the Spanish Dagger.

"Nanny made it look easy. Something he sniffed that time though. Wind moving smell was something crossed the path and the wild grass that grew in thatches of violet-sparked hay. He was whinnying, then jumped. Fate took larger rhythms. Next thing I knew wires and tubes on my hands. Flying followed by pain. The way of the world."

Louis grunted. Lila pulled hard on the bottle. Her mother clucked.

She droned on, already drunk-ish. "When I woke up I asked about Shenanigans, my Nanny boy, and they said hush and when I woke again they told me he had to be destroyed. Not because he hurt me because he was broken, legs, mercy killing. Cruel to be kind. I asked why they didn't kill me. Daddy got angry, don't ever talk like that again. Later when he used to beat his smartass teenage girl he said it hurt him more than it hurt me but he had to be cruel. Cruel to be kind. I used to say, 'You can control my body, but not my brain.'"

"How did that work out for you?" Louis asked.

"You tell a story then."

Louis sniffed the air. "I think Texas is somewhere near."

"What, you serious, sniffing him? Listen then. A favor from you, I want," she said a little slurry Yoda voice. "But first a story from you."

"Come here. I don't know why you stand so far away."

"Always telling us what to do," she said, leaning on him, a little flirty. "Boys. I've been watched over by them and all I ever learned was what was s'posed to be good for me. Instead of sympathy I got advice. My father and my grandfather built a fortress around me, my father tried to be my friend, my boyfriend was afraid of my father, and the only man I ever loved ran off with my mother. My mother. And now my husband. Don't tell me about Mexico. Why do the flowers grow here in all this heat?" she asked pointing at an incongruous green spot with blooms.

He was stung. Afraid? How drunk was she?

"Louis, why?"

"I don't know," he answered, angry. "I suppose there are artesian wells or some deepwaters that will abide the planet's collapse. I wasn't afraid of your father. You ran away from me. And your husband. What about old Tex?"

"Texas. Nobody calls him Tex. She pulled on the bottle yet again and drank and coughed at its strength. "I came for a… for a favor, like I said. But I came to save you too. Later. Even in all this heat."

"Meanwhile, I'll save you?"

"Now. Mister Monster. Tell *me* a scary story," she said as they walked, producing a flashlight and turning it up on her face, which might have been scary if it wasn't still light enough out. "Okay, tell me the bees. The real stuff. The lake. That one," she said pointing to the dry bed.

"Please," he said. "I don't want to remember it. Surprised you do."

"The lake story. A lake back when there was water here. Bees back when there were bees. Young Lila May was there and saved your life. You can do the same for me."

"You drove me to the hospital," Louis said, dulled now by dulled anger.

"We were skinny dipping over there on the treeside," she said ignoring dull protest, addressing her remarks at Gwen. "Where the trees used to be, that is. Dangling our naked legs over the edge. Back when there was an edge, and water."

It was futile to resist. "We drank wine coolers back then," Louis said having reprised the old yarn enough times to know the proper entrance. "But that wasn't the horror part. I was stoned and babbling and the day was perfect and all ears seemed tuned into me. I had just finished reading this fucking Canadian professor's book and I was explaining…"

"Mansplaining.

"Fuck you. Sorry Gwen. Stoned and explaining how the romance novel held precedence over all other genres and how all fictive modes are just tributaries. From epic to horror. I batted away the bees. I picked up the wine cooler with everybody screaming 'no' around me thinking it was a group groan at some joke I didn't even remember telling. Then I took a huge swallow of the sweet alcohol and I knew something was wrong. It started in my mouth. Sharp pains like a caricature of carbonated fizz. One two three four. It happened so fast and then there was motion in my mouth. Crawling, rolling horrible motion. Stabbing pain. I swallowed and froze four five six seven. Fuck! My mouth opened and a bee flew out. Meanwhile pains I never knew I could feel began ratcheting up. I panicked and it all turned surreal. I flailed around like a rag doll, woozy. I felt my wind pipe swell up and I couldn't breathe, drowning in sunlit air. Everybody laughing. Probably swallowed a dozen bees. The world from comic to horror flowed, from romance to epic, stoned to horrified. And everybody laughing. And I fainted. When I came to my friends were afraid but you drove me to the hospital though why you didn't call an ambulance is still a mystery. Those friends couldn't look me in the eye afterwards. Trauma is supposed to be bad, ask any halfwit academic, but embarrassment is worse."

He snorted, continued. "I got in your car and what did you say to me as we drove to emergency?"

Lila laughed and apologized. Hiccupped.

"What?" Louis said.

"Maybe you'll bee more careful next time you try to get a buzz on."

"And what else?"

"Tell the doctor your blood type is bee positive."

She squeaked an insincere apology, again. Gwen laughed too. Louis thought his stupid life ruined by one big gulp of shitty soda pop wine then later he met a mad dog in the bush of Central America. Creatures of destiny made him alike. He walked toward the Moon Tower. The moon peeked out halfway up. He smelled Texas again. "I'm gonna scout ahead," Louis said and took off on another trail.

"You see," said Lila to Gwen, "he's not a wolf. He's a man who tricked himself into thinking he is. He's crazy. The bees made him do all this weird stuff. Then Daddy."

"Don't count on it," Gwen said. "Just tell me you are ready to do what I asked. The gun is loaded. And soon as the turn happens, the turns happen…"

Lila was accumulating regrets. "I'll do it. Though. It's not right," she said. "Cruel to be kind. Mama, like Nanny."

"Mexico," Gwen said. "He says it happened in Mexico. He can't remember where it happened to me. On my front porch."

"Where is Louis?" interrupted Lila May.

"I'm here," the man himself said strolling out of the dark. "And I can smell someone waiting nervously at the Moon Tower."

"Heightened senses? Almost turned? she thought. "It's Texas, I bet. He's a creeper," she said. "What would you have done with him you were in wolf form?"

"I don't know, kill him."

"I didn't ask you to kill anyone. Just protect me and Mama. And that means not leaving me and Mama alone in a getting dark park."

Louis looked hurt. Gwen started talking, "Do you know, Louis, that the Moon Tower was invented here in the late 19th century to prevent serial murders, to make the world more safe by night? In Austin? Our innovation. Serial murders started here too. An Austin man, I assume a man not a woman or a wolf, began it as a thing, killing nurses and hookers. Some paranoid theories suggest that he got chased off by the police and the Moon Tower and shipped out all the way to London, his nurse and hooker spree here done, and transformed into Jack the Ripper over there. There is even a little evidence, some say. We invented the Moon Tower to scare off monsters and now we monsters live under it."

"I'll stay until I turn. It's the clouds," Louis said assuming drivel. "Has to be clear…"

"Jesus, let it go. I tell you what, I can help you turn," Lila sputtered and took off her sunglasses. Her left eye was shot with blood, ringed with an inflated bruise. Bad black eye. Her lashes were gluey.

"Who did this to you?" Louis said.

Tears started rolling over her black eye. "We did it to each other."

"You telling me it was your fault? In a way?" Angry now metamorphosis rumbled inside, thought he felt it, help was on the way. The moon emerged.

It would happen. Everything was tingling like a struck funnybone. Just then the whole dinosaur village, the roses, the planted path with the labels in the edible gardens with little plaques its Beauty Berry, Cleaver, Hackberry, etcetera painted silver by the Moon Tower and the real moon. The clouds raced away. Fuck the tower, Louis thought, there it is. "I smell him, the wifebeater," Louis said between clenched teeth. "He's near, isn't he?"

It began the moment Louis saw her face. The moon was round and silvery, far away but near enough to cast shadows. He pulled away from Lila's feeble grip. It brightly cleared the hilltop, the clouds parted, Louis doubled over in sweet agony, bones small and little cracked as he seethed and yelped, hopped up and now a monster stalked down the arboretum path towards prey away from Lila, proscribed by pack rule.

Lila pulled out her gun and aimed at his back, but the couple from the creek broke in on the clearing lit clearly. "What's fucking going on here?" asked the beleaguered man, pulling out his own gun.

Gwen then started to change from elder hostile to ghostlike wraith and finally to wolf. Snarling after the high lonesome crying.

The couple were dumbfounded by the sight and sound, froze still until a fully transformed Louis leaped out of dark and made short work of their throats. They were on the ground, Lila May screaming. Gwen in the moon's rays became that hill country beast that ran from Wulfhardt down to the river running through Austin. The real reason Leo Wulfhardt had a werewolf obsession. She likes my boyfriends. Lila sobbing as transformed Louis' lips ran blood and saliva, then turned to his bloody business at the Moon Tower not far away. Lila looked in both directions but not at the nice couple gagging out liquid ends. She whirled, resolved, and put a bullet into her mother who squealed like a pup stepped upon then snarled—afraid and confused.

"This hurts me more than it hurts you."

Gwen snarled, ripping herself from the bonds, face covered with fur, a wail forming in her lips, stood and then stumbled. Lila turned and left as her mother collapsed back into the wheelchair crying. Lila didn't feel like offering comfort.

Meanwhile the wolf formerly known as Louis felt great. He sang out Lila's name over and over with his new vocal cords, an echoing ominous drawn-out howl. So be it. Civilization was falling away. Finally. His stride was low and he could hear a long time away from here from Texas to Lila on the other end of the park path. Broken leaves of grass sharpened to phrases then into clear statements. Empty space became un-ponderous as movement led to the feed. Like the deserted world of dreams when shook awake he ran from dark into whatever odd lonesome fate awaited him. It. Wolf hit fence and tumbled tripping. There was lightning crackling his interior landscape. Its lungs took in a large quantity of multi-scented air and let out a growl. He was changed all the way and innocent now. Sin was irrelevant. But that didn't really matter.

"What's that, who's there?" I asked the Moon Tower, fearful of the dark and the light, fearful of the echoing.

"Lila?" My quavering tones sang into the arcing light. "Texas is here."

I brought out my bottle of Beam, but it tasted thin and inadequate. Then in false moonlight I saw something.

Herd him, "thought" the wolf selecting an approach along the obstructing chain link fence erect in some places pushed over in others, awakened now to animal anger under bright electric light. Herd him into a cul de sac said the insects chiming the grass. The moon is rolling one way and the clouds across it in the opposite direction. Walking apace creep Louiswolf sees Texasman, but not the other way around.

"Baby?" I asked the air, hoping it was her. I sensed an enormous unknown factor, a harbinger of profound disruption. My life was about to be changed.

This long supernatural courtship with death was becoming a drunk cotillion now, a coming out. Everybody dance, she thought, and I am the date. Mother in the chair. She went back felt guilty. Gwen slumped. Lila started toward the tower again, rolling the heavy wheelchair chair with its slumped form. She tried not to think about the dead couple. She tried her phone but there were no bars. I did what I was told, she thought, cruel to be kind. The warm night air stirred.

"Baby," she answered. She can hear the sharp high talk of bats overhead.

I backed off towards the tower. A buzzing sound came from the artificial moonlight overhead. The wolf rose from the bushes near the chain link.

"Nowhere to run," I said.

"Nowhere to hide," I heard Lila say as she came into the circle of artificial light. She screamed when she saw the wolf.

He was a lopsided sight. More like a man but there was hair and teeth.

I regarded the iron rungs and bars. I stumbled backwards trailing clouds of fear, sweat, and booze. The creature retreated into dark cautiously regarding. Back to the fence.

"Nice doggy, good boy?" I said, surprised at my own quavering pitch. "Louis?"

Looked down and could see nothing but a wind moving the dry weeds around disturbing the air with the deep incense known to cowboys and rattlesnakes.

"Baby," I whispered.

The wolf who doesn't remember any sins was watching the whole scene from the outside like a film shot from outside a rocket ship. The wolf had killed two people. This man was from the werewolf's pack but somehow okay to kill. Puzzling development. He felt tangled in hunger, then leaped toward the puzzling prey now running.

The werewolf cut my leg tendon. In horror, I fell back sobbing gulps of air leg dragging beast in low pursuit. One leg flopping the pain throbbing I made it under the tower's glow, stopped, and barfed volumes. Then considered the tower as refuge above the rumpled fence.

She pulled her handgun from the bag remembering to target the furcovered heart. "This is for you, Louis. I waited for you, Louis, so long. Why couldn't you be brave? One day you will thank me for this. Cruel to be kind."

The wolf creature, more like a man, now stooped, broad faced, long hair covered mouth full of sharp and curved teeth, stalked low into the light. At first she could not.

A wolf cannot climb I thought.

I pulled myself up where a picnic bench butted against the Moon Tower.

And the moon's silver light of the world fell and showed me a man on all fours. No a wolf that rushed into light and up the tower and then the wolfman, sharing the lower pegs of the pole, found a tendon at my other ankle, biting down felt blood well and another tendon snapped. I screamed. He leapt up and was on my arms, teeth sunk in so deep and the flesh torn along sliding lines, blood sluicing into the wolf's mouth. Release and reattach, then it tore as I looked down in shock, arms mangled bone, shreds of tissue hung, anatomy revealed. The creature tearing me apart. It will never be the same, I thought. Me without an arm. Tingling, I was going into shock. Me without me hadn't occurred to me yet. The wolfman pulled me down into the dust.

Lila horrified was paralyzed solid, the wolf went for my neck but missed and tore a corner of my face up, then yanked it away and chewed the skin. Jabbering in shock with a rag of my faceflesh in the werewolf's mouth and beast crouched over writhing victim. The cruelty in the heart of things. She saw and screamed. The wolf now all wolf under the white moon turned towards the woman he could never kill but wanted. The wifebeater was dying, so be it.

The wolf spat out the face chunk turned and was trying for more flesh around the ear. Lila froze at the frightening sight; her husband, apparently not protected by herd instincts and taboos, a writhing corpse coughing, not far from the end. She had fallen like a collapsed puppet, sang oh God over and over again. The wolf snarled as he looked up at her. He reared up, threw another bloody bite down. The manwolf up on his haunches looked closer at Lila.

Me too? she wondered, and came out of her paralysis, an electric shock, she was half aware of aiming and pulling the trigger. The projectile pushed the creature back, his hide hard to penetrate, though penetrate it did. The gun's kick sent her from kneeling onto her back. She stood up fast though. Lila moved closer and shot again point blank, a second bullet just in case. She wasn't a hunter. She missed the heart but hit well enough, well enough, it turned out. The wolf screamed. The betrayal and the metal point hit his sternum.

I could barely breathe. My face burned and one eye was apparently blinded flashing unbearable hurt. Blood ran out. My pounding heart needed more air, and my thoughts sped fast past panic but were crowded together by blinding pain, signals from four different areas, increasing in a sickmaking crescendo. And then the agony hit a wall, slowed until fear was all that was left. This is taking me where? The pain was hard at first then started to spin away. There was a sense of heavy atmosphere pressing down on me while I felt paradoxically light. Noises seemed more like waves crashing on my ears, and I could not smell. It was a curious and slow realization, an absence, no scents of the Austin air, the loamy dry earth, or anything. My head was lying next to the offensive pool of vomit, nothing. I arched my head back for air, and the pain made a comeback but I was spinning, an orbit out. The moon was paper now up and low over the hills, larger than it ever was before.

Tried to move my head again but I couldn't really feel. The wiring inside usually worked. It always did before. I was keenly aware of how hard my lungs *were* working but there was no sense or sensation, out or in, just air out and in. The paste coming apart, the place was the last. Why here? All I have left is forever and nothing, which makes sense all of a sudden. The beginning of real death frightened me. It was a peculiar feeling like a crooked arrow in my heart. I tried coughing. My life was mine, at its slipaway. Birth in reverse. A spin a centrifuge and parts of me spun off. Fingers, toes, hands, feet, arms and legs, torso leaving a head, which snapped off. There it was, my vision clouding on the only thing in my eyes the moon. So perfect round and white at this low declension with the shadows of mountains and the craters and the well known man in it. A man walked on the moon, left a flag. Why can there never be a restaurant on the moon? There's no atmosphere. Lila May walked in this park with me. I saw the city at the end of Stranford Drive to Lou Neff (Luna) to the

Colorado River. She doesn't want me to go. Poison plants down here with labels, poison ivy, poison sumac, elephant ear, diffenbachia, pothos ivy, oleander, and lily of the valley. How I know all this? I'm the Wulfhardt gardener's son. How I met Lila? Her teasing me. I come back to the moon's face. Cain, Mani and the Great Wolf, I lived a long time and under the moon I was eaten by a wolf. Then I think a long dream, peacefully the city on the Colorado banks.

After some time, moments, Louis came to but I did not. He felt something give, something, released. But he didn't want this. He wanted something back. In his chest a dart, a bullet, lodged slightly inside his skin. Felt sad like when the good drugs wear off leaving just us behind.

Pain built around the bullet hole, and it felt like something had been torn away a gobbet was gone. Dizzy cold. Faint. He drifted.

But when he woke up a third time he knew what it was.

Louis was alive, in pain, but alive.

The wolf was dead.

Lila saw my eye socket exposed and the side of my face including the cavern of mouth, tongue, and teeth exposed, drool running out one side and then Lila stopped ran gathering me into her arms. "There there," she said. "There there." A monster created a monster. Texas me fell into dying like the citizens on the path.

"Where's the missing skin? Oh here. Let's take him to my daddy's hospital. My hospital. I can fix you."

"Hush. There there," said Lila. "Shit there's no bars, no satellites above, no service for the phone. I did something worse."

"You cured me?" asked Louis.

She bent down eye to eye. "Saved you from eternal life."

"How?"

"Silvered bullets."

"Silver bullets were invented by Hollywood," Louis said. "Some fucking director."

"*Silvered* bullets. Okay, darts. Part of it is the formula for making silver. And John Shaney's DNA supplied the rest. They took it from his arm but it didn't work. They found a bag of bloody sheets in a pillowcase in his car. Air plus werewolf blood. It worked. My father's butler and Maria Ygnacio found the sheets."

"What?" Louis asked, coughing.

"Yeah. His system fought the virus, and the R&D people working on it and tried it on some of the monsters you turned. Monsters Daddy kept. You and Daddy."

Louis wasn't feeling well, kept shaking his head as if to clear his vision. It wasn't working. "Please start from the beginning."

"It was Shaney, honey. He was immune to the werewolf virus, not a curse, came from a disease that jumped off feral cats in the Central American jungle. Almost turned but never did. That's what silvered the bullet. A formula developed to block this novel form of this hyper-something hypertrichosis. Identified it, cured it. Found some DNA anomaly they called a magic gene. John Shaney stopped the plague. Well Daddy did," she said. "Daddy," she laughed.

He was struggling to keep up.

Lila said, "Shaney is coming for Mama."

Gwen lay prone across the wheelchair blinking up at the moon. "When is John coming?" The heat from earlier shone on her face reddened.

"Why are we leaving? I'm still dizzy or something," Louis said. He was suddenly remembering deaths. He killed so many. They were adding up with a ping like a pinball score. They now weighed in him.

There were no satellites above now, said her phone. They were walking, pushing Gwen, who asked, where is he? A kind of haze moved across the ground and the dim light spreading from the east went incandescent in it. Low there, it rolled down an embankment. There was a menagerie of animals, time running out while she was preoccupied with her phone. "There," she said. "I've got a signal." They were in the parking lot.

Her face glowed in the smartphone light, concentrating. Louis saw the tear tracks on her face and wanted desperately to care. He saw himself and he wondered what a self was, much less two.

John Shaney pulled up in a Jaguar sedan.

"Here he is," said Gwen clapping her hands.

"What happened? What happened to Gwen?" he said. Shaney saw her. He was worried because it looked like Gwen was having a particularly rough time. Some time with my daughter, she had said, try to make a wrong thing right. His beautiful wife, and here her beautiful daughter. He crossed the parking lot. He was worried she was on her own when the old affliction arose he watched over Gwen, ever since she watched over him ever since jail.

"I'm cured," said Gwen.

"There there," he answered. John couldn't be happier. "Your monthly problems. Over."

Gwen snickered; loved his clunky sense of humor. Shaney lived love's monstrous sense of humor. He could not resist Gwen. And though their life together pained others, they were happy. Love is a monster. They could go home to the nice beach house in California that Gwen bought them, where Shaney worked at the state school. Before they drove off in the Jaguar; Gwen tried to hug Lila, but she smiled and started crying. So long, Mama.

And then air sucked back into my lungs. Gasped with feeling, reborn with extreme prejudice, you might say. My eyes saw something. A big bright 3D circle blocking everything behind it, all. What was behind? Reached up to bat it away. My arms worked. Blinked twice. Still there. The moon. Both eyes online. Got up slowly after a long few moments considering how the cruelty locked in the heart of everything can occasionally relent. Remembering the mother nothing. But here it was strange. Nothing hurt. My neck and face had rough spots and dried blood. Stood up and tried to walk. Fell down hard.

Lila got Louis to stop bleeding. In her car, windows rolled up to spite the heat, she saw the end. They would get off scot-free, Mama gone and Louis here. She drove up to his car but he looked so green and shaky, she said, "Come home with me."

Didn't mean it like that or did she? She knew the end, knew the dead lying alone in the park, the moon that was not quite down. She knew the shirt he wore, the green one went with his red hair. She'd bought for him. He probably put on the shirt to get into her pants. She rolled the Audi Fox forward and saw there were three deaths on her conscience. But she could drive away free.

She got her phone working. "Want to report an attack; looks like three people dead."

"What are you doing?" asked the hoarse and wounded former wolf.

"Can't leave him to die." Lila kept talking to the cops. She told them who she was. She hung up and sighed.

"He beat you."

"He punched me in the eye after I told him that Townes Van Zandt was overrated. On the other hand, I ghosted him. It was cowardly. After all, I married him."

They got out of the car and heard a siren. Not too far away.

"Wouldn't it be funny if that was our siren?"

"Let me do the talking; you lay in the car and act hurt."

"I am hurt, I'm fucking decimated."

"You know Texas once told me that 'decimated' technically means reduced by ten percent. It was based on the Roman centurions."

"What are you fucking talking about?"

"Never mind. That *is* our siren." Indeed it was, the strange thing just kept getting louder, and when the cops came lights splashing around in joyous color, Lila told the former werewolf to sit in the car. She went to talk to the police. After a few moments one of the police came over to the car and asked Louis if he was okay. Lila was praying he wouldn't say anything. Two or three more cop cars arrived, meanwhile. A bunch of them with flashlights walked down the path Lila pointed. They wouldn't let her come.

One of the cops asked Lila if she remembered him. She said maybe. The night we picked you up and brought you to the station and you told the joke about the man with five penises.

"That doesn't sound like me," she said. "That sounds like my husband."

God, my husband. They might think I did it. Just then one of the cops came running out, said they found two people. He stopped talking, choking on the word "dead" in front of a civilian. Lila said, there were three. Her husband, she thought. All of the police went into the park except one woman standing with the cars, radio in her hand. She was calling ambulances, probably from Wulfhardt too.

Trying to stand up again was easier, strength gathering and something about the relative silence of my surroundings forced me up on my knees in a hushed moment. The moon was going down. I would always be in debt to it. I got up and walked out, trying to remember where my car was and how to drive. There were a lot of cop cars at the other end of the lot. I waited a while and they all ran into the park. I started it fast and drove out the other exit.

I was weak and when I got to a cheap hotel, the clerk laughed when I said my name was Texas, so I said, Robert Weston Smith, but you can call me Jack. I slept around the clock. I woke up and tore some teenage boys apart. Then I called Shaney next morning and I scared Louis to death with the next phone call. I made him tell me everything I've told you. Made him.

Tell you one last what: I made up stuff about Lila May. She was very nice. I couldn't bring myself to speak to her again even though I'll likely live forever. I already died and it wasn't so bad and coming back wasn't so good but I will be monstrous in my cravings forever. Price you pay. This was how it ended, Louis said. She stood in the morning sun with the police. The little flowers that grew around the park belonged to her, and these unopened morning blooms were like those closing buds near her Daddy's hospital that the fading sun bent and huddled.

The cops let them go. Into the declined aspect of civilization they rode.

Temperatures of 118 degrees Fahrenheit scoured the earth that was Texas with appalling regularity that summer. There were a few scientists that believed the massive killoff might impact favorably, but Lila May knew a lot of other experts thought otherwise. People were tired of the plague too, what the media called the werewolf pandemic that shut down all the cities every full moon for five years now and wrecked the economy. Most folks went out into the city without masks on craving death.

Found out a few months later my wolf isn't fooled by locked doors in storage rooms. So they are not safe.

That night, Lila drove Louis to the hospital and then went to sit in the ER waiting room, fell asleep waiting. Light grew in the window. Long wait take a nap between life and death.

She had a little game she played to go to sleep. Told me about it on our honeymoon, other moons ago.

People never know the forces that unravel them, she said. Before she went to bed, Lila would start a list of all the things that she could not control. Mortality, for instance, and the when of it. Misfortune, like a chipped tooth you get on late Friday night when the dentists are off. Gravity, always working. Time, slippin, slippin. The chemical balances that spin our hormones and moods, tides up and down the spine according to some ancient clock we never wound. And as she got sleepy the big abstracts trailed off into little specific things: the effect of winter light on an impatient heart that loves the sun; the smell of popcorn and air conditioning when you walk by a movie palace you cannot enter cause of bidness you must tend; a bad crush on someone too young for you the hurting fool in old married age; the phases of the moon; obviously, the fire, water, earth signs that tug us from the newspaper columns; and, last but not least, the hitch that caught the horse's hooves.

There, there. And mop your eyes and smile, she always does, the ghost girl long ago seeing the flowers that the fading sun in the field bent and huddled, something like a sweet death wish after troubles end. Maybe Lila is fated to meet some somebody, a dream of that life carried forward on some firing neurons that turn into another kind of wish. A blink and a memory, it could come again with no hitch, a smiling period of graceful movements, like we all believe, a run at living happily ever after the everything that changes.